THE MARKOFF WOMEN

THE MARKOFF WOMEN

A NOVEL BY JUNE FLAUM SINGER

M. EVANS AND COMPANY, INC.
New York

This is a work of fiction. Any resemblance between characters and persons living or dead is purely coincidental.

Library of Congress Cataloging-in-Publication Data

Singer, June Flaum.
  The Markoff women.

  I. Title.
PS3569.I544M3   1986   813'.54   85-27546

ISBN 0-87131-464-9

M. Evans and Company, Inc.
216 East 49 Street
New York, New York 10017

Design by Diane Gedymin

Manufactured in the United States of America

9 8 7 6 5 4 3 2 1

For my second daughter,
 Brett Eve,
and for my grandmother,
 for whom she is named

I want to thank my father, Mike Flaum, for all the wonderful stories he has told me . . . those tales of the old country without which *The Markoff Women* could never have been written.

PART ONE

1880 – 1898

1.

The Family Markoff claimed Eve Brodkin as a bride in a manner completely alien to usual shtetl procedure. There was no matchmaker, no dowry, no period of courting. What happened was that one wintry day the Markoffs, who rode the countryside surrounding the town of Slobodka on the handsomest of horses seeking out livestock to buy and resell, galloped into the town where the Brodkins lived, and David, the only unmarried Markoff son, laid eyes on Eve in the marketplace. She was only seventeen, and her magnificent red-gold hair hung down her back blazing in the cold clear light. David Markoff was struck dumb. Never, never had he seen such a vision. Suddenly the ground beneath his soil-encrusted boots was no longer frozen and the sun shone as hot as it did for only a few short weeks each summer.

As the youngest of the five brothers, David hardly ever dared address his cantankerous, fiery-tempered father who ruled his brood with an iron fist. Instead he whispered to his older brother, Yacob, who whispered into the ear of *his* older brother, Hershel, who spoke to Shlomo, who took the eldest brother, Abraham, aside and told him how things stood with David. Then it fell upon Abraham to speak to Chaim the father.

Chaim Markoff growled as was his custom and rode around the marketplace sizing up the girl as carefully as if he were considering buying a young heifer. He had heard stories about this Eve Brodkin, about how highly educated she was, and now he was not unimpressed with her beauty. As a matter of fact he found her stimulatingly beautiful. So much so, as a womanizing widower, he even considered for a few moments acquiring her for himself. Young as she was, she appeared to be more woman than his youngest son could handle. (Chaim was a man who held respect for no man, certainly not for his own sons.) Then he shrugged, then he spat. Let the mewling, driveling pup have her! Maybe she'd make a man of him.

Accordingly, Chaim Markoff stood for a few drinks in the tavern, which loosened a few tongues which ultimately revealed a few more facts about the girl. Facts and speculation. Besides her obvious beauty—that incredible hair and those green eyes with the slight upward slant to them—there was a dignity about her unusual in so young a girl, a certain strength of character. Certainly strong-willed . . . And there was the matter of her learning: Not only was she learned in Hebrew, it was said she had read not only the Mishnah and the

3

Gemara, but the mysterious Cabala as well. It was a fact that not only did she read and write in the Hebrew of the prayer books but in the everyday Yiddish that most Litvaks, those poor Lithuanian Jews, conversed in. But most couldn't read or write; who had time, after all, to learn everything? More, she was able not only to speak Polish and Russian, the official language of the land, fluently, but was able to read and write in those languages as well. It was true that her family were learned men—scholars and rabbis all the way back—but what did any of the Brodkins know of Russian? Enough to speak a few words when they were forced to. Learned men, more so than ordinary Jews, tried to lock themselves away from the gentile world. Wasn't that so?

Someone even whispered in Chaim's ear that the girl had a sixth sense, that she sometimes knew something was going to happen before anyone else did . . . When Chaim looked at this fellow with amused contempt, the man shrugged his shoulders: *Who knows? Sometimes God, for His own reasons and in His infinite wisdom, chooses some people to bear certain gifts . . . It's a waste of time to question His will.*

How much all of this Chaim believed was questionable. But it didn't matter. He had heard enough and he had seen the girl with his own eyes and he liked what he saw. Accordingly he turned to his sons who stood huddled together awaiting his decision and he grunted, nodding his head. The Family Markoff would demand the daughter of the Family Brodkin in marriage. And immediately! Just as when he bought a cow or a horse, he had neither the patience nor the inclination for lengthy negotiations. He would even waive the dowry. What did he care about a few rubles? He'd even pay for the celebration himself. Everyone knew Chaim Markoff was a sport.

When the Markoffs, all six of them uncommonly large, with mops of yellow curls and silky golden beards, presented themselves at the household of the Brodkins, those gentle souls trembled. Oh, they had heard of the wild Markoffs! Who had not? They were infamous in all the nearby towns and villages for their hard-drinking ways, for their feats of strength, for their propensity for brawling at the drop of a questionable word. Each son, as well as the father, was credited with the ability to flatten an offender with a single blow, not to mention their success as a group at routing a whole mob in a matter of seconds. Any one of them was able to bend a horseshoe in half as easily as he could crush a nutshell within a beefy fist. Clearly the Brodkin males—the father who was past eighty and the two sons who spent their days praying, studying and interpreting the Talmud—were no match for the Markoffs.

The Brodkin brothers looked at each Markoff, from one to the other, and then at each other in amazement and helplessness. What was to be done with these Markoffs? They knew what these madmen were capable of—flinging furniture through windows, tearing a house down by its rafters, even razing it to the ground. (It was said that that was exactly what they had done to the abode of one hapless farmer who had been so misadvised as to try to give Chaim the short end of a stick in a deal.) Everyone knew they were like a bunch of crazy

Polacks, these wild men! Should they let Eve marry into this family of crazy men? *Could they?*

What happened then was what usually happens when intelligent, studious men are forced into decisions based on fear—they rationalized. This rationalization took the form of *pilpuling* or hairsplitting—that ancient Yiddish practice of debating the meaning of the ancient writings. They went round and round, each Brodkin brother seeking to convince himself and the other of why their motherless half sister Eve, less than half their own ages, should become the bride of David Markoff.

There *was* the matter of the dowry. Where once they had been a rich family when their great-grandfather, the learned Rebbe Elijah Brodkin, had boasted a great rabbinical following (they still lived in what was considered a fine house), they were now genteelly impoverished. Their grandfather, Rebbe Elijah's son, and then their own father, had never been politically astute enough to maintain that following, and now there was no money for dowries, hardly enough for their own daughters, much less for Eve.

And what was to be done with her, after all? *If* there had been a substantial dowry, Eve, with her beauty and erudition, could have been married off into one of the finest rabbinical families. Even into the family of the great Vilno Rebbe. But as matters stood, Eve's beauty and erudition were liabilities. Most families who would accept a bride without a dowry were suspicious of a girl with too much knowledge, not to mention being intimidated by such beauty. They wanted obedient, hardworking wives to keep the Sabbath and to mother sons—not an Eve with her airs and graces. And there was her strong will that was not fitting in a woman. It was seen as stubbornness, even impudence. Most scandalous of all were the whispers that she had been known to utter French words, of all things! But it really was not so strange. Two years before, they had had a Yeshiva student boarding with them—a young man from Morocco who was familiar with that language. Before anyone noticed, there was Eve conversing with him in French, and reading his books as well.

So actually, what was to be done with her? A woman was born to do God's will, was she not? And she could do God's will by bearing David Markoff's children as well as anyone else's, and without a dowry to boot. While the Markoffs were certainly not what *they* would call learned men, rumor had it that they were, nonetheless, pious. Come sundown on Sabbath eve, it was said, they would quickly terminate any deal even if it were nowhere ready to be terminated, even if the method used to complete it questionable. (The clapping of the buyer's palm against the seller's palm always meant the deal was made, and heaven help the fool who didn't honor this. Sometimes, people said, Chaim Markoff would just wait for the seller's hand to be up, waving around in the middle of the bargaining process, and he'd catch the man's palm there in midair, smacking his own against it. Sometimes spitting into his palm first, sealing the transaction twice over.)

Moreover, in addition to not demanding a dowry, Chaim Markoff was prepared to finance the wedding celebration himself. Prosperous, as well as hearty eaters and heavy drinkers, the Markoffs would undoubtedly do both families proud in the way of food and libation.

So it was settled. Not so much a consent as a surrender. The Brodkin brothers assured their old father, who deep in his heart was proud to have fathered such an exquisite creature as Eve and was therefore especially fond of her, that it was truly a match made in heaven.

Sealing the betrothal with a glass of spirits, Chaim Markoff decreed that a week was long enough to complete the wedding preparations. Accordingly, he and his sons would return the following Friday. They would stand beside the Brodkins in the synagogue on the Sabbath eve and then on the Sabbath itself. Come sundown, the wedding would take place with drinking and dancing the likes of which the town had never seen before. As a matter of fact, Chaim and his sons would perform the kazatska themselves in honor of the occasion. No one in all of Mother Russia, Chaim proclaimed, could do the kazatska with more proficiency or sustain the performance for as long a period of time. Also, they'd do their balancing trick for which they were famous. They'd balance glass upon whiskey bottle upon glass upon bottle until glasses and bottles reached the heavens!

"And my son makes only one request—" Chaim said, at the same time picking up the iron poker that was used to stoke the fire.

"Yes?" Simcha Brodkin inquired with trepidation, his eyes on the poker, his hand clutching at his beard, while David looked at his brothers with questioning eyes. He had made no request.

"When the bride's taken to the ritual bath her hair's not to be cut." Chaim said it confidently, as if there were absolutely no question his request would be honored.

The Brodkin brothers were scandalized. "But—"

"I've given my word to my son that your sister's hair will be spared," Chaim roared out. "Surely no one wishes me to break my word." He smiled slyly. "Why concern yourself? Where is it written, after all, that we should cut off what is most desirable? We cut off the foreskin of the baby boy's pecker but we leave the best part," he laughed raucously, brandishing the poker. "And it *is* only custom and not the Law that the hair be cut off. Correct me if I'm wrong," he said threateningly.

The Brodkin brothers looked at each other. *This was really an outlandish demand.* Still, which one of them would dare correct this Chaim Markoff?

"Custom," Mendel Brodkin muttered. "To avoid the covetous eye." His long bony fingers combed his beard.

The prospective father-in-law roared. "Covetous eye? *Who* would dare cast a covetous eye on the bride of a Markoff?"

Mendel and Simcha exchanged looks. This uncouth Jew, this *bulvon*, was no fool. Sly as a fox was more like it. When they didn't answer, Chaim did . . . for them. "No one!" he bellowed, and for emphasis took the fire poker he was holding and bent it in half with no more exertion than it took to stroke a cat.

"No one," Mendel Brodkin mumbled into his beard.

"Then it's settled. The hair's not to be cut. Agreed?"

This time the brothers looked first at the twisted poker and then at each other. "Agreed." They were eager to be done with the matter. After all, what was to be done with these Markoffs? Only a crazy man argued with another crazy man.

As for David, he couldn't figure out why his father had, in his name, insisted that his promised wife's hair not be cut at the *mikvah*. It had never even entered his head that such a request was possible. But whatever his father's reason, he was grateful.

Eve couldn't believe what was happening to her. Her father and her brothers giving her in marriage to a wild man, the offspring of a crude, ignorant family? It was as if they were selling her for a few pieces of silver. Worse . . . *that*, at least, would have implied she had value. As it was, she was being used only as the pawn of cowardly men in appeasement of wolves nipping at their heels. What they were saying in effect was that she was nothing more than a piece of meat used to fend off the attack of wild animals.

Oh, she'd seen the Markoffs in the marketplace! She'd seen them riding through the town like a small mob of Jewish Cossacks, blond beards flying, great masses of yellow hair blowing in the wind. And every last one of them with eyes the color of the blueberries that grew wild in the forest. Oh, they were handsome, it was true. Even that father, commanding as he was with his towering height and bristling with muscle. And the one she was promised to—that David— he was probably the handsomest one of all, with more of a gentle look to him. Perhaps, if he came from a different family . . . Perhaps, if he were an educated man . . . But as it was each one of them was roughly dressed and roughly spoken, and each one of them had the reputation for being as brutish as the creatures they dealt in.

How could they do this to her? Didn't her father love her? Didn't the Torah stand for mercy? What mercy was being shown her? And justice! What of justice? The Book spoke of justice over and over again. Oh, she had known that someday she'd be wed, but she had never expected to be promised without her consent. And if she would have been betrothed without being consulted, she surely would have thought she could trust her father and brothers to choose well for her—a gentle, learned man who spoke softly and sweetly. At the very least she would have thought she could have trusted them to choose for her a man who didn't smell of horses!

In the week between the betrothal and the wedding day, the preparations went on about the bride-to-be without her cooperation. Chaim Markoff, true to his word, sent a sleighful of provisions for the wedding feast. The bride's sisters-

7

in-law threw themselves into a flurry of cooking and baking and urged Eve to make a wedding dress for herself. She had always been adept with the needle, had always, since she was a little girl, sewn dresses for herself the likes of which the townspeople had never seen but for glimpses of the aristocratic women who sometimes had cause to ride through the town on their way to a ball at the Squire's. (Much to her brothers' discomfiture, Eve had copied styles from worldly books of fashion she had acquired surreptitiously. It couldn't be denied that a certain vanity was her vice.) But now she steadfastly refused to do anything about a wedding gown. Finally the sisters-in-law called on neighbors to help, and then Eve, in turn, refused to stand still for fittings. She raged that she wouldn't participate in her own betrayal.

What she *did* do was lay siege to her father who had a soft heart and especially for Eve, the daughter of his late, second marriage. She begged, cajoled, even cried piteously for him to have mercy on her. He became heartsick but still was forced to tell her, "But it's already promised." Then he locked himself in his study so that he wouldn't have to look at her mournful face or listen to her pleas. Secretly he appealed to his sons. "Perhaps it's the wrong thing we're doing?"

The sons shuddered at the very thought of how the Markoffs would react to a cancellation of the wedding and reassured their father that of course they were doing the right thing. They enumerated, for their father and for themselves, all the reasons for the match once again: One, the Markoffs made a very good living. They'd provide handsomely for Eve who, after all, *was* spoiled, for which their father had to assume responsibility since it was he who had allowed her to spend her time reading and studying when he should have insisted she be more concerned with household duties. And the worst of it was that the books she had read had not always been the *right* kind of books. And what about the many worldly dresses she'd been allowed to sew for herself? Dresses that were not at all seemly for the daughter of a pious household. Why did their father think they themselves had never allowed Eve, who *had* offered, to sew such dresses for their own wives and daughters, God forbid? But wed to David Markoff, she'd be able to indulge her fancies and it would no longer be on *their* consciences.

Two, the Markoffs were vigorous men. There would be many grandchildren. And wasn't that Eve's duty in life? To produce many strong children?

On and on they went. When it came to sophistry the Brodkin brothers were resourceful men and they didn't come up short with reasons for the marriage. They concluded by comparing her to a balky calf. What did one do with a balky calf? One put a rope around its neck and led it around until it learned the proper way for a cow to behave. But like their father, they too avoided Eve for the entire week.

Eve first learned that her hair wasn't to be cut when she was escorted to the ritual bath to be purified for her wedding day. At first she felt relief, even joy. She *was* proud of her spectacular hair. But then the spite and rage within her rose stronger than vanity and pride. David Markoff might own her body and be able to force her to perform her functions as a wife, distasteful as even the thought was, but she was determined he wouldn't have the comfort of her beauty as well.

"Cut it off!" she screamed at the bath attendants who hadn't known what to make of their instructions not to shear the bride's hair to begin with. Now they didn't know what to make of Eve's insistence on being shorn.

"We were instructed by your brothers—"

"I don't care. I want it cut off! All of it! It's my hair and it's my right to be a proper matron just like all of you!"

But not one of the women moved to pick up the shears. It wasn't a seventeen-year-old girl who had to be obeyed. Spotting the small scissors that were used to cut the finger- and toenails, Eve snatched them up. "Very well! If you won't do it, I'll do it myself!"

One of the matrons rushed forward and grabbed at Eve's hand to stay it as she made blind stabs at her hair. "Don't be a fool!" the woman whispered. "In the end, whom do you spite? Nobody but yourself. It is, as you say, your hair and such lovely hair it is . . ." The workworn hand smoothed back the tendrils from Eve's forehead. "If your mother were alive she'd tell you the same thing. You probably have the most beautiful hair in all Lithuania, maybe in all Russia for all I know. For all any one of us knows. Keep your hair! Be glad Chaim Markoff insisted your hair not be shorn."

"Chaim Markoff? Not the son?"

The woman shrugged. "The father speaks for the son, I suppose. That's the way it is in that family. The father does all the talking."

She might have known, Eve thought. In her family it was her brothers who did whatever speaking was necessary due to her father's age and infirmity. But Chaim Markoff? He was a much younger father, a strong, intimidating presence. He was powerful, overwhelming, frightening. She shuddered just thinking about him. She allowed the woman to remove the scissors from her hand though she still wept bitter tears.

"Good," the elderly woman said. "You'll see. You'll be glad later on. And he, that David Markoff, he's not so terrible. A good-looking young man." She looked around to make sure the other women didn't hear her. "You'll see. The youth and good looks make the marriage bed easier and that's of no small consequence, believe me. They could have married you off to worse—an eighty-year-old man who shuffles around in slippers and with crumbs in a long, gray beard." She winked. "It happens all the time. Those kinds relish a beautiful young virgin as well as the next one."

Eve looked at her unbelieving, and the woman laughed. "It happened to me! My own father was on his deathbed and he wanted to see me married before he left this world for the other. So there I was, only sixteen, and they wed me off to the man I just described, right at my father's bedside. Lucky for me he didn't last for more than two years."

9

The two sisters-in-law, Deborah and Leah, dressed the silent, finally passive bride. Leah's daughter, Sarah, nearly Eve's age herself, arranged Eve's hair, adjusting the wedding veil as best she could without Eve's cooperation, whispering at the same time, "You don't know how lucky you are. Everybody's talking about how crazy your husband-to-be is about you."

Her mother heard her and added encouragingly, "Yes. They say he fell madly in love with you the moment he saw you in the marketplace."

"Just like in a storybook . . ." Sarah said, her eyes shining.

"God willing," Deborah told Eve, "you'll be with child in a month's time and you'll forget all this nonsense about choosing your own husband. Believe me, that's the way it goes. Wasn't my own marriage with your brother arranged without my ever seeing him? And wasn't I pregnant before the month was out? Soon you'll have a houseful of children and you won't have the time to think about yourself so much. That's the way God planned it."

Eve didn't answer her, unconvinced. But Sarah said she hoped that she herself would get as good-looking a husband as David Markoff. For this remark, Sarah's mother threw her a dark look. A man's good looks were certainly not to be discussed in the Brodkin household.

Later, out of earshot of the bride, the two sisters-in-law consoled each other. "She was always too high and mighty for her own good. And willful. It's better this way."

The wedding guests agreed that Eve, in her white, lace-trimmed wedding dress, was probably the loveliest bride any of them had ever seen, although all brides were lovely. No one took notice that as she stood under the wedding canopy she barely repeated the vows after the rabbi or that her lips scarcely brushed the rim of the wedding wine cup. But no one could mistake the bridegroom's joy as he shouted his vows and smashed the ritual glass under his foot with such vigor the floor actually trembled. The guests applauded and cheered. A good omen. Surely their union would prosper!

Then the food was brought out in such quantity it excited the glummest of the assembled. The Markoffs had provided not only chickens but the succulent geese and fat-laden ducks Chaim preferred to deal in. (Chickens were for dealers of lesser standing than he.) And there were huge, tender briskets of beef. Unaccustomed to such abundance the guests almost scorned what they now considered lesser dishes—the mounds of chicken livers, chopped with onions and moist with chicken fat; the kasha varnishkas and dumplings yellow with many eggs; all the different kinds of fish—chopped and pickled, smoked and fresh, kippered and salted. And the liquor! Brandy and vodka and slivovitz and Cognac! Cognac! They could have gone a lifetime without the taste of Cognac on their tongues. Where had Chaim Markoff obtained it? A miracle, really!

No one drank as much as the Markoffs themselves, including the bridegroom. They matched and topped every man there, drink for drink, as the toasts proceeded in rapid fire. The assembled drank to the father of the bride, to the father of the groom, to the bridegroom and of course, the bride, the most beautiful woman in all of Russia. They drank to life. *L'chayim!* They carried the bride and groom around on chairs hoisted on their shoulders.

Then Chaim called for a plain wooden chair and ordered it placed on its back on the floor. He crouched in a knee bend and grabbed but one leg of the chair by its very tip and with his arm held straight out, elevated the chair and himself until he was standing tall and the chair was stiffly and steadily in the air on a level with his chin. The guests cheered but only in polite nervousness, not understanding why this was some kind of feat. *What kind of a trick was this for a strong man?* They looked at one another. *Who couldn't pick up a plain wooden chair? A little child could pick up a chair . . .*

Chaim, showman that he was, was counting on his audience's stupidity about the principle of leverage involved—that picking up the chair in this manner made the chair as heavy as a thousand times its actual weight. But they would soon find out that you needed an arm of iron to pull it off. Grinning, he had his sons repeat the stunt, one after the other. When David performed he looked to his bride for approval, but her eyes were averted.

Then Chaim turned to the guests. "Which one of you is strong enough to pick up a simple wooden chair?" he jeered. He thrust the chair at one of the burlier guests. "Here. Try it." The fellow grabbed it with two hands easily and almost laughed. *It's so light this whole thing must be a joke!* Then Chaim took the chair back and laid it on the floor and the victim went into a knee bend and grabbed hold of one leg with a bent arm, held close to his body. "Oh no, straight out!" Chaim warned. "Don't bend your arm or I'll break it off!"

The hapless aspirant, terrified now, did as he was bid and for a second the chair lifted crookedly, rising perhaps an inch before it crashed back to the floor. Chaim roared with laughter as the man blinked and smiled foolishly. *What had happened to the chair? It had become like a stone when picked up in that manner . . . like a rock . . . a boulder!*

"Who'll be next?" Chaim demanded.

One after the other, they tried. As each failed, Chaim laughed drunkenly, each time louder than the time before, until one stocky guest rushed forward and without pausing, grabbed the leg of the chair but not at its tip, but close to the seat. With one rapid motion he lifted it high in the air!

The crowd grew silent as Chaim screamed, "Cheater! Horse's asshole! Charlatan! The tip of the leg! *The tip!*" His fist came down on the contender's arm like an anvil, so hard that both the man and the chair fell to the floor.

Stunned, the guests looked at the crumpled creature lying on the floor, hugging his hurt arm to his body. Then they started to laugh too, along with Chaim, louder and louder. *A dolt deserving of no sympathy. What had he been thinking of? Trying to beat Chaim Markoff and by cheating yet! Didn't the horse's asshole realize you needed an arm as strong as a mountain to lift the chair as Chaim had?*

11

The triumphant Chaim had another slivovitz, a long draw straight from the bottle, and called out for the musicians to start their fiddling. He went into a crouch and with his mighty arms folded across his chest broke into the kazatska, followed by his sons.

Then the handkerchief dance followed, with the dancers each holding on to the edge of a scarf rather than touching hands since no male was supposed to touch the flesh of a woman who might be impure. By now the brothers Brodkin were agonizing that the Markoffs might be too drunk to leave town right after the celebration, as originally planned, with the couple's act of consummation taking place not at the bride's home, but at the bridegroom's. *It was amazing that, with all the liquor they had consumed, they hadn't already passed out.*

Finally they were departing and Chaim was barking out orders for the trip back home. Since he and David had come to town on horseback, with the rest of the family arriving later in sleighs, there were two horses that had to be ridden home. Chaim directed Abraham, the oldest son, to ride one horse and David, the other. He himself would drive the sleigh with the bride and her belongings, leaving three sons, four wives, and a mob of children to fill the remaining two sleighs. David briefly wondered why it wasn't he, the husband, who would ride with his bride in the sleigh instead of his father, but with all the confusion he dismissed it from his mind. Finally they were off, leaving the Brodkins to breathe their sighs of relief.

David and Abraham arrived home first, followed by the other brothers and the families. The women hurried to put the children to bed, and the brothers gathered in the front room with a fresh supply of vodka to await their father and the bride. Again and again they toasted the bridegroom who by now was in a frenzy of impatience. He was about to bed the most desirable woman in all of Russia! Where were his father and his bride? Chaim, directing the others, had been the last to leave but still—

Nervously David went to check if the room for his bride had been readied. All the Markoffs lived under their father's roof, a rambling one-story structure that had grown helter-skelter along with the family. As each son had married, another room had been added on, and every now and then an additional room was built to accommodate all the children. While the house was certainly no architect's vision, it still was one of the symbols of Chaim Markoff's prosperity since many families not any smaller than theirs were forced to live in houses not one tenth the size of theirs, right on their very street. While all the houses had some kind of a yard where the families raised vegetables and kept a few chickens, and possibly a barn, the Markoffs had the largest yard, a piece of property easily the size of three of the others, with a barn, a stable and a storage shed.

Presently, another room would be added on for David and Eve. In the meantime the brothers' wives had readied a room by emptying it of children (sticking one in here and two there and another over here) and had moved in a large bed. David looked at the bed now and visualizing what would soon happen there, grew even more frantic in his anticipation. He ran back to the front room hoping that his brothers would retire so that he could go straight to the bedroom when his bride arrived, but his brothers were still going strong and they pressed yet another drink on him. Then, at last, he heard the sleigh coming to a halt at the front door and he ran outside to assist his wife in dismounting. But she ignored the hand he held out to her and climbed down by herself, walking stiffly into the house.

Eve was determined that no one see how tired she was, how cold and frightened. The ride had been a nightmare for her as her thoughts had raced ahead more recklessly than the horses whipped on by the drunken Chaim. She hadn't been able to think of anything but what lay in store for her that very night. The four sisters-in-law whom she had barely taken notice of at the wedding rushed forward now to greet her, to welcome her. She could not force herself to respond. It was hard enough for her to stand on her two feet when all she wanted to do was to collapse and die!

The women escorted Eve to the bedroom while David waited in the front room, as was the custom. They would assist her in removing her coat and shawls, would help her don her nightdress. While they did all this, they kept chattering, trying to put her at her ease. They introduced themselves—they were Hannah, Miriam, Ruth and Dora. Tomorrow, they told her, they'd sort it all out for her, tell her who was who and which husband belonged to which wife and give her all the names of their children. But tonight! Tonight was her wedding night and it was already half way to morning.

Eve didn't respond. The women looked at each other with significant smiles, lifted eyebrows. They took both her silence and passive resistance as a sign of modesty, the new bride's nerves.

The youngest one, the one called Dora, offered shyly, "You'll be happy in the morning . . ."

"It's true," the one called Miriam, round as a butterball, said and laughed heartily. "It's better to be a married lady than an old maid."

"Yes," Dora agreed. "No one wants to be an old maid."

For a moment Eve considered disputing this statement but in the end remained silent. Then the one called Hannah, obviously the oldest and seemingly the most dignified, patted her shoulder reassuringly. "There's nothing to be afraid of. The whole thing will be over before you know it. A few seconds, that's all and it's over. Especially in the beginning when they're overanxious."

They all giggled at that and then the tall, thin one, Ruth, observed with a little smile, "We all lived through it and most likely you will too."

"What a thing to say," Miriam challenged. "*Of course* she'll live through it. And who knows? Maybe by tomorrow morning you'll already have a seed in your belly."

"Oh, God willing!" the pretty Dora breathed, her cheeks pinkening. "It should only happen to me."

The women were reluctant to leave until they had at least a small sign that this new sister-in-law could talk. *Was she a mute?* But Eve looked back at them, determined to be proudly silent. Her green eyes glistened as if to say: *This is all a terrible miscarriage of justice and nothing will ever be right with the world again!*

Even as she knew that her predicament was in no way their fault and they were treating her as kindly as they knew how, she still wanted to display her defiance, to shock them, ridiculous as she knew the notion was. She reached up to the coronet of braid that encircled her head, yanked, and the hair tumbled down in a great, whirling mass, all the whole golden-red length of it, and as it did, the women gasped. Not suspecting that the great circles of braid were real, not one of them had even looked closely enough to discern that this girl, certainly as strange as she was beautiful, wasn't wearing a matron's wig at all. Never, never had they seen or heard anything like it—a married woman with hair falling past her knees, and what a fall it was!

For a moment, Eve's eyes flashed with amusement at their reaction and she laughed. But within seconds her laugh turned hollow, haunted, like the laugh of those who, reputedly, danced on graves.

Among all civilized people there are certain rules for the behavior of a bride-groom, especially so when the bride is of a particularly sheltered background— rules and niceties and considerations. But no one had ever explained this to David Markoff and he had never known the gentling touch of a mother. She had died after delivering her last son into the world, he who had been larger at birth than most babies, even larger than the other big Markoff sons. So, in the absence of any instruction and forgetting, if he had ever known it, which was doubtful, that copulation was supposedly a divine matter, David went at his bride as primitively as any godless infidel might have. He had been waiting for this moment for many hours and he was flushed with drink. Also, he was very young and at the height of both his carnal desires and his sexual powers. Most of all, Eve was so spectacularly lovely.

He immediately crushed her to his chest, then quickly proceeded to tear at her nightdress from both ends, one hand at its high-buttoned neck and the other at its hem. It was as if he had lost his senses, and certainly all control.

So unrestrained was his attack that Eve thought it was even possible she might die. She fought back courageously, albeit futilely. At the same time she tried to cover her nakedness as the torn nightgown fell away in tatters. But this seemed only to fire David to even greater abandon. He flung her down on the bed and threw himself on top of her. He buried his face in her hair and in her neck and then as if propelled by a life of their own, his lips moved voraciously to her breasts, sucking at them as if the twin vessels were truly the source of life's sustenance. And while his mouth did that, his hands moved insistently to the space between her thighs.

Nothing, *nothing* Eve had ever read in all the many books she'd ingested

14

had prepared her for this—this attack upon her person and her dignity as a woman! At the same time it was her dignity that wouldn't allow her to cry out. Even as she was no longer able to fight back, she was determined that the last thing she would do would be to scream or cry. She would endure it all in stony silence.

She felt his mouth probing, his lips caressing with a violence; she even felt his teeth gnawing like a rabid wolf's. She felt his hands everywhere—at her breasts, her belly, her buttocks, the soft inner flesh of her thighs. Finally she felt him penetrating her, and she felt mortally wounded as if by physically entering her core, he was searing her body to his, branding her like one of the cattle his family bought and sold.

Flushed with satisfaction and the heroism of his triumphant male organ, David Markoff fell asleep. Eve, beside him, still didn't weep. Rather, she listened. She listened to his sleeping, waited for his breathing to become regular, listened for the revelers several doors away, waited for them to go to their rooms or perhaps to fall into a drunken sleep on the chairs and benches of the front room. When everything was quiet she intended to run! She was sure that when she told her father to what she had been subjected, he too would be appalled. He'd denounce the Markoffs as barbarians. He would shield her, protect her and never, never allow her to go back. So when the house finally lay in stillness, she crawled out of bed, put on her heavy boots, then the shawls and fur-lined cloak over the remaining rags of her nightgown.

Let them see what had been done to her body! Let them all see! Her brothers and their wives and her father! Surely they'd all be revolted and shocked. Her father would tear at his beard and declaim to the heavens: "Hear my voice, O Lord, and witness the degradation of my innocent child and deliver us from persecution by these heretics, these unbelievers, for certainly this is what they must be!"

Eve crawled through the window ready to run through the night on foot rather than take the time to try and hitch up a horse to a sleigh. But as luck would have it, Abraham or David, drunk as they had been, had left one of the horses milling about in the cold, untended, to search the hard, snow-covered ground with his muzzle. Seeing the horse, Eve both thanked a merciful God for His bounty and expressed a word of contempt for someone who would leave a horse out in weather like this. She mounted the chestnut beauty, dug her heels into the animal's flanks and looked up into the heavens. The night was well lit, the sky thickly strewn with stars, and there was a large slice of moon ensuring that she would find her way home with no trouble. Surely that was an omen that she was meant to flee before another day dawned.

As she rode through the night, Eve could think of nothing else but how her father would decry the unholy manner in which she been violated. True, she had stood under the marriage canopy but she had been raped just as surely as if she had fallen into the hands of the Cossacks. Surely no daughter of Abraham

15

was meant to endure this kind of violation and especially at the hands of a man supposedly chosen for her in heaven, as the words went . . . No, her father would most certainly denounce *all* the Markoffs and demand a divorce.

It was almost day when Eve ran into her father's house, arousing the entire household. One by one they assembled, speechless with astonishment to watch as Eve yanked the scarf from her head to reveal her hair, a crazy, wild mass of tangles and curls. Then, as she flung off all the layers of outer clothing to reveal her near naked form in the torn nightdress, they gasped. The brothers turned their eyes away from her exposed breasts, the glimpses of white thighs and bare rounded hips. Her father shrieked and covered his eyes with his hands. "Daughter! Cover yourself! Have you lost your senses?" He sank into a chair as if he no longer had the strength to stand.

Her sister-in-law Leah wailed: "She's gone mad! It's happened before to other brides when the shock's too great . . ."

"Yes!" Eve cried. "You're right. I have gone mad and is it any wonder? Look what he's done to me, this husband you've chosen for me!" She looked at her brothers but they wouldn't look at her. "I've been ravaged!"

Her sister-in-law Deborah murmured under her breath, "She's right. Clearly she's been ravaged." She went to Eve and hugged her. "Cover yourself," she whispered. "They won't look at you until you're covered. They're forbidden to look at you like this. And they won't listen to your words until—"

Then for the first time through the long day and night, Eve wept. She had held out for hours. She had been outraged as a mature woman and not as a child and she had run in the night as even a courageous male might have done, but she was hardly more than a little girl and now she sobbed like one. She sobbed and heaved against Deborah's breast.

When she was finished weeping she looked up to see her father wet-eyed too, the tears rolling down his old, parchmentlike cheeks, his lips moving silently. She wasn't sure whether he was praying to God or cursing the infidels but still, she was gratified. She saw her brothers with their heads together, talking heatedly, and she knew with satisfaction that they too were outraged, both for her and for her family's honor. Now they were surely going to demand that she be granted a divorce

With that settled in her mind, she marched herself off to bed. When she awoke there would be time enough for everyone to console her, to apologize for what they'd done, to arrange for her to go to the rabbi for the bill of divorce. She was too exhausted to consider whether a divorce would be granted to a wife upon request or whether it was the husband who had to demand it, or at least acquiesce.

As Eve fell asleep the Markoff household was already coming awake. David, naturally, was the first to note her absence and he raced through the house looking for her and then went outside calling her name. Hannah went to the outhouse to look for her; when she wasn't there either, they sent Dora to search the nearby woods. Then Abraham noticed that the chestnut mare was missing too and the deduction was made that Eve was indeed gone, and where would she go on the horse but back to her father's house?

Chaim Markoff had not yet sat down to his morning meal when Abraham told him what had happened. The other brothers were dying to tease David about how with one *shtup* he had driven his wife away, but Chaim was directing murderous eyes at the lot of them and they didn't dare. Then Chaim fixed his stare on the humiliated David. "Weak-livered, weak-bellied arsehole!" he spat out contemptuously. "Aren't you even man enough to hold on to a bitch of a heifer? Hitch up the horses to the sleigh, you sniveling heap of dung!" A few minutes later he and a red-faced David were off to reclaim the bride.

Just a short while before father and son arrived at the Brodkin door, Deborah shook Eve awake. "Your brothers and father want to speak with you. Dress yourself."

Although she had hardly slept, Eve came awake immediately and jumped out of bed. They were probably impatient to take her to the rabbi about the *get*, the bill of divorcement. Eve bathed and dressed carefully, relaxed enough now to take her time in brushing and braiding her hair and arranging the braids in coils around her ears and in a knot on top of her head. When finally she entered the study where her brothers and father awaited her, she sensed that things were not as she had imagined when she had gone to bed.

"You've disgraced us!" Mendel began immediately. Eve pulled back in anger; she couldn't believe what she was hearing.

She looked at the old man sitting at the table, his body shaking with agitation. "Father!"

He didn't look at her. "But you stood under the wedding canopy with David Markoff, daughter . . ."

"Father!" she cried out again.

In a quavering voice her father continued: "What came to pass was only the obligation of the married woman. It's true . . ." his speech faltered for a moment, ". . . that the bridegroom acted in astonishing fashion. Well, that's true," he looked to his sons but they looked away. He passed a trembling hand across his forehead and said appeasingly, "It must be his youth—"

Eve thought she must be going crazy. Her father couldn't actually be saying the words she thought she was hearing. "Father!"

"You must return to your husband, Eve. You must fulfill your duty as a married woman. So it is written."

"No, Father! You can't make me! Don't make me! I beg you!" She fell to her knees in front of him, picked up his cold hand. It was the color of yellowed ivory and she pressed it to her lips.

He snatched his hand away as if she had burned it. "Stop! Get to your feet! We're not gentiles after all!"

"Father, I beg you!" She looked at her brothers. "I'll just run away again, I warn you!"

At that moment there were noises from the front room. Angry voices. The door was flung open and Chaim Markoff filled the doorway, with his son behind him. "Who do you think this bitch of a girl is making a fool of? Not Chaim Markoff! What kind of men do you think you're fooling with? Wiggling worms like yourselves? Pieces of dirt? Pieces of *drek?* We're taking her back and if there's anyone here who wants to stop us, let that fool dare to tell me that!"

The air in the room was thick with silence. Eve, still on her knees, stared at the floor, consumed with shame for her father and her brothers. As God stood witness, she was being abandoned by cowards, thrown to the wolves in allegedly human form.

Then Chaim strode across the room in his heavy brown boots and looked down on Eve with contempt, as if she were nothing more than a bug. She stared up at him with eyes that were wet with rage, so dark green as to be almost black. Chaim ran his eyes disdainfully over her body as everyone watched and held their breath, and then Chaim reached out a huge paw and dug thick fingers into the crest of Eve's braids and yanked, until her hair came loose and tumbled down. Then, pulling her along by the length of it, he dragged her across the floor into the front room while David hung back, awash with shame. He'd fallen in love with a beautiful princess but he had treated her as if she were a slut, and instead of earning her love, he had only incurred her hatred. He was ashamed of his father, whom he had always unthinkingly respected. He realized that his father should have been ashamed of him, his son, ashamed of his behavior. But he wasn't. All that concerned him was that Eve had made a fool of them all by running away. Now his father was treating this lovely, brave girl worse even than he had himself. And he, coward that he was in front of his father, was saying nothing, doing nothing.

He was filled with loathing for himself. Yet when his father yelled at him, "Stupid yellow-livered arsehole, open up that door!" he ran to do as he was bid, just as he always had.

Then they all heard Eve say in a voice rich with derision, "You can let go of my hair, Chaim Markoff. You can even allow me to stand. After all, what do you have to fear from me? I'm only a female, hardly more than a child, and as anyone can see, without any protectors. And you're so big and strong and brave! You can make me go along with you very easily. You don't even have to put me in chains! Surely you're not afraid to let me get to my feet?"

Everyone in the room squirmed with embarrassment at her words. Even Chaim, for a second, was taken aback. Few men in his lifetime had spoken to him this way, but a woman? Never! Still he laughed and let go of her hair. She was a bitch of a girl, but she'd learn her place as any bitch of a dog that belonged to him would.

Eve, her hair freed, got to her feet with all the dignity she could muster under the circumstances, and looking straight ahead, said in a clear proud voice, "Deborah, would you please hand me my coat and shawls? I'm going out into the cold world and I'm sure no one is that heartless he would wish me to be cold too."

Deborah was so distressed she couldn't hold back her tears as she scurried to get the coat and shawls. They all watched wordlessly as Eve slowly and deliberately dressed herself. Leah rushed forward to cover Eve's head with a large black scarf and murmured, "Time will take care of everything . . ."

Eve could hear her father weeping as she walked to the door but she gave no indication she heard. David ran to open the door for her but Chaim followed her through first. As she walked through the snow to the sleigh, David jumped ahead to assist her, but she ignored him and climbed into the sleigh without his assistance. When he tried to cover her with the bearskin rug, she still ignored him, looking straight ahead. Helplessly, he sat down beside her.

As Chaim was about to crack the whip, her father came shuffling out the door, through the snow, in only his felt slippers, his frail figure struggling with a great brass samovar. He stumbled up to the sleigh and held the samovar up and out to her. "For your new home, Evele," he entreated. As she made no move to accept the urn, he implored: "Evele!"

"Either take it or don't take it!" Chaim roared. "But one way or another, we're off." He snapped his whip for emphasis. "So? What's it going to be? David, take the fucking thing already, you horse's behind! How long are we going to sit here freezing our asses off?"

David looked from Chaim to Eve, afraid of disobeying the one, afraid of offending the other.

Suddenly, the tears rolled down Eve's cheeks and she turned to her father and held out her arms to receive the samovar. "God be with you, Father." She smiled at him through her tears, not wanting him to berate himself too harshly after she was gone. *He* wasn't the beast; he was only a poor timid lamb.

Then Deborah came running out of the house with a pair of brass candlesticks, with Leah right behind her. "I forgot all about these. They were your own mother's. Every bride must have her own candlesticks."

Eve set the samovar down on the floor of the sleigh and took the candlesticks. "Thank you." She forced herself to smile. Her sisters-in-law had tried to be good to her in their own way.

"God will bless you, Eve. You'll see. He'll send you many children to love."

"Enough already!" Chaim yelled into the cold air. "Giddyup!" The horses' breath sent steam toward the gray sky.

"Goodbye, Papa! Deborah! Leah!" She turned to wave. "Father, I understand," she cried out, wanting to spare him further grief. But they were already several lengths away and her words were carried off on the wind.

Another sleigh came toward them as theirs sped along, skidding from side to side from the excessive speed. Chaim gave not an inch, forcing the other sled off the road, screaming at the same time, "Give me the road! Give me the road, you piece of a bitch's miscarriage!"

19

David shook his head in despair. Not only didn't he respect his father, he obeyed him only because he feared him. He glanced at Eve sideways, thinking *she* was more worthy of respect than anyone he had ever known. He wished he could find the words to tell her this and the words to beg her forgiveness. If he could do that then maybe he could also tell her he loved her. Then, maybe, one day she would tell him that she loved him too. After that, maybe the day might come when she'd respect him.

He asked her if she were warm enough and even though she didn't answer, he fumbled with the lap robe trying to pull it closer about her. When she still wouldn't look at him, he sighed in anguish.

Good! Eve thought. Let him suffer! She wanted him to suffer! It was only fair. How dare he think that he could simply *seize* another human being for his own? It was only right that he endure all the torments of hell! Then she let out a moan of a sigh. No matter how much *he* suffered, her own fate was sealed.

Clearly it was useless to try to escape from the clutches of the Markoffs. They'd find her no matter where she went and they'd drag her back. Ordinary men would probably allow her to leave if she wanted to; they'd weary of her and her attempted escapes. But not Chaim Markoff! With him it would be a matter of family honor that she remain under his roof.

She'd seen that look in his eye when he dragged her across the floor by the hair. He had relished it! *He* was her enemy, not this boy sitting beside her. She glanced at David out of the corner of her eye. He *did* seem miserable. She sensed that he was sorry for the way he had treated her. He did seem to be trying to make up to her. She had to concede that whatever he had done was not entirely his fault. It was his father's. How could one expect anything more of a son with a father like that? And he had been motherless, as she herself had been. She knew how painful that was. And he was young, probably only a few months older than she was.

She thought of all the things people had said about him—how he had fallen in love with her on sight; how mad he was about her; how good-looking he was. Yes, she had to admit that he was handsome. She saw now that her brothers wouldn't have hesitated at marrying her off to the dotard with crumbs in his long gray beard and hands that were shiny with yellowed old skin, hands that would shake as they touched her. Oh yes, that could easily have happened. Her brothers were capable of doing exactly that! Blushing, she thought of the marriage bed with that old man and she had to admit to herself, embarrassing as it was, that for all her rage and indignation, she would choose this David, with his uncontrolled passion, over the other.

Then she asked herself: *Do* you want to spend the rest of your life in bitter recriminations, railing against a harsh God and a harsher fate? Surely that was a sin, she told herself. And if it wasn't a sin, surely it *was* a waste of her life. Hardly the kind of life she had envisioned for herself. Life was too precious to throw it away like that—a sea salted with bitter tears. Besides, she was supposed to be so smart. Everyone had always said she was smart. Her brothers had always said she was too smart for her own good. Well, what would a truly clever woman do in a situation like this? Wouldn't she find a way to make life good? For herself, and even for her husband? For the children that would come along?

Yes, a clever woman would try to make the best of a situation, would try to make a good life for herself, and even for this wild man who sat beside her now, he who had been so determined to make her his own. After all, was he really that impossible? She had read worldly novels where the couplings had been almost as savage and at the time she had thought the love scenes wildly romantic, exciting. In those novels all the maidens dreamed of a strong, handsome stranger falling in love with them and carrying them off, mad with impetuous desire.

While her sense of the romantic reacted to this new vision of her husband's passion for her, her head told her she was being ridiculous. Theirs was hardly a storybook marriage. For one, the existence the Lithuanian Jews led in this provincial corner of the Russian world was hardly the stuff fairy tales were made of. Still, she *could* make an effort, she *should* make the effort. It was the intelligent thing to do.

She looked at David again from under her lashes. He seemed so crushed, so repentant. Perhaps it was meant to be that they should make a life together. Some kind of preordained destiny. Perhaps it was all written down somewhere.

David felt her gaze, smiled at her tentatively, his eyes begging for forgiveness. She quickly looked away to stare at the huge, awesome back of her father-in-law. *He* was the obstacle to her and her new husband finding happiness together. She was convinced of it. She'd have to think how to deal with him, this brute who was so accustomed to having his undisputed way. He raised a strange feeling in her. It was more than fear. It was a kind of unhealthy dread. There was an essence emanating from him. What was it? The scent of potential evil? Or was she just being melodramatic? Perhaps he was nothing more than a mean, cantankerous man.

But still she had to deal with him. She'd have to be very clever, and she'd have to be brave. He *was* intimidating. But now she was determined to find a way to contend with him. She would! Her future life, the life of this boy sitting beside her who would share her future, depended on it.

2.

Upon arrival at the Markoff house, Eve went directly to the room she was going to share with her husband. She carried the candlesticks herself, directed David to follow with the samovar. Eagerly he did as he was bidden. He was just glad that she was speaking to him at all.

She placed the candlesticks on either side of the samovar on top of the dresser and proceeded to unpack her straw suitcases which held both clothes and books.

"Don't you want the samovar and the candlesticks in the front room?" David asked.

"If that's what I wanted I wouldn't have placed them here."

"I thought that's where people usually put things like that," he mumbled. "In the front room . . ."

"It's not *my* front room. When I have my own maybe that's where I'll put them."

"But this *is* your home," he said, subdued, not wanting to fight with her but at the same time wanting to keep up a conversation.

She cast him an oblique look. "My home? I hardly think so. Who rules the roost here?"

He had to say his father.

"Then this is your father's house."

"That's true, but we all live here—my brothers and their wives and their children. Nobody questions whose house it is."

"Exactly. *Children* don't question their father's authority. That's understood. I guess you and your brothers are children. Not men."

He was stung. "But your own brothers live in *your* father's house," he retorted.

She tossed her head. "A different situation entirely. Our family has the tradition of a rabbinical dynasty where many families lived at one court. And too, my brothers live in at least equal stature with my father, which certainly doesn't seem to be the case around here. Besides, who said my brothers are men? Do real men allow infidels to carry off their daughters or their sisters? Actually my brothers are no more honorable men than you and your brothers."

David blushed at this reference to his honor. He had *not* acted in an honorable manner. He couldn't refute that. But at the same time he was honestly perplexed. Did she really expect him to challenge his father's authority?

22

She hung up several dresses, all in different bright colors. Without looking at him she said, "I'll need a place to put my books. A bookcase . . ."

Eager to please her he ran to find something that would do. If there had been a bookcase in the house, he would have emptied its contents to the floor, flung them to the wind, hurled them to the sky. But there wasn't a bookcase since there weren't any books. He returned with a long table which he carried above his head as easily as if it were a bag of feathers. "Will this do?" he asked anxiously.

"I suppose. It will have to, if there's nothing else." She gave a small sigh.

He watched as she arranged the books to her satisfaction, she taking her time and he wrestling with his eagerness for her to be finished.

In an attempt at making conversation, he said, "You have so many books. Where did you get them all?"

"Where do you think? Most of them I bought off the wagons of the second-hand book peddlers in the marketplace. Or from the bookstalls in Kovno." She smiled slightly in a somewhat superior fashion. "Surely you must know they do *have* bookstalls in Kovno?"

"Of course . . ." he muttered. Actually, although he was often in the city of Kovno—it was right over the bridge—he had never once taken notice. Why would he? He had never bought a book in his life.

"And occasionally I've been given a few books by people who are cultured enough to have had them in the first place."

Cultured? He didn't know what she was talking about. Now he was eager to drop the conversation about books. She *was* talking to him, which was what he wanted, but it was hardly a *friendly* conversation. Her manner was barely polite, more cold than not. He wondered what he could say next, *do* next. Technically, one might say it was *still* his wedding day since twenty-four hours hadn't yet elapsed since they had stood under the wedding canopy. Yet, under the circumstances, how could he even *suggest* to her that they—no, of course he couldn't do that—and he certainly wasn't going to repeat his behavior of the night before. He would as soon kill himself as do that. Well, he would have to await a clue from her as to how to proceed.

Finally she seemed to be finished with the books and she requested a basin of water and a piece of soap. Instantly he ran to get her what she wanted. When he came back with the soap and water, she picked up the piece of soap and sniffed at it delicately, wrinkled her little nose. "Oh my, your father's soap smells terrible. It smells of lye. It's laundry soap. Isn't there any other kind?"

He shrugged, perplexed. What did he know about soap? Whether it smelled terrible or if it was sweet-smelling? He had no idea if there were two kinds of soap in the household.

She asked him to leave the room so that she might undress and perform her toilette. He had never heard anyone use the word before—*toilette*. But he gathered what it meant. The word and the very notion of her undressing left him both blushing and atremble. Despite her less than friendly tone, it seemed she *was* preparing to receive him in a manner suitable and proper for a bride of her refinement. He left the room quickly, both elated and aroused, almost unbearably aroused. He thought of asking when he could return. Five minutes? Ten? He decided it would be better not to ask. She'd probably call him when she was ready.

But the minutes passed. It seemed to him that it was a half hour at the very least. He was beside himself with anxiety, shivering with desire and longing. But he cautioned himself to keep his head, to move slowly. Now it had become as important to him to make her love him as it was to take possession of her body. If he didn't wait for her to indicate that he might approach her, the very small progress he had made would be lost. He would *not* hurl himself upon her again. He'd go slowly, he'd be gentle, as difficult as that might be.

He waited in front of the closed door a few more minutes. Then, unable to stand it any longer, he called out, "Eve?"

"Yes?"

"Can I come in now?"

"If you must."

If you must? What kind of an answer was that? He threw the door open and practically hurtled inside. To his amazement he found her sitting up in bed attired in a nightdress with a high, lace-trimmed collar. She was reading, of all things! And next to her, where he envisioned himself, was a pile of books.

He didn't know how to deal with this turn of events. "You're reading?"

"Does it look as if I'm asleep?"

"But you're in bed and it's the middle of the day—"

"I didn't think it was night."

"Are you sick?"

"You might say I'm not well."

He was drowning in a mass of confusion. Did she mean then that her body was in its flux? "You mean that—"

She looked at him sideways. In amusement? In contempt? He wasn't sure. "No, I don't mean *that*." She turned back to her book.

"What *do* you mean?"

"The body is not the only part of a person that can sicken, you know."

He didn't say anything in answer to that. He had no idea what he could say. He decided he didn't feel all that well himself. He had assumed that she'd been ready to—now he was convinced that he knew nothing. Not knowing what else to do, he just stood there at the bed while she continued to read. It occurred to him that he could climb into the bed too, but at the same time he realized that might be a very foolhardy act.

He cleared his throat to get her attention. She looked up at him, patiently waiting for him to speak. "Do you mean that it's your spirit that's not well?" he asked.

Well, she thought, the situation does improve. "The spirit . . . the soul . . .

24

It doesn't matter what one calls it," she said airily. "But the soul *can* sicken and die quicker than the body, you know."

He muttered something unintelligible.

"I don't understand what it is you're saying," she said. "Is it possible that you wish to apologize? Is it that you're saying you're sorry for your unforgivable behavior? If that's so, I suggest that you speak out like a man instead of mumbling."

He fought for control. He wanted to scream. He was beset with frustration. "Are you saying that I'm not a man?"

She was enjoying herself. "I'm not sure *who's* saying it. Perhaps it's the voice of my body. But then again maybe it's the voice of my spirit."

His face turned so vivid a shade of red she wondered if he was thinking possibly of striking her. Actually, for the few moments while the blood pounded in his head so furiously, it was not completely inconceivable. But he controlled himself, desperately trying to emulate her airy tone. "You can tell them," he said, "your body, your voice, your spirit—that David Markoff is a man!"

"Ah! Then you are apologizing? Good!"

He stared at her in disbelief. Somehow she had maneuvered him into expressing something he had never said. He *was* sorry for his behavior—that was certainly true—and he had been groping for a way to express this, but he had never come close to saying it. Still, she had said it for him and now that she had, he was relieved. It was done and he hadn't had to utter the difficult words, words that men didn't usually say to women. Oh, she *was* clever as everyone said. Now he wished only that he could find the words to tell her that he loved her. Or that somehow she'd manage to say those words for him too.

He saw her open her mouth to speak and his heart raced. All she said was, "Well, at least that's a step in the right direction. Perhaps one of these days you'll even find the courage to let your father know that he has a grown man for a son."

He staggered with disappointment. Now she was back to his father and the matter of whether he himself was really a man or a weak boy. At least that's what he *thought* she was saying. "How do I tell my father that?" he mumbled.

She smiled the barest of smiles. "You tell him that only a child lives in his father's house."

He could have wept with his frustration. What could he possibly say to her to make her understand that what she wanted of him was impossible? Then he thought of the Ten Commandments. After all, she was a pious girl. "The Commandment says to honor thy father, doesn't it? If I go against my father that would be breaking the Commandment, wouldn't it?" He hoped she'd be impressed with his logical and brilliant answer.

But no! She only laughed in an affected manner before she said, "Do you really think you honor someone by demeaning yourself? In the end one honors one's father best by honoring himself first."

He didn't even know what she was talking about. If he followed her meaning at all, it wasn't words he wanted to hear. In fact, he had lost all taste for their conversation. His head ached, he felt sick. But he had to say something. He had to give her some kind of an answer. Finally he asked her, "What do you think my father would say if I told him all this?"

"What would he say?" she asked softly. "*I* have an idea but there's really one way to find out for sure, isn't there? Perhaps one of these days you'll have the courage to find out." And with that she turned back to her book.

At nightfall he announced to her that the family was ready to eat. She told him that she wasn't joining them. Rather, she continued reading until it was late and then prepared herself for sleep. When David came back to the room when dinner was over he undressed and then made tentative motions of getting into the bed with her. She lifted her eyebrows at him. "Oh? Shall I assume then that you've spoken to your father about your intentions to make your own home for your wife and yourself?"

David made a guttural sound, looked at her with desperate eyes.

"Was that a yes or a no?"

"A no!" he shouted.

"Then unless it's your intention to get into this bed by brute force I suggest you take your body elsewhere to sleep."

Anger and desire wrestled with prudence and shame. "I'll not force anything," he said proudly.

"Good. I'm glad to hear that. You can sleep in the front room on one of the benches."

He closed his eyes in terror at that prospect. What would his father, his brothers, even the wives, think of him if he did such a thing? It was the most humiliating thing he could possibly do. He'd sooner kill himself. For a moment he wished he had never laid eyes on her. He was beginning to wonder if he had married a real girl at all or some kind of demon. If only she weren't so beautiful. But then some people, those who believed in demons, said that often they took the shape of beautiful women the better to fool people. . . .

"I can't go to sleep in the front room," he said desperately. "I'd be the joke of the whole family. My brothers would laugh at me. My father would spit on me. Look here. I'll sleep in the bed but on the edge only. I won't touch you, I promise."

"I'm sorry but it would only be possible for you to sleep in this bed if you forced your way in."

He was too weary to argue anymore about it, too weary and too heartsick. Not knowing what else to do he threw himself down on the floor. He didn't even have a comforter but he didn't care anymore if he froze to death. Just as pride kept him from sleeping in the front room and also kept him from forcing his way into the bed, it kept him from searching out some kind of cover.

Eve went promptly to sleep, well satisfied with her own progress. It would only be a matter of days, she thought, before David would declare his independence from Chaim. But David lay awake all night, shivering with cold, while all sorts of thoughts scurried around in his head. He was caught in a dilemma—too terrified to stand up to his father, yet yearning for his wife's submission. Not only her submission but her love as well. And he could not deny it, he yearned to hear her call him a man. Still, it never occurred to him to wonder at how his thinking had changed in less than twenty-four hours. All he could think of was whether there was an answer to his problems.

When his father and brothers rode out just after dawn in their search for livestock, David went with them, leaving his bride in her bed. Gazing at her as lovely in sleep as she was awake, he was consumed with wonder and longing. He prayed that by some miracle, by the time he returned that night, she'd be in the kitchen with the other wives, preparing the evening meal. She'd greet him with a secret smile, with an invitation in her spectacular green eyes.

When he did return that evening, only the sisters-in-law were in the kitchen with their children and Eve was still in her room. Hannah told him that she'd been there all day excepting for the time when she emerged to use the outdoor facilities. Solemnly Miriam told him that Eve hadn't eaten all day and Dora added, "Except for two cups of tea." Ruth who was very thin herself, said with a little smile, "If you're not careful your bride's going to be as thin as a stick."

While his brothers looked on with a combination of leers and amusement and his father fixed him with a contemptuous eye, David headed for the bedroom. He found Eve sitting up in bed again, reading. Her hair was in a loose knot, with tendrils prettily escaping here and there. She looked not at all ill. As a matter of fact, she looked as fresh and perky as a spring flower growing in a meadow. Still he asked, "Are you well?"

"I'm not unwell."

"You haven't been out of the room all day except for—"

"That's true."

"Why not?"

"I had no reason to leave it except for—"

"But they said you haven't eaten all day—"

"That's true."

"But why not? You *have* to eat." He was at a loss as how to cope with this latest development—a fasting wife.

"I can't eat."

"Why not?"

"I can't eat food I haven't helped prepare. That would be most unfair to your sisters-in-law."

"You *could* help prepare the food. Then—" he said hopefully.

"That's an impossibility."

"Why?" he almost screamed.

"Because it's your father's kitchen. I can't prepare food in your father's kitchen."

"Then you'll starve," he said spitefully, losing patience.

She smiled a little, showing even white teeth. "A possibility—"

"But then you'll die!"

"That too is a possibility," she conceded cheerfully.

"That's against the Law, you know," he cried triumphantly, thinking that at last he had her. "The Scriptures say that it's one's duty to live. Life is sacred, after all. I'm really surprised that an educated girl like you doesn't know that."

She smiled to herself. This was more like it. She was even enjoying herself. He might be uneducated but he wasn't dull. "Ah, but you're talking about my body. What if in saving my body, my spirit dies? What do the Scriptures say about that?"

He had no answer. How could he? He wanted to shake her, to force her to eat, to force her to eat her very words as well. Most of all he wanted to make love to her, but he knew that was impossible. He slammed out of the room. After dinner he returned to find her presumably asleep. He made no attempt to get into the bed, reconciled to sleeping on the floor. But this time he found himself a cover. He slept the night through very pleasantly dreaming of a room shrouded in candlelight with a table at which only he and Eve sat, feasting. And while he dreamt, Eve planned her next move.

The next morning the men went off as usual and the wives went about their chores wondering what was going to happen with their new sister-in-law. She was a strange one all right. Would she spend the day in bed again? they wondered. But it wasn't very long before Eve made an appearance, wearing a bright green dress the likes of which they had rarely seen, and her hair was elaborately arranged in a cascade of curls. They were put off by her grand appearance and mostly ignored her as she fixed herself a glass of tea and sat herself down at the kitchen table to drink it. But Eve smiled at them beguilingly and they had to smile back at her, one by one. But why shouldn't they smile at her? That she looked like a queen couldn't be counted against her, after all. But her family was said to be poor so where did she come by a dress like that?

"What a beautiful dress!" the youngest one, Dora, breathed shyly. "I've never seen such a beautiful dress in my entire life." She came over and tentatively touched a sleeve with its flounce of lace. "I could die for a dress like that!" she said longingly.

"Thank you. I made it myself."

Hannah looked Eve over carefully. "So? You sew that well? And I thought you spent all your time in bed reading . . ." Her face was devoid of expression but her eyes sparkled.

Eve laughed. This Hannah had a sense of humor and that was encouraging. "No, not all my time. Only part of it. Sometimes I sew."

"I wish I could sew," the round, pleasant-faced Miriam said, but without any envy. "Not so much for myself but for my girls."

"That's all she has, you understand," Ruth said quickly. "All daughters and not a son among them."

Miriam shrugged, seemingly amiable. "It bothers *her* more than it does me. I like my girls."

"I'd take a girl happily," Dora blurted. "I'd gladly take anything that was sent to me—"

"She's barren, you understand," Ruth explained, not unkindly.

"What kind of a word is that to use?" Hannah demanded. To Eve she said, "Dora's only been married two years. She's barely twenty. She's got plenty of time before she's called barren."

Eve nodded. This Hannah's the keeper of the peace, she thought. And the oldest. Ruth, who was holding a very large baby to her breast, seemed to have a sharp tongue. While Miriam appeared to be very good-natured and without guile, Eve didn't doubt that her plump sister-in-law had her cutting edge too, as far as Ruth was concerned anyhow. Poor Dora was so sweet and obviously without any authority, since she was shy, the youngest, and the only one without a child.

Miriam brought a glass of tea for herself and joined Eve at the table. "Do you make all your own clothes?" When Eve nodded, she observed, "It's a gift from heaven, golden hands."

"But on the other hand, I don't know how to cook at all. Maybe I'll teach you to sew and you can teach me to cook."

Miriam laughed heartily. "Me? Sew? I have ten thumbs. But I'll be glad to show you how to fix a few dishes. Why not?"

"I'll say why not!" Ruth said sourly. "We can certainly use a few more hands in this kitchen. With all these mouths to feed all we do practically is cook and wash up. I wish *I* had a little time to sew or read—"

Miriam laughed. "*If* you could read in the first place."

Ruth, sitting at the table now with her glass of tea, still nursing the baby, appeared not to take any notice of this jab. "Just you wait, Eve. After you have a few children, God willing that they should all be sons like mine and not all girls like some *other* people I could mention, you won't have so much time left over to sew fancy dresses." She moved the baby to the other breast, smiling grimly. She had gotten *her* jab in. "But if you're not worried about getting that dress dirty, I'll be glad to teach you to cook myself."

Hannah joined them at the table. "I think before you start cooking, Eve, you better start eating a little something. You know what they say about a new bride? She has to keep up her strength."

They all smirked at her implication and Eve laughed. "No, thank you. This tea will do me just fine."

"At least have a piece of bread with something on it. Or at least a few cookies to go along with the tea. Dora, get out the cookies and don't just stand there hovering,'' Hannah directed. "Get yourself a glass of tea and sit down.''

Dora ran happily to get the cookies and the tea as if she had only been waiting to be asked.

"Now tell me,'' Eve said as if it were a matter of the highest importance, "who is married to whom?''

Hannah began, "I'm married to Abraham who's the oldest son. Next comes Shlomo, Miriam's, and next is Hershel, Ruth's, and just before David comes Yacob, Dora's. As for the children—'' she leaned down and wiped the nose of a four-year-old sitting on the floor nearby, playing with a wooden toy, "you'll get acquainted soon enough. Just be careful they don't get your dress dirty. Are you sure you won't have a little something to eat? An egg? A piece of cheese?''

"No, thank you.'' Eve made up her mind that since her dress seemed the focus of all their attention, she'd make each one of them a new dress, one as grand as her own. Besides helping her to make friends with them, it seemed the right thing to do. "As soon as I finish my tea I'm going to the marketplace to buy some material, the prettiest piece of cloth I can find—''

They looked at her with bemused expressions. Yesterday she had stayed in bed all day reading and today she was buying material for another pretty dress and she sounded as if she were waiting for them all to cheer. Not that they minded, still—

"—And then when I return I'm going to start sewing immediately. I'm going to make *one of you* the most beautiful dress I've ever made.''

They all looked amazed, each face reflecting the same thought. *A dress for one of us? Well! But which one?*

"Which one of us?'' Ruth demanded. She snapped the cheek of her son who, falling asleep, had stopped suckling.

"Well, I intend for each one of you to have a new dress. One at a time, of course, as fast as I can sew.''

Now the women were really shocked. She was going to make *four* fancy dresses . . .

"Which one of us will you start with?'' Dora asked longingly but without any real hope. She knew it wouldn't be she. She was always last . . .

Eve wished she could say, "I'm going to start with you, Dora, so tell me, which color do you most absolutely adore?'' But she couldn't. Obviously it was Hannah who had to be first. "I'm sure you all agree Hannah should be first. Then I'll make one for Miriam and then Ruth.'' She looked at the forlorn Dora. "I'll sew as fast as I possibly can,'' she promised. "It really won't take that long.''

But Hannah shook her head. "No. I don't think we can allow you to do this. Who, after all, has the time to make such a dress for another? And four of them? No . . .''

Dora's face fell a mile and Miriam's mouth suddenly turned down. Ruth shot an angry look at Hannah.

30

"But that's the point," Eve smiled. "*I* do have the time. Especially since I won't be helping with the cooking right away. So tell me, Hannah, what color do you love?"

Still Hannah hesitated while the others fixed her with beseeching eyes. "*Nu?*" she said finally. "Do I have a choice then? God forbid I should stand in all of your way. You'll kill me. You pick the color, Eve, and the material and the style of it since you know about such things." The other three women circled around Eve, fingering the fabric of her dress, offering suggestions for Hannah's dress.

"But I insist that you have something to eat first before you start in with the sewing. How about some chicken soup with noodles?" Hannah urged. "We made it fresh yesterday."

"I can't."

"And why not? Are you sick, God forbid?"

"I can't eat because if someone should ask if I've eaten today I don't want you to say yes. But I don't want you to lie for me either."

So, Hannah thought. *She wants poor David to worry that she's starving. So, it's her business. Their business.* "Well, I can't force you to eat—"

"No," Ruth agreed. She thought too that the no eating business had to do with David. Then she smirked. "If anything we should be forcing Miriam *not* to eat by the looks of her." As she spoke she was trying to push her nipple back into her son's resisting mouth.

"Better you should worry more about why you're forcing that child to nurse when he doesn't want to," Miriam retaliated with a spiteful smile.

"Oh? You're trying to say something? Spit it out!"

But instead of answering, Miriam maddeningly hummed a little tune.

"Stop it, you two!" Hannah commanded. "Do you want Eve to think all we do is quarrel around here?" She turned back to Eve. "All right. If you're going to market I'll give you some money."

"I have a little," Eve said, thinking of the three rubles she had brought with her.

"No need for you to spend your money. We'll take the money from the household funds." She removed a jar from a shelf.

Eve's interest was aroused. "The household money? And do all the husbands contribute?"

"The husbands?" Ruth snickered. "Where would they get the money to contribute? Only Chaim contributes. He's the only one who has two coins to rub together."

"You mean no one gets paid any wages? They work and . . . all of you . . . don't have any money of your own?" By now she knew the answer.

"Not a kopeck," Ruth answered vehemently.

"Chaim says we have whatever we need," Miriam explained. "A roof over our heads, food on the table, warm coats—"

31

"Yes," Ruth sneered. "*His* roof, *his* food and *his* say if we need a new coat."

"I see," Eve was thoughtful. "It's *his* purse and his purse strings."

"If you want to put it that way," Hannah acknowledged. "But what's the use of talking? That's the way it is. But to give the devil his due, he usually doesn't say a word about how we spend the household money. All he cares is that whatever he wants to eat is on the table and that there's plenty of vodka."

"But what would happen if you spent all the money at once? Used it all up? What would happen if you had to ask for more right away?"

Hannah shook her head. "It's never happened. Who would be so foolish as to spend it all and have to ask for more?"

"I'd gladly die before I'd ask for more," Dora rolled her eyes.

"On the other hand, he'd probably die from shock if anyone had the nerve to ask him," Ruth said, giving her son a shake. "Look! Would you look at this child? Look at how he won't eat!"

"Is it any wonder?" Miriam asked Eve. "Every time he takes a breath she sticks that swollen udder back in his mouth. How happy would anyone be to eat if he's eaten all day?"

"I'd say very happy if it was *you*," Ruth quickly countered, looking pointedly at Miriam's plump figure.

Miriam laughed in an affected manner. "Why don't you tell Eve why you insist on giving that child the tit day and night when he's already as big as a horse?"

"Why don't you shut that mouth of yours that's as fat as the rest of you?"

"Girls!" Hannah rebuked them. "*Sha* already! I'm ashamed of both of you!"

"Well, if she didn't pick on me I wouldn't have anything to say to her," Miriam said defensively. "Everyone knows how good-natured *I* am!" She smiled widely to show that it was true. "Here, Ruth darling. Give me the baby and let me put him in the cradle for you. We'll give him and those poor tits of yours a rest." She took the boy from Ruth's arms and surprisingly enough Ruth didn't protest except to say, "You'll see. As soon as you lay him down he'll start to scream. That's why I keep feeding him."

But the baby gave a gurgle or two and promptly went to sleep. Even Ruth had to laugh. "He's doing it out of pure spite. To make a fool of me. You'll see, Eve, after you have a couple of your own. They live to see how they can make a fool out of you. Eve—?"

Hearing her name, Eve looked up. She had been lost in thought. Now she continued aloud the conversation she'd been having with herself. "The household money? It belongs more to all of you, you know, than to Chaim. He's only *one* person and all of you, and your husbands, all labor in his vineyard."

"Vineyard?" Dora was puzzled. "But he doesn't have any vineyards."

"She doesn't mean an actual vineyard," Hannah explained. "It's an expression from the Bible." And Dora said, "Oh," not understanding any better than she had before.

Well, they'll all understand better when I'm through, Eve thought. Action would explain better than words. She held out her hand. "Well, give me the money. Since it's really your money more than Chaim's, I'll buy a really beautiful piece of material for your dress, Hannah, no more than you deserve."

"Ah!" Hannah's eyes twinkled. "One deserves only what one can get."

Eve laughed. "I couldn't agree with you more."

Eve found the marketplace easily. As in all towns, it was the hub of the wheel, with the streets of houses the spokes. In the middle of the marketplace were wagons and stands, while shops and small stalls made up the perimeter. Everyone milling about took notice of her right away. Chaim's new daughter-in-law was a looker all right. Eve nodded and smiled at everyone and they couldn't help but smile back.

The very first thing Eve bought was a large piece of cheese and two rolls which she consumed ravenously. Then she purchased an apple and a pear which she ate more leisurely, walking around. She had no guilt feelings about spending the money on herself; her husband worked for Chaim, therefore the money belonged to her too. Now when David asked his sisters-in-law if she had eaten, they could say no without lying. It was unlikely that he'd ask her if she'd eaten in the marketplace, so now he could continue to be concerned about her.

She rummaged among the stalls until she found a length of cloth that pleased her; it was the color of a summer sky for the fair, blue-eyed Hannah. Then she purchased a piece of sheer white lawn, some filmy lace and a length of red ribbon, and hurried back, eager to get to work. Four dresses were a large order, and in her spare time, in the privacy of her room, she'd work on her own new chemise—one with a low-cut bodice, ruffles of lace, trimmed with the red satin ribbon. Even to herself it sounded irresistible.

She set to work while the women crowded around her.

"Don't you need a pattern?" Hannah asked as Eve cut directly into the blue cloth.

"No, I never use a pattern. I like to make my own designs. I just use my eyes."

"It's all in the hands," Miriam nodded her head. "Golden hands, like I said."

Eve pointed to her head. "I think it's up there. Everything's like that, I think. You have to see something very clearly in your mind first and if you see it hard enough and clear enough, that's half the battle."

Hannah looked at her speculatively. "I have a feeling that everything you see in that head of yours usually turns out just the way you see it."

When David returned that night the sight that greeted him was enough to make him giddy. Eve, with her hair in a bustle of curls that fell clear down her back and dressed in an incredibly pretty dress, sat by the kitchen fire sewing! She was up and about and *sewing* of all things! Seemingly gay! *What could that*

33

mean but—? His heart pounded with excitement and the joy quickly spread down to that place where, at least, *he* knew he was a man. He detected a specially festive mood in the kitchen. Even Ruth, usually glum, was smiling and Hannah, usually serious, was humming. The children were playing contentedly instead of screaming. He had no way of knowing that Eve had entertained them all, women and children alike, with fanciful stories all afternoon as she sewed, but still he had a feeling that it was she who was responsible for the pleasant atmosphere.

Chaim was also taking notice, David saw. He was peering suspiciously about and his gaze under the bristling yellow-gray eyebrows seemed to center on Eve too. What was in his expression? It wasn't his usual glowering disapproval. Rather it seemed a mixture of disapproval with—? David wasn't sure but he didn't care either. *If Eve was performing such a homey task as sewing and so attractively turned out at the same time, it could only mean one thing. She was sending him a message.*

He wouldn't even inquire if she had eaten today. Perhaps at dinner she'd even slip an especially delectable piece of meat onto his plate as she helped serve to indicate further that she felt affectionate toward him. He'd seen the other wives do that from time to time and the sight had always made him feel particularly lonely, bereft. *But tonight? Tonight was his night!*

As the women brought the steaming platters and bowls into the dining room, David saw Eve rise from her chair. But instead of going to help them, she gathered up all the bits and pieces of her needlework and went toward their room! Without even a darting look in his direction! *What did she expect him to do? Follow her? God knew he wanted to! Gladly he would have given up his dinner to follow her, to find her undressing in their room, to take her in his arms as she modestly yet passionately submitted to him.*

He looked around, saw his father watching him with a peculiar expression and narrowed eyes. He tried to figure it out. Finally he interpreted it as: She's only a female, you idiot! Eat your food! Drink your whiskey! A man takes a woman when he's ready. On a full stomach!

As for his brothers, they were smirking. No, he couldn't follow her now like a sniveling little boy toddling after his mother. He'd have to force himself to wait, wait until all the eating and drinking and talking was over, until the household slowly bedded itself down for the night. Then and only then could he go to his wife. He'd bear the waiting while his desire mounted, while he kept himself going by envisioning what awaited him at the end of the evening. . . .

An evening meal in the Markoff household was no simple matter nor was it of brief duration. First the women carried in all the food that had been prepared that day. Of necessity it was a prodigious amount. There'd be many different dishes—herring or some other kind of fish, smoked, pickled, boiled, to start, maybe even two kinds. There'd be at least one soup, maybe mushroom with

evening—bright as primroses, lutescent as sunshine. He thought that she really was no ordinary mortal being. Rather she was a golden angel and the very sight of her forced his heart up into his throat where it stuck, making him audibly suck in huge gulps of air in order to keep on breathing.

Seeing him, she rose and picked up all her sewing things, murmured a few words to the two small children pressed up against her legs in a half-daze, lost as they were in the imagery of the story she'd been telling them, and went quickly to her room. Making up his mind as quickly, David followed her. To hell with his brothers' snickers and the smirks of his sisters-in-law. To hell with whatever his father thought. Tonight he'd wait for no man to eat before he claimed his wife!

He ran into the room to find Eve already unbuttoning the neck of her dress. Her fingers were on the third button down, revealing the swell of her bosom and the sight of her exposed breasts left him unable to breathe. But Eve's fingers stopped unbuttoning. Rather her arms crisscrossed her bosom as if to hide even that small glimpse of her beauty from him.

"Yes?" she inquired as her emerald eyes sparkled, blinding him almost as completely as the golden vision of her had done only minutes before. He opened his mouth to speak but nothing came out and he gestured with his hands helplessly. Boldly she removed her arms from her breasts, placing her hands on her hips. "You've something to tell me? Is it that you've told your father that you're a man, after all? Is that why you're here now?"

He shook his head desperately, not being able to find his tongue.

"I see," she said, lowering her lashes and eclipsing the shining lights of her eyes, leaving fluttery shadows high on her cheekbones. "That's very disappointing," she whispered.

A sigh of anguish escaped David's lips and then she sighed too. A tiny sigh of disillusionment. Then she went to the shelf where his comforter was stored, removed it and threw it on the floor. He stared at it for a moment before turning on his heel and walking from the room.

He left the house by a side door, trying to avoid being seen by any member of the household. He slouched off to the barn, pulled a fur blanket out of the sleigh and lay down wearily on a pile of straw. He'd spend the night here rather than on the floor inside and he didn't care if he froze to death. He probably would. And he didn't give a damn about his dinner either. No matter what he did, whether he ate or didn't eat, he already knew that he was going to be hungry, hungrier than he had ever been.

After matters went on in much the same way for some time, Eve decided it was time to revise her strategy. Maybe if a woman wanted a boy to act like a man she had to treat him like a man in the first place.

At sundown that Sabbath day the other wives readied the evening meal for the men coming home from the House of Worship but Eve readied only herself. When David entered the house, his eyes scanning the front rooms for her as had become his habit and, finding her not there, he went in search of her with an air of gloom which too had become habit. The door to their room was closed and while he called out her name he had no real hope of being asked to enter. Or not with any show of enthusiasm. But wonder of wonders, tonight her voice came to him softly, even invitingly. Trembling, he entered the room. What he saw made him doubt his own sight. He must be dreaming! There before him stood his wife as no other wife ever appeared, he was sure. Was it an angel? No, not an angel but a siren! A spellbinder, barefoot and alluring as a temptress. She wore some kind of garment made of some thin material adorned with lace and red ribbon. Did a flesh-and-blood woman appear before her husband like this?

Pale slender arms. A throat enticing in its white hollows. Softly curving shoulders. When his eyes dared to glance down from the shoulders—the sweet round swell of creamy breasts. Then, as if that vision were insufficient to stun him, the lovely arms lifted, the fingers entangled themselves in the mass of hair and with one graceful gesture her hair unfurled and the brilliant abundance came tumbling down. The dreamlike vision tossed her head, sending the glistening waves swirling all around, enveloping her in a fiery golden splendor.

He attempted to speak but his mouth was too parched. He heard the vision say: "Who will make love to me then? A boy or a man . . . ?"

He came toward her as if in a trance. She closed her eyes. She felt his hands so hot they seared through the cloth of her undergarment. He picked her up and gently laid her on the bed. In what manner would he make love to her? she wondered. Would he tear the chemise from her unresisting body? Or would he remove it slowly, savoring each touch? But then, before anything else, she felt his warm breath upon her throat and she waited. Soon she felt his warm lips kiss each toe, one after the other, and then his lips moved up her thighs and her lips curved into a smile. . . .

Later he asked, "Whom are you married to?" and she opened her eyes wide. "I think that after all, I'm married to a man."

3.

Now that she and David were truly man and wife, both in body and spirit, Eve was ready to advance to the next step in her plan. She was determined to establish David as a man in his father's household. One step at a time, she told herself.

Accordingly, she insisted on helping to prepare that evening's meal, offering to make the small mountain of potato pancakes that were needed to fill all the many mouths. "But I'll need instruction."

"Latkes aren't difficult. I'll show you how to make them," Miriam offered.

Immediately Ruth objected. "*You* always put in too much egg and then they come out too soft. Latkes have to be crisp."

"But if you don't put in enough eggs, they fall apart. As a matter of fact, *yours* always fall apart," Miriam flashed a retaliatory smile.

"*Sha,* you two!" Hannah waved them away. "I'll show Eve myself."

"Oh, pardon me," Ruth huffed. "*You* always put in too much onion."

Miriam placed her hands on her hips. "Much as I hate to say it, Hannah, I have to say Ruth's right. When I eat *your* latkes, I'm never sure if I'm eating potato latkes or onion latkes."

Hannah was taken aback, offended. "The chick doesn't teach the hen," she said haughtily.

Eve looked from one to the other. What had she started? Affection for one another was the binding quality in a family, much as the eggs were to the potato pancakes. And that's what she wanted for them—to be bound together in affection, *united.* In unity there was strength! Everyone knew that. If she wanted them to be unified the better to defy Chaim, it was for their own sake as well as hers and David's.

She saw that Dora's eyes were tearful from the strain of *not* offering her services as instructor. Dora was her solution. "You know what? The three of you are much too busy to bother with me. You have more important things to do. Why doesn't Dora show me how to make latkes? She can spare the time more than the three of you. Isn't that right, Dora?"

Pink with pleasure, Dora nodded her head. Eve put her arm around her. "Let's be careful not to use too many eggs, as Ruth said. We don't want the pancakes too soft. But we also don't want them to fall apart, so we have to make sure we use *enough*, just as Miriam does. But I do love lots of onion in mine just like Hannah does. Don't you love a lot of onion flavor?"

Under Dora's grateful instruction Eve peeled, grated, added, mixed, molded and mounded the cakes into shape, then placed them on the great paddles that went into the oven again and again until all the cakes were baked and ready to be kept warm until dinner. Then over the sisters-in-law's protests—they really wanted Eve to proceed with her sewing as they wanted their dresses more than her help—Eve gathered wood for the stove and fireplace and hauled in bucket after bucket of water from the well. In answer to their objections she said, "Oh, but I have to sing for my supper," which was completely enigmatic to the women.

Then she asked where the tablecloths were kept since she wanted to set the table. "So I can make my choice," she told Hannah.

"Choice?" Hannah laughed. "We have *two* tablecloths. One for everyday and one for the Sabbath. Here—"

Eve looked from one to the other. She couldn't see that the Sabbath one was any nicer than the everyday one. They were both old and worn and spotted with the stains of years of use. "Isn't there a really special one? Of damask or lace?"

Hannah laughed again. "Damask. Lace. You know we don't have such a fancy household."

Eve smiled faintly. Here was more ammunition with which to build her case against her father-in-law. It was necessary for the whole family to rebel against Chaim if her plan was to work. "Really! But these are such poor tablecloths and I was told that this isn't a poor household. Even poor Jews have a special cloth for the Sabbath. In my father's house, we didn't always have meat on the table but we always had a lovely cloth. That's how civilized people live. Obviously Chaim only doles out enough money for all of you to live in a very primitive fashion, not much better than the poorest of peasants."

Hannah looked at her skeptically. She pointed out that poor peasants lived in huts and not in a big house as they did, not to mention that they had a dining room separate from the kitchen, not to mention that they not only had meat on their table but fowl as well. So—

"But man does not live by bread alone," Eve blithely quoted. "And besides, by the time you women sit down to eat, how many times do you find all the meat and fowl gone?"

She found a length of pink fabric among her own things that would do for a tablecloth and she ran outside to break off a few boughs of pine. Coming back inside, she asked for a vase.

"We have no vases," Hannah said flatly.

"Not even one?"

"Not even a cracked one," Ruth commented.

"Most likely if we spent money on vases Chaim'd crack us over the head with them," Miriam joked.

Only Dora took Eve's request really seriously. "We *should* have at least one vase. We must be the only house in town without one."

Hannah threw her a look. "Well, we can always run over to the Squire's manor and borrow one. Why not?"

"Couldn't we use one of the pickling crocks?" Dora begged Eve.

"Yes, Eve," Hannah said dryly. "Please say yes. I'm sure no one will be able to eat a mouthful if we don't have *something*. . . ."

But Eve was determinedly cheerful. She arranged the boughs of pine in the brown crock Dora brought her, placing it in the middle of the table. She studied the effect of the pink cloth and pine boughs. Dora inclined her head and studied the effect too. "Lovely," she cried, and Ruth and Miriam agreed: *it was nice.* Hannah said nothing; she just stood to one side, a rusty smile on her face.

"Of course, it would be even lovelier if we had flowers instead of the pine boughs. If it were spring we could take the children and gather some wild flowers," Eve said.

"Oh yes, if only it were spring—" Dora echoed, wistful, caught up in the vision Eve painted.

"Yes," Hannah sucked in her cheeks. "That's all we have to do—all of us traipsing around picking flowers!" But then she had to laugh finally, kissing Eve on the cheek. "You're a one!"

"I'd gladly help you pick the flowers," Dora offered.

"I know you would," Eve said, giving her a hug. "And I wouldn't dream of picking flowers without you."

"Would you pick flowers without me then?" Ruth asked quickly, jealously.

"Of course not," Eve said.

But Miriam jeered, "But how could you go with that one?" indicating the baby rooting at Ruth's breast. "Unless you'd go along with it stuck to you like a bat, as if it were glued on." She gestured comically with her hands at her chest.

"So how about you? You'd go out picking but you wouldn't be able to bend down what with all that blubber surrounding you—" Ruth puffed out her cheeks and made circular motions with her free arm to indicate fat hips.

"*Sha!*" Hannah ordered. "Since the snow covers the wild flowers by only ten feet I don't think any of us will be running to pick flowers. That table looks beautiful enough for the Tsar himself, but how long are we going to stand here admiring it?" Still she herself lingered. "*Nu?* I wonder what Chaim will have to say about all this fuss and feathers?"

"Perhaps he'll say, 'Oh, how lovely! Why don't you ladies go out and buy us a proper vase and tablecloth so we can really eat like civilized people? So our table will be lovelier still,' " Eve exclaimed, and they all laughed. Then she went off to change her dress for dinner.

The pretty table wasn't the only surprise she had in store for Chaim that night.

Although the women were accustomed to seeing Eve in one splendid dress after the other, when she returned to the kitchen in a pink dress that oddly enough didn't clash with her hair, they were taken aback.

"It's the New Year maybe?" Hannah asked.

"Oh no," Dora answered. "The New Year's in the fall and now it's winter."

Ruth threw her a withering look. Dora was sweet but really impossible. "So, tell us, Eve, what's so special about tonight?"

"It's special because it's the first time I'll be sitting down to dinner with all of you." Actually, she *was* rather tired of eating her dinner in quick bites and gulps before the men came home from work.

Hannah nodded. Since Eve had helped with the cooking that day and made the fuss over setting the table, she should have known this was coming. Although none of them had questioned her, they'd all guessed that her not eating with them had something to do with a private matter between her and David. Their period of adjustment. So everything must be settled between them now. *So . . . That was good.*

"Tell us," Ruth smiled slyly. "How come we're being so honored tonight?"

Eve blushed and Miriam said, "Why shouldn't we be so honored? Maybe you better feed your son for a change and not ask so many questions."

"And maybe if you had a son, you'd feed him too instead of stuffing your own mouth for a change," Ruth quickly struck back.

The first thing David saw as he came in was Eve in a ruffled, delicious pink dress that rustled as she walked. And with green ribbons in her hair! If the sight of her wasn't enough to make his heart beat wildly, she ran up and kissed him full on the mouth for many seconds, making his ears roar, reminding him of their intimacy of the night before, as if he could have forgotten. He was overcome with emotion. He was also embarrassed in front of the family. At the same time he was delighted and magnificently proud. He couldn't remember ever being this happy. He didn't give a damn that his brothers were laughing at him, making rude comments. He didn't even care that his father was looking at him with narrowed, scowling eyes, as he embraced Eve.

The second thing David saw was the dining table covered with a pink cloth and adorned with pine boughs. Instinctively he knew that it was Eve who was responsible, and his spirit was further uplifted. There was no end to the wonder of her. He wondered if his father would notice. But Chaim merely sat down at the head of the table and waited for the women to start serving him, drumming his heavy fingers on the table impatiently. The women started their running with the bowls and the platters and the huge pots. While they did this, Eve was fetching extra chairs from wherever she found them and fitting them into place around the table.

They all stared at her—Chaim, the brothers, the sisters-in-law, David. Even the children. *What was she up to now, this crazy Eve?* She ignored the looks and after putting a last chair in place, sat down herself without so much as a glance at anyone. Elaborately arranging her dress in place around her, she smiled beatifically at Chaim, remarked, "Don't you think the table looks nice, father-in-law? I do so love sitting down to a pretty table."

There were gasps but no one said anything, even the children grew quiet. They, too, knew that no one sat down at the table with their grandfather, except for their fathers, and they only after Grandfather was through eating and ready for his first glass of tea. Then everyone looked at David to see how he was taking this. David, it seemed, had turned to stone. Next, they looked at Chaim, and he too was as if struck dumb although his eyes were full of rage. It was not inconceivable that he would hit Eve, hammer her with a mighty fist, flatten her with a swipe of a mighty arm, maybe even maim her or strike her dead.

Eve's lips were unnaturally stretched into a smile as she gaily called out, "Come, David! Sit down here beside me so we can eat this wonderful dinner together. I made the latkes myself, with Dora's help of course." Even as she spoke her heart went out to her husband. She knew she had placed him in one of the most difficult situations of his life.

David shuddered. He couldn't even bring himself to look at his father, much less— Not usually particularly intuitive, he realized at that second something that had never crossed his mind before. For every man there is a moment of painful truth when he has to make a terrible decision. His own moment had come. It was so quiet in the room, deathly quiet, as every person there waited to see what he would do, waited for him to choose between his father, whom he had never once challenged before, and his wife.

If I fail her now, she'll be vanquished, shamed, made to appear ridiculous. She won't ever again look at me as she did last night. Never again will we share what we shared last night—passion, laughter, intimacy— The seconds passed and still he didn't move.

If anyone had told him before last night about the special intimacy that could occur between a man and woman, he would have scoffed. He wouldn't have known what they were talking about. Most likely he would have laughed scornfully the way people do when there is mention of something of which they have no understanding.

Only a fool would turn his back on what I shared with Eve and by God, I'm not going to play the fool.

He strode over to the table and sat down beside Eve, took her hand. The trembling smile she gave him was more than beautiful, more than grateful; it was proud.

Everyone was looking at Chaim, including David, just waiting to see what he would say, *do* . . . After a second or two, Chaim slammed the table with the flat of his hand and the noise was like a clap of thunder. The wooden table groaned in anguish and threatened to split; the dishes clattered; a glass tumbled to the floor and crashed; the soup sloshed out of its tureen onto the pink tablecloth, and fear chilled the air as well as the wives' blood.

Then there was a silence again. Eve broke it. She called out, "Come everybody! Sit! The food's growing cold." At the same time she ladled out some of the steaming soup and handed it to David, who took it and set it down. Then she said, "Let me help you, father-in-law. Would you like lima bean or some of the mushroom and barley?" She smiled into his eyes, "It smells heavenly . . ."

Chaim's face turned a deep purplish red but he didn't answer. Eve filled a bowl with the mushroom and barley soup and held it in midair, waiting for him to take it from her. When he didn't, she set it down and called out, "Come children! Sit!" The children—all those old enough to do so themselves—climbed up on chairs, enjoying the novelty of the proceedings. Eve filled another bowl, handed it to David who took it and passed it to the child nearest him. "How about a little help?" Eve called over her shoulder to the women who stood transfixed, mentally wringing their hands.

Not one of them moved until Hannah shook her head in despair. Then Dora wailed. With tears running down her cheeks, she ran over to the table and took a filled bowl from Eve, ran around the table with it to place it in front of Ruth's son, Daniel. Ruth sighed deeply, and with the baby Gershon on her hip, grabbed the hand of her two-year-old, Aaron, and pulled him over to the table, lifted him to a chair with one arm, grabbed a bowl of the soup and plunked it down in front of him. "Eat!" she commanded him and turning, called out: "Miriam! You've got girls sitting at this table! Maybe you want to feed them if it's not too much trouble?"

Miriam laughed nervously, glanced at her husband Shlomo whose face gave her no answer. She said, "*Nu?*" to no one in particular and advanced slowly to the table. "Certainly I want to feed them. You think I'll let them starve because they're girls?"

"So who's keeping you from feeding them? Feed!"

Hannah's sigh filled the room. She moved forward slowly. "Where will it end?" she asked under her breath.

As if in answer to her question, Chaim hit the table again and got up, pushing his chair back so violently it crashed to the floor. "I don't eat with women and children!"

"So tell me something new," Hannah muttered, wiping at her son, Joshua's, nose. She looked at Abraham furiously, as if to say: *For God's sake, do something!* It was as if all the men except for David had removed themselves from the situation, waiting for either God or Chaim to resolve it all.

"I don't eat with women or children," Chaim said again, this time his voice ominously low.

This time Eve answered him. "I'm sorry to hear that. It would be nice if we could all break bread together, but if you choose to eat later, after we're through, we'll all understand—"

There was a communal gasp. Surely this time she'd gone too far. David himself was convinced of it, convinced that Chaim would strike Eve dead. He got up, his chair scraping the floor. Most likely his father would kill him too, and his brothers wouldn't even lift a finger to stop him.

But what was taking his father so long? *Is it possible he's going to do nothing?*

Why, he simply doesn't know what to do! He doesn't know how to cope with this situation! That's the truth of it! David wanted to laugh. His father, who ran roughshod over everybody, rabbis and farmers and butchers, slaughterers and thieves, liars and doubters, plain men and clever men, had met his match in Eve!

Then Chaim sprang up, graceful as an animal in the wild in spite of his size, and moved around the table pouring the filled bowls of hot soup over the heads of those children nearest to his hand. The children screamed, Dora wailed, someone gasped but the others were frozen speechless.

Then Chaim grabbed a bottle of vodka by its neck, spat on the floor and said, smiling viciously at Eve: "*I* don't eat after anybody. *I* don't eat leftovers." He left the room, his boots making a terrible noise. David made as if to go after him but Eve put a detaining hand on his arm. Her eyes huge with the shock of Chaim's unspeakable violence, she murmured, "You have to let your brothers deal with this."

But the brothers, running to help the women clean up the children, to see if any one of them was actually burned by the hot soup, were not inclined to pursue the matter with their father. Rather, they were angry with themselves for letting things go so far, angry with their wives for abetting Eve who was clearly a troublemaker, angry with David for allowing his wife to start the trouble, certainly angry with Eve herself. It was true what people said. An educated woman, especially a good-looking one, only meant trouble for everybody.

"The man's an animal," Eve said, rubbing Ruth's Asher's head with a towel. She was conscious of everyone's hostility.

"Oh, he is!" Dora agreed, sniffling.

"At least no one's really hurt." Miriam was mopping up soup from the floor. "The soup wasn't that hot anymore."

"I don't know what you were thinking of," Hannah mumbled. "Sitting down at the table with him . . ."

"Did you really think he'd take that like a sheep?" Abraham shook his head. "And you, David? What were you thinking of?"

"I was thinking that Eve was right. That's what I was thinking."

"You were thinking all right. You were thinking with your *shmuck!*"

"Abraham!" Hannah admonished, her face red.

"Do you know what else I think? I think *you're* the *shmuck!*" David stuck his face in that of his brother's. "A man who lets his father spill hot soup over his child's head and does nothing about it isn't even a man!"

The other brothers cheered up, backing away a little, thinking that at least they were going to have a little fun watching Abraham and David go at each other. But Hannah jumped between them and Eve murmured, "No, David. Please!"

Abraham backed off, deciding to make a joke of it all. "Look who's calling names—my little brother. The baby!" David decided to laugh too. "Maybe the baby can teach the old man a few things. . . ."

"*Nu?*" Ruth said, wiping her hands on her apron. "The food's on the table and it's getting colder every minute. Is anybody hungry?"

Several of the children piped up that they were, and their mothers went to serve them. Soon everyone sat down and began to pass the food around, filling their plates, eating. For a while it was fairly quiet as everyone ate self-consciously, but soon the nervous pall began to lift and gradually conversation began.

Well, Eve thought, things hadn't turned out exactly as she had planned but everyone, with the exception of Chaim, *was* eating together and that had been one of her goals. She hadn't really expected Chaim to do *nothing* . . . It wasn't exactly a victory but it wasn't a defeat either. "Well, David, you haven't told me what you think of my latkes . . ."

"Delicious!" he said with his mouth full. "The best I've ever eaten."

"He's right," Hannah acknowledged. "They are delicious and they've got plenty of onion, I'm happy to say."

"Not bad," Ruth admitted, sticking food in her two-year-old's mouth as she ate with the baby Gershon lying across her lap. "I'm glad to see you didn't make them too soft like some people I know do—"

"They're almost as good as if I made them myself," Miriam allowed. "At least they're not falling apart like—"

Eve broke in quickly. "Thank you all. But most of all I have to thank Dora. I couldn't have made them without her expert instruction."

Dora turned pink with pleasure and Eve thought, Oh yes, Dora. Thank you for being so brave. I'll never forget how you, of all of them, rushed forward to help serve the children with Chaim sitting there glowering like a devil. It took courage. Especially to do it before the others did it. It's hard to be first when one has never been first before.

And you, Ruth. You jumped into the battle quickly too. Thank you!

But she harbored no resentment against Miriam and Hannah for waiting to come to her aid. They had lived under Chaim's thumb for so long. It was a habit difficult to break. Perhaps when one became accustomed to living with tyrants, living in fear of them seemed as natural as breathing.

But most of all, thank you, David. Last night you made love to me like a man but tonight you proved you were one. I couldn't love a man I didn't respect but tonight you made me respect you for all the time to come.

That night David made love to his wife again . . . the triumphant lover. He had stood up to his father and he had honored his wife. He was filled with pride in himself, even as Eve murmured in his ear, "I was so proud of you, David, so proud!" But as soon as she said the words she was filled with pity for him. Poor David, she thought. The battle has just begun. . . .

The next evening Eve began to put all the spare chairs around the dining table before the men got home.

"What are you doing, Eve?" Hannah demanded.

"Putting chairs around the table, as you can see. Enough chairs so that we can all sit together as we did last night."

"You're a crazy person, Eve, that's what you are. A *meshugane!* After what happened last night! After Chaim spilled the soup over the children's heads. He could have scalded them! God knows what he'll do tonight if you start the same thing again."

"But Hannah, we made a gain last night. Can't you see that? If we retrench tonight we lose whatever we gained."

"Excuse me." Hannah's voice was thick with sarcasm. "I'm only an ignorant woman. What does this 'retrench' mean?"

"It means pulling back. Going backwards. Chaim's a tyrant. As much a tyrant as the Tsar. If you don't fight back against tyrants they become even stronger. Bigger tyrants. If people don't fight back they cease to be human beings. They become dogs, whipped dogs."

"And you think by simply sitting down at the table with Chaim we're going to be people and not dogs?" Hannah scoffed. "This great pleasure of sitting down to eat with Chaim is going to do this? I'm not so sure I *want* to eat with him."

"I don't think I want to either," Dora piped up. "To tell the truth I don't even think I could eat a bite with him looking at me. I think if he looked at me while I was swallowing I'd probably choke to death!"

"Oh, no you wouldn't," Eve said furiously. "Maybe dogs choke to death so easily but people don't, I assure you. Don't you see? None of this is really about eating together with Chaim. It's about respecting ourselves. If we're willing to eat last and to eat scraps, we're saying something about ourselves. We're saying we're nothings! Your daughters, Miriam! Do you want them to grow up thinking you're nothing and they're nothing? And you Ruth! You feed the baby from your body. Wouldn't it be wonderful if you could feed him something else besides your mother's milk? If you could feed him the knowledge that his mother is as good as anyone else—even a man! Last night, no matter what Chaim himself did, we gave everyone present—Chaim, the children, our husbands— that message! Now do you want to take that message back?" she implored.

They stared at her until Hannah sighed deeply. She threw up her hands. "She's a *meshugane* but she's right. I have to say that, even if I'd like to forget that it all happened. Last night when my Golda went to bed she said to me that when her Aunt Eve sat down at the table with her grandfather, she was frightened for Eve. She was scared Chaim would hit her. Then when her Aunt Dora and her Aunt Ruth came running over to help she was so happy for Eve. And proud! Then she said something very funny. She said that in addition to being happy for Eve, she was happy for *herself. Nu?* What can I say except that she, Golda, young as she is, got the message. Then she said something that made me ashamed. She said she wished that *I* had run over to help Eve first, right away. So, God help us, I have to say Eve's right—"

Eve threw her arms around Hannah and hugged her tight.

47

"That's all fine and good," Miriam said. "But how do we know what Chaim will do tonight? God forbid maybe he'll even hit someone and cripple them. Wouldn't it be better to compromise? To let Chaim sit alone and eat and then after he's through we can sit down with our husbands and children? That way, we wouldn't be eating last."

Eve shook her head. "No, we can't do that either. That way we and our husbands and children will still be eating Chaim's leftovers. But wait! I have another idea. We can give him his own small table, which will be a kind of compromise—acceptable, I think, to him and to us. He can eat all by himself but at the same time we'll all be eating at the same time."

The women helped her set up the small table in the dining room several feet away from the long main table. They laid out cutlery, a plate, a glass, a bottle of vodka. Ruth looked doubtful. "What makes you think he'll be willing to sit here?"

"Because I think he'll take it that we're bowing to him by allowing him to eat in solitary splendor, like a king. For the time being that will be enough."

"What do you mean? For the time being?"

"You'll see. I have a hunch how things will work out." She ran to the kitchen and started laying out small serving dishes, in addition to the large ones they normally used.

"Now what are you doing?" Miriam asked.

"These are to be used for Chaim's table. Separate serving dishes."

"Why?"

"So there'll be no running back and forth with the large serving dishes from the big table. The idea is that once we bring all the food out and set it down, we all sit and eat, like the men do, like the children do, like Chaim does. No one jumps up and down like a chicken without its head. Everybody sits and eats with dignity."

"*Oy vey!*" Miriam clapped both hands to her head. "I hope all this is worth it."

"I think it's worth it," Ruth said and Dora rushed to say, "I do too."

Hannah nodded. "Last night we took a step forward, just as Eve said. Only a fool goes backward . . ." She left the room and when she returned the kerchief that usually covered her head was gone and in place was the blond wig that was saved for the Sabbath and special occasions. And in place of her everyday dress was the special blue one Eve had made, complete with tucks and pleats. At first no one said anything except for Hannah's Golda who had just walked into the kitchen, "Oh Mama, you look pretty!" and then Miriam said, "So, Hannah! You must *really* think this is a special occasion."

"Oh I do," Hannah laughed. "Tonight I'm going to eat like a person and not like a dog."

Still, they were all very nervous as the men arrived home and went to the porch off the kitchen to wash up. And they were all very nervous as they started filling the large bowls and platters and running to the table with them. Eve busied herself sitting the children down around the long planked table so that when Chaim first walked into the room there'd be no misunderstanding. He'd see the children sitting at the big table at the same time he saw the small table with the single setting.

The brothers came into the dining room first, before their father, and immediately there was a tension when they saw the children sitting. Abraham was about to yell, to tell the women to get the children out of the room, but before he could speak Chaim appeared in the doorway. He took his time sizing up the situation. He scratched at his beard, plucked at an eyebrow with two thick fingers, grimaced and tugged at his nose. Then he threw himself into the chair at the small table and gave the surface a sharp rap with his knuckles, signaling that he was ready for his food. Eve took it upon herself to go to the kitchen and bring out his single serving dishes. Placing them down, she looked Chaim in the eye while he looked back at her from under his heavy eyebrows and it was almost as if the two of them were alone in the room.

Oh yes, Eve thought. *We understand each other, Chaim, you and I.*

Then Chaim uncharacteristically smiled, and Eve saw the naked malice in his eyes. Apparently, just as she had thought, he was accepting her small act of servitude as a symbol of surrender, of obeisance, which served to negate his own compromise of eating in the same room at the same time with the whole family. *Good. Let him . . . for now!*

The others, all of them, were oblivious to everything but the fact that Chaim was actually sitting there, allowing Eve to serve him! They breathed a communal sigh of relief and slowly, self-consciously, sat down too. Equally self-conscious was the silence in which they started to eat, a silence punctuated only by this child's demand and that one's fussing, and emphasized by the very noisy sounds of eating and belching emanating from Chaim's table. Finally, ignoring the strained atmosphere, Eve cheerfully inquired of David, "Tell me all about your day."

David was startled. No one had ever inquired about his day before. Hershel immediately jeered, "Yes, David. Do tell us. We're all dying to hear, aren't we?" He winked at the other brothers who snickered.

David turned to Eve. She was looking at him expectantly, a bright smile on her lips. To the devil with his brothers! She really wanted to hear about the day's interesting happenings and he *wanted* to tell her! But what would interest her? Certainly not how many chickens they bought from Moishe Grushkin or the two cows they had bought from a farmer on the other side of the river, then sold to Kushner the butcher almost immediately after. But something funny *had* happened when they'd been invited into Kushner's wife's kitchen for a glass of hot tea to warm them from the chill of the day. Yes! *That* would make an amusing story to tell Eve.

"We sold two cows to Kushner the butcher today," he began and Eve nodded in encouragement. "As you know, it was very cold today, exceptionally cold . . ."

"Cold?" Chaim spat out from his table. "Cold, you horse's ass? I can remember a day only last year when it was so cold the eyes ran, and the very second the tears came out, they froze on the cheeks like hailstones on the ground! You don't have the brains of a half-wit if you call today cold!''

David flushed. He didn't even want to continue with the story but Eve nodded at him, touching his thigh. "Go on," she said softly.

David cleared his throat. "Well, Kushner's wife, Reba, invited us into the kitchen for a glass of hot tea to warm us. And there by the window was the Kushners' new baby boy, naked as the day he was born, lying in his cradle—''

"Imagine that!" Miriam interrupted. "*Her* baby actually lies in a cradle. *She* doesn't carry it around all day giving it the breast!''

Ruth dropped her spoon. "At least *she* has a son—''

Eve gave them both a look and said to David, "Oh? Why was the baby naked?''

"Reba Kushner said he had a rash, that the sun coming in through the windows would be good for his little pecker.''

Now the brothers leaned forward with smiles of anticipation, all except Shlomo, and David opened his mouth to continue, gratified now to have his brothers' rapt attention. But Dora said in dismay, "The baby was naked on such a cold day? Is the woman crazy? Surely her kitchen wasn't warm enough for that?''

Exasperated, David explained: "They have double windows as we do. When the sun shines through the two sheets of glass, it's hotter than a stove.''

"For God's sake!" Hershel shouted, knowing the end of the story and eager to have David tell it so that they could all laugh. "Let him talk!''

"So the baby's lying in the cradle naked and Shlomo here," David crooked a thumb at his brother, "walks over to take a look at the new baby, and he leans over to give the baby's cheek a tweak"—David broke into laughter along with the brothers—"and the little stinker peed right up into Shlomo's face!''

When Eve and the other wives broke into laughter, joining David and the brothers, even Shlomo, red-faced, laughed too. The children laughed the hardest, and Miriam clucked amiably, "My Shlomo the *shlimazl* . . .'' But she touched his arm affectionately.

"Driveling, puking, cretinous horse's behind!" Chaim muttered, but no one paid any attention. They were all busy searching their memories for a similar story, reminding each other, laughing and talking all at once.

"Tell Eve the one about the chickens and the trough," Abraham urged David while Shlomo flamed a brighter shade of red and protested, "No! It was a long time ago—''

"Not so long ago," Yacob hooted. "A few months maybe.''

"I want to hear," Eve prodded David and he, enjoying his new role as raconteur said, "All right, but no interruptions this time. It was last spring, I think. We'd just bought a large lot of chickens. A hundred maybe—''

"A hundred?" Chaim bellowed. "More like two hundred, you ass's dung!''

David's face flushed a deeper shade of red than Shlomo's. "Maybe it was more like two hundred—"

"Go on," Eve said. "Whatever. It doesn't matter."

"Well, we had to round them all up and put them in crates and pile them in the wagon, which meant we had to chase every last bird around the barnyard. It took us hours and it was already getting dark but finally we were down to one last hen. She must have been a very smart chicken because no matter what we did she kept getting away from us. So Shlomo here takes off his jacket to throw over her and at the same time he takes a flying leap in the air, intending to land on top of her. But what happened was Shlomo leaped right into the pig trough!"

Chaim's "Half-witted, drooling idiot of a jackass's crud!" was completely lost in the laughter that ensued. Even Shlomo was laughing so hard he didn't hear Chaim either.

Then everyone had a story to tell. There was so much talking, one voice over the other, no one paid any attention to Chaim's loud coughing, obnoxious belching, his gurgling as he drank the vodka straight from the bottle, his vicious banging and rattling of dishes. By the time they were drinking tea and munching on sugar cookies and sponge cake, Chaim was broodingly silent. Perhaps it was that he was more drunk than usual. Whatever it was, when Eve came to clear away his dishes, he fixed her with a glance that was so hateful, so evil, she felt a chill. But what had she expected? She knew that he and she were locked in a contest of wills and she also knew that Chaim wasn't a man of grace who could admire or respect an adversary, least of all, *like* one. No, the situation was only what she could have anticipated.

As his eyes swept over her, she was aware and not for the first time of another emotion revealed in Chaim's dark blue eyes. She found the expression of that emotion—even though she couldn't exactly put her finger on what it was—even more disturbing than his animosity. It wasn't until she and David went to their room that it came to her clearly what it was she had seen reflected in Chaim's eyes—

As she undressed, revealing first voluptuous breasts, then rounded flanks, and then slender, shapely legs, she looked up to see David's face cast in shadow as he watched her, even as his eyes centered in on the triangle between her thighs. She saw the gentle look of love darken over with lust, and she knew then what she had seen in Chaim's eyes. Just as David's spiritual love for her was coupled with sexual yearning so was Chaim's hostility toward her laced with carnal desire.

Her blood chilled with the realization. If this was true, then Chaim Markoff had taken on a new role. He was more than the obstacle to David becoming a man—he was the beast of prey, a hunter with the smell of danger about him. And she was his prey. How could she fight back? To fight for her own and David's independence, even the whole family's independence of him, was one thing. But this other thing? How was she to cope with that?

51

She felt David's mouth on hers and she closed her eyes, as she tried to close up her mind against all the scary thoughts, all the frightening possibilities. Slowly and gradually they faded as her body responded to David's. As he entered her, as her body reached up and arched to meet his, she wasn't thinking of Chaim at all.

Afterwards, she dismissed the whole thing as utterly ridiculous. She had allowed her dislike for Chaim to distort her thinking. She had let her imagination run wild. The notion of Chaim lusting after her was just silly. She wouldn't allow herself to think of it again.

Hoping for things to proceed according to plan at a brisk pace, Eve was disconcerted when for several evenings things went on in the very same manner —Chaim, sitting at his private table, listening with one ear to the pleasant conviviality at the big table, while he busied himself with gusty chewing, chomping, gurgling, grunting and table-slamming, at the same time punctuating their conversation with caustic, denigrating and vulgar remarks.

Then one night, when she had almost given up on Chaim's further capitulation as far as the seating arrangements were concerned, he plopped himself down at the head of the main table, albeit with a great show of nonchalance. *This* was exactly what she had counted on—Chaim being unable to tolerate anything but the complete attention of his household, or accept not being at the center of things. He wanted to dominate the conversation; he wanted to be the one who told the stories, to elicit the laughs and the applause. But the important thing wasn't that he sat down with the family, it was that he had *capitulated*. He was eating with the family, and the women were no longer eating his leftovers. Although it was only the beginning of the war, a mere skirmish in the scheme of things, it *was* a victory.

She thought about what would come next even as she ate that night, watching Chaim trying to obscure the fact of his surrender by ignoring the women and children, addressing only his sons in conversation that was more monologue than not. He even performed one of his tricks in which two forks were supported by a coin balanced on the very edge of a glass. It was a trick none of the boys had ever attempted and now when Yacob did attempt it and actually pulled it off, Chaim mocked his performance, calling him a clumsy blockhead.

"Oh no, it was wonderful," Dora cried before realizing that she was actually refuting her father-in-law.

"Wonderful?" Chaim growled contemptuously. "Maybe in a hundred years he'll do it wonderfully, that asshole." He threw Dora a look of such withering magnitude that she immediately suffered a coughing fit of enormous proportions.

When they retired to their room David was very enthusiastic over what he viewed as Eve's triumph. "You knew, didn't you, that it would turn out this way? That Father would eventually sit down with the rest of us?"

"I thought . . . possibly . . . maybe . . ." She began to undress.

52

"I can't believe it—" David exulted.

Eve wanted to tell him that this was hardly the end of it but only the means to a much more encompassing conclusion, but she saw that David was already aroused by the sight of her naked flesh and was moving toward her, all thoughts of his father forgotten. No, she decided, this was not the right moment. . . .

Later, as they lay in the dark, David's face buried between her breasts, she whispered to him. "Remember, David, what it was we talked about that first night I spent under this roof? Do you remember what I said it was that I wanted?"

Reluctantly David came back from the edge of sweet sleep. "Yes, I remember. You said you wanted me to act like a man. To stand up to my father. Well, I've done that, haven't I?" he asked uneasily. He rolled over on his back. "When you sat down at the table and I sat down next to you . . ."

"Oh yes, David, you did . . ." She covered his face with kisses. "But—"

"But what?" What was it that she wanted now? More proof of his manhood? He wondered if she would ever be satisfied. Would she always want *more?* And he? Was he capable of giving everything she wanted?

She felt his anxiety. She stroked him. "It's not enough, David, that we all sit down to eat with your father. That's only a beginning. You and I can't really be man and wife in the full sense of the words until we're living with you as the head of our household instead of your father."

A sigh of anguish escaped his lips. "But that's impossible! I mean it's impossible for now. . . ."

"Why, David, why is it impossible?"

"You know why. Because we don't have any money to set up our own household. We don't even have a groschen . . . You know that none of us gets any wages. How could I have any money?" he asked bitterly, and then was startled by the bitterness in his own voice. Had it always been there? he wondered. He tried to remember . . . He couldn't remember ever thinking about it before. But yes, he had worked since he was a child and never received a kopeck in wages. Oh, once in a while his father had thrown a few coins on the ground for his brothers and him to scramble over—a few groschen, a few quarter-kopecks. Usually, since he was the youngest and easily pushed out of the way, he ended up with nothing. "How can we get a home of our own without a kopeck of our own?" he demanded of her angrily out of his own frustration.

"It's terribly unfair, David, that you and your brothers work and don't receive anything for your labors. It would be different if you were a poor family. If the whole family had to work just to put bread on the table. Even I . . . even as a little girl . . . always got a few kopecks to buy myself something, no matter how small. And we hardly were as prosperous as your family. And your brothers—with families! Abraham! How old is he? He must be almost twice your age and he doesn't have money of his own to buy his children a toy or his wife the smallest trinket? It's ridiculous! And what happens if one of you wants to go to the *kretchma* for a drink like the poorest peasant might?"

"We *don't*, unless Father's along to pay—" He was angry now, but more, he was ashamed. He couldn't fault Eve for finding the situation ridiculous, for finding him ridiculous.

"It's not fair, David. It's not right."

Right? Fair? No, it was neither right nor fair. But his father wasn't a fair man. Fair was probably the last word that could apply to his father. "Of course it isn't but what's the use of talking about it? Maybe—"

"Yes?" she turned to him eagerly. "Maybe—?"

He groaned and turned away from her. He *knew* what she wanted him to say . . . that maybe he'd ask . . . no, not ask . . . *demand* wages from his father the very next day. Real wages, with which they could buy their own food and pay for their own roof. *But she wants too much, more than I'm capable of. Oh Eve, I love you but you want too much. Or maybe it's that you were right about me that very first day. Maybe I am only a boy and not a man. A boy without the courage to demand what's due a man.*

His back was to her and she put her cheek to it, aware of the doubts and anxieties that were assailing him. She had to reassure him. "I know what you're thinking," she said. "You want to go to your father and demand that he pay you wages. You want to do it this very minute. But you mustn't. You can't act hastily. . . ."

"I can't?" he asked in relief, in gratitude for the stay of execution.

"No. We have to think this through. It would be much better if your brothers were to join with you in making this demand—"

"Ah, that's a problem."

"Why?"

David laughed. "Because they don't have you for a wife."

"Oh, David I do love you. And we will get what we want. A home of our own. Our very own family. I know it here—" She placed a hand on her brow. "And I know it here." She laid his hand on her breast.

In a few seconds David forgot about his father and about the dilemma of making the impossible possible. With eager hands he parted Eve's thighs and once again entered her. But this time even as she closed her eyes and felt David surge and tremble within her, she wasn't able to erase from her mind the specter of Chaim the Terrible and the task that lay ahead.

4.

By morning Eve had figured out her next step. It had to do with the purchase of the material for Ruth's dress, which she was ready to work on since she had just completed Miriam's dress. Dressed for the marketplace, she asked Hannah for the money to buy the fabric.

Hannah took some coins out of the money jar and handed them over. Eve looked at the money doubtfully. "Surely you can spare a little more. Chaim can afford it."

Reluctantly Hannah gave her two more coins. "Chaim can. The question is whether the jar can."

"Remember when I asked you what would happen if you spent all the money in the jar, and you said you didn't know because it had never happened? Well, why don't we find out?"

Hannah laughed. "Thank you but no thank you. I don't think I want to find out."

Miriam snickered. "What do you think would happen? He'd holler and scream and generally carry on as he always does."

"But in the end he'd probably give it, wouldn't he?" Dora asked.

"Maybe . . ." Ruth answered her sourly. "But he'd throw it on the ground for us to pick up."

"But Yacob says he often buys drinks for everyone at the tavern. Doesn't that mean he's generous?" Dora didn't want to believe that Chaim was completely mean.

"No, not really," Eve told her. "That's just showing off. Real generosity begins in the home and I see very little of that around here."

"I agree! How often do we get a new dress around here anyway that we have to be stingy with the money?" Ruth laid her baby down in the cradle. "I think I'd like to go along with you, Eve, to help pick out the material if Dora will keep an eye on Gershon—"

"Of course I will," Dora said quickly but Eve said just as quickly, "No, Ruth. I want to surprise you. Trust me. You won't be disappointed."

Reluctantly Ruth agreed to be surprised and Eve's relief was so obvious Hannah looked at her with suspicion. *She's up to something . . .*

"Oh, I can't wait for Ruth's dress to be finished so you can start on mine,"

Dora breathed. "I wish you could buy the material for my dress too so you could work on both dresses at the same time— You know, a little on Ruth's, then a little on mine."

"Oh, I don't think that would be fair," Ruth quickly interjected. "Since I'm next in line my dress should be finished before Eve even sticks a needle into yours."

"Ruth's right," Hannah said decisively. "Besides, if we spend the money on material for two dresses it'll leave us short for the rest of the month. And while you, Eve, might be interested in seeing what happens when we run out of money, I'm not. I need that trouble like I need a hole in my head."

"Whatever you say, Hannah. You're the boss," Eve laughed.

"Some boss I am. With Chaim around I'm a boss like Dora's a boss . . ."

"Me?" Dora's eyes opened wide. "*I'm* not a boss!" Then she realized that Hannah hadn't been serious. She laughed. "Oh, you . . ."

Hannah patted her cheek. "I wish you *were* the boss, darling. Speaking of the boss, that reminds me. We barely have a piece of pickled fish left and that's Chaim's favorite. While you're at the market, Eve, get some fish. Whatever there is that's good for pickling. Here." She handed over some more coins. "While you're at it you might as well buy enough to last us a while."

The women gathered around Eve eager to see the material for Ruth's new dress. Unable to wait another second Ruth grabbed for the shopping bag and pulled out a length of fabric. Horrified, she stared at a piece of red and white checked gingham. "*This* is the material for my new dress? You were right when you said I'd be surprised, Eve! I couldn't be more surprised!" She threw the piece of cloth on the floor.

Eve laughed. "The gingham isn't for you. I just happened to see it and I thought it would make a pretty dress for a little girl. Then I saw that it was big enough to make matching pinafores for Miriam's girls." She picked the cloth up and gestured to Rebecca, the oldest of Miriam's daughters. "Come here, Becky." She held the fabric up to the girl. "There . . . Pretty, Miriam?"

Miriam shook her head from side to side. "Beautiful! What else?"

"Really beautiful," Dora echoed as Becky beamed and Ruth screamed: "What about my dress? You're going to make dresses for Miriam's brats instead of for me?"

"Of course not. These pinafores will take no more than a few hours."

"So then where's my material?"

"The truth is I couldn't find anything I liked enough so I thought I'd go to Kovno tomorrow. After all, how far away is it? A half hour. There I'm sure I'll find exactly the right thing. After all, does the Squire's wife buy the cloth for her dresses in Slobodka? No, I'm sure she goes to Kovno. Ruthie, you're going to have a dress fine enough to go to the Squire's ball."

Ruth, mollified now, laughed. "Oh, I'm sure Count Makowski and his guests would be delighted to have me at their ball. They'll curtsy and say, "Oh, Madam

Markoff, you're so lovely in that dress, so grand. We're absolutely thrilled to have you here tonight even though you're a lousy Jewess!"

Eve, in turn, bowed deeply, declared in a deep bass: "Madam Jewess, I am Count Igor Petrovski Petrokov! Will you do me the honor of joining me in a polka? I won't even cut off your head with my sword since you are such a *lovely* Jewess."

They linked arms and began dancing around while Miriam and Dora clapped their hands in accompaniment and the older children, quick to pick up their mood, skipped in a circle around them.

Suddenly Hannah blurted, "Where's the fish?"

The dancing stopped and Eve clapped her head. "The fish! I forgot about it completely. I don't know where my head was."

"Neither do I," Hannah grunted suspiciously. "So give me back the money."

"The money?" Eve repeated as if she had never heard of the word.

"Yes, Eve, the money. The money I gave you for the fish."

"The fish money. I'm afraid I spent it." She smiled disarmingly.

"On what?" Hannah demanded. "On that red and white *shmatte*? That rag? Then where is the rest of the money?"

"The rest of the money?"

"Yes, the rest of the money," Hannah cried. "And don't keep repeating after me like a dummy. You're no dummy and I'm no fool. You spent the fish money on the gingham so where's the money for the cloth for Ruth's dress? Do you have it or don't you?"

"No, I don't. You see, I also bought these—" She pulled four books out of her shopping bag. "I thought it would be all right. I used to get new books all the time."

"Something smells and clearly it's not fish. You spent both the money for Ruth's dress fabric and the fish money on a piece of rag and a few stupid books?"

"I'm distressed to hear you refer to my books in that manner, Hannah. I'm surprised at you. Besides, I bought something else." She dipped into her bag again and with a flourish pulled out a pair of scissors.

"But *why* did you buy them? What's wrong with the old ones?" Hannah's voice shook with agitation.

"They were dull. Very dull."

"They could have been sharpened."

"No. They were rusty. Hopeless. I couldn't take the chance they would ruin the material I'm going to buy tomorrow in Kovno. And these new ones—they'll cut beautifully." She waved the scissors in the air. "We needed them, didn't we?" she appealed to the other women. Ruth and Miriam nodded and Dora said, "Oh yes. They're wonderful. So new and shiny."

Hannah gave them all a dirty look. "They're only scissors, not the Tsarina's jewels. So tell me, Eve, what do you intend to use for money when you go to Kovno tomorrow?"

"I was hoping you'd give me more money—"

"Spend it all then? Empty out the jar? So we'll have nothing left for necessities? That's what you want, isn't it? So we'll have to ask Chaim for more money before it's time for him to refill the jar. You already have us sitting at the table and eating with him. But now you just want to stir up trouble. Now you want just to poke the hornet's nest . . ."

"No, not just to stir up trouble. To make a point. That we should have money to spend on ourselves as we see fit. And that if he paid our husbands wages as they deserve, then it wouldn't be necessary for us to use up the household money . . ."

"Pay our husbands wages?"

"Yes. Wages. Men earn wages and children only their keep."

"So that's what this is all about!"

"Eve's right, Hannah," Ruth said slowly. "She's right. If we spend all the household money then Chaim would want to know why and then we could tell him our husbands should get paid wages! They should!"

Eve was grateful for the support. "You see, if Chaim pays our husbands a fair wage then we could all contribute to the household funds. In other words, pay for our own keep and still have a few kopecks left over to do what we want with. Each couple could decide for themselves what they want to do with those extra kopecks. It's fair."

"Very fair," Dora agreed.

Miriam nodded. "What do you think, Hannah?"

"I think that it all sounds very fair and wonderful. I also think that if all the money is gone someone is going to have to explain to Chaim why . . . all this business about the wages. So I want all of you to tell *me* something since you all agree how fair and wonderful this is—I want you to tell me who is going to do all this telling to Chaim? You, Miriam? You, Dora? Or will it be Ruth or Eve? Because it's not going to be me. I'm not going to be the one who gets this house torn apart—"

"Please, Hannah, don't get so upset," Eve tried to reassure her. "I will tell him. Trust me. It will all work out."

"Oh, I trust you even if you are crazy. It's Chaim I don't trust not to kill us all. . . ." Still she went to the shelf, took down the jar and poured all the money that remained out on the table. "Take it! Spend it! And who knows? Maybe God will help us all!"

"He will, Hannah. He will." Eve counted up the money. "You know, since I'll be in Kovno I might just as well buy the material for Dora's dress. Just to save the extra trip. Maybe there'll be a tiny bit of money left over for a couple of other things like a nice cake of soap. Did you know you can buy *French* soap in Kovno?"

Dora, delighted that Eve was going to buy the material for her dress too, after all, exulted: "French soap! But what is French soap like? Have you ever seen a piece?"

"Yes. It's heavenly."

"Heavenly, is it?" Hannah shook her head. "*God* is heavenly. *Saints* are heavenly. You sound like a foolish peasant girl, Eve, instead of an educated female from a pious Jewish home."

Eve refused to allow Hannah to be angry with her. She threw her arms around her sister-in-law's solid form. "Oh, come on, Hannah. I didn't mean to sound sacrilegious. And I know it sounds silly, but if you ever smelled French soap you'd know what I mean. It smells like . . ." she groped for a word. "It smells like . . . *heaven!*" She giggled and her mood was contagious. Miriam, Ruth and Dora giggled too.

Hannah, still encircled within Eve's arms, remained unsmiling. "French soap!" she muttered. "You've lost your mind entirely, you little fool. How far do you think you can push Chaim?"

"Just far enough, Hannah. Just far enough."

While Eve handed out the few toys and trinkets she had brought back from Kovno for the children, the women's excitement mounted. Still, Hannah stood off to one side, frowning. When Eve unfurled a length of royal blue velvet, and the other women gasped, Hannah complained, "Velvet of all things!"

Ruth threw her arms around Eve. "It takes my breath away!"

"My breath too," Hannah drawled. The dresses Eve had made for her and Miriam, while lavish in design and execution, had at least been fashioned of sturdy and practical material. "Tell me, Eve, what will Ruth do with such a dress? Nurse Gershon or wear it to visit the Tsar?"

"Oh, Hannah, don't be such a sourpuss!" Ruth hugged the material to her breast. "I've never seen anything as lovely before!"

"Yes, Hannah," Eve said. "Don't be such a sourpuss. What's wrong with Ruth that she can't have *one* beautiful dress? Is she so terrible she doesn't deserve to—?"

"*Nu?* Who said she was terrible? All I'm asking is *what* is she going to do with such a dress? Give her baby the tit in it? Wash the clothes? Scrub the floors?"

"She'll wear it on special occasions. On the Sabbath. On holidays. Passover is coming. She'll wear it to the services."

"*Gutteniu!* To *shul?* Her dress will make that place look like a barnyard in comparison."

"Oh Hannah," Eve pleaded. "Maybe she'll wear the dress just to make herself feel beautiful or to please Hershel."

She unwrapped the other package of cloth and revealed several yards of deep plum taffeta. Again the women gasped and Dora's eyes filled with tears. Hannah made a guttural sound deep in her throat and Miriam sighed, "Is that a color!"

"Fit for a queen," Ruth said, fingering the fabric, trying to determine for herself if Dora's cloth was more magnificent than her own.

"I could die without ever having anything as beautiful again." Dora's voice was full of wonder.

"And you probably *will* when Chaim finds out we've spent his fish money on dress material that's good for nothing," Hannah said with sarcastically cheerful enthusiasm. "Taffeta! Of course you and Ruth can always wear your dresses to the marketplace where the wagons can splatter them with mud and the horses can make *drek* on them! For that they'll be just right."

Then Eve took out a few pieces of soap, each wrapped in French tissue paper that was beautiful in itself, covered with red and pink roses. "There's a cake for each of us." Then she brought out a flacon of eau de cologne. "This we'll have to share. I only had enough money to buy one bottle . . ."

So it's done, Hannah thought. She really has spent every last groschen.

"French perfume!" Dora gently took the bottle from Eve's hand and opened it. "I can hardly believe it!" She sniffed at it delicately, touched her fingers to the opening and then to her throat. "Am I doing it right?" Eve nodded and she breathed, "Oh, I feel like a princess!"

"A Jewish princess yet," Hannah muttered. "What else?"

Ruth yanked the bottle from Dora's hand. "Here—let me." She touched her fingers now to the bottle's mouth and dabbed at her ears. Then Miriam grabbed the flacon from her and applied the perfume liberally to her ample chest directly from the bottle. "Cow!" Ruth screeched. "That way you'll use it all up at once! You're so ignorant you don't even know the proper way to apply it."

"See, Madam Eve," Hannah said in disgust. "You've made them as crazy as yourself. And us without a drop of pot cheese in the house and with not a piece of pickled fish either."

Eve laughed at her. "God isn't going to bring the world to an end because of a little pot cheese or a piece of smelly fish. And that's the idea, isn't it? That Chaim *misses* his old fish and asks for it . . ."

"It's *your* idea, not mine. And anyway, no matter whose idea it is, I was hoping it would be a few days yet before the big moment arrived. A few days grace, you might say. But the way it's going to smell in this house tonight . . ." She shook her head in despair.

"Oh, come on, Hannah. Don't be a stick-in-the-mud." Eve took the bottle of perfume from Miriam and with her fingers applied a few drops to Hannah's throat and ear lobes while Hannah fussed, pushed her away. But Eve persisted, giggling all the while, touching her perfumed fingers to Hannah's temples as well. "Oh, just sniff it, Hannah! Admit it! It *is* heavenly, isn't it? I bet Abraham will think so too!"

Hannah, giving Eve another push, began to laugh. "You're impossible! You're going to be the death of us all!"

When everyone gathered for the evening meal a heady mixture of odors infused the dining room. The eau de cologne blended with the aroma of simmered meat, sautéed onions, garlic, freshly baked dark bread. Chaim sniffed the air as if something was offending his nostrils, but he didn't say anything. Then, when Hannah placed the dish of salt herring in front of him in the hope that he'd

60

simply take a piece without asking for some of the pickled fish he was so fond of, he did just that with only a grunt and no comment. Hannah breathed an inward sigh of relief but Eve was disappointed. However, she brightened when Chaim refused a bowl of soup and instead demanded a piece of boiled carp with onions.

"We didn't make any boiled fish today," Hannah said quietly.

"Why not?"

Hannah shrugged. "One doesn't make boiled fish every day."

"Then I'll have a piece of pickled fish."

This time before Hannah could answer, Eve said, "We didn't make any pickled fish either."

Pointedly ignoring Eve, Chaim asked of Hannah, "Why don't we have any pickled fish either?"

Hannah threw Eve a look which plainly told her to be quiet. "Because we didn't get any fish in the market today."

"Why is that?" Chaim asked quietly enough. "There was no fish in the market? Or did all the rivers dry up? Or the sea for that matter?"

Hannah's hands fumbled with her apron as she wondered what to say. Then she decided that *nothing* was as good an answer as any and she gave Eve another warning look.

Reluctantly Eve leaned back in her chair in silence. She couldn't very well do what Hannah's expression explicitly forbade. If Hannah wanted to put off the moment of confrontation she'd have to allow her that.

Chaim took a swig from the bottle of vodka and growled, "Since a man can't have a piece of fish in his own house, what *can* he have?"

Hannah rushed to fill his plate with *tsimmes* and flanken, boiled potatoes flecked with black pepper, barley tossed with fried onions, while Eve sat silently. Tomorrow was another day, she told herself. And tomorrow there still wouldn't be any boiled fish or any pickled fish or smoked fish or any other kind of fish besides the salted dried herring that was a staple. But in addition to the fish, there should be *another* item missing from the table, something that would be missed even more sorely than the fish.

Suddenly, Chaim, holding a short rib of beef in one hand and wiping the grease from his mouth with the other, sniffed at the air again and grimaced. "What in blazing hell do I smell in here? If I didn't have all my brains I'd say it stinks in Chaim Markoff's house like a fucking whorehouse!"

"The children!" Miriam blurted into the shocked silence and quickly covered the ears of the daughter sitting next to her. Dora tittered and Eve asked sweetly, "Why, father-in-law, how would you know what a whorehouse smells like?"

Ruth giggled, Hannah had a coughing spell and Dora began hiccupping. David seemed to be choking. Eve pounded him on the back, not sure if he was really choking or trying to stifle a laugh. She poured herself a little vodka, raised her glass to the table at large and offered, "*L'chayim!*" No one was sure if it was a toast or a taunt.

Then, looking directly at Eve, Chaim squeezed his own glass of vodka so tightly it broke within his hamlike fist. The liquid seeped through his fingers, pieces of glass fell to the table. Smiling, Chaim opened his hand. There wasn't a drop of blood.

As the sisters-in-law bustled about with their morning chores, Eve sat by the kitchen fire pinning together the pieces of royal blue velvet which would make up the bodice of Ruth's new dress. She was still mulling over which particular item she'd like to see missing from the table that evening. It had to be an item of *particular* significance.

"I could have died when the old man said it smelled like a whorehouse in here," Miriam chuckled, sticking a forefinger into a plump hen's cloaca, feeling around, determining that it was after all, a good bird.

Ruth, expertly plucking feathers from another chicken, laughed. "Personally, I thought I'd choke to death when Eve asked him how he knew what a whorehouse smelled like."

"What *does* a whorehouse smell like?" Dora asked, peeling potatoes. "I've never been in one."

"I didn't think you had," Eve giggled. "And I'll tell you a secret—neither have I. But I'm sure it was the odor of our cologne that Chaim was referring to; I'm sure whorehouses smell heavily of perfume."

"*Sha!*" Hannah said, looking significantly at the children playing on the floor. "Maybe we should get another chicken from the keeping shed. Since we don't have the fish we could make a sweet-and-sour fricassee to have first. What do you think, Miriam?"

"We don't have that many chickens left either. And only a couple of ducks and a few geese. I'm sure they'll come back with an empty wagon again. They haven't brought anything back with them in the last week."

Eve's ears perked up. She had never taken notice of what the men brought or didn't bring home for the family's own use. "How is that? If they usually bring home fowl or meat why haven't they this last week?"

"You don't know the business, Eve," Miriam said, washing the chicken. "If you did you'd know that every year around this time, near the end of winter and just before spring, everything dries up." She salted the chicken. "Whatever is left people will keep for themselves until supplies become more plentiful again. Haven't you noticed that the men have been coming home later and later? That's because livestock has become almost impossible to find. And if they find it, usually the farmer won't sell it. Soon they'll stop going out altogether until spring is truly here."

Hannah gave Eve a significant look. "It's true. And the only reason there's a fish to be bought—*if* one has the money—is that they can always cut holes in the ice. Of course if one has money one can also buy dairy. . . ."

"Well, good," Eve said cheerfully. "As soon as Chaim realizes he has to pay our husbands wages and does so, we can all put money into the household fund and buy fish and dairy, whatever's available at market. Really, Hannah, instead of putting it off, it's better if we get it over with. Tonight—"

Hannah merely sighed heavily.

When Miriam and Hannah went to the storage room to check on exactly how many chickens *were* left, Eve went with them. Her attention, however, was not on the chickens or ducks or geese or on the cuts of beef, but on the many bottles of vodka lined up in a row.

"So what is it you're doing there by the open door, Eve?" Hannah called, feeling icy drafts rushing through the kitchen. "You're freezing out the whole house." She went over to see what it was exactly that Eve was up to and stopped short as if struck dead in her tracks. "My God!" she shrieked. Eve was emptying out a bottle of vodka into the snow, and lined up by the door just waiting were what appeared to be every last bottle they had. "Are you insane? What do you think you're doing?"

"Creating a shortage."

"Crazy woman! Stop this minute!"

"There's no stopping now," Eve said, picking up a second bottle and un-corking it, even as Hannah struggled with her. Hearing the commotion at the back door, the other women came running over to see what was going on. They saw Hannah and Eve actually grappling—Hannah trying to grab a bottle of vodka from Eve's hand.

Out of breath, Hannah let go of Eve's arm. "Here I've been worrying myself sick about tonight as it is, and this crazy person is spilling all the vodka out in the snow and in the meantime is letting in the freezing air so we'll all catch our death. When Chaim finds out there's no vodka, as well as no fish, it'll be the end for sure!"

"The end of *what?*" Eve asked.

"The end! The end of us all!"

"Is he going to kill us then, do you think? That would be the absolute end."

"While we talk about how Chaim is going to kill us, why don't we shut the door so the cold won't?" Ruth said dryly and closed it.

"Oh no!" Dora put her hands to her head. "He wouldn't really kill us! I don't believe it."

"No, he won't kill you darling," Miriam answered her. "*You* he'll kiss. *Us* he'll kill."

"Think about it calmly, Hannah," Eve said. "What can he do? Spill some soup over our heads? Mostly all he can do is scream and rage and maybe break a few glasses."

"So what's new about that?" Ruth tossed her head.

"Don't worry so, Hannah," Eve pleaded. "He won't know we actually spilled the vodka into the snow. All he'll know is that there isn't any because we didn't have the money to buy more when the supply ran out. Just like the fish."

"So then why must it be vodka too?" Hannah demanded. "Why isn't the fish enough?"

"Because we're trying to make a point, and the vodka will make a stronger point than the fish alone will. And I told you—I'm willing to take all the responsibility for spending the money myself."

The other women looked at Hannah and Eve almost as if they themselves were not involved at all, as if the matter were completely between the two of them.

"*Oy vey,* you're killing me," Hannah wrung her hands. Then she herself flung open the door again, pulled the bottle out of Eve's hand and quickly emptied it. "Let's get this over with before we die from the cold, saving Chaim the trouble of striking us dead, God forbid!"

Then they each picked up a bottle, poured, and watched the vodka form a puddle over the icy crust of snow. "Vodka doesn't freeze, you know," Eve said for no reason at all.

"Lessons yet . . ." Hannah muttered. "For that she's good."

A new dense snow began to fall, building on top of the old quickly, and the men were very late. Finally the women fed the children and put them to bed. They agreed to wait for their husbands before eating themselves. "God forbid Eve shouldn't have the pleasure of sitting at the table when Chaim discovers there's not only no fish but no vodka too. . . ." Hannah tried to make a joke of it but there were wrinkles of tension in her forehead.

"Oh, my God!" Miriam clutched her head as if only now remembering there'd be no vodka. "What a night we picked to be out of vodka! When they're already hours late, frozen to the bone, starving like wolves, tired as dead ones, and most likely without even a chicken to show for their day. . . ."

And with every temper honed to a fine edge! For the first time since they had spilled the vodka into the snow Eve felt a twinge of doubt and remorse. It did seem she had chosen a particularly bad day. For herself, she would have exulted in this heightened element of danger in the confrontation with Chaim, but for the others? She had led them into this situation like sheep, and she knew that with every minute that passed their anxiety was growing. And what about David? As tired, cold and miserable as he would be when he finally came home, what sympathy could she expect from him for the crisis she herself had created? It was even possible that his rage might equal his father's.

Only Ruth appeared cool. She went to the cupboard. "It occurs to me that we have a half bottle of plum brandy here— Yes, here it is." She held up the bottle triumphantly.

Miriam checked the level of liquid with a knowing eye. "It won't go very far but it will be better than nothing."

"It doesn't *have* to go very far. There's enough here for a drink for each of us. I propose we drink a toast to *us*. We're going to need it," she smiled cheerfully, getting out the glasses, while Eve thought: *Oh, Ruth I could kiss you. Maybe everything will still turn out all right.*

Hannah accepted her glass from Ruth. "Why not? Hanged for an ewe as hanged for a lamb! So, Evele, make the toast."

"Ruth should make the toast."

Ruth held up her glass. "To all of us!" she said grandly. "And I say *if* we're making a point, tonight's the night for making a point that *is* a point!"

They hit their glasses all around and drank.

"But what *is* the point?" Dora asked hiccupping, having tossed her brandy off in one gulp. "Spilling out the vodka?"

"*Oy vey!*" Miriam rolled her eyes.

"No, never mind," Ruth told her. "Just remember one thing. We spilled it out but we're pretending that it was all gone, drunk up. And God help you if you tell one single person that we actually spilled it out! You can't even tell Yacob because then all our husbands will be angry with us, not even to mention Chaim."

"Don't worry. I won't tell anyone. It's our secret. To tell you the truth I'd rather Chaim was angry with me, even Yacob, than any of you. I think I'd die if all of you were mad at me."

"Who could be mad at you, sweetheart?" Hannah patted Dora's cheek. Then she got up from her chair to go over to the window to look out into the dark.

It was almost eleven o'clock when the men trooped into the house, looking more like figures sculpted in ice than humans. "Look at those faces. Don't even ask if they bought anything today," Miriam warned the others.

As weary and frozen as he was, David still managed to hug Eve, grateful she was there to welcome him. She gave him back a lingering kiss, the better to warm him and sustain him in the painful moments to come. As he collapsed in a chair, she pulled off his wet boots and the trousers that were heavy and stiff with frozen moisture. She brought him a comforter to wrap himself in and a basin of snow to rub into the frostbitten hands.

Finally all the men were huddled into comforters and gathered around the dining room table, wanting only to eat and drink, too tired to talk. The women ladled out the beet soup first, its red hue burnished with the addition of browned morsels of beef. "Nothing like a hot soup to warm a person," Miriam clucked.

"True," Hannah agreed. "When a person's cold it's better than a piece of bread or a potato." She served Chaim his bowl, her face pale, her hands trembling as she set the bowl down.

Chaim shoved it away roughly, causing it to slosh over the rim onto the tablecloth where it spread looking much like bloodstains. "Vodka!" he growled. "Where the hell is the damned vodka? On a night like this a man wants his vodka first! Not borscht, you cow!"

Hannah's white face turned red and Abraham's face turned white. Though everyone was accustomed to Chaim's curses and name-calling, he usually didn't so address Hannah. But Abraham only sighed wearily and huddled deeper into his blanket.

"Is it too much to ask why you idiots didn't put out the vodka?"

Hannah's mouth opened to speak but closed again before anything came out and then Ruth began, "It's that—"

"Let me," Eve interrupted. It *was* her responsibility even though she was no longer feeling as brave as she had, now that the big moment had come.

"Well? Where is it?" Chaim bellowed.

Eve put a hand on David's shoulder. "There is no vodka. There isn't a drop in the house."

She could feel David's body tense under her hand in the thick silence. Then, even before Chaim found his voice, there was an undercurrent of disbelieving angry groans from the brothers. They, as well as Chaim, needed not one shot of vodka but several.

Everyone was amazed to hear Chaim speak in a controlled dulcet voice. "And *why* isn't there a drop in the house?" The brothers' jaws dropped. Ruth, Miriam and Hannah exchanged looks. *Unbelievable!* They'd been expecting something not unlike the wrath of God—floods, plagues, thunder and lightning—but here was Chaim speaking so softly. *Had this long, terrible day softened his heart?*

"There isn't any vodka because there wasn't any money to buy it with." Eve's voice picked up more assurance as she went on. "Not a kopeck, not a groschen, not a quarter of a kopeck."

The brothers stared at Eve, their faces scowling far more than Chaim's. They were beginning to sense that it was David's beautiful but without a doubt trouble-making wife who was at the bottom of their vodkaless state. Who else's fault could it be? They had had terrible days before, many of them, but they'd never once been without vodka before she came. Deep inside him, David groaned. He too sensed that in some way Eve was responsible for there being no vodka. And his father must be thinking the same thing! He was scratching at his beard and ominously eyeing Eve.

Still, Chaim spoke softly, more softly than anyone had ever heard him speak. "Not a kopeck? That's strange. It can't be more than a few days, maybe ten or twelve, since I put the monthly allotment in the jar. Why was there no money left for vodka?"

The whole room waited for Eve to answer. Ruth wondered why Chaim was acting better on a bad day than he ever had on a good one. Miriam reasoned that since Chaim was being not only reasonable but fairly polite, it must be that the terrible day had not only softened his heart but his brain as well. As for Dora, she was sure Chaim had been taken with a fever from being out in the blizzard so long. But Hannah realized, as Eve did, that Chaim's manner was only the calm before the storm and that his behavior now was more threatening than if he were raging.

"There's no money left because we spent it all," Hannah blurted, wanting to get the whole thing over already and wanting to spare Eve from bearing the complete burden.

But Eve refused to be spared. She held up a hand to Hannah, saying, "If you want to know what we spent it on, I'll tell you. On dress material. For a beautiful dress for Ruth and one for Dora. Because they're good wives and they've never *had* a really beautiful dress. And we spent it on dress material for Shlomo's daughters because little girls need pretty dresses too. It's important for them to look nice too."

"Yes," Ruth cut in. "Children aren't lumps of clay either," she said feelingly, even though this was a new thought for her.

"And we bought new shears to cut the material with because the old one was rusty," Miriam said, eager now not to be left out.

"After all, are we paupers that we have to use a rusty shears?" Hannah asked reasonably. She looked at Abraham who was trying desperately to signal her to be quiet. She shook her head at him. "And we bought books—four of them—for our minds. Our minds have to be fed as well as our mouths. We're not creatures with stomachs only."

"And we—" Eve tried to speak.

"Excuse me, Eve," Hannah said curtly. "I'm not finished. You'll forgive me if I remind you that you're not the only one God gave a mouth to. We bought toys for the children . . . only a few because—"

"Because children don't only have stomachs either," Ruth interrupted although Hershel glared at her furiously.

"And don't forget the soap. We bought sweet-smelling soap because the soap we make ourselves smells terrible," Miriam said matter-of-factly.

At that David, although his body was tight with tension, had to fight hard not to laugh, remembering how Eve had turned up her nose at their terrible-smelling soap her first day under the Markoff roof. It didn't take much to guess whose idea the soap was.

"And don't forget the perfume," Dora cried, eager to put in a few words too. "We bought French perfume. Lovely!"

At that there was an audible reaction from the men—sounds of surprise, anger, distress, irritation, disgust, even despair, and still Chaim was silent. He had been looking at each woman in turn as she spoke, calmly, even with interest.

Now, Eve thought, was the time for her to give her planned speech of *why* they had spent the money, now that everyone knew on what it had been spent. The *why* of it was the point, after all, and it was as important for all the husbands to hear as it was for Chaim. Then Chaim finally started to speak and although his voice was still low, she easily heard the threat in it. "So! It was because of all these things including French whore perfume that you weren't able to buy vodka for my table. . . ."

"And not fish either." It was as if Dora was reminding him.

"And not fish either," Chaim repeated slowly, his voice picking up volume. "So, I take it you decided it was more important to buy material for dresses for your stinking female bodies . . ." he picked up the bowl of borscht and dropped it to the floor, "and soap to wash your stinking female bodies . . ." he picked up a bowl of groats and sautéed onions and smashed that to the floor, "and French perfume no less, so that all your stinking bodies could stink to high heaven like those of stinking whores!" He picked up a roast chicken and heaved it against the wall. "That for your stinking female bodies!"

Even Eve was too shocked to speak. Even she hadn't expected Chaim to react this violently. David jumped up and put his arm around her, both in protection and consolation.

But it was Hannah who spoke: "You forget yourself, Chaim Markoff! I remind you that this is a Jewish house and there are innocent Jewish children sleeping in the other rooms, and we, whom you speak of in this disgraceful manner, are Jewish wives and mothers."

"It is you who have forgotten yourself, woman!" Chaim stood up and with one motion picked up the heavy table and flipped it over, sending it slamming to the floor where for a few seconds it rocked on its side. Dishes crashed, glasses shattered, and borscht, wine red, splattered everywhere.

After the first few seconds of shock, confusion reigned as the women raced back and forth with towels and rags and the men uttered exclamatory phrases of disgust and anger, not sure anymore at whom they were angrier, their wives or their father.

Eve could have wept with frustration. She had not even had the chance to make her point. Well, she was going to! No matter what! Even as David was trying gently to push her down into a chair. Ignoring the din and David's efforts to restrain her, she called out: "Is this the only answer you're capable of giving, Chaim? Breaking dishes, insults? An intelligent man might ask *why* did we spend the household money on what you refer to as our 'stinking' bodies. And then we could answer you: We spent the money on our *beautiful* bodies for the simple reason that we don't have any money of our own to use."

The room grew hushed at her repetition of Chaim's word, and the choice of her own. *Beautiful bodies*. Who used words like that?

Eve was inspired by the silence to go on, even to be fanciful. "With these beautiful bodies we work in your kitchen and your house, we care for the children and keep the Sabbath. And when we're finished with the work, we make love to our husbands with our bodies . . ." Ignoring the gasps, Eve tossed her head. "Yes, with our bodies we comfort our husbands and grow babies both for our husbands and for God because the Talmud says of a man without a child that he is alive but at the same time dead. I would say that makes our bodies very beautiful! And I would say we've earned the right to have some money of our own to spend as we see fit. But since we're not asking you to pay *us* for what we do, we think it's only fair that you pay our husbands for their labor. Then we'll all contribute a fair share to the household money and then we'll have what's left over to spend in any way we choose . . . on our beautiful bodies, or whatever—"

There was a groan or two from the husbands but Chaim himself only rocked on his heels. Then suddenly Dora started clapping her hands for Eve, caught up in the excitement of her words, whereupon Yacob, fearful eyes on his father, rebuked her. Dora looked as if she might cry.

Eve herself glanced quickly at David to see if he was angry with her. But no, his face was full of pride! Impulsively she kissed him full on the lips.

But Chaim was laughing! He was laughing at her! How dare he? Anger? Yes. But his laughter was contempt as if she were nothing but a tiny flake in the cosmic snowfall and her impassioned words nothing more than the drivel of a child.

Then abruptly, Chaim stopped laughing. In a harsh voice he ordered Hershel to go to the stable and bring him back his saddlebag. Bewildered and reluctant to go out into the black icy night again, Hershel nevertheless put his wet boots back on, and with but a blanket thrown over his head and back, he trudged out to do as he was bid. Then Chaim ordered Shlomo to pick up one of the roast chickens from the floor and hand it to him. As they all watched in silent fascination, Chaim, holding the whole chicken in one hand, tore into the meat with his teeth again and again, biting off large raggedy chunks, chewing gustily as small pieces of flesh flew into the air and bright yellow fat smeared both his face and fist. When he had nearly demolished the bird, he broke off a leg and gnawed at that until he was down to the bone, which he crushed between his teeth and then spat out the pieces.

By this time Hershel had returned with the saddlebag, and Chaim bade him to stand holding it while he proceeded to devour the chicken's remaining leg. Finished with that, he threw the remaining carcass over his shoulder and demanded a towel. Hannah handed him one, and he slowly and deliberately wiped his hands and face and then let the towel fall to the floor. He gestured to the waiting Hershel who handed him the saddlebag. From out of the saddlebag, Chaim withdrew a bottle of vodka nearly three-quarters full! While Eve's eyes burned with the tears of frustration—he had managed to outwit her after all—Chaim smiled triumphantly and pulled out the bottle's cork, and with a *"L'chayim"* he put the bottle to his lips and drank for a full thirty seconds.

The sons watched longingly as Chaim drank. Eve knew that every word she had so loftily offered was completely obliterated by that spare bottle of vodka. She felt ill with the desire to go up to Chaim and beat him with her fists. Oh God, she wanted to kill him!

Wiping his mouth on his sleeve, Chaim said, "Not only won't there be a groschen of wages, neither will there be a groschen put into the money jar until this month is up. And then, the usual amount will be put in minus the amount I'm forced to spend on vodka for myself. But I'm a generous man," he smiled with big teeth. "I'll not deduct the money I'll spend feeding myself at the inn. As for the rest of you, what you eat is your own problem. Next month, if the money is gone on even the first day because some wanton bitch chooses to spend it on perfume and whatever else her evil spirit tells her to, then all of you will do without for that month too.'' With that, he lifted the bottle again, this time very much in Eve's direction, took another gulp and went off to bed taking the bottle with him.

The instant he was gone Abraham turned to Hannah. ''So? What did you expect? That he was going to kiss you on both cheeks?''

''Sometimes you don't do because you expect,'' she answered, picking up some broken pieces of crockery from the floor as she spoke. ''You just do because you must.''

''And what *did* you do in the end?'' Shlomo asked. ''I'll tell you what you did—'' He turned to Miriam. ''What you *did* was leave us without a drop to drink and our dinner on the floor. And for what? For French perfume? And when do we get to smell this very expensive perfume?''

Miriam shrugged. ''Last night. When Chaim said it smelled like a whorehouse in here—that's when you smelled it.''

''It's almost all gone,'' Dora said sadly.

''Instead of talking so much, do you think one of you strongmen could pick up the table so we can straighten up a little and see if there's anything left that can still be eaten?'' Ruth demanded, her hands on her hips. ''Or is that too much for you?''

''Maybe without our dinner we're not so strong,'' Hershel answered his wife crankily while Abraham and David righted the table. ''And never mind the food. How about that we're frozen to our guts, to our bowels, to our assholes and we don't have a drop of something to warm us?''

''Listen to that mouth on him,'' Ruth complained. ''My husband has a mouth on him like his father's.''

Hershel smiled bitterly. ''And if I didn't have a mouth like my father's would it help me? Would it get me some of that comfort of a beautiful body Eve was shooting off her mouth about? Maybe David doesn't mind giving up his supper and his vodka. At least he's got something to look forward to when he goes to bed. And what do I have? A woman I can't touch because she's nursing . . .''

''*Oy vey iz mir!*'' Hannah cried. ''Have the decency to save that kind of talk for when you're alone together in your room, please!''

''You're complaining about talk, Hannah?'' Abraham laughed with uncharacteristic sarcasm. ''That's good because that's what I usually get in *our* bedroom. Talk and not much else.''

''*Oy vey iz mir!*'' Hannah cried again.

Eve thought that she'd be sick for sure at what was going on. ''Please! Everyone!'' she begged. ''Let's not fight among ourselves. We have to stick together.''

''If *you* didn't start all this trouble in the first place we wouldn't have to be sticking together,'' Yacob accused. ''We'd be eating right now, and drinking.''

David threw him a murderous look. Yacob was his older brother by two years, but he'd kill him if he didn't shut up.

70

"It's the truth, isn't it?" Yacob insisted, defending his position to the others. "Did we have this trouble before *she* came?"

David made a dive for Yacob's legs, picked him up off the floor and in another quick motion elevated him to over his head. Then he started to spin. The other brothers perked up visibly. *This was more like it!* Any moment now Yacob would go flying, maybe even through the window!

Dora screamed and Eve pleaded: "David! Put him down please!"

Reluctantly David set Yacob on his feet. The brothers turned away in disappointment and disgust. Nothing was going to save this night from complete disaster; they weren't even going to have the small pleasure of seeing Yacob hurled through the air.

Dora breathed a sigh of relief. "You mustn't talk against Eve, Yacob. She's a wonderful person."

"Oh, what do you know about anything?" the disgruntled Yacob complained, drawing his blanket around his shoulders again. "For one thing, you're not very smart. Everyone knows that. And for another thing, you can't even produce a child. And what did your wonderful Eve say about a childless man? He is not dead but not alive."

Dora burst into tears and Eve ran to comfort her while Ruth yelled, "Enough!" She was on her knees, scrutinizing an oatmeal pancake for damage. "If everyone would stop fighting and saying nasty things and instead would pick up maybe we'd find enough here to make a meal. Then everyone would feel better."

Miriam picked up a chicken. "At least Chaim missed this one. There's really no reason we can't eat it. A little wipe and it'll be as good as new. Well, almost as good."

"Who can eat?" Abraham asked, sitting down at the table. "Who has an appetite?"

Hershel threw himself into a chair too. "It's not even good to eat so late at night. It lies on the stomach like an anvil."

Shlomo joined them at the table. "It'll be time for breakfast soon."

Yacob came over and slumped down in a chair dejectedly. "Breakfast is for when you wake up and this night is nearly over and we haven't slept yet."

"What a mess I've made of things," Eve whispered morosely to David who was kneeling alongside her, helping to pick up whole boiled potatoes. Miraculously, half of them had remained in their unbroken bowl. "I've accomplished nothing outside of making everyone angry with everyone else. In fact any headway that we made before by forcing Chaim to eat with the whole family has been lost tonight. Chaim is the victor for sure. . . ."

"No, no." David tried to reassure her. He tipped her chin up with a finger. "It's not all over yet." He kissed her mouth, then her cheeks, then the tip of her nose. "Tonight Father's won but that doesn't mean he's won out for good. You're not giving up, are you?" He popped a whole potato into his mouth. "I'm not!" His voice was thick with potato.

"Oh, David!" *Every day he becomes more and more the man I dreamed of—He's not even angry with me and maybe for tonight, that's victory enough.* "If your mouth wasn't so full of potato I'd kiss you."

"And if I were you," he said with his mouth still full, "I'd do it anyway."

So she did and they both laughed and tried it again. As they kissed, Eve could see out of the corner of her eye the brothers looking at them, clearly resentful of their kissing and giggling.

"Oh, David! Your brothers are *really* angry with me and with their wives too. And that's because of me too. Those women have been so wonderful—they backed me up, they trusted me. They even had the courage to speak up to Chaim and say *we* did this and *we* bought that, when it was really only me who made all the trouble. I put them into this position and now they're going to suffer for it and, on top of that, have their husbands mad at them. Oh, if only your brothers weren't so angry. If only they could laugh at everything just a little. . . ."

"I think we can arrange that."

"How?"

"Like this—" He picked up a potato and threw it at Abraham, hitting him on the cheek. Abraham turned to look at him with disbelief! When he saw David laughing, he broke into laughter himself and picking up a slice of pot roast that had just been salvaged, he moved quickly across the room to slap it against David's nose. But David got to his feet and ran, and as he did so, he threw another potato, this time at Hershel. The potato landed in Hershel's thick thatch of unruly curls and Hershel picked out the pieces, reached over and rubbed them into Shlomo's beard. Shlomo sat there patiently waiting until Hershel was thoroughly finished. Then he stood up and pushed Hershel off his chair. From his position on the floor, Hershel's hand searched out and found a slice of pickle which he threw without aim. He hit Yacob who was by this time sitting on David's chest. Within seconds, the room was a great free-for-all with food, including handfuls of wet noodles, flying in all directions.

Miriam, still hugging the chicken she'd rescued from the floor to her breast, viewed the action dispassionately. "I think they'll be busy for quite a while. So, in the meantime, why don't we go into the kitchen and have a little something—a piece of breast, a leg."

"All she thinks about is filling her stomach. What are we going to do about this room?" Ruth asked the others.

"What will we do? We'll clean it," Hannah told her. "Tomorrow. Tomorrow is another day and tonight is tonight. And tonight," she looked at the brothers wrestling on the floor, wildly laughing and happily smearing each other with food like young boys without a care in the world, "tonight did not turn out so bad after all."

"I think tonight's been very exciting," Dora said enthusiastically. "Probably the most exciting night of my life!"

72

"Is that so?" Miriam put the arm that wasn't hugging the chicken around Dora as they walked to the kitchen. "More than your wedding night?"

Ruth elbowed Eve. "You hear her? See what she thinks about, that Miriam? Day and night it's two things—what goes into her mouth and what goes on when the lights go out."

Too stimulated to sleep even though it was nearer to morning than to night, Eve and David lay talking. "You saved the day, David. I never would have believed your brothers would have ended up laughing this evening."

But David was more thoughtful than exhilarated. "The hardest part is yet to come, Eve."

"You mean when there's nothing left to eat and Chaim won't give us any more money?"

"Yes, that too, but I was thinking in particular of our next step. So far you've gone about things in a roundabout manner. Father's a man who only understands direct force. Now that he's already laughed in our faces, there's really only one solution . . ."

"Yes?"

"If he refuses to pay us wages, we have to refuse to work. Isn't that right?"

Of course David was right. She'd been thinking the same thing but after the evening's disaster she'd been reluctant even to suggest it. "Yes, David. That's exactly right!"

He was exultant only for a moment that she agreed with him. "It's not going to be easy."

"Of course it won't. But Chaim's only one man. And all over Russia the people are beginning to fight back, to strike against much more terrible odds."

"I know," David said, but without much conviction. "But I think it would be easier to get my brothers to join in a national strike than to go against my father. And for me to strike by myself means nothing. Isn't that right? It only means something if all of us refuse to work."

"Yes, David." It was amazing how far David's reasoning had come.

"So how are we going to accomplish that? Convince my brothers?" He really didn't expect an answer.

"We'll have to persuade them."

"Easier said than done," he sighed. "I know you think you can do the impossible," he laughed forlornly, "but my brothers aren't going to listen to anything you or I say. They're terrified of father for one thing, and for another, they're as stubborn as asses, every last one of them."

"Maybe they'll listen to their wives."

"I doubt that too."

"Oh, I don't know," Eve smiled. "Maybe they will. We women have our ways."

"*You* do, but I don't know if *they* do. Besides, first the wives would have to be convinced. And after tonight, I don't know. . . ."

"Oh, I think they're convinced all right. It's only a matter of letting them know that they are."

"Sometimes I think it takes a crooked head to figure out what's going on in *your* head."

Playfully, she pounded him with a fist while he cowered in mock fear. "At least we'll have some time to work on it. Every year around this time we lay off for about a month since there's no livestock to be found."

"I know. Miriam explained that to me today."

"Well, tonight on our way home Father said he was ready, that today was our last day until spring."

She snuggled up to him, pulling the comforter around them in such a way that they were in a little cave. "That's wonderful! It must be an omen!"

"How do you mean—an omen?"

"It must be an omen from heaven that we should have a work strike since tonight's the night Chaim refused to pay wages, and it's also the beginning of the period when no one can work anyway. Don't you see? We have this period to persuade everyone that they can't go back to work when the period's over. An omen!"

"As I just said, it does take a crooked head to figure out what's going on in your head."

She giggled. "I don't know. Your head doesn't seem so crooked to me."

When David was asleep she got out of the bed and went to the window to look out at the night. It was still snowing. She thought about the five or six weeks they had to lay the groundwork for their work strike. Time enough . . .

She turned around to look at David lost in sleep. *Oh, David, I haven't told you about our baby yet. Do we have time? You and I? Enough time for our baby to be born to parents who answer to no one but each other?*

She looked out the window again as if possibly she might find an answer there. But she only felt the icy winds coming through the cracks. It was as if the winds blew right through her chilled heart. Oh, she was such a little fool! She and David and Chaim, too, were only the tiniest of specks of all the millions of specks that covered Russia. A baby born to freethinking parents? With Chaim or without Chaim, how could that be true of any Jewish child born into this land of toil and trouble?

She ran back to bed, pulled the covers back over both of them. "David—"

He came awake. "Sweetheart, what is it?"

"Oh, David! We do have to hurry! We're going to have a baby . . ."

5.

By morning the blizzard had passed but the icy winds continued to blow out of the distant steppes, swirling the freshly fallen snow into great clouds that obstructed almost all vision. Since there was no reason to get up, the men slept on while the women went about their chores—preparing the breakfast, attending to the children, kindling the fires. Eve lit the samovar. It was the kind of day that called for endless glasses of tea, and she was already planning on much conversation and discussion.

When Chaim awoke, he never came into the kitchen at all. Watching him leave the house, the women assumed he was headed for the Inn where he'd find all the food, companionship and vodka he desired. Or maybe he was headed for Olga Shakov's house. Olga, aided by a pretty friend, was known to keep a room or two available for a special boarder. The two ladies were said to provide whatever it was a man needed that the Inn didn't.

When the brothers awoke they ate their breakfast and discussed what chores there were to be done and which chore had priority. A fence needed mending but obviously it was a bad day to tackle that, with the winds howling like a pack of wolves. The barn wall had to be repaired but for that they would need materials and it was clearly a very bad week to be asking Chaim for money for lumber. They *could* start the addition of the new room since David and Eve had supplanted four of the children, but that necessitated a foundation and it was definitely a bad month to lay foundations, an impossible month to lay foundations. That would have to be done late into spring. Slowly their list dwindled. Then they decided it was already too late in the day to do anything since before they knew it the Sabbath would be upon them. Accordingly they put on their heavy jackets and boots and went off to those places where the workless men of the town congregated on a cold, bleak short winter day—the Inn, the butcher shop, or maybe at Ilya the blacksmith's.

Miriam and Ruth set about straightening the chaotic dining hall—picking up the broken dishes and glasses, scrubbing the floor and even the walls, even attempting to fix a couple of broken chairs themselves, while Dora with a couple of the older children was dispatched to the barn and chicken house to search out any hidden eggs. Hannah and Eve began the preparation of the Sabbath loaves. Hannah sighed. "It will be a poor Sabbath dinner we'll have tonight."

"It doesn't have to be—"

"Well, since we'll have no more money until the month is up, we have to conserve whatever food we do have. And the men will be complaining about you know what not being on the table."

"Maybe we can make it so pleasant they won't notice the missing vodka. We'll set a pretty table and light the candles and—"

Hannah snorted. "You're dreaming. Like Chaim was going to pay wages that's how they won't notice we don't have any vodka . . ."

Hannah seemed so downcast Eve wondered what she could possibly say or do that would cheer her up. "You know, Hannah, after I went to bed last night I couldn't sleep. And you know how it is when you can't sleep—the thoughts whirl around and around. I thought of what you said to Chaim about us buying the books. You said that *we* bought the books for our minds because our minds have to be fed as well as our mouths. That was wonderful, Hannah. But then I thought how it wasn't true. I bought those books for myself and not to feed yours or the others' minds at all. I remembered how you told me that you had started lessons when you were a girl but that you had to give them up. And Miriam said she has already forgotten the little she had learned. And Ruth and Dora—why, no one ever taught them anything. And here I was, lucky enough to have been taught to read, reading for almost my entire life—reading and learning. Then it occurred to me that I could be teaching you, all of you, to read, sharing with you the things I've learned. So I was thinking that since there's no time like the present we should have daily lessons starting today."

At first Hannah seemed interested, but then she scoffed, "Where would we get the time? And even if we found the time it would take forever for us to learn to read. Better you should just tell us your stories about the world. You know, how once in a while you give us a little lesson in history."

"No," Eve said decisively. "I mean, I'll teach you history and anything else you want to know that I know, but I insist you all have to learn to read for yourselves. No one can think for herself if she can't read for herself. And not just Hebrew either. I'm going to teach you to read Yiddish since that's what we speak."

"They speak Hebrew in Palestine, don't they?"

"Yes, but what of it?"

"Palestine is the land of Israel, isn't it? And we're all Israelites, aren't we?"

"Yes, but we live here and it's Yiddish that Jews speak here, so though we pray in Hebrew, it's important that we read Yiddish."

Hannah smiled with irony. "We live in Russia and while we speak a little Russian and a little Polish, mostly we only speak Yiddish. Mostly we don't speak Russian at all except for the few words we exchange with the gentiles. I know *you* can read Russian and I suspect that you speak it well, but how often do you really use it? So here we are—Israelites who live in Russia, pray in Hebrew but speak Yiddish. It's funny." She had fixed two glasses of tea and they sat down at the table. "So what do you think, Eve? Do you think maybe we Jews will all speak Hebrew someday in the Promised Land?"

76

"I don't know if it will happen in our lifetime, Hannah. I don't know if any of us will ever see the Promised Land . . ." She looked down into her glass of tea as if there might be an answer there.

"So tell me, Eve. Are there any countries where the Jew speaks the language of the land and not Hebrew and not Yiddish?"

"Well, I think they do in Germany. But Yiddish and German are very similar. Yiddish comes from the German. They say that in America the Jew is really starting to speak the language of the country. The old Jews still cling to their Yiddish, but their children are learning—"

"Tell me. If you could leave Russia tomorrow, would you? Or do you think that someday even Russia will be free, a good place to live?"

"In order to answer that question I'd have to ask another. Even if Russia was free, would the Jew ever be? Even if we weren't despised by the authorities, wouldn't we always be *the Jews,* always apart from the others? Could it ever truly be our land?"

"So I take it you would leave? But where would you go? To Palestine? At least it was once our land. At least a Jewish person could feel a little at home there. The people wouldn't all be such strangers. There, at least, we'd all pray in the same language."

"Yes. It would be better than here. It's warm and they can't send you to Siberia. But I don't think Palestine would be my first choice. Here in Russia, even if we were free of the authorities we'd still have the peasant to spit on us and the gentry to accuse us of all kinds of unspeakable things. And we'd still have our own men who would say that as women we're their inferiors and they still wouldn't let us sit with them in the synagogue. So then I'd have to consider if it would be much better for me in Palestine even if it were Israel again. There we'd still have the Palestinians who, while they might be no more powerful than the Jews, would still despise us. We'd still have our own men who would still think of us as inferior, not worthy even to be called up to the Torah. All we could hope for would be a *slight* improvement in our position. There we might even rank on a par with a goat."

"Ah, so it *is* America you'd choose. Where they don't speak American but English and where they say the streets are paved with gold."

"You know better than that," Eve laughed. "But yes, I would definitely choose America."

"And what about the gentiles there? They don't despise the Jews there?"

"I guess some do. But not as much as they do in other places because they themselves aren't oppressed. They're just people who went there to make a better life for themselves just as the Jew would."

"And our own men? Do you think in America they let the women go up to the Torah?"

"I don't think they do . . . *yet.* But in a country where you live free you grow as a person and your ideas change. I think that someday in America they *will* call women up to the Torah. They will let them speak . . ."

"You're dreaming," Hannah laughed. "The men would as soon allow that as they'd let you take away their penises."

Eve laughed heartily. "You may have hit the nail on the head, Hannah. Maybe that's exactly how Jewish men regard the Torah. Like their penises. Look at it this way. All through the centuries the Jews have been oppressed, driven from country to country. As a result they became a fearful people, living in the shadows. It was hard for the Jewish male not to lose belief in himself as a man. Yet no matter how they were persecuted, they held on to their Torah. So, like their penises, the Torah became a symbol of their manhood, and they won't let us come near it. They keep it for themselves. They want to make sure that they come first, at least with God." Eve smiled impishly at Hannah. "But in America, things will be different. They'll see. In America, our men will find out that they'll have to allow us our place in the sun or we'll turn our backs on them. In America all people can have an education—even if they're poor, even if they're Jews, even if they're women. And an educated woman can pick and choose. Once she's choosing, would she choose to be a second-rate person? No! She'll demand to stand beside the man even when God is looking."

Hannah stood up reluctantly. Interesting as the conversation was, they couldn't very well sit there the whole morning. "All right. So we'll learn to read and then we'll be educated women. And then we'll pick and choose," she laughed. "Tell me, Eve. Do you think all men are afraid we'll steal their Torah, their penises?"

"Come now, Hannah. I might be better educated but I'm sure you're far wiser. I'm sure you know as well as I do that there are all kinds of men. Some are too weak to give anything to anyone and others are strong enough to share everything—the world, their place in the sun, even their standing before God."

"Ah! If only all of us could find a man like that!"

"I would think," Eve smiled, "that a wise woman would look first in her own bed. Maybe if she searches hard enough—"

Hannah nodded. "Is that what you've done, Evele?"

"I've been lucky. And at first I didn't even know my own luck."

Hannah laughed, a half-sigh. "I wonder if Chaim's wife, may the poor soul rest in peace, ever searched her bed. Come to think of it, Eve, maybe *that's* Chaim's problem. Maybe he's worried *we'll* steal his penis!"

They both laughed and then they heard Dora giggle. "Are you two *really* talking about penises?"

Dora had just come in the kitchen door with the basket of eggs she had been to search for, and she was breathless, her cheeks red from the cold. "I know a rhyme about penises—'If you take four times the nose, then you've got a good-sized hose!' "

The three of them giggled.

It wasn't until later that Hannah suddenly asked Eve, "If you think America's so wonderful why don't you and David go? It's not impossible, after all. People go all the time. And you're both young and strong . . ."

78

"Oh, I want to go. Some day I will. Actually I yearn for it. I want to see it with my own eyes, smell it, live it with every breath in my body. But I don't think it's time yet. There's my father who's old. And there are all of you whom I look on now as my very own sisters. And still, even as I hate so many things about it—there's this damn land. I know it sounds silly but there's something inside me, deep inside, that wants to leave this murky, muddy, frozen place better than I found it, even if it's better for only a few people. Oh Hannah, I'm going to have a baby and wouldn't it be wonderful if he or she could be born into a Russia that's even a tiny bit better than it is today?"

"For the baby, *mazel tov*. For the other—" she shook her head. "Empty Russian dreams. Even I, who haven't read anything, know that Russian dreams never, never come true. All they do is break your heart."

"No, Hannah. For me America is the dream, and Russia—Russia is my dark reality."

After the women had struggled with their first reading and writing lesson—recognition of the letters, the pronunciation and, especially hard for them, the copying, they stopped for tea and cookies, and they asked Eve to tell them some stories. Eve searched her mind for some historical tale that would relate in some way to the message she was eager to get across to them—that since Chaim had refused to pay the wages they asked for, the next step was for their husbands to refuse to work, and it was up to them to talk them into it.

So while the women were expecting to hear perhaps a biblical story, Eve told them about the Americans' fight for independence against the British. She related how they chafed under the rule of England, and how, ultimately, they moved on to their Declaration of Independence and to the ensuing Revolution.

"What was so remarkable was that this pitifully small band of men were able to defeat all the king's men although they weren't trained and had very little in the way of supplies. They were starving and in tatters. Why, they marched through the heaviest snows of winter with only rags covering their bloodied feet—"

"So? *Nu?*" Miriam shrugged. "What's so special about that? That's just like here—"

Eve ignored her and went on. "Why did they do this? Because man's need to be free is perhaps his strongest need of all. And how were they able to defeat the English? Because they were unified. In unity there's strength."

"Tell me one thing," Hannah said reasonably. "If man's need to be free is so strong how come all the peasants of Russia don't rise up and fight?"

"Not to mention the Jews . . ." Ruth added.

"But they have *tried*. Many times. Right this very minute in Moscow, in St. Petersburg, right here in Lithuania, there are people talking, planning. If you take a look at history you'll see that the time comes for everyone when they fight back simply because they can't stand being pushed around anymore. As we ourselves did last night. As *we* fought back against Chaim . . ."

"You're comparing Chaim to the Tsar?" Miriam asked, incredulous.

"Yes. Because the Tsar's a tyrant and Chaim is one too. Chaim's only a petty, Jewish tyrant but a tyrant is a tyrant. And last night *we* fought back!"

Ruth laughed. "Yes, we fought back using a piece of fish and a bottle of vodka as weapons. Some revolutionaries we are! Besides—Chaim!" she scoffed. "He's nothing but a bully."

"But that's what every tyrant is! A bully that tries to get away with as much as he can, as the others will let him."

"So we fought back against our bully," Hannah said. "We fought back and we lost. And now we have to live with it."

"No, we don't! We can go on fighting!"

"And how do we do that?"

"We asked for wages for our husbands and Chaim refused. So now it's our move. We say to him that if our husbands don't get wages, *they refuse*. They refuse to work!"

The women looked at her as if she were truly *meshuge*. Their husbands refuse to work for their father? It would never happen in a thousand years.

"So this is what our history lesson was all about?" Hannah wiped her hands on her apron. "I should have known. You're not one to talk without a point, after all. But there's one thing—how do you propose that we get our husbands to refuse to work?"

"All of you have to talk all of them into it."

"How do we do that?"

"One way or another . . ."

When the men returned late that afternoon Eve immediately asked David if he had said anything to his brothers about not going to work with Chaim once the time came.

"I mentioned it in passing, making a joke of it more than anything, just to see how'd they take it. Even as a joke it went flat. They looked at me as if I were some kind of a fool. And you—? Did you mention it to the wives?"

"Yes."

"And?"

"I think it's too soon to tell."

It was a relief to all that Chaim, true to his word, didn't come home for the *Shabbes* dinner. Still, it wasn't the cheeriest of meals despite the fact that the women wore their holiday dresses and their wigs and used up the very last of their eau de cologne. After the men departed for the evening services and the children were bedded down, the women set about clearing away and cleaning up. Hannah said, "See Evele, I told you. All they know from is what's *not* on the table."

"They didn't even notice that we were wearing the perfume," Miriam added.

"Hershel did . . ." Ruth said, biting off her words. "He didn't say it smelled like a whorehouse as Chaim did, he just said it stunk."

Hannah clucked her tongue and Ruth said bitterly, "I should have told him what really stinks—male scum!"

80

The others stared at her, truly shocked.

"Well, don't look at me like that! It's true. Their *stuff* stinks to high heaven and they think it's so precious, every stinking drop!"

"Stuff? What stuff?" Dora asked but no one paid any attention to her since Miriam was smirking slyly, asking, "Is that why you'd rather have your husband spill his juices into the snow instead of into you?"

Ruth gasped, for once speechless in the face of a verbal attack from Miriam. But Hannah said, "Shame on you! What kind of talk is that?"

Miriam spread her hands. "But everyone knows Hershel goes off into the woods to do for himself what she won't."

"Oh, you bitch! You obscenity!" Ruth rasped, finding her tongue.

Miriam turned to the others as if in innocence. "Am I wrong? Everyone knows the only reason she keeps nursing that overgrown horse of a son is because a nursing mother is impure and her husband can't come near her. The way she's going, she'll still be giving that child a tit when he has a full set of teeth in his mouth already.

"When he's already running off to *heder,* she'll have to come running to the Hebrew school to make sure he takes the tit. When he's ready to be called to the Torah for his *bar mitzvah* she'll be right there giving him her breast rather than giving Hershel his rightful place between her thighs. And when he's ready to stand under the *chupah* with his bride, he'll have to come to her for a suck before he sticks it into the girl . . ."

"Miriam!" Hannah cried, covering her ears. "Have you no decency?"

"Decency? You expect decency from *her*? From that fat cow who can't give birth to anything except girls? At least I've produced sons!" Ruth beat her breast. "And she's so anxious to get that hole of hers—which I might add is as big as a barn—*filled,* she's willing to go on having girl children until she's dried up like a prune!"

"Enough!" Hannah ordered. "The two of you are a disgrace!"

Eve, who was always upset at the spectacle of Ruth and Miriam fighting, was even more upset to hear Dora murmur, "I'd be more than willing to go on having even girls until I dried up like a prune. I'd gladly take anything."

"Do you hear that, Ruth?" Eve cried out. "Now you have Dora saying *even girls,* as if having daughters was like having less than nothing, as if all of *us* were nothing."

"First of all," Ruth said in a voice strangely quiet now, "Miriam started up with me first. And second, it's *true.* We are nothing. We're dirt. We're less than dirt."

"No, Ruth! It's not true."

Ruth burst into tears. "Yes. It's true. We're nothing. We're less than nothing!" she sobbed.

Hannah put an arm around Ruth consolingly as she threw Miriam a dirty look. "Do you see what you started?"

"Yes," Eve agreed, "you did start this time, Miriam." But even as she spoke she realized that what Miriam had said about Ruth continuing to nurse her baby Gershon in order to be impure, to stop Hershel from making love to her, might very well be the truth. Otherwise, why would she be reacting to Miriam's taunt this way? She had been angry with Miriam before but she had never cried. She had never suggested before that she thought of herself, of all of them, as nothing.

Gradually Ruth's sobs subsided but she went on in a drone, "All of you know it's true even if you won't admit it. The men just use us to empty themselves into. They stick it in and we lie there like dummies and receive it. They enjoy it and then because they're hypocrites they attach a holy reason for doing it. They say it's only to have children and not even at their own will. It's God's will, they say.

"God's . . ." she sneered. "Does anyone ask us if we want to do it? Or if we like it? God forbid! It's our duty! And we're the ones who have to live with the results—the children. Child after child. We're the ones who have to spend the rest of our lives wiping—wiping up, wiping away. First we have to wipe their stinking juices from our thighs and then we have to wipe the babies' behinds, their dirty faces, the running noses, the fevered brows, the sick bodies. We wipe up the vomit and the shit, the tears from the cheeks and the pain from their hearts. Wiping and wiping . . . It never stops until we ourselves are worn rags only good enough to wipe the floors."

Her voice wore down and the other women sat motionless and mute before their sister-in-law's obvious torment. Eve wanted to say something, anything that could possibly assuage the pain Ruth was feeling, but what could she say that wouldn't be taken as colossal conceit on her part? She herself had been married only a short time, had no children and was probably spoiled, just as her brothers had said so often. How could she presume to say anything?

The silence in the room was broken by Hannah who approached Ruth, towel in hand. "So? This one time let *me* do your wiping," she said, half joking, half forlorn, as she dabbed at Ruth's tear-stained cheeks.

Then Dora started to weep, a soft mournful sound, a low aching wail and Eve wondered whether Dora cried because of what Ruth had said or for herself . . . *Or is it that she cries only because Ruth cries, not even understanding Ruth's words, but feeling Ruth's pain?*

"So?" Hannah said, smiling a little, looking at Dora's cheeks stained with tears too. "Ruthie is right. The wiping never stops." And she mopped at Dora's cheeks too.

Then the baby Gershon cried out from his cradle angrily as if to remind his mother of his presence. Miriam, most likely in atonement for making his mother cry, picked him up and placed him high on her shoulder. "I'm sorry, *mameniu*, a tit I can't give you." She patted him gently on the back, looking at Ruth, a half affectionate, half sheepish expression on her round, Slavic-featured face. "I'm sorry, Ruthie . . ." she said. "I guess it's that I'm tired of the cracks about having only girls."

Ruth nodded. "I'm more to blame than you. Everyone says I'm sour and you're pleasant. It must be so. And God knows I've twitted you enough about those girls of yours. It's really *their* fault—the men. They say we're good for nothing if we don't produce sons and I play along. I make myself a big shot because at least I did one thing right—I had sons. You know what I was doing? I was making myself more than a nothing at your expense. And if you want to know the truth, I envy you. Your girls are sweet and they'll be a comfort to you in your old age more than my sons will be to me. That's how it is with daughters. With sons—who knows?"

The two women smiled at each other, and Eve watched them. *And I think I'm so smart. I thought with all my words and education I was going to teach them about unity. I'm the fool and they can give me the lessons. I have yet to learn about real life. The real unity is their shared spiritual strength—their capacity for enduring a shared pain, a shared laughing through the tears.*

"I think we should have a glass of tea and finish cleaning up later," Hannah said. "Dora, get the glasses and the cookies."

I've seen them as nice but essentially simpleminded. I've confused their being unread with ignorance. And it's really I who am simpleminded with conceit. They're wise enough to survive and endure with grace. . . .

Eve glanced up to see Hannah smiling at her over the rim of her glass. "So, Evele, what are you thinking about so hard? That we're eating up all the cookies? And that in a few days we'll be out of eggs too and unable to make any more?" Hannah's eyes were crinkling around the edges, smiling like her mouth.

Endure with grace and with humor too. Eve smiled back at Hannah. "I was thinking very important thoughts. About these glasses of tea. Did you know that in the Tsar's palace they don't drink tea out of glasses at all? They drink out of teacups of French porcelain, the most beautifully painted teacups you can imagine. Delicate, thin as eggshells."

"Thin as eggshells!" Dora repeated in amazement. "And French!" Her eyes went big and round as she mulled the idea of it over in her head.

"And why were you thinking about French teacups?" Hannah asked as if amused at the workings of Eve's brain.

"I don't know. Why not?"

"Why not indeed?" Hannah laughed.

"What a one you are, Evele!" Miriam shook her head.

Then, piteously, Ruth's son cried out again, Miriam's shoulder in the end being no substitute for his mother's breast and Miriam handed him over to Ruth.

Ruth put the boy to her breast and said, "Yes, you're one of a kind, Eve. Maybe if there is one woman that *isn't* nothing, it's you."

"Oh yes!" Dora cried out. "Eve could never be nothing!"

Eve looked from face to face. They were gazing at her with admiration. With more than admiration, with love. She was filled with shame. She had come here so full of herself, so vain, with her long hair hanging, mocking their own poor cropped heads, flaunting her fancy dresses and showing off constantly. She

83

was trying to force her own ideas on them because she was so conceited she insisted on thinking she was smarter than they. And how did they reward her arrogance? By offering her admiration, love and complete trust.

What did she give them in return? The very doubtful privilege of sitting down at the same table with a nasty, rude and vulgar bully. She sewed a few dresses—elegant, frivolous dresses—when they lived in a world that had no room for either frivolity or elegance. She filled their heads with her silly notions—French teacups and soap and perfume, when they lived in the dregs of Russia where life was hard and where they could barely exist as human beings, much less as Jews. Then instead of helping them in some concrete fashion, she ended up making their husbands mad at them. And she offered to teach them to read, not so much for themselves as for herself, to suit her purposes, partially because their inability to read and write offended her sensibilities.

Oh, if the eye offends, by all means, Eve, pluck it out! As long as it isn't your own eye. Oh, I am selfish! Now I'm preaching revolution to them! A work strike! And what kind of a work strike? A work strike against one petty man, and for the gain of David and myself, and only incidentally for them. . . .

She was overcome with emotion. She was overwhelmed suddenly by her love for these women whom she had known for so short a time. She was filled with a yearning to give them something real, something truly fulfilling. Yes, she wanted to free them from Chaim's oppressive thumb but she wanted to give them more. She wanted somehow to show them that they deserved to inherit the earth even while they still lived.

She turned to Ruth, "*Who* was it who said you're nothing, Ruth?"

Startled, Ruth nearly dropped her glass of tea. "Are we back to that?"

"Who was it?"

"Everyone. My father said it when he didn't think I was even worth teaching, didn't he? And my husband thinks it even if he doesn't say it because he lives by what his father thinks. And the men in the synagogue. Don't they say it when they won't even let us sit with them? They won't even touch us when it's that time of the month. Oh, they want to put their things into us and they want to plant their seeds inside us; they want us to grow babies and feed them at our breasts but at the same time they call us unclean, impure, because of it. And my mother—she loved me but she thought I was nothing too because I was a girl. Why not? She thought she herself was nothing."

"Exactly," Eve said excitedly. "And it won't end until *we* ourselves think we're something. Now, *I* don't think you're nothing, Ruth. And Hannah doesn't and neither does Miriam nor Dora. Do you?" she challenged the three women and they shook their heads.

"There! None of us think you're nothing!"

Ruth laughed scornfully. "But all of you are women. All of you are nothing. It doesn't matter what you say. It's only what *they* say that counts. The men! They're in charge of the world."

"But naturally they say it. Don't you see? If they say *we're* nothing, that makes *them* something. That makes them everything. But we ourselves let them get away with this lie. We mustn't believe them!"

"Doesn't the Talmud say they're better than we are?"

"But who wrote the Talumd?" Eve demanded. "Men!"

"But it's God's word—" Miriam interjected.

"But who says it's God's word?" Eve countered. "The men. Even the Christians' Testament says 'give honor unto the wife, as unto the *weaker* vessel.' But where did they get that phrase? From *our* Testament. It's one group of men repeating the words of another group of men, and between them they make it out as truth among all men. It becomes more of a truth as it's repeated by one generation after the other through time."

"But doesn't it say in the Book that God made Eve from Adam's rib?" Dora asked.

Eve laughed. "Do I look like a rib to you?"

Dora blushed. "I didn't mean you . . ."

"That's all right. You don't look like any man's rib to me either."

"But God made man in His image. Therefore, it follows then that He must have thought men *were* better than women too," Ruth said dolefully.

"Oh, I don't know about that for sure. That's the way men wrote it down. But just suppose, suppose the man who wrote *that* down lied, or just guessed. Or not knowing exactly if that was so, preferred to *think* that was the truth. Just suppose it wasn't. What if the truth is God made *us* in Her image?"

"God forgive you, Eve!" Hannah gasped. "You're talking heresy!"

"No, I'm not. I know there's a God and I believe in the Almighty. All I'm saying is I personally couldn't swear the Almighty wears a man's face. As it is, we're only taking a man's word for it—"

Ruth laughed. "God a woman? That would be some joke on the men if that were really so . . ." But then the laugh stopped and the smile left her face as her tone changed. "No. It's impossible. After all, *we* were the ones picked to carry the children and to deliver them in pain. We're only the bearers, just as when we were slaves in Egypt."

"Ah, the children. We *were* the ones chosen to bear the children and I think right there is the answer to our puzzle. But I don't think we're the bearers in the same way the Jews were when they were slaves in Egypt. I think we women are the *creators,* truly the chosen. All of creation lies within *our* bodies. *We're* the special ones because we're the creators of all mankind!"

Dora giggled. "No, not mankind, Eve. Don't you mean we're the creators of all *womankind?*"

The women stared at Dora dumbstruck. Then Eve laughed. "Oh, my! Womankind! Oh Dora, that's wonderful!"

Ruth gazed at Dora in a bemused fashion. Then she smiled and then she laughed. "Womankind! That is kind of wonderful!"

6.

The days passed slowly for Eve. She continued with the lessons. At the same time she continued trying to convince the women to convince their husbands not to go back to work when the time came, unless Chaim changed his mind about giving them wages for their labor. But it seemed like a losing battle. The women were, it seemed, more concerned with the daily counting of their dwindling food staples.

She and David became more and more pessimistic about the situation day by day.

"Did you find out where your father's staying?"

"He was at Olga Shakov's. Now he's with the Widow Rabinowitz. She's been a widow for several years and father's visited with her before from time to time."

"How convenient for him," Eve said with uncharacteristic bitterness. "He receives all the comforts of home and then some—cooked meals, vodka, plus. Tell me, is the Widow Rabinowitz also the kind of woman who pulls off his boots?"

"I wouldn't doubt it," David laughed but without real mirth.

"He probably figures that by the time he returns home, ready to go back to work, and refills that damn money jar, everyone around here will be so desperate they'll kiss the ground he walks on. And he's right about that, I guess. No matter what I say to the women they go right back to counting how many potatoes are left in the bin. That's all they think about."

It occurred to Eve one afternoon to tell her sisters-in-law the story of *Lysistrata*, a story that had captured her own imagination when she first came across a description of the play, which told the tale of the women of Athens who had banded together in a common cause.

They were doing the laundry—a chore that in the winter went on for endless hours. First pots of snow had to be melted and then heated to almost boiling. The clothes had to be scrubbed, rinsed, wrung out, and hung outside where the articles quickly froze dry. Then the stiff-as-a-board laundry had to be brought back into the house to thaw, and then completely dried over the fire. The air in the kitchen was heavy with moisture and redolent with the odor of wet wool.

"In ancient Greece over two thousand years ago, a story was written—" Eve began the daily lesson. "Actually it was a play about what one group of women did to bring peace to their embattled city. I don't know if the play was written about real women or not, but it *was* about real times in Greece when the country was constantly at war, one city against another. Well, these women wanted peace so much they took matters into their own hands. As a result of their joining forces, uniting together, these women were able to force the men into doing what they wanted—to make peace. But there's no reason that any group of women couldn't do the same thing to accomplish whatever they want. . . ."

"What was it exactly that they did?" Dora asked, seemingly fascinated.

Hannah chuckled. "By chance did they spill vodka out into the snow?"

Eve laughed. "I doubt it. But maybe it was wine they poured into the Aegean Sea."

"Now, if it were *you* who wrote this play, I'm sure that's exactly what they would have done." Hannah wiped steam from her face with her arm.

"So tell us already," Ruth demanded, holding the baby Gershon to her breast as she stirred a pot of clothes with a thick stick with her free arm. "What *did* they do?"

"You have to understand, I never read the play itself but only an article discussing it."

"So? How come you didn't read the play?" Hannah teased. "Is it possible that you don't read Greek?"

"Hannah! Will you stop fooling around?" Ruth said sharply. "I want to hear what these women did."

"Well, for one, they laid siege to a citadel, a fortress that guarded their city much like the garrison that looks down on us. Well, the women took control of this citadel and from the way I understand it, they wouldn't perform any—no services at all for their men."

"What does that mean?" Miriam asked, stopping her scrubbing.

"They didn't do *anything*. They wouldn't cook, they wouldn't wash, they wouldn't—they withheld—"

"Withheld? What does that mean?" Miriam's expression indicated that she knew exactly what *withheld* meant.

"It means what you think it means. They refused to sleep with their husbands."

Dora's eyes grew very round and Miriam puckered her lips and shook her head from side to side. "So!"

"Just hold on a minute here, Eve," Hannah said, spreading a shirt out on top of the stove. "This is serious business you're getting into here. Maybe you'd better think twice before you start handing out that kind of advice. It's not very nice to come between a husband and a wife. . . ."

Eve was hurt. "What a thing to say! I have no such intention!"

"No? You didn't tell us this story for no reason. You're suggesting that we do what those women did, aren't you? That's what it sounds like to me."

Actually Eve had been considering just that, that the wives could convince their husbands not to work by withholding their services, including themselves, but she saw that it would never work out. Hannah refusing to cook? Or Ruth refusing to wash clothes? Or Miriam or Dora refusing to allow their husbands their bodies? It would never come to pass. Besides, hadn't she at first tried withholding herself from David? It had worked out much better when she had tried the opposite—offering, loving. "What I have in mind is exactly the opposite—"

That took a moment to sink in.

"You mean?" Miriam asked and when Eve nodded, she said, "Isn't that what we always do?"

"You do it, but do you *offer?* Do you take the first step? Do you do it willingly? Joyfully? With a passion?" She herself blushed. "What I'm thinking of is for all of you to be the ones to *start*, not wait for your husbands to—What I'm thinking is that you have to be especially . . . loving. And make yourself especially . . . alluring, as Queen Esther, as—"

"Enough with the examples," Hannah said dryly. "We get the idea."

"What about Ruth?" Miriam pointed a finger. "Her husband can't touch her since she's nursing."

"Why don't you worry about yourself?" Ruth asked irritably. "Worry about how you're going to make yourself—what was it you said, Eve? alluring. I'd think you would have your hands full with *that* without worrying about me and Hershel." Abruptly she removed Gershon from her breast and put him down on the floor. He immediately started to scream.

"Maybe it *is* time for you to stop nursing, Ruth. Gershon's well over a year and it *is* a long time for Hershel to go—"

"How *dare* you?" Ruth stared at Eve icily. "Are you so anxious to have your own way that you're giving me advice about something that's none of your business? You're no more than a snot-nosed—"

"Oh Ruth, forgive me!" Eve cried. "I only wanted to—"

"Yes, I know what you want. You want to tell everyone what to do." She scooped the screaming child up and stalked from the room.

Eve turned to Hannah. "Did I say something so terrible?"

"Not terrible, but not good either. You went too far."

"I would say so," Miriam huffed. "I would certainly say you went too far."

Eve swung to face Miriam. She was shocked to see hostility reflected in Miriam's eyes. "I'd say it's way too far when a seventeen-year-old snip starts standing behind my bed and tells me how to do with my husband what I was doing when she couldn't even wipe her own behind!"

"Miriam! I never meant to tell you what to do in bed! Really!"

"No? Maybe then I shouldn't believe my own ears? It certainly sounded like you were telling us all to act like whores!" And she too slammed out of the kitchen.

Eve turned to Hannah. "Did I—?" Before Hannah could answer Dora burst into tears. "Now what?" Eve asked in desperation. Was it possible she had also offended Dora of all people?

"I've always acted the way you say to Yacob. I've always acted like I loved him *in that way*. And what good has it done me?" Dora wailed. "Yacob despises me because I haven't given him a child. I still have no baby and Yacob blames me. It doesn't matter what I do!" She fled from the room sobbing.

Eve sat down at the table and buried her face in her hands. Then she sat up. "What did I do wrong, Hannah? All I suggested was that they act in a loving way to their husbands. What's so bad about that?"

"You touched painful places in their hearts, those places better left alone. With all your cleverness, *tsotskele*, you're young and you've got a lot to learn."

Eve nodded. She didn't doubt that Hannah was right. "And what about you, Hannah? Were you offended by what I said too? Are you angry?"

Hannah looked around at all the various stages of doing the laundry that had been abandoned. "Only at all this—" she laughed. "As for the other, I figure I'm not so old that I can't learn a few new tricks from a smart young pup."

Eve stood up, threw her arms around Hannah. "I do love you!" And she turned to leave the room.

"Where are you going?"

"To make up. To tell everyone I'm an impossibly arrogant wretch. To talk to them . . ."

"Good. That's good. Go talk. But one thing. Talk, don't lecture." Eve nodded. "When you're through talking be sure to come back in here. Whether the men should go on a work strike or not, I'm not sure. About *how* exactly they should be convinced I'm not sure either. But one thing I'm sure of is that I'm not going to finish doing all this laundry by myself."

Eve found Dora in her room still crying, so she murmured words of comfort, feeling especially guilty that she had brought such anguish on poor, sweet Dora. And she felt guilty too that as she sat on the bed mouthing trite words of consolation, she herself was proudly, smugly pregnant.

"I've tried everything—spells, potions. One tasted so awful, Eve, you wouldn't believe. It was made from the insides of a fish I think." Dora lowered her voice to a whisper out of some assumed sense of shame. "Chaim *himself* has dragged me to every Wonder Rabbi within fifty miles. And you can see the results—my belly remains as flat each time. Now Chaim and Yacob want me to go to this Wonder Rabbi in Vilno. He's supposed to perform miracles where all the others have failed. But I'm terrified to go. These rabbis scare me to death with their beards down to their shoetops and with their fierce eyes. And even so, they don't help. What do you think, Eve? Should I go? Hannah says it can't hurt—"

Eve considered. Vilno was the largest city in all Lithuania and one of the oldest. It had always been a seat of learning, a sophisticated city. Whatever existed that could possibly help Dora would most certainly be there. Wonder Rabbi, or whatever else it took. She had an idea.

"Yes, Dora, I think you should go. You have nothing to lose . . ." *And please, kind fate, just possibly, something to gain.*

"If only you could go with me, Eve, I wouldn't be so afraid."

"Oh, I intend to go with you!"

"You do?" Dora's voice rose in pace with her spirits. Then it plunged. "But will they let you? Chaim will most likely expect Yacob to go with me even though Yacob doesn't like going to the rabbis any more than I do."

"Good. In that case I'll go in his place."

"But we have to go on the train and we'll have to stay overnight. I'm afraid that Chaim won't be willing to pay for you . . ."

"If he won't, I'll pay for myself. I still have three rubles of my own."

"Oh Eve!" Dora hugged her. "It won't be so bad if you go with me. I've never been on a train before. Have you?"

"No. But Dora, please, you mustn't get your hopes up too high. Even the greatest of . . . Wonder Rabbis . . . can fail."

"No! Not this time! Not if you go with me! I just have a feeling! This time the miracle is going to happen!"

Her idea a miracle? *Please, God!* But she didn't know whether it was feasible. Maybe she was just being arrogant again, a know-it-all. Well, it *was* worth a try.

"When will we go?" Now Dora was in a frenzy of impatience.

"Mmm . . . maybe the week after next. I need a little time to—" she broke off her words.

"To what?"

"Oh, just to see if I can find out a few things about Vilno. You know, so we'll be able to find our way around easily. There's nothing like being prepared."

"Of course," Dora beamed. "There's nothing like being prepared."

"May I come in, Ruth?"

"So come." She was sitting on the bed, holding Gershon in her lap. "I was just sitting here doing nothing. I never just sit doing nothing. I was just seeing what it was like."

Eve smiled at her. "So? What is it like?"

"Nice. Quiet. It feels a little funny but it's nice."

"Here. Let me hold Gershon for you so you can sit by yourself."

"He can sit on the floor. I guess if I let him sit on the floor more he'll start to pull himself up and try to walk. The other boys started by his age already. Do you think I'm holding him back?"

"Well, you could do both. Hold him sometimes and sometimes put him down to sit or crawl."

"Yes. That sounds reasonable."

Ruth put the baby down and he started to crawl away from the bed. "I guess he's ready for a lot of things."

"Ruth, may I apologize? I spoke without thinking. I know I was wrong to speak about such a personal matter. Will you forgive me?"

"Yes, you were wrong. But you weren't totally wrong. That you said it was wrong, but *what* you said wasn't. I guess I've realized . . . known . . . for a few weeks already that it's time to stop nursing . . ." She sighed deeply. "It's easy for you to talk but it isn't easy for me to do. What do you know? You're young and you're beautiful and you haven't even had your first yet. But you'll see. When you're in the same boat as I am you won't be so anxious either to have your husband put it in and start the babies all over again. One second is all it takes! After that it's another one starting all over again. Some die the minute they come out and break your heart. Some live and break your back. You're so smart. You tell me. Do you know how a man and woman can go to bed and not end up each time with a bundle that's too much of a good thing?"

Eve sighed. "If I knew I would tell you. It seems there should be a way—"

"You see. It's easy to give advice to others. But when one really wants to know something, there's no answer." Her voice dropped. "It's not fair."

No, it wasn't, Eve thought. Conception itself didn't seem fair. There was Dora who so desperately wanted a baby and couldn't get pregnant, and here was Ruth who already had as many babies as she seemed emotionally able to cope with and who became impregnated as she herself said, the second she had intercourse. How many times had she heard the stories that circulated in all the towns and villages about those unfortunate unwed maidens who had to slip but once, *once*, to end up shamed and burdened for life? Conception seemed more than unfair. It seemed malicious, spiteful.

But there *was* one thing to do that seemed obvious to her and it should have been obvious to Ruth who, while uneducated, was no fool. Still, Eve hesitated to point it out since she had already made Ruth both angry and sad with her interfering tongue. On the other hand, if there was a *bare* possibility that she could help, wasn't it her duty as a human being to try and do that? She took a deep breath. In for a kopeck, in for a ruble.

"There is one thing I can think of, Ruth—"

"Yes?"

"You won't get angry with me again?"

"Speak."

"When a man and woman make love there is that point before—" Eve paused, trying to phrase what she had to say as delicately as possible. "Before the man . . . lets go . . . of his semen, he can . . . withdraw from the woman . . ."

Ruth stared. "You mean pull out?"

Eve nodded, unable to tell if Ruth was shocked, angry or what? But why should she be? Hadn't Miriam said that Hershel, frustrated at not being able to make love with Ruth since she was nursing, had gone into the woods to spill his semen just as Onan in the Bible had? Was what she proposed worse than that or worse at all?

Finally, Ruth said, "Isn't that supposed to be wrong?"

"Wrong? It's wrong to have more children than you want or than you can take care of. And it's wrong for a man and wife not to make love at all. They tell us making love is only to have children, but it's hard to believe that there

91

isn't more to it than that. I think that it was a gift given to men and women to help them better stand all the painful moments of life. A little joy to balance out . . .''

Well, she had done it again. She had started out talking and ended up lecturing. But Ruth didn't seem angry. Rather she was thoughtful. Gershon, who had crawled under the bed and was stuck, screamed out. Ruth got down on her hands and knees and retrieved him, sitting down on the bed again, automatically giving the child her breast. "I think it sounds right. I wonder if Hershel would go along—"

"You'll have to explain it to him. The pros and the cons."

"If only *you*, with your big mouth, could do that for me."

"I think this is one time I'll keep my mouth out of it," Eve laughed. "But keep in mind that—"

"Yes?"

"There are two ways of persuading a man to do something. If one way doesn't work, you try the other— And since you've tried one way, well—"

"Yes."

Miriam was back in the kitchen pressing a shirt with three black irons which she alternately used and then heated on the stove. Hannah stood by folding clothes at the table.

"Miriam, I want to apologize for—" She had to stop; she didn't know exactly what she was apologizing for. She knew she had offended Ruth and upset Dora but in what way had she insulted Miriam? She glanced at Hannah for some possible guidance but Hannah left the room, leaving her piles of folded articles where they were.

Miriam slammed an iron down hard on the shirt. "You don't have to say anything. You weren't in the wrong. If you must know, I'm jealous of you."

"Jealous?"

"You were talking about how we should carry on with our husbands to convince them to do what we wanted. That we should show passion, should offer, be more— What was the word you used? Alluring. And I thought to myself—*ahh, easy for her to say.* But me? How was I going to be as beautiful as Queen Esther? *You* can be young and beautiful and alluring, but me? I'm too old and too fat. So I got mad at you. That's all there is to it. I was jealous of your youth and your beauty, even of your hair. So don't tell me you're sorry. I'm the one who's sorry." She slammed the iron around so viciously she drove it into the hand that was stretching out the fabric. "*Oy!*" she screamed. "Now I burnt myself!" And she stuck two fingers into her mouth.

Eve ran to the door, flung it open, grabbed a handful of snow, rushed back with it to Miriam. "Here. Let me—" She held Miriam's finger against the snow. "Better?"

"Yes. I guess so. You see? I'm so clumsy I can't even iron without burning myself."

92

"Oh, Miriam, don't. Don't do this to yourself. Don't you know you're beautiful?"

"Please. I know you mean well but don't insult me. I might not be as smart as you but I know a lie when I hear one."

"But there are many ways of being beautiful. Just because one person isn't as young as another doesn't mean—"

"It means . . . it means . . . And besides," she laughed a little, "I wasn't beautiful when I was a young girl so why would I start being beautiful now? Do you think a person who isn't beautiful to start with grows into it like an old shoe?"

"Oh, Miriam, you're being foolish. I've read many novels by many great writers. They write often of older women who are beautiful, inside and out."

"Books! They aren't life!"

"But they're about life. If the things in books weren't at least partially true, how would the writer know to write about them in the first place?"

Miriam waved away her words. "Your books aren't written about me. I'm fat. Even you can't deny that."

"You're *zoftig*, pleasingly plump."

"So, even so, how does a *zoftig* lady not look like a fool jumping around a bed alluringly?" Miriam laughed forlornly.

"Famous artists *chose* to paint very round ladies because that was their ideal of beauty."

Miriam dismissed this with a pooh-poohing sound.

"It's true," Eve insisted. "What you are is voluptuous, round and with a feminine softness that men find very attractive. And you have full breasts. You *know* men love round, soft women with large breasts. *Everyone* knows that."

"You're just being nice. That's your problem. That's why you make other women jealous. It's not enough that you're beautiful *and* alluring," Miriam laughed again, "but you also have that gorgeous hair and you're smart, and then you're nice." She shook her head. "It's too much. I have to hate you."

"I don't believe you. You don't hate me."

"So, all right, I don't hate you. But you're still beautifully slim and I'm not. That remains."

"I bet Shlomo thinks you're beautiful," Eve smiled slyly. "I just bet he loves those wonderful big breasts."

Miriam's lips curved into a bit of a smile in modest acknowledgment.

"There! I knew it! And look at your skin. Flawless! Like summer cream. And your disposition. Your disposition shines through. It's worth a million rubles."

"I'd rather be slim like you."

Eve had an idea. "Just wait right here and don't move. I'll be back in a minute."

"Where would I go?"

"Here—" Eve brought back her treasured book of paintings. "There's a painting here I want you to see."

She thumbed through the pages carefully since the book was old and its pages fragile. She found the picture she was searching for—a reclining nude by Rubens. The woman in the painting was a radiant splendor of more than ample, roseate roundness, whose sweet pink face even resembled Miriam's to a degree. "See! This is what this famous artist considered the height of female beauty."

Miriam gaped. "She's naked!"

"Yes. Artists consider the female form a work of beauty. In the time of the Greeks—"

But Miriam wasn't listening. Eyes shining, she asked, "And you're saying I resemble *her*? This work of beauty?"

"Yes."

"I want to show the others." She ran with the book to Hannah, to Dora and to Ruth. Even Ruth did not deny a certain resemblance. The women grew so entranced with the book, turning its pages for other paintings that might bear a resemblance to one of them, they almost forgot about preparing dinner. Miriam, with a show of embarrassment, asked if she might keep the book overnight. Blushing as pink as the lady in the Rubens painting, she said that she'd like to show the picture to Shlomo.

Eve thought that even if they hadn't made any progress that day as far as the work strike was concerned, it still had been a wonderful day, all things considered.

Even as the weather turned a bit warmer, David couldn't report to Eve that his brothers were any more receptive to his pleadings and arguments. "They curse, they grumble. They're simple men. All they care about is eating their fill and drinking more. And besides everyone is getting edgy hanging around day after day instead of working. The truth of it is they're more inclined to fight with each other than with Father. We saw Father at the Inn today. When Hershel and Shlomo got into a fight over nothing at all and Hershel threw Shlomo out the door, Father laughed . . ."

"Did any of you speak to him?"

"At first only Yacob did. Something about Dora going to Vilno to see the Wonder Rabbi there. Then Father bought Yacob a drink and before I knew it, they were all drinking—Abraham, Hershel, Shlomo." Then David smiled, knowing the question Eve wanted to ask but wouldn't. "No, *I* didn't have a drink."

"My poor David."

It seemed more and more obvious that Chaim was going to win and she and David were going to lose. She should have realized that any plan of hers was no match for the mindless Markoff appetites. David was right when he called them simple. Simpleminded. Obviously their brains didn't function until their stomachs were bulging and their brains besotted with liquor, the barbarians!

"If only we could figure out how to get some money—enough to feed everybody and fill my brothers' bellies with whiskey," David said as if reading her mind. "Then they might listen to some sense. I'd do anything to get a few kopecks, but everything is at a standstill here and everywhere else. No one is working and all the butchers are idle." He banged his fist against the wall with frustration.

Eve thought about her three rubles. How far would they go?

"How much do you think it costs to go to Vilno?"

"*Vilno?* Why are we talking about Vilno?" Then he remembered that Yacob had talked to his father about Dora going to Vilno. "Do you have something to do with Dora going to see the Miracle Rabbi in Vilno?"

"I promised her I'd go with her."

"You? I wouldn't have thought you believed in Wonder Rabbis."

"I don't."

"So why are you going? Just to give her comfort? Or are you up to something? That's it, isn't it? You have something up your sleeve."

"Oh, David," she laughed. "You're beginning to know me too well. Now I know we're truly married."

"We had better be. Just to make that baby kosher." He placed a gentle hand on her belly.

"Oh yes." She took his hand and pressed it to her cheek. "So what do you think it costs to go to Vilno? Dora says Chaim wants her to go so he'll pay her expenses, as well as provide the tribute for the rabbi, but I'm sure he'll be too spiteful to pay my way."

"I don't know how much it costs. Half a ruble? We'll have to think about where to get it."

She got out her three rubles and showed them to him.

"Where did you get them?"

"I brought them with me from home. I was saving them. I'm not even sure for what. Maybe I wanted to give them to you as my dowry since you didn't receive one for taking me off my family's hands." They smiled at each other, remembering their wedding day. "I think I'll keep one for my trip with Dora and we'll spend another on some food for the house. If I shop carefully maybe it will buy enough food for a few days."

"And the third ruble?"

"That *is* your dowry. For you to treat your brothers to drinks at the tavern for as long as it lasts."

"Don't you think it's more important to spend that ruble on food too?"

"I've always believed it's as important to feed the spirit as the stomach. And since your father's standing treat I want you to do the same. It's a—" She waved her hand. "Call it a gesture. Let them all, including Chaim, wonder where the money came from."

David turned away.

"What is it, David? Are you angry with me?"

"Not with you. With myself. I'm twenty years old. I'm a husband and I'm going to be a father and this is the first time in my whole life I have a ruble in my pocket. This is the first time I'm going to treat anybody to anything. And *you're* giving me the ruble—you, to whom I haven't given the smallest thing. You, to whom I should give everything . . . the world."

"But, David, you have. You've given me everything that means anything. You've given me your love, for one thing. Haven't you?"

"Oh, Eve." He shook his head. "You always put things nicely but it doesn't change the truth. I've never given you anything real."

"Oh, yes you have, David. What do you call a baby? A baby is the realest thing I can think of."

And more. A baby is the promise of the future.

7.

Eve and Dora took the train to Vilno and then a droshky to a very handsome townhouse. When Eve rang the doorbell a liveried manservant answered the summons and admitted them into a long waiting room.

"Where are we?" Dora asked in a whisper as she looked around in awe. She had never seen a room like this before. The walls were paneled in a dark wood and decorated with gold carving, the tall narrow windows were shrouded in deep red velvet draperies and there was a row of chairs with high balloon backs, covered in brocaded fabric. Tentatively Dora touched a wall with her fingertips, then the draperies. She bent down to touch the multicolored patterned rug. "None of the other rabbis I've gone to see lived in a house like this—"

"We're not at the rabbi's. Take off your coat," Eve told her as she removed the shawl from Dora's head herself.

Underneath her heavy coat Dora wore the new plum taffeta dress which Eve had completed only a couple of days before. Eve was eager for them to make a good impression. She didn't want the doctor to think they were country yokels without the means to pay for a consultation with a professor of renown. She herself wore one of her grandest dresses; it was bottle green velvet. She had a new hat to go with it, one with a long white plume. She had made the hat at the last moment especially for this visit, using bits and remnants from her treasured store of trimmings.

Dora held her coat out, not knowing what to do with it. It seemed much too shabby to put down on one of the grand chairs. "Where shall I put it?" she whispered. "And if we're not at the Rabbi's, *where* are we?"

Eve spotted a coat rack in a corner where she hung both Dora's coat and her own. She realized she had made a mistake in not telling Dora earlier that they would visit a doctor—a gentile one at that—before seeing the Wonder Rabbi. Now Dora was bound to panic; she was already overwhelmed by her surroundings but only slightly more so than Eve herself. Eve had had no idea that Dr. Golov was not only a professor, but obviously one of the gentry to boot. She wondered if gentile doctors were in any way deterred by virtue of their profession from being as anti-Semitic as any member of the aristocracy might be. . . .

What had she gotten Dora into? Or herself, for that matter? But she had had no choice, really. When she had asked the doctor in Kovno for the name of a

97

professor in Vilno who specialized in "women's problems," he had given her only the name of Ivan Golov. "He is known for it," Dr. Gottesfeld had told her. When she asked him if Dr. Golov would be averse to treating a Jewish woman, the kindly doctor had only half-smiled and shrugged his shoulders helplessly. Obviously he wasn't sure.

"Dora," Eve began, sitting down next to her, wanting to inform her of what they were doing here before the servant returned, "we're at a professor's . . . a doctor . . . a famous doctor . . ."

Dora's hand flew to her mouth. "But I've never been to a doctor before!"

"I know. But you mustn't be afraid. A doctor's duty is to help people."

"But what will he do to me?"

In her own growing anxiety, Eve blurted, "What do you think he'll do—kill you?" She was instantly contrite. "Oh, Dora, he'll try to help you. First he'll examine you and then he'll be able to tell us what he can do for you."

Dora began to cry.

"Oh, Dora, don't! Please!" Eve was terrified that the servant would come back and see Dora crying. What would he think? She wondered if gentile women ever cried in this waiting hall, or if they had some kind of shield that protected them from this particular kind of fear.

"Dora, if you don't stop this minute I'll start crying myself!"

The idea of Eve joining her in her tears shocked Dora so, she stopped instantly and only sniffled. "You can't cry, Eve. If *you* cry, I'll die."

"All right. If *you* die, so will I!"

At that, Dora's lips curled up in a smile and she even laughed softly, dabbing at her eyes with a small handkerchief. "I guess I won't die then."

"That's a relief. I'm glad to hear it. Here, let me—" Eve took the handkerchief from Dora and wiped a tear stain away. "There, that's better." She straightened Dora's curled blond wig. "You look lovely."

For a moment she considered pulling the wig from Dora's head, replacing it with her own hat. She'd tuck the short ends of Dora's real hair under it. Then, without the identifying wig and with Dora's bright blue eyes, Slavic cheekbones, and short, broad nose, who'd be able to tell her from any Russian woman? It would make things go easier and there was nothing wrong with making things easier . . . But then she was flooded with shame; she couldn't possibly commit such a prideless act.

"Eve, what will I say to him?"

"Not much. He doesn't understand Yiddish."

The truth dawned on Dora. "You mean we've come to a goyish doctor? A gentile doctor that lives in a house like this? Oh my God!" Her astonishment couldn't have been greater if Eve, her own darling Eve, had turned her over to the Cossacks.

Eve put her hand on hers. "If I tell you everything's going to be all right, will you believe me?"

Dora thought for a moment. "Yes. I'll always believe you."

"Good. I tell you everything's going to be fine."

Dora folded her hands in her lap and sat up straighter while Eve wished that she herself had more faith in her own words. "I know this isn't easy for you, Dora. It isn't easy for me either. But if Dr. Golov can help you— If you end up getting pregnant, well then, it will be worth everything."

"You will do most of the talking, won't you? Since I don't speak or understand Russian that well." Then she smiled. "Won't the doctor be surprised to hear how well *you* speak Russian?"

Eve looked at her in surprise. Dora had never heard her speak more than a few words of Russian at any one time. "How do you know how well I speak Russian?"

"Oh, I'm sure you do. I mean I don't know for sure but I'm sure you do."

A gray-haired woman with an equally gray skin stretched tautly across the bones of her face, wearing a white uniform, came back with the manservant. She looked first at Eve, and then at Dora, turned to the servant and whispered furiously while she pointed at her own head. It was obvious to Eve that the nurse was angry with the servant for allowing a bewigged Jewess to enter the house. He responded by mimicking a shawl-draped head.

Eve's heart sank and she could feel her face burning. Her impulse was to pull Dora out of the chair and run for their lives. But she couldn't do that either. It would be more humiliating than their present position. All she could do now was wait with Dora for the inevitable confrontation and deal with it, holding on to as much dignity as she could muster. *Oh, damn them to hell!*

She stiffened her spine and sat, waited silently for the nurse to approach them. Her mouth a straight, unyielding line in her face, the woman informed them that the Professor wouldn't be able to see them. He was much too busy.

"We'll wait," Eve answered resolutely, "until he's no longer busy."

"That might be a very long time."

"We'll wait."

Other patients came and went and Eve and Dora sat for what seemed like many hours. When the waiting room was empty once again the nurse returned and said, "Professor is still occupied. We're closing the waiting room for the day." She went and stood by the door, indicating that she was only waiting to lock it up after Eve and Dora left.

"What time do you open in the morning? Six o'clock? Seven? Well, no matter. We'll be back at six in any case, wig and all." Eve smiled pleasantly. "We'll wait on the doorstep and we'll tell whoever comes to see the doctor that the door is still locked and that they'll have to wait too . . . *behind us!* We'll wait all day if necessary."

The woman bit her lip, considered, mumbled she'd be right back and left the room. After several minutes she came back and ordered them to follow. Eve took Dora's hand, and they followed the woman through a series of rooms, all handsomely furnished, to end up in one that was lined with books and had a great polished desk. Behind it sat a tall, dark man of indeterminate age. He had a black pencil-thin moustache, a high forehead and a piercing gaze with which he quickly dismissed Dora and centered on Eve. His eyes widened for a moment or two and then he spoke without heat in a voice without inflection. "My nurse tells me you wouldn't go away. It's necessary that you understand that owing to reasons I won't go into, none of which is maliciously intended, I assure you, I'm not in the practice of treating Jews."

"I never *thought* you were in the practice of treating Jews, Doctor. What I did assume was that you were in the practice of medicine."

His face darkened, his eyes narrowed and his fingers played with a pen. "You speak Russian fluently, Madam. It is Madam?"

"*Oui, Monsieur. C'est Madame,*" she answered haughtily, feeling an overwhelming need to show off for this snob, to put him and his gentile condescension in place.

His expression reflected a piqued interest, which was what she intended by answering him in French. His eyes took in her meticulously arranged red-gold hair, her elaborately designed dress.

"I take it then that *you're* not Jewish? And—" he indicated Dora only with a movement of his head, "this young woman is your servant?"

Deliberately, Eve smiled. Deliberately, she dimpled. "No, Doctor. If I weren't Jewish, I'd hardly be in a position to have a Jewish servant. Jewish servants almost never enter the employ of a gentile. They'd consider that beneath them."

This time anger flashed in Dr. Golov's eyes. He took her answer to be insolent as indeed Eve intended it to be. But then she was sorry. *What's wrong with me? I'm only antagonizing him. And I'm here to get help for Dora, not to show him how quick I am with an answer.*

"I'm sorry if I offended you, Dr. Golov. I didn't come here to spar with you. I'm Eve Markoff and this is my sister-in-law, Dora Markoff. We're both Jewesses although I don't wear a wig. I brought my sister-in-law to see you because I was told you're a specialist in women's problems and Dora has been unable to conceive. Since, besides being Jewish, she's a human being in need of help, I thought you, as a physician, would be willing to try to help."

His very dark eyes moved about rapidly as he studied her, his expression revealing that in spite of himself, he was enjoying the conversation. He smiled a little. "Don't you Jews usually go to one of your special rabbis for *this sort of thing*?"

Eve had to control herself not to scream. She had to be polite for Dora's sake no matter how severely he tried her patience. "I repeat, Dr. Golov: I came here because you're a physician and I assumed physicians tried to heal. Therefore I'm surprised to hear you refer to your own medical specialty as 'this sort of thing.' Then she couldn't help herself. She said, "One would think you had never even heard of the physicians' Hippocratic oath . . ."

Dr. Golov laughed aloud. "Hippocratic oath, is it? You *are* incredible, Madam Markoff. I can see that you're a Jewess, after all. You most definitely are, as they say all Jews are: pushy, arrogant, and decidedly clever. If you've set out to intrigue me I must confess you've succeeded. So, tell me, Eve Markoff, what do you know about the Hippocratic oath?''

She was tempted to tell him but to what avail? To what end? Just to prove to him that she was indeed clever? He had already mocked her and insulted both her and Dora. To continue this verbal duel would only lead to further mortification. She glanced at Dora who seemed bewildered by the rapid-fire exchange of Russian which she wasn't able to follow. Still, Dora looked at her with complete trust. *And I've failed her!* The only thing she could possibly do for both herself and Dora now was to cling to whatever remnants of dignity that remained.

"Whatever I know about the Hippocratic oath, Doctor, is sufficient for me to understand that if you have indeed taken it, you betray it. We'll go now and leave you in peace to pursue your very peculiar kind of medicine—'this sort of thing,' as you yourself call it.'' She rose from her chair.

The doctor jumped to his feet. "One minute, Eve Markoff. I'll make a bargain with you. If you'll tell me what you know about the Hippocratic oath, I'll examine your sister-in-law and if I find there's something, anything I can do, I'll do it.''

"But why, Professor? Since you don't usually treat Jewesses, what can it possibly matter to you what I know about the oath? What is this? Some kind of gentile game?''

"As I said, I'm intrigued. Well, do you accept the challenge?'' His eyes sparkled.

Her first instinct was to take Dora and sweep out of the office but a second instinct told her he was sincere, that now he was prepared to try to help. And there Dora sat, still gazing at her with those trusting eyes. She couldn't let false pride stand in the way now. "Very well. But I have a condition of my own.''

"Yes?''

"If, after examining Dora, you find that you can't help her, you're willing to say that to be a gentile gentleman is not necessarily better than being a Jew—''

He threw back his head and laughed. "Agreed. And what will *you* be willing to say if I *do* help your sister-in-law?''

"On the day the baby's born I'll make a toast. I'll drink to Ivan Golov— long life! Even if he isn't a Jew.''

The doctor laughed again. "And will you ask the mother to name the baby after me?''

"It will be a pleasure, Dr. Golov. But you do realize that a Jewish child can only be named for the soul of one who's passed on to the other world?''

"Once again, touché, Madam Markoff. Will you begin then? The oath—''

Eve put her hand on Dora's shoulder, certain now that whatever there was to be done would be, even if she herself had to perform like a trained monkey to assure that it was.

"The Hippocratic oath is part of the *Hippocratic Collection,* a body of medical works that was circulated by what was known as the Alexandrian medical school, sometime around three hundred years before . . . well, B.C., shall we say? The oath prevails to this day and Hippocrates himself is still venerated, both as a physician and as a man of high character, which is something, unfortunately, that cannot be said about *all* physicians,'' she lowered her lashes, making a point.

Dr. Golov nodded, smiling, acknowledging that he hadn't missed her point, and Eve continued with assurance: "It's said that Hippocrates was the first to separate medicine from philosophy. The most famous line of the *Hippocratic Collection* is, 'Art is long and life is short.' What's most notable about the *Collection* is its aphoristic style, which means that its conclusions are set forth in short, easily remembered sentences.

"I'll pass over the beginning of the oath since it's not relevant to our situation. The second part goes, 'The regimen I adopt shall be for the benefit of my patients according to my ability and judgment, and not for their hurt or for any wrong—' You will note, Dr. Golov, there's not a word differentiating between Jew and gentile . . .

" 'I will give no deadly drug to any, though it be asked of me, nor will I counsel such, and especially I will not aid a woman to procure abortion . . .' " She interrupted herself to smile. "Isn't it wonderful for you, Dr. Golov, that you're asked to do exactly the opposite of that in Dora's case?"

When the doctor's face didn't move, his eyelids didn't even flutter, she continued: " 'Whatsoever house I enter, there will I go for the benefit of the sick—' " She smiled again. "Now, Doctor, don't you think *that* could most certainly be interpreted as 'for the benefit of the sick, *either Jew or gentile?*' "

Without waiting for an answer, she went on: " 'Refraining from all wrong-doing or corruption, and especially from any act of seduction, of male or female, of bond or free. Whatsoever things I see or hear concerning the life of men, in my attendance on the sick or even apart therefrom, which ought not to be noised abroad, I will keep silence thereon, counting such things to be as sacred secrets.'

"As for myself, Doctor, *I'll* keep it a sacred secret if you help Dora so that you won't feel compromised in aiding a Jewess . . . Now, shall I go on? Shall I recite the *Aphorisms?* Or would you rather hear the treatise *On Wounds of the Head?* Yes . . . ? What do you say?"

He spoke softly, "I say, 'Bravo! Bravo! Madam Markoff.' A virtuoso performance."

Eve looked quickly to see if he were mocking her but she saw only sincere, shining admiration.

"A dazzling performance! You dazzle the mind as well as the eye."

"Please, Dr. Golov, don't overestimate my capabilities. It's no more than a Jewish trick for which, as you know, we're famous. It's only that I merely have to read something and it is committed to memory. A stunt, a Jewish stunt. That's all."

"I see. And now *I'll* do my gentile stunt."

102

He went to the door, called to his nurse. "Prepare Madam Dora Markoff for the examining room." He turned back to Eve. "I'll do whatever is possible. When a woman doesn't conceive it can be any number of reasons, not all correctable. It may even be the husband— Then, of course, there's nothing I can do—"

"I understand. I know you'll do whatever you can."

The husband? What male would ever accept that conclusion?

She told Dora that she was to go with the doctor's assistant. Dora grabbed for her hand. "Oh, Eve, you have to stay with me. Please! I'm afraid to be alone with them."

"Of course I'll stay with you. But you mustn't be afraid. Dr. Golov is going to do his best for you. I'm sure of it," she whispered in Yiddish.

Switching back to Russian she said, "I told Dora I'd stay with her the whole time. You understand? She's afraid of you." She smiled faintly. "It isn't only the gentile who fears his blood will be stolen. There are those of us who have reason to put that particular shoe on the other foot—"

In acknowledgment of this pointed jibe, Dr. Golov raised an eyebrow and bowed from the waist.

Eve's suspicion, born out of hope, that Dora's problem might be a simple medical one, proved true. Discovering a thin tissue of skin partially obscuring the cervix, the narrow outer end of the uterus, Dr. Golov was able to correct the problem easily in his own surgery. Dora remained overnight and Eve stayed there with her. They'd be able to go home the following day.

"Dora, I want you to listen to me carefully. At first I thought we'd go to the Wonder Rabbi *after* we had seen Dr. Golov," Eve explained as they were ready to leave. "You see I thought we'd only have to give Dr. Golov a small fee from the money for the Rabbi, and we'd still have enough left over. But now that the Doctor's performed surgery we won't have enough money for the Rabbi. And we really don't need him since Dr. Golov says there's no longer any reason why you won't be able to conceive."

Dora threw her arms around Eve. "I have you to thank for . . . for this miracle!"

"No, not me. Dr. Golov!"

Dora shook her head. "I know I'm not clever, Eve. But I do know certain things. If it wasn't for you, Dr. Golov would never have seen me, would never have made me, well, *better*."

"That's all that counts."

"But, Eve, what will I say when they ask me about the Rabbi?"

"You'll say that you've been truly blessed. And that's all you'll say. And it won't be a lie."

Dora's face lit up. She was delighted to share a secret with her darling Eve.

"Now give me the money Chaim gave you for the Rabbi."

Dora handed over the little leather bag and Eve counted out the money. Forty-one rubles in all, including the ruble for their accommodations at an inn.

It seemed that Chaim was being tightfisted only with his own family. When it came to giving money to the rabbis, he was positively princely. She asked the nurse what the doctor's fee was and the woman, obviously disapproving, said, "Professor says there's to be no charge."

"That's very kind of him but what would be his usual fee?"

The woman calculated. "A consultation? A procedure? Twenty rubles . . ."

Eve laid down the twenty rubles. "Tell the professor I insisted." It was not without irony, she thought, that the Rabbi's miracles came higher than the doctor's skills.

Now there were twenty-one rubles left. Actually they could still go to the Wonder Rabbi with the remaining money. The rabbi would accept whatever they gave him. Most probably even twenty rubles was more than he usually received. But what would be the point? Just to keep herself and Dora honest? Why give away twenty rubles for something that was already *fait accompli*? With Dr. Golov's surgery, all Dora needed now was a bit of luck.

Eve put the money away in her purse, unable to suppress a smile. Chaim's rubles were going to help them hold out against Chaim.

"Now don't forget," Ivan Golov told Dora. "If it's a boy you're going to name him after me."

Dora smiled politely while Eve laughed. "Ivan Golovitch Markoff? Why not if *you're* willing to take the chance? Remember I did explain to you that a Jewish baby is named after someone whose spirit has gone to heaven but whose body lies in the ground."

"I'll chance it," the doctor's eyes sparkled. "Since I know you'll put in a good word for me with your God. Even He must tremble before you . . ."

"Dr. Golov," Eve lowered her lashes modestly, "I think you overestimate my powers."

"I think not," Ivan Golov said, suddenly sober. He bent his head, taking her hand and pressing his lips to it. "There's only one thing about you that I regret, Eva Markova," he said, Russifying her name.

She looked at him quizzically. "Yes? Is it that I'm Jewish?"

"No. Only that you're married."

Even though the manservant was scandalized, the maid startled and the nurse highly disapproving, Ivan Golov personally came out into the street to help them into the droshky that would take them to the railway station.

"Really, I will never forget your kindness," Eve told him.

"And I, I fear, will never forget you."

"Fear?"

"Yes. Fear. It can only be painful to remember someone you have known for a pitifully few short hours for the rest of your life. . . ."

During the train trip back Eve rehearsed Dora so she'd be prepared for questions about the Wonder Rabbi. She was to be generally evasive. But this proved unnecessary. When they arrived back in Slobodka late in the afternoon, they found a raging controversy going on that commanded everyone's attention, so much so that no one asked them anything.

"What is going on?" Eve asked David.

"If the whole thing wasn't so serious, it would be funny. Father was at the Inn yesterday morning when Feifke the fiddler came in. Since Feifke's a traveling musician he gets around. He frequently hears things no one else does and he often gives father tips about a farmer who has a few cows or a gaggle of geese for sale and father gives him a finder's fee. Yesterday, Feifke told father about a single cow for sale. The farmer who had the cow lived some distance away and ordinarily father wouldn't go so far for one cow but under the circumstances—that there's been no meat in town for so long a time—it seems he decided to go by himself and get the cow and present it to the townspeople as a gift, which for father, is incredible in itself."

"Mmm . . . not so incredible," Eve murmured, thinking of the forty rubles Chaim had apportioned for the Wonder Rabbi. But she would tell David about that later. "Obviously your father thinks charity is going to buy him a place in heaven since nothing else will. Besides, this would make him a hero to the townspeople. A hero and a philanthropist! And you know how your father loves applause . . . But go on, I'm dying to hear what happened."

"Well, without a word to anyone father started out immediately to get the cow even though it was already late in the day for such a trip—about eleven o'clock in the morning. Then he didn't come back until six *this* morning after traveling all night. As soon as he was back in town he went straight to Kushner the butcher. They called in the ritual slaughterer and the minute the cow was finished off and skinned, Kushner started cutting.

"By this time word had already spread that the meat was going to be distributed to every Jew around—a present from Chaim Markoff. Needless to say a huge crowd gathered at Kushner's with everyone standing around talking, joking, singing father's praises. Suddenly, Kushner screams, "There's a needle in the stomach. The cow's *tref!* She's not kosher and we'll have to give her to the gentiles!"

"Really?"

"Yes. You can imagine! The crowd went crazy! Not to mention father who looked as if he wanted to kill and skin Kushner himself. But right away there were those who said Kushner was wrong, that the needle didn't make the meat unclean. Those were the ones who cared more about getting something to eat than about the dietary laws!"

Eve laughed. "You mean they were more interested in what would be going into their own stomachs than what came out of the cow's."

"Exactly. But the more pious ones, like Pincus Rubinstein for one, agreed with Kushner. Well, father had made up his mind, he was going to give that meat to the townspeople even if it killed them!"

"He must have been furious. I daresay he hadn't traveled day and night to give away meat to the peasants—"

"Right! Then Yonkel Lieberman said maybe it would be a good thing to give the meat to the gentiles, that they'd be grateful and would spare us a pogrom in the future."

"So what did your father say to that?"

"He almost spat in Yonkel's face. And he sent for Rabbi Maloffsky. I think he meant to scare the Rabbi into saying what he wanted, but the trouble was he never got a chance to speak to Rabbi Maloffsky alone. And you know the Rabbi . . ."

"Yes. He never says a definite yes or a definite no to anything."

"Right. And he didn't this time either. He said he couldn't remember such a thing happening before and maybe the answer was yes and maybe the answer was no."

Eve giggled. She knew it was a serious business but it *was* funny. "Then what?"

"Then someone suggested they send for a rabbi from Kovno and right away the two factions couldn't agree on which rabbi it should be so they ended up sending for—"

"Two rabbis," Eve burst out.

David laughed. "You know this story better than I do. Yes, they sent for two rabbis, with each faction getting the rabbi of its choice. Now, do *you* want to tell *me* what happened next?"

"Certainly I do. Since there were two rabbis, one said the cow *was* kosher, and the other said it wasn't—"

"You're impossible!" He ruffled her hair. "How did you guess?"

"Simple. Two rabbis, two opinions. Then what happened?"

"Nothing much. The two rabbis went back to Kovno just as you arrived home. Now things are at a standstill. When I left Kushner's they were talking about sending someone to Vilno to discuss it with the rabbis there . . ."

"One minute . . ." Eve closed her eyes tightly. "I think I remember something— Was that needle simply lying there in the cow's stomach? Or was it sticking into it? Piercing it?"

"I haven't the slightest idea. Why?"

"Well, if the needle was standing on end with the point actually sticking into the stomach, then the cow isn't kosher. But if the needle was just lying there, doing nothing, so to speak, then the cow's flesh can be eaten."

David smiled at her ruefully. "It won't work, Eve. I'm sorry. If the rabbis can't give a positive opinion what makes you think that bunch is going to take *your* word on it? *I* do, but they're not going to—"

She was indignant. "Really, David! Do you think I'm that arrogant to think they would take *my* word on this? But they *will* take the word of the great Reb Yisroel, the Vilno Gaon, who lived over a hundred years ago. They had the same situation then and that was *his* decision."

David couldn't suppress a smile. "Oh, and has the great Vilno Gaon been in touch with you? I know you have many talents, Eve, but I didn't know that you were able to converse with the dead.''

She rolled her eyes heavenward at his joke. ''Really, David! It's all written down in a volume of commentaries by the Talmudist Jacob Shmuel ben Abraham Binyomin—''

''Believe me, Eve, I don't doubt you— But if *you* know about this decision how come the rabbis don't?''

Eve laughed. ''I guess we don't read the same books. Or perhaps they've read it but have forgotten—''

David made a mock bow. ''In that case, my darling Eve, let's go down to the butcher's and find out what position the damned needle was in.''

''No, we can't do it that way. We have to have the book of commentaries ready to back us up. I mean, if even you were skeptical, didn't quite believe I knew what I was talking about—''

David started to object but she shook her head teasingly. ''Admit it, David Markoff! You were making fun of me. You were just a little doubtful—''

''Doubt you? Never! Well, just the tiniest bit. Do you have the book of commentaries?''

''No. It's at my father's. We'll have to go there first thing in the morning and get it. Unless you think we should start out now?''

''No, morning will do just fine. I have some other ideas about what we should do right now.''

They were back in Slobodka before noon. David wanted to go straight to the butcher's but Eve told him to take her home first. ''I want you to go to Kushner's by yourself. But don't say a thing until you read the decision *first*. And read it with a flourish. *Then* ask Kushner very dramatically—'Was the needle lying . . . or sticking in?' If you do it that way, I don't think there's any doubt about how Kushner will respond.''

''You mean if he hears the decision read first, he'll decide that the needle was definitely *not* sticking into the stomach . . .''

''I think that most probably with all the excitement, he doesn't even know for sure anymore. But under the circumstances, I think he'll make the right choice.''

''But why should I do it instead of you? It's you who—''

She put a finger to his lips. ''It will sound better coming from you. It's your place. Today you become a man of destiny . . .''

There was a celebration in town that night, festive with vodka and music and dancing. Everyone drank toasts to David Markoff who had saved the day, and that's how Eve wanted it. A man thought of as a hero will act accordingly.

Chaim drank along steadily but he didn't join in any of the toasts. Rather he fumed that it was he who had furnished the cow in the first place but it was David who was grabbing all the glory. He went around the room, grabbing this one by the arm and that one by the lapel, punching shoulders, reminding everyone he could collar just who had done what for the Jews of Slobodka. For the most part he was congratulated for having such a clever son. No one had ever guessed before that David was such a scholar. Imagine! Quoting the great Reb Yisroel! David had turned out to be a learned Jew, a person of worth and substance.

Chaim snickered at the absurdity of the thought. He burned with hate. Not for David, who was nothing but his new wife's fool. She was the one at the bottom of this, the one who was responsible for diminishing the credit *he* was entitled to.

Eve looked up from a conversation with Hannah to catch Chaim staring at her from across the room with such a look of malevolence it took her breath away.

Hannah, taking it all in, sighed heavily. "And what did you expect? His thanks?"

8.

While the incident with the cow and the needle was a personal triumph for David, it did nothing to advance the cause of obtaining wages from Chaim. Eve could see that, if anything, it had only made things worse as far as that matter was concerned. By stealing Chaim's thunder she and David had most likely only strengthened Chaim's resolve to see them thoroughly brought to heel. Eve didn't doubt for a moment that if it was at all possible, her father-in-law would have liked nothing better than to have her broken body splayed on the ground before him so he could grind his mud-spattered boot into her face.

It always seemed to be two steps forward and then one back, she reflected. Or maybe it was *one* step forward and then two back. One way or another, they weren't making any progress. When she questioned her sisters-in-law about how they were doing in their efforts to persuade their husbands not to go back to work for Chaim, she got very little back in the way of answers. Miriam only smiled, shrugged her shoulders as if to say: *Who knows?* And Dora had her mind on only one thing—conceiving. As for Hannah, she was only concerned with what there was put on the table to eat. She thought of nothing else.

Only Ruth, who *had* stopped nursing Gershon, had anything of consequence to say. "A little loving means they'll say 'yes' today but then tomorrow they're just as likely to say 'no.' " Eve realized that she was probably right.

The one ruble from her original three that had gone to buy provisions had hardly helped to alleviate the grumbling at the table. They weren't eating much more than potatoes and salted herring with black bread, most of the ruble having gone for the flour so that they could at least count on having the bread. There *had* been a tiny amount left over to buy a small quantity of tea, but not enough to buy the cracked sugar to sip the tea through. As for the ruble she had given David to treat his brothers at the tavern, it went in a single afternoon since the brothers shared both a lack of restraint and a huge capacity. The only visible result of that afternoon was the teasing the brothers gave David about where he had obtained the ruble.

At this point they had only one weapon left—the twenty rubles she had secreted away, the Wonder Rabbi's money. It had seemed such a fortune to her then but she saw it as woefully inadequate now. How long could twenty rubles last against the resources of Chaim, who most likely had a small fortune salted away and enough venom and spite to enable him to hold out for years against his sons' defection?

Eve could see that the biggest obstacle to her scheme was that the brothers were men without imagination, without vision. They knew that on the day they started working with Chaim again, rich and plentiful foods would reappear on their table and the money jar would be filled. They'd start eating like kings again, and drinking like lords once more. No, she could see they wouldn't be willing to chance doing without again. She was just fooling herself if she thought it would be any different.

In the meantime there were signs that the long winter was finally coming to an end. The snow that had remained frozen hard to the ground, seemingly impenetrable to any stray ray of sunshine, was finally softening under foot. Soon it would be spring in Russia as it was already all over the world. It was hard for her to believe that she had been married so short a time, that she and David had come so far in that short a time. It was even hard for her to realize that she hadn't even been pregnant for that long a time, only a matter of weeks. She had been married in winter, had conceived in winter, and yet, it was not *quite* spring.

Any day now Chaim would return home from his stay at the Widow's and roar for his sons to mount their horses, to hitch up the wagon, and they'd be off. And everything would be the same as it had always been. No, she wouldn't get the chance to spend the twenty rubles on food to prolong the strike against Chaim because there would never be a strike! Their only chance was to spend the twenty rubles on something else, something that offered a very real and practical alternative option for the brothers Markoff.

She pondered this alternative option for a couple of days. Then, as they lay in their bed in that very special time before sleep overtook them, the best time for good and sweet pillow talk, Eve said, "David, I think the time has come for us to make a move . . . into our own home and our own business. . . ."

David said nothing, only placed his hand there where their baby was growing almost imperceptibly as yet, but growing just the same. It was his assent and again Eve was reminded of how far they, she and David, had come in so short a time.

They rented a house of four fairly large rooms with a barn and a well and enough of a yard to keep chickens and raise some vegetables. It was only a street away from the Markoff household. Looking around at the small quarters and the roughhewn floors, Eve told David, "When I didn't want to marry you everyone kept telling me what a lucky girl I was because the Markoffs were a prosperous family with many horses. Then when I came to live in Chaim's house which is without the refinements I expected a prosperous family would enjoy—lace tablecloths, satin comforters, brocade chairs—I thought everyone had lied about your family being well-off. But now, comparing this house to your father's— Well, I guess he's a rich man, after all."

"No. He's not. I'm the rich one." David said, putting his arms around her. "Sometimes I think I must be the richest man in the world."

The first thing David wanted to do in the new house was to sand the dirt-stained splintered flooring. "You're the Princess Eve," he proclaimed, "and as such, you deserve to walk only on the finest, smooth-as-satin floors."

"That's sweet, David, and I appreciate the thought, but since we're short on time and money we'll just clean the floors for now. The quicker we're finished fixing up, the sooner you can get started looking for livestock. That way you can get the jump on your father. It's not going to be easy."

"Oh, I know. But I'm not going to be too particular about what I buy. I intend to buy anything that moves."

The sisters-in-law couldn't have been more shocked to hear that David and Eve were moving into their own house than if Eve had announced they were leaving for America. Hannah immediately wanted to know how they proposed to pay the rent on the new house. "With the money David earns trading in livestock. He's going to do just what Chaim and his brothers do. Only now he's going to keep all the profits from his labors." She let the words sink in before she added, "Just as all your husbands will if they decide to join him."

The women couldn't believe their ears! Now Eve wasn't talking about a work strike anymore. This was a whole other story. She was talking about all of them having their own business directly in competition with Chaim!

Eve knew better than to expect an immediate response, especially an affirmative one. She knew by now that it took them a little time to get used to an idea.

"Tell me," Hannah said, musing. "Where will David get the money to pay for what he buys before he sells it?"

"That's simple. He'll buy one chicken and sell it. With the money he gets he'll buy two chickens and sell them. And so on . . . That's how it works."

"Yes," Hannah agreed. "That sounds simple. But what isn't simple *is* where will he find the money to buy that first chicken?"

Eve wasn't ready yet to discuss the twenty rubles from the Vilno trip. That would entail a big discussion about whether it was strictly kosher to keep that money and use it against Chaim. Besides, neither she nor Dora had divulged that they had visited a doctor rather than the Wonder Rabbi.

"I still have a ruble left from the money I came here with—"

"That will buy a chicken surely." Hannah nodded. "But the rent? How will you pay rent until David gets started buying and selling?"

"That's simple. By sewing. I'm going to take in sewing."

"Oh, Eve!" Dora wailed. "I'm going to miss you so. It's hard to think of not seeing you every day."

"And how about the lessons?" Ruth wanted to know. She was the one who had taken to the lessons avidly. "You started teaching and now when I'm first beginning to learn you're going to stop—"

"Hold on! All of you! You're missing the point. We're moving into the new house because David is going to work on his own. But the whole idea is that if the brothers will refuse to work for Chaim, they can work with David. It will be their business as well as David's, and the profits will be equally divided. Since it would be difficult for all of you to live in Chaim's house while refusing to work for him, we're fixing up the new house to accommodate as many of you who choose to join us."

"And this house you've rented? It's big enough for all of us?"

"The house is not big. It's the old Kazinsky house. You know it. But it will do. We're going to partition the rooms. It will do for a while, at least. Until we all decide to buy it if we can and make it bigger, or until we make enough money for everyone to have his own house. That will be up to each individual family. We'll be a democracy."

"And if we don't move in with you, there'll be no more lessons I take it," Ruth said bitterly.

"Oh Ruthie! Do you think I'd do that? There will always be lessons for whoever wants them. Whether she lives with us or not. And that goes for visiting too, Dora. You'll always be welcome no matter what."

"But I want to come live with you," Dora cried. "It would be so much fun!"

"Yes. And I *want* you to come live with us. You're going to have to try and talk Yacob into coming in with us." She looked at the others as she spoke. "Tell Yacob that now he's no more than a peasant working in the fields of Chaim Markoff. Tell him to come work for the Brothers Markoff and he'll be his own master."

They partitioned the house to afford a kitchen large enough to hold an extralong dining table, which they'd need if everyone came to live with them. The remainder of the house was divided up into six tiny bedrooms—one for each couple, and one left over which, with the built-in benches lined up against the walls, would sleep the children. Then David built the dining table, fashioned rudimentary chairs, and over Eve's objections, several bookcases.

At first she had protested. "We can't spare either the time or the lumber for extra refinements." But David said, "I married a princess and I've never given her earbobs for her shell-like ears or bangles for her lily-white arms, not even a tiara to rest on her flowing tresses. The least I can do is give her a damned bookcase."

She giggled. "Where did you learn those fancy words? *Shell-like ears?*" She scoffed but she was pleased.

She sewed curtains, fashioned mattresses and pillows out of straw, stuffed *perinas* with feathers and even began hooking rugs out of rags although that was a task that would stretch on for months. They bought only what they couldn't possibly make themselves.

"I guess we'll have to buy a wagon, whatever it costs, because I just know you're going to find so many chickens, you'll need one that will hold hundreds—"

"From your mouth to God's ear," David said. He was more concerned about getting a horse. He could do nothing without a horse. And a horse cost a fortune. "What do you think?" he asked Eve. "Does my mare Chessie belong to me or does she belong to Father?"

"Are the trousers you're wearing yours or your father's?"

"I'd say they were mine."

"How long have you worn them?"

"Almost a year."

"And how long have you been riding Chessie?"

"Going on three years."

"Then Chessie is yours."

When the house was as warm and as hospitable as they could make it, Eve invited the whole family, including the children, for Sabbath dinner. If there weren't quite enough chairs to seat all the children there *was* a lace cloth on the table, there were candles in brass sticks, and the samovar gleamed. The children could double up or sit on a parent's lap. The sisters-in-law were overcome with admiration for what David and Eve had done with the small house. "Lovely!" Miriam said and Ruth acknowledged, "Cozy!"

"Cozy?" Dora gushed. "It's beautiful! Oh Yacob! Please! Let's come live here. It's like a dollhouse . . ."

"No, not a dollhouse," Eve smiled. "The women who live here will have to be flesh and blood and work like horses." She looked at Hannah who hadn't said a word.

Finally she did. "Very nice," she said thoughtfully. She turned to her husband. "Isn't it?" She wondered if he could consider coming here to live. Would he consider throwing in his lot with his youngest brother, defying his father at the same time?

Abraham seemed bemused and bewildered. He scratched at his beard, crinkled up his soft blue eyes which were not as dark a blue as any of his brothers'. "Nice?" he asked. "It's more than nice. My little brother seems to have gotten farther along in life than his big brother. I would say David has made himself a real home."

"Isn't that just like a man?" Ruth snickered. "David *and* Eve have made themselves a real home."

"It was never our intention to make a home simply for ourselves. This house is for all of us . . ." Eve felt she had to make that clear. "For whoever will come here to live and join with us in making our living." She was talking more to the brothers now than the sisters-in-law, but Miriam wanted to know if they couldn't talk about all this later. "We were invited for dinner and it's already past sundown."

"There she goes again," Ruth laughed. "She's interested in only one

113

thing—food." Then she added, "Well, *almost* one thing. We all know what the other thing is," she leered and everyone laughed.

David said the prayer over the challah. Each adult and child had a piece of the egg bread and wished each other a "good *Shabbes*." There was a bottle of vodka on the table and a decanter of a ruby-colored wine. The meal began with stuffed fish and Miriam and Hannah exchanged raised eyebrows. *A delicacy yet!* The fish was followed by a steaming tureen of cabbage soup with slivers of beef floating on top. *What an aroma!* Then came a huge bowl of broad egg noodles flecked with bits of fried onion and a *tsimmes* of burnt-orange sweet potatoes and sliced yellow carrots studded with dark purple prunes. *Good to look at too!* Finally, Eve brought to the table her crowning triumph—four crisp-skinned, fat and succulent capons surrounded by delicately browned whole potatoes.

"Oh my God!" Miriam breathed. "It's been so long since we've had a piece of chicken I can barely remember what it tastes like."

The brothers were no less enthralled.

"Where did you get them?"

"How did you buy them?"

"Where do you think I got them? How do you think I bought them?" David exulted. "I'm not a chicken thief yet."

"They're the very first purchase of the new business," Eve said proudly.

"The very first purchase of the new business and we're eating them up instead of you selling them and making your profit. What do you call that?" Hannah demanded.

"It's called eating up the profits," Ruth offered.

"No. It's called a celebration." Eve was thrilled that things were going so splendidly. "A hard-won celebration. Those capons weren't easy to find, as you can imagine. David had to search hard and long. For hours and hours. Things would go easier, of course, if he had some help. A lot more ground could be covered naturally . . ." she said, affecting an ingenuous air.

"Oh, naturally," Hannah chuckled. "What else? But tell me one thing, Evele—how come when you make a statement it's never simply a statement? There's always a point hanging from it, like a horse's tail."

Eve smiled demurely. "Perhaps the problem is your ears, Hannah darling. Perhaps you don't *hear* things simply."

"I've never had complaints about my ears before." She picked up the large carving knife and began sectioning a capon, forgetting that she wasn't in charge of the kitchen. "But speaking of ears, I think it's time they heard a toast. Abraham!" she pointed the knife at him. "You're the oldest. I say you make a toast to the new house and the new business."

Abraham smiled expansively, got to his feet, held out his glass. "To the new house, to the new business, to this excellent vodka and to the four beautiful capons!"

Everyone laughed as if he had said something very funny and Dora gave

Yacob a gentle shove. He looked at her questioningly and she nodded her head up and down, encouraging him.

So he got to his feet as Abraham sat. He cleared his throat noisily, unused to the floor. "I have a toast too. To the new house, to the new business, and to my new son!" he shouted. "Dora's finally going to have a baby!"

There were cheers and congratulations while Eve quietly exulted. Then Dora rose from her chair, her cheeks bright pink. "I would like to make a toast too. To my darling Eve who is re–"

Quickly Eve cut her off. "I think we should toast the Wonder Rabbi of Vilno—"

Dora sat down and Shlomo stood up. "If you ask me, I think it's Yacob we should toast. The rabbi maybe made a miracle but it was Yacob who did all the hard work."

They all roared in appreciation of the sally and Hannah cautioned, "*Sha!* Little pitchers . . ."

The children were temporarily put to sleep in the different rooms while the women cleared the table and started washing up. The men stayed at the table finishing off the wine and vodka. "And what's Father said to you about all this?" Hershel asked, spreading his hands to indicate the house but meaning the new business too.

"Nothing," David said. "How could he? I haven't spoken to him. I haven't seen him. Has he come home or is he still at the Widow's?"

"As far as we know he's at the Widow's. But I did see him at the Inn. He says we'll be riding out in a few days."

"And he didn't say anything about me and Eve?"

"Not a word."

"Still he must have heard," Abraham said. "All Slobodka knows you've moved in here. Someone must have said something to him—"

"Without a doubt," Shlomo added. "He must be burning. I wouldn't be too surprised if he came calling on you one of these days."

"No!" Hershel shook his head vehemently. "More likely he'll act as if he never heard of you."

"Or that he heard of you but that you were dead," Yacob added.

Shlomo laughed. "Maybe not so much David as Eve. I'm sure he'd like to think of Eve as dead . . ."

Everyone laughed but David. He wasn't amused.

"On the other hand," Hershel said speculatively, "maybe he doesn't care that you and Eve moved out. Maybe he's even happy about it, considering . . . Maybe he'll only get mad when he learns that you're riding around buying up livestock, cutting into *our* business."

"Yes," Shlomo agreed. "He probably won't like that, especially since you're already working and getting a jump on us."

"*Us?*" David demanded. "You said getting a jump on *us*, Shlomo. And

115

you, Hershel, you said I was cutting into *our* business, meaning yours and Father's. So that's the way it is. You're all staying with him. I offer you a way out and still you're all sticking with him." His voice was rising. "Well, if that's it, you can all go to hell! You're all so chicken-livered you make me sick! You're all scared to death of him, scared to death of your own weak-bellied shadows! Not one of you is a man!"

It occurred to David to throw them out of his house. If it weren't for the children asleep, he'd do just that. He was sick to death of the lot of them. Big, strong men and terrified of Chaim! As he himself had been, but at least he had found his courage. He *would* throw them out of his house and the children could stay!

Abraham put a hand on his shoulder. "Easy, David, easy. You've got to give a man a chance to think."

"God damn it, you've had a chance to think for twenty years! How long does it take to decide that you're tired of being shitted on?"

But the moment of extreme passion, of near violence had passed and he slumped back in his chair. "Just let him come here . . ." David muttered. "I'll spit in his face."

"Just think of the pleasure it must be for once in your life to sit down at a table and afterwards not to have to wash up . . ." Ruth complained, fiercely scrubbing at an encrusted roasting pan.

"Maybe if our business goes well, we'll all have that pleasure one day. We'll get dressed up and go eat at the Inn in Kovno, or at a café there," Eve said, trying to get David's attention, to indicate that he shouldn't lose his temper. "The Jews who live in the big cities do it all the time, I understand. In Moscow. They say they're forever eating in restaurants there, drinking at cafés." But her mind wasn't on what she was saying. She was more interested in what the brothers were saying at the table.

"In the meantime, we ate up the first merchandise," Hannah said regretfully. "Now what will David use for money to buy with the next time? How long can a couple of rubles stretch? Have you gotten any orders for sewing yet?"

"Monday I'm going to the Squire's. I hear that the Countess Makowski's pregnant. I'm going to offer my services as a seamstress to make her a wardrobe for her pregnancy. I should be able to earn quite a few rubles from her . . ."

"Are you completely out of your head?" Hannah was angry. "Why do you want to start up with them? If the gentry doesn't bother you, don't bother them! The less you have to do with them the better!"

"It's that kind of thinking that's kept us on the outside. Maybe we have to mix more with the gentiles so they'll learn to like us better. Or at least they'd find out we don't wear horns, and that we can be trusted not to drain their children's blood for our matzohs."

Hannah made a derogatory sound. "What makes you think she'll like you enough to trust you enough to hire you in the first place?"

"Because I have a new idea for a dress to be worn during pregnancy. Now, women just wear *big* dresses, and they just keep wearing bigger and bigger dresses as they go along—if they can afford it. But even these bigger dresses don't fit them otherwise. They're uncomfortable and make a woman look her worst. Now I think the Squire's wife, the Countess, will be interested in this dress that I've made for myself. See—'' She lifted her bodice to show the top of her skirt. ''The waistband's gathered on a drawstring and as my waist grows so does the waistband and the skirt is made extra full so there will be no problem when my stomach gets bigger.''

The women marveled and Eve went on to explain. ''What I did was take an old dress and made it into a two-piece outfit. But if the Countess orders a dress, I'll sew an outfit that's designed in two pieces to begin with—a skirt and a bodice, or a jacket.''

''Oh, I wish I could have one of those too,'' Dora said wistfully. ''But if you're going to be sewing for the Squire's lady I guess you won't have time to . . .'' her voice trailed off.

''No, she won't!'' Hannah said. ''You can't expect that—''

''Yes, she can, Hannah. She can expect. She's my sister so she can expect. And I will. I'll find time for Dora, always. As I would for any of you.''

''Oh, Eve . . . You know what color I would love. Yellow. Like sunflowers that cover the earth . . .''

''Then yellow it will be.''

''Not one of them said he was coming in with us,'' David told Eve after everyone had departed. ''I don't give a damn anymore. I'm sick to death of them. Scared of their own shadows. I'm just sorry we spent all that time fixing up the house to accommodate them.''

''It's not over yet, David. I have a feeling that at least one of them will come over to our side. Maybe even two or three. Now, at least, they have a place to go. I think that makes all the difference, having a place to go.''

9.

It was some time after David had left with his horse and wagon but still early in the morning when Eve set out on foot to call on the Countess Makowski. It was at least an hour's walk, and the road leading to the Squire's manor was still half-frozen and muddy. As she walked along, Eve passed the Squire's fields, which stood apparently forsaken, desolate and dormant in the cold morning light. Here and there, she could see a peasant stumbling along, a lone black figure swathed in rags from head to foot. It seemed impossible to believe that in only two to three weeks the land would be dotted with peasants—bustling about, planting, even singing as they sowed. Russians loved to sing.

Eve had never seen the Count or his Countess but she had heard that he was elderly and liked to dress in the uniform of his former regiment, and that she was much younger than her husband, pretty and forever making pilgrimages to St. Petersburg. In St. Petersburg, life itself was a party—teas, socials, dinners and grand balls. But this was of no consequence to Eve; she only cared that the lady would be currently in residence at her manor house and would grant Eve an audience, and then give her an order for at least two dresses.

Actually, Eve wasn't completely without a sense of trepidation. Any Jew would be stupid to suffer *no* apprehensions at all over seeking out a member of the nobility.

As she plodded along, trying to avoid both the deeper ruts and the remaining drifts of icy snow, at the same time struggling to keep her skirts out of the mud, Eve passed that juncture in the road which led to the towering hillside where at its pinnacle stood the old fort overlooking the territory it guarded. She glanced up at the gloomy structure, then quickly looked away and hurried by. It was hard for her not to equate the more oppressive aspects of Russian life with the huge, bleak edifice. Each time she viewed the fort, even from a distance, she was filled with a dark, vague fear.

When she was a couple of hundred feet past the juncture she heard an enormous clatter and clanking and the hoofbeats of horses. Turning to look, she saw a large wagon pulled by four horses, careening wildly as it made a sharp turn to the right, then beginning its steep ascent up the hill. The horses seemed to be having difficulty making the climb, while the wagon, piled high with sacks, crates and boxes, appeared as if it might fall apart at any moment. She realized that this must be the wagon that made the monthly delivery of supplies to the Cossacks manning the fort.

She continued on her way, not really interested in whether the horses would successfully complete their climb, or if the wagon would even stay in one piece. She still had quite a way to go and she was trying to figure out what she could charge the Countess if all went well and she did get an order.

Off the main road to her left was a secondary road barely wide enough to accommodate a wagon, which led to the manor house, still some distance away. Eve passed barns and stables, carriage houses and chicken coops, storage sheds of different sizes and ice cellars, arbors and bowers, and a fenced-in riding circle. It was almost a village of its own. Here, peasants appeared to be working although what precisely they were doing in all the snow and mud, Eve couldn't determine.

Finally she reached the stone mansion and taking a deep breath to give herself courage, wielded the huge knocker. After several minutes, a woman dressed in black with a white apron and a ring of keys hanging from a cord around her waist opened the door. She looked Eve up and down and decided that she was a lady. Then she looked around Eve to see what kind of carriage she had come in. Seeing none, she determined that Eve had come on foot and was no lady after all. Her manner immediately grew brusque. She demanded to know what it was Eve wanted.

Eve explained and the woman, disgusted, waved her away. "Go . . . We already have girls that sew . . ."

"I just don't sew or mend. I'm a dressmaker."

"We don't need dressmakers. The Countess has dressmakers in St. Petersburg, in Paris. Go!" And she began to close the door on Eve.

"No! Wait! Please . . . Tell the Countess that I make *special* dresses. Maternity dresses."

The woman considered whether or not to bother the Countess, twisting her face disagreeably at the same time. "All right," she said finally. "I'll tell her. You wait here—" Then as if suddenly realizing that Eve was at the front door instead of the back, she scolded: "What idiot comes to the Squire's front door? Only ladies and gentlemen come to the front door!" She shook her head in anger at this infraction. "Even a peasant knows enough to go around to the back."

Eve waited for more than two hours in a long, unheated hall until she was bidden by the woman in black to a wooden flight of backstairs not illuminated by lamp, candle or window. Then suddenly she was in an upstairs hallway so brilliantly splendid it easily put the house of Dr. Golov to shame. Eve didn't know where to look first. The walls were painted a delicate silvery green and there was furniture that Eve instantly recognized as in the style of Louis XV although she had never seen anything resembling it outside of books. Oh, how these Russian aristocrats admired those things French, she thought, as her gaze focused on a *bombé vernis Martin* commode and then a gold and plum damask marquise. She would have loved to stop to examine everything in detail but the woman hustled her along the hallway until they came to a sitting room, small but exquisitely furnished, where a blond woman in a flowing boudoir gown sat at a writing table.

Both the servitor and Eve waited patiently until the Countess deigned to look up and take notice of them. "You may go, Truska." The woman left and Eve said, "What a charming room, *Madame!* What a beautiful *canapé à corbeille!* And what a magnificent screen!" She ran over further to examine the panels which were decorated in a seascape. "Italian, isn't it?"

The Countess smiled icily, suspiciously. "Perhaps. I always assumed it to be French. And how do you know about such things? Are you traveled?"

"No. I've just read about faraway places."

"I see. What's your name?"

"Forgive me for not having introduced myself. I'm Eve Markoff, my lady."

"Then you're Jewish?"

"Yes, my lady."

"And yet you can speak French and differentiate between Italian and French art and you're not even from a large city. How is that?"

"I have a knack for languages and I've always read and studied . . . whatever books I could lay my hands on. And I have a good memory, my lady. I always remember what I've read."

The Countess frowned and Eve's heart sank.

I've done it again! Showing off, trying to make myself stand out. While I might have aroused her interest, I've also made her dislike me. And probably distrust me. I know they don't trust Jews who are too bright. Why couldn't I just keep my mouth shut and let my dressmaking speak for itself?

"And you're a seamstress?"

"Yes, ma'am."

"Truska said you make maternity dresses. What exactly is a maternity dress?"

"I'm wearing one."

"You're pregnant?"

"Yes, my lady."

"I couldn't tell. You can't be very much along. Well, come over here and let me take a look at your dress."

The Countess's eyes lit up when she examined the drawstring waist and the way the bodice fitted ingeniously over it with a peplum that hid the excessive fullness. Her manner changed immediately from distantly cold to friendly. "I've never seen anything like it. I'm not far along myself but I've been wearing nothing but peignoirs for weeks already. And still I look like a house."

Eve demurred but the Countess's laugh tinkled out. "No, don't deny it. It's true. To tell the truth, I don't think the Count even likes to look at me in this condition. But now you'll make me a dress . . . two, one for day and one for evening. And if they come out well, we'll talk about additional ones. Come—"

The Countess took Eve into her boudoir where Eve took her measurements. Then she followed the Countess into a storage room, its walls lined with shelves that held more fabrics of more colors than Eve had ever seen in a market stall. Linens and silks and satins and fine wools . . . a yellow brocade, a spring green taffeta, a mauve sateen, a fawn gray velvet, a burnt-orange bombazine, serges and broadcloths . . . Then there were the boxes of decorative trimmings—beads and feathers and fringes, maribou, spangles and paillettes of all sizes and colors, seed pearls and flowers fashioned of silk. And the laces! Mignonette and Alençon and Chantilly, Venetian point and Valenciennes . . .

"I usually go to Paris once a year and order dresses and coats, even fur coats for which, of course, I bring the pelts with me. But in addition, I always buy bolts of cloth and boxes of trimmings since one never knows when one won't be able to travel to Paris. The Count's such a worrier. At the least sign of anything he won't let me go. He says that one never knows when war will break out and I suppose that's true enough. This year I didn't go to France because of my pregnancy but last year I did. The year before I didn't because I was pregnant then too. This is my third child. I have a little girl of two and a boy four. I wanted to go to Paris this year even with my pregnancy. To tell the truth I was desperate to go; it's so dull here, one can go out of one's mind. But the Count wouldn't hear of it. We did go to St. Petersburg just before I became pregnant. We usually go to St. Petersburg twice a year. I'm related, you know, to His Imperial Highness on his mother's side . . ." Then her voice trailed off as if she suddenly remembered to whom she was talking and realized that it wasn't appropriate.

They discussed at length which of the fabrics should be used for the day dress and which for the evening. Finally it was decided that Eve would begin with the day dress and would use a rose-colored watered silk. The Countess called the color "terra rosa." Then, when Eve returned for the fitting, they'd decide on the fabric for the evening dress. Perhaps white, the Countess thought, although white did make one look larger, didn't Eve think? And since one was already large enough with child, one didn't *need* to look larger still. Didn't Eve agree? Perhaps the evening dress should be blue? Pale blue satin . . . Or did Eve think *taffeta?*

The Countess asked if Eve's child would be her first. "It must be—you're so young. So young and so clever to have thought of this expandable waistline. But my husband says that all of you Jews are clever. He says that the Germans don't even mind the Jews because they're so clever. Especially with money. The Rothschilds, you know. In Germany the Jews are even allowed to put a *von* before their names. I met the Rothschilds in Paris. The French branch of the family. Such style! You'd hardly know they're Jewish . . ."

"I understand they're true adherents," Eve murmured, not wanting to say too much. The Countess looked surprised. "Is that true? Well, that's all to the good, isn't it? Better than being heathens, I would think . . ."

The fabric for the dress was wrapped into a neat parcel and Eve set off for home. When she again approached the site of the fort, a thought occurred to her. If the ascent of the wagon up the hillside was so difficult—she herself had seen the contents of the wagon being tossed from side to side—it stood to reason that sometimes things must *fall off* the wagon, unnoticed by the driver . . .

She considered whether it was worth crossing the road and taking a look. It *was* getting late. She had to start dinner for David and she wanted to clean the mud stains from her coat and dress before they set and became almost impossible to remove. Well, she decided, it was worth a quick look.

She crossed the road, walked in the course the wagon had taken, her eyes searching the ground. Yes, she was right! There were some potatoes that had rolled into the deep ditch at the side of the road. A sack must have broken. Much as she disliked picking up the now filthy vegetables and putting them in her clean marketing bag, it would be foolish not to. Pride and poverty didn't mix and the former had to make way for the latter.

She started up the fires—one in the hearth, one in the stove. Then she removed her coat and dress and using a small stiff brush and a bowl of cleaning solution she mixed, she stood in her chemise and petticoat and worked away at the stains. Suddenly her door flew open. She heard it rather than saw it since her back was to the door.

David, home sooner than she expected!

"Darling, I have wonderful news! I saw the —" She turned. It wasn't David but Chaim! He was grinning at her wickedly, his bulk seemingly filling the room! He was grinning at her with big white teeth but his eyes weren't smiling at all . . .

She couldn't find her voice. She was terrified even though it hurt her to admit that to herself. Finally she managed to say, "How dare you enter my house without knocking?" Even as she spoke she was painfully aware of how inadequate her words sounded. "What do you want?"

He advanced a step or two closer.

"You're not welcome here! Get out!"

At that he laughed raucously. "So you thought you'd make trouble for me! You and my milksop of a son!"

"Don't you dare speak of David like that!"

He spat. "Phooey. A mama's boy and you're the mama . . ." he growled contemptuously. "You're the troublemaker. You're the one who's trying to set my sons against me! You're the bitch! A whore! A stinking bitch of a whore!"

He advanced another step, menacingly closer.

"I want you out of my house!" She tried to speak calmly, coldly, the better to sound strong. It was important with an animal like Chaim not to let him smell the stench of her fear.

"I made a mistake letting David marry you in the first place. I should have seen what a bitch of a whore you were with all your fucking airs, your dresses, your hair!"

She sneered. "Oh, but it was you who made sure I kept my hair, wasn't it? And why? Because you've had your disgusting eye on me—"

Oh, dear God, a mistake! She knew it as the words left her mouth. The smile left his face and he took another step toward her. Dropping her dress and the brush she was cleaning it with, she backed away, into a corner. A tactical error. *Oh, God, another mistake!*

"Bitch! You flaunted yourself, didn't you? Like any bitch in heat! The trouble with you is that David's not man enough to keep you in your place. What you need is a real man to teach you, to fuck you, to show you what a woman like you is meant for! Just to be fucked like the cow you are. To give birth to sons to suck those bulging tits! That's what you're good for—"

His eyes ran over her, taking in the swell of her breasts emerging from the ruffled camisole, her white shoulders. He reeked of alcohol; he wasn't only full of rage but vodka too!

He reached out a red paw and grabbed her camisole tearing it to the waist, exposing her breasts. She tried to cover herself without even thinking, criss-crossing her arms over her chest. She had never felt such terror but at the same time she was outraged! "You'll pay for this!" She didn't even know what she was saying.

She tried to move out of the corner, to get something to cover her nakedness, but he quickly blocked her. She realized that he wouldn't leave until he had released some of the violence within him. Perhaps if he struck her, beat her, it would satisfy some of that rage so that he would spare her body a more lascivious attack. Perhaps she could even make that choice for him. "You wouldn't dare touch me, you disgusting drunk! You wouldn't dare strike me!" she taunted.

"You still don't have the sense to keep that bitch's mouth of yours shut!" With that, he hit her across the cheek with the flat of his hand and her head rocked with the blow. Would that satisfy him? she wondered. No, it wasn't enough. She forced herself to grin at him with derision and he hit her again, this time with the back of his hand. For a moment, she was more giddy than pained, then strangely numb and light-headed, as if she were going to lose consciousness.

"Who were you expecting, slut? Standing around in your underwear . . . A Cossack from the fort?"

Then she thought, *David!* She had to get Chaim out of the house before David came home! If David came home and found the two of them like this . . . her face bruised and welted, her breasts spilling from her torn chemise, there'd be the most brutal kind of fight and who knew how it would end? Who would end up dead?

She wondered how many blows it would take before Chaim left or killed her.

"Answer me, you piece of shit, you piece of a whore's miscarriage! Who were you waiting for in your slut's underwear?"

Maybe she'd try *not* answering him. Not looking at him. Maybe he'd get tired of calling her names and leave?

Dear God! He was unbuttoning his trousers. *Oh God!* How stupid of her to think that hitting her would be enough for him, would satisfy him. Ravishing her was what was on his depraved mind; nothing else would suffice.

Tears of anger at her own impotence rolled down her cheeks. She was boxed into the corner; she couldn't even get to the knives. There was nothing she could do to stop him! She could struggle and she would. She could scream, but what of it? Neither her screaming nor her struggling would help. She was powerless against him . . .

His phallus was out of his trousers now, red and turgid. She would faint, she thought. She would retch! "David will be home at any minute," she cried out. "He'll come home and kill you!"

Chaim laughed in her face. "That weakling! That mewling, gutless, marrowless, gelded son-of-a-bitch! Don't make me puke! With one finger I'll lay him out!"

For those words alone she wanted to kill him! "David's a thousand times the man you are!" She spat in his face.

Taken by surprise, Chaim fell back and she dashed out of the corner, across the room to the table where a paring knife lay. But as her hand found it, he was on her again, twisting her wrist until the knife fell, and he was laughing once more. "When I'm through with you, fancy lady, you'll be begging for more. You'll see what a real man is."

What she saw was that it was all over for her. He'd take her and she'd never be able to tell anyone about it. Especially David. David would set out to kill his father and it was more than likely Chaim would kill him instead—not because David was weak or gutless but because Chaim was a savage animal with more hate and viciousness in him.

Chaim had her bent back on the table, taking his time, increasing his pleasure by toying with her, bruising her breast with meaty, harsh fingers.

What was more terrible, she realized, was that she would be, bound by her enforced silence, completely at Chaim's mercy . . . forever. He would be back again and again, to take her whenever he wished, enjoying her ineffectual thrashing, her meaningless protests, relishing his mastery over her. Unless she killed him before the next time.

He was all over her now, his weight crushing her hard against the table. And she was so weak! *Oh God damn her, she was so weak!* His hand was under her petticoat and she kicked out at him but the harder she fought the more pleasure she saw in his face.

He lowered his face to hers, his beard covering her face, his red lips seeking hers. She screwed her face away in an attempt to evade them but they went instead to her neck, her throat, her heaving breasts. Yes, she fought back, and she would curse him as he penetrated her and she'd fight him with all her available but inadequate strength even as he pumped and poked and violated, taking sadistic joy in her curses, her squirmings, her strugglings and grapplings. But in the end she'd still be his—marked, dirty, soiled—indelibly despoiled. And he would be back. She would have to be ready the next time, waiting, ready to kill him!

But he was removing his body from hers, pulling her up from her bent-back position on the table. "This way is too easy for you. I want you on your knees, you stinking slut!"

He grabbed her by the hair, forced her down to her knees until her face was at a level with his swollen male organ. *Oh God, she wouldn't!*

She wrenched her head back. She cried, "The townspeople! The Rabbi! When I tell them what you've done you'll be stoned, driven from town!"

He laughed like a deranged creature. "They won't believe you! They'd sooner believe you're a whore! They won't dare believe you because they know I'll kill the man who believes you!"

With that he threw her kneeling body to the floor where she flopped like a limp doll. He pulled her petticoat up and her underdrawers down and threw himself on top of her. Physically unable to move any more, she searched for other words that would stop him. "The Squire will believe me!"

"Squire? What makes you think the Squire will care about what happens to a Jewish whore?"

"He'll care! I was there today. They like me—the Count and the Countess . . . They'll be delighted to believe me and *they're* not afraid of you, are they? They have the Cossacks to take care of you! The gentiles aren't afraid of you. They'll love nothing better than having a Jewish rapist to serve up to their people as an example of the Jew's immorality. You'll be the official scapegoat to offer up for Easter—a Jewish father who rapes his son's wife, a Jewish devil capable of anything, even raping, fornicating with their own wives and daughters. They'll torture you and send you to Siberia."

As she started to run down, to run out of words there was noise in the street—a kind of noise she didn't recognize, had never heard. But Chaim did! Suddenly, in front of her eyes she saw fear in his face. She saw his penis grow as flabby and as limp as if he'd been thrown into the icy river. She managed to wriggle out from under him now that he was immobile. She scrambled to her feet and ran to the window. She saw a mob of peasants running through the street, armed with rocks and sticks and clubs and pitchforks, rakes and whips— old men and young men, even little boys, even a few old crones—twenty of them or maybe thirty. *My God! What was happening?* Then she knew! She had never seen this kind of demonstration before but she had heard of them, mostly in whispers because it was nothing one wanted to talk about too loud. Talking about it made it too real, too vivid, almost as if it were happening all over again. It was not exactly a pogrom with Cossacks or soldiers. Rather, it was a minor pogrom. Not organized, not official, but instigated by the authorities—a lesson, a warning. It was a party for the peasant who too needed an outlet for his pent-up rage, *his* need for violence, not unlike Chaim himself.

She saw a little boy struck down with a club, old Nahum Pinsky struck repeatedly with a stick until he fell. An old woman, lying in the road, was kicked in the head. They were running past her house now and the rocks came flying. One broke the window and hit her in the chest before it fell to the floor.

"Get down!" Chaim cried. "Away from the window! In a few minutes they'll pass. They attack only what's in their path!" Chaim shouted at her. But she ignored him. She didn't even look at him. She'd never fear him again. The oppressor had been vanquished by an oppressor stronger than he, even more terrible.

She saw that she was bleeding where the rock had hit her. She wiped at the blood with her hand. Still not looking at Chaim, she went to her bedroom to wait for the mob to pass. She sat on the floor just praying. Praying that no one would die, that no house would be put to the torch. When it was quiet she redressed herself and went back into the kitchen. Chaim was gone. She knew he wouldn't be back. He'd never be back.

She opened the door to the street. She saw two men trying to extinguish the flames from a barn; Nahum Pinsky's wife sitting in the mud with her husband's head in her lap, crying; the small boy who had been attacked with the club being carried away. Now there were other bodies lying in the road, some quiet, some wailing, some just bleeding. The demonstration that had not been quite a pogrom was over and she went into the street to see what had to be done.

10.

David had brought home a gift for Eve and as it was his very first present to her, it was hard to say who was more excited, she or he. "Close your eyes and hold out your hand!" he commanded.

"Which hand?" Eve asked, her eyes screwed shut.

It has to be a ring, she thought. *It's a wedding ring to replace the one Chaim supplied for our wedding.*

"Which hand?" she asked again since David hadn't answered her.

David laughed. "I don't know. I guess it's the right one."

She was going to correct him, tell him that the left hand was the one for a wedding ring, but she didn't want to ruin his surprise. Accordingly, she stuck out the right hand.

David laughed again. "Now I don't know which finger to put it on—"

Her eyes flew open. It was a thimble.

"It's silver," David said proudly. "*Real* silver. When the man said that true aristocrats always had *real* silver thimbles, I knew I had to buy it for you. I told the man there was no one in the world more aristocratic than *my* wife."

"Oh, David, it's beautiful! I love it!" And when they sat down to eat she wore it exactly as if it were a ring.

After David said the prayer they began to eat. "It's nice . . ."

"What's nice? The dinner?"

"No . . . Yes . . . Of course the dinner. But I was thinking how wonderful it is to come home after a long day, having done a little business, to have had a little left over to buy my wife a present. To be here with her in our own place—warm, eating, talking. Not to have to look at my father glowering and listen to him screaming and cursing and complaining. Belching! It's like a little slice of heaven."

She smiled at him to show that she appreciated his words, agreed with him. But at the same time she only toyed with her food, his words a reminder that indeed they were alone and that she had not managed to bring her sisters-in-law along to share in this heaven, as David had so poetically put it.

"What do you hear around? Have they, your father and brothers, started working again?"

"Yes. One farmer told me today they had just been to his place before me.

That he had sold them a horse and that I had just missed out. A horse! As if I had enough money to buy a horse!"

"You will, David, you will."

But she couldn't stop thinking about Ruth and Miriam and Dora and Hannah. They hadn't even come to visit. They were only minutes away and she hadn't seen them at all, not since that day of the demonstration that had been almost a pogrom. She had spent her days working on the Countess's dress, hardly leaving her house at all. Certainly she couldn't go to Chaim Markoff's house to see her sisters-in-law.

"I guess they won't be coming here to live after all, David. Your brothers are going to stay with Chaim, aren't they?"

"Let them! If that's what they want, who needs them?" For himself he was just as glad to be alone with Eve. His brothers had had their chance. He was only disappointed because Eve was. "They're stupid, thickheads. Some people you just can't help. To hell with them!"

They were almost through with dinner when there was a violent pounding on the door. For a moment they sat motionless with that nameless apprehension that accompanied an unexpected visit in the night, an instinctive animallike fear that froze the blood. Eve looked at David. *Was it a pogrom? Dear God, not again! Or is it soldiers come to drag David away to fill the conscription? A requisitioning of our horse? An interrogation? A gentile had been found dead and they were investigating, starting with Jews . . . Or is it only one drunken Cossack, ready to torch our house, but politely extending us the courtesy of allowing us to leave first?*

David went to the door, opened it a cautious crack, peered out into the black night. But it wasn't any Russian official, no drunken Cossack! It was Yacob and behind Yacob, Dora! And behind Dora, Yacob's horse loaded down with packages and bundles.

"Are you going to let us in or not?" Yacob demanded querulously. "Did you tell us to come or didn't you?" Over Yacob's shoulder Dora called out: "Eve! Eve! We're here! We've come to stay with you!"

Dizzy with relief, Eve ran to the door. "Welcome! Oh, welcome!"

"He hit her! He actually hit little Becky so hard she fell down and just because she spilled a glass of milk! So I said to Yacob I can't stay here anymore. I can't have my baby born in a house with a man like that! And I told Yacob that even if *he* wouldn't come, I was going to, by myself. Isn't that right, Yacob? Didn't I say that? I was going to come here in the morning by myself . . ."

Yacob glared at her. "That wasn't the only reason we came. We came because *I* decided to come."

Dora flushed and looked down at her hands folded in her lap. She knew why *she* had come. Maybe Yacob had to have his own reasons.

Yacob poured himself another vodka. "Tonight, tonight I told Father for the first time that Dora was pregnant. And what do you think he said?"

"What?" David asked, knowing already that it must have been something disagreeable, one way or another.

"He said, 'So, you *shlep!* You *shlimazl!* The Miracle Rabbi at ninety is more of a man than you'll ever be!' " Yacob drained his glass. "Ordinarily a remark like that from Father I ignore. Who ever questioned Father? But this time . . . this time something clicked in my head. Something which wouldn't let the remark pass. So I said to him, 'What do you mean by that? What do you mean that he's more of a man than me?' And do you know what he said—this man who's my father? He said, 'Apparently the rabbi's able to stick his wick in better than you, you *shtik drek!*'

"All of a sudden I saw red. Besides what he's saying about me, even about Dora, he's also saying something about my son who isn't even born yet. I wanted to kill him! If he was any other man I wouldn't have hesitated. Still, was I going to do nothing? So I said to myself, 'Yacob, you may be your father's next to youngest son, but you're not a *shtik drek.* You're a man and it's time to go where you'll be treated like a man, spoken to like a man. You don't have to live with insults anymore, Yacob. Now you have a place to go.' "

The tears streamed down Yacob's cheeks. "A place to go made all the difference—" Abruptly he threw his arms around David, threw his head down on David's shoulder. For a moment, taken by surprise, David sat stiffly. Nothing like this had ever happened before. But then he wrapped his arms around his brother, hugged him close.

Watching them, Dora laughed with joy. "Oh, Eve, I've never been so happy in my life! This is the most wonderful thing that could have happened—for me to live here with Yacob and you and David. And soon there'll be your baby and then mine. Our babies will be more like brothers, or sisters, or whatever, than cousins, won't they?"

Eve nodded. *Friends . . . sisters . . . brothers . . . cousins . . . It's all the same.*

"And just think! If Chaim hadn't hit poor Becky, making me decide that I couldn't live in a house with a man like that anymore, we wouldn't be sitting here right now—"

Yacob lifted his head from David's shoulder and stared at her as if he couldn't believe his ears. He made a fist, shook it, slammed it down on the table. "We came because I'm a man!"

Dora looked down at her hands again. "Yes, Yacob, because you're a man . . ."

At dawn the brothers set off on their rounds of the countryside. David told Eve that they'd be back late since now that Yacob was with him they'd be covering a larger territory. Eve helped Dora to unpack and generally settle in while she inquired about Miriam and Hannah and Ruth. How they were getting along and what was happening there.

"Oh, it's like a *shiva.* Like everyone was mourning for the dead. Just

129

yesterday morning while we were doing the chores Ruth was saying that while spring may be coming, on the day you left, the sun stopped shining . . .''

Two hours later there was a commotion at the door and there was Ruth herself, holding Gershon on one hip, and carrying a bundle with the other hand. At her side were her other three boys, the two older ones dragging bundles, and the smaller one holding a rag doll. Ruth was grinning widely. "A short walk . . . yes. But probably the longest one I've ever taken. Here—" She thrust the baby at Eve and the bundle at Dora. "I have to go back and get the rest of my things. Keep an eye on the boys. Give them a piece of bread to chew on. They haven't had any breakfast. And you can give Gershon a piece too; he both sucks and chews now. And you can put him down. He walks but watch him. He's just as likely to fall down and crack his head. I'll be back soon. Is the samovar lit?"

"Last night after Yacob and Dora left, Chaim let loose with a stream of curses you wouldn't believe. Then he got up and bellowed, wanting to know who else was leaving because we could all get the hell out right then and there as far as he was concerned. Nobody said a word. I guess everyone was too stunned.

"Then he stormed out of the house for who knows where? The rest of us sat. Then I said, 'Yacob and Dora have done the right thing. Yacob, at least, acted like a man.' Well, Hershel chose to take offense at my remark. Mind you, at his father's he doesn't. At mine, he does. He demanded to know in a very nasty tone of voice if I thought *he* wasn't acting like a man because he didn't choose to come here like Yacob did. I told him I didn't like the tone of his voice. I also told him not only had Yacob acted like a man but now he and Dora were going to be free people. Then I said that he and Shlomo and Abraham and us, their wives, *weren't* free. We were all serfs, quaking in our boots and wetting our pants. Then I appealed to Hannah. 'Isn't that right, Hannah?' I asked her. I'm sorry to say Hannah didn't answer me. You know Hannah. When she's aroused she has a lot to say but mostly she likes to keep peace in the house, which I suppose is important too.

"But at the same time that she kept silent, she *did* look at Abraham, *a look* . . . It was as if she was hoping *he* would say something but you know Abraham; he's not the type to say anything if he doesn't have to. Actually I'd say he's the gentlest of the brothers. He must have taken after the mother, may she rest in peace."

Personally, Eve thought David was very gentle and she liked to think he was the most genteel of all the brothers, but she didn't want to interrupt Ruth by saying anything.

"So not getting any answers from that corner of the room, I turned to Miriam and I said, 'Isn't that right, Miriam?' Well, Miriam just shrugged, saying nothing, as she usually does. She doesn't like to stir the pot, that one. She doesn't want to shake anyone up if she doesn't have to, least of all herself. That's how she saves herself. She'll live to be a hundred and eight, that one, just by staying placid. It's her way. She refuses to get excited even if the house is burning down. She lets other people get excited. But at the same time, while she doesn't say a thing, she does lots of looking. But she doesn't look at Shlomo, who would be the logical one for her to look at— Am I right? He's her husband and who should she look at if not him? But instead she's looking at Hannah, as if waiting to hear from her before she takes a position, before she says a word. But since Hannah wasn't talking, neither was she.

"Well, I look at Hershel again but now he's not talking to me at all so I get up and I say, 'You know what? You're all *shtik drek*, every last one of you. You, Hershel; you, Hannah; you, Miriam; and you, Abraham and Shlomo. You're all nothing but pieces of shit and I feel sorry for you. And at the same time I feel sorry for you, you all make me sick to my stomach. You know why? Because given a choice, you'd all rather be *shtik drek* than real human beings, free human beings. As for me, I don't want to be a *shtik drek* anymore, living with this horrible person and at his mercy. Being afraid of him and accepting whatever he chooses to say or do, however he wants to treat me. And you know what? I don't have to anymore. *I* have a place to go!'

"I didn't say another word to Hershel, not last night and not this morning. I just waited until he rode out with the others this morning, then I started making my bundles . . ."

"And Miriam and Hannah?" Eve asked. "What did they say to you this morning?"

"Not much. Once I started bundling things up they helped me."

"And Hershel? He doesn't know you're gone?"

"I guess he didn't think I'd really leave. But he'll find out soon enough. Tonight. I gave Hannah a message to give him from me. I told her to tell Hershel that I had gone to be a free woman and to bring up my sons to be free men. i hope she'll tell him in exactly those words. What do you think of that message?"

"It does have a ring."

Ruth laughed a little, proud of herself. "It does, doesn't it?"

"I wonder what Hershel will do when he finds you gone." While she was delighted that Ruth had come, she was also worried. The last thing she wanted was to cause trouble in Ruth's marriage. Surely that was a sin—to come between a husband and wife. "What do you think Hershel will do?"

"Either he'll stay with his father or he'll come here to be with his wife and his children. One or the other."

"Yes, I've gathered *that*," Eve offered dryly. "One or the other. But *which* of the two do you think he'll do?"

Ruth considered. "I don't know. What do *you* think? After all, it was you who suggested I stop nursing so I would be . . . you know . . . available. And then you suggested that in order not to get pregnant, I should suggest to Hershel that he shouldn't . . . you know . . . let himself . . . inside me . . . And that worked out pretty well . . ." she laughed. "So all in all, I'd say you're pretty smart. So what do you think he'll do?"

"I just bet he'll come. He won't stay without you," Dora said, bouncing Gershon on her knee.

"Yes, I think he'll come," Eve said. "But maybe not right away."

"But what will you do, Ruth, if he doesn't? Ever?" Dora chucked Gershon under the chin.

Ruth gave her a baleful look. "You just said you'd bet he'll come. God, you can be exasperating, Dora."

Dora hung her head and Ruth turned to Eve, "What *will* I do if he never comes?"

"I'm not sure. Why don't we think about it when and if it's necessary, which I'm sure it won't be—"

"If he doesn't come will you ask me to leave? We're a lot of mouths to feed without Hershel—"

"Oh Ruth! What a question! Of course we wouldn't ask you and the boys to leave. I'm thrilled that you're here, but at the same time I don't want you and Hershel to be separated . . . unless . . ."

"Unless what?"

"Unless you decide that's what you really want—"

"I don't want to be separated from Hershel, but at the same time I won't live in Chaim's house any longer. No matter what." She took a big gulp of tea. "It's a pleasure to be here, to be a free person. And if Hershel doesn't come I'll do whatever I can to earn our way."

"Oh, Ruth, don't. There'll always be a place for you and the boys, but I'm sure Hershel will come."

"Well, I have to think about if he doesn't. I can always sell pickled herring in the marketplace. All I'd have to do is buy the herring and pickle them. I wouldn't mind selling herring in the marketplace. I wouldn't earn much but it would be something."

"It won't come to that. Hershel will—"

Dora cut her off. "I'll be glad to mind the boys for you when you're selling."

"Just a minute—" Eve protested.

But Ruth said, "Thank you, Dora. I appreciate your offer."

"Oh, don't mention it. It will be my pleasure."

Eve sent up a silent prayer that Hershel would come, and soon.

Each day David and Yacob rode out, and the women settled more or less into a routine. For the most part, Eve sewed, now working on the Countess's second maternity dress, and Ruth and Dora did the chores and looked after Ruth's boys, and they all cooked. And they all waited for Hershel to come. Seven days passed and Eve was beginning to wonder if he ever would and what could possibly be done to prod him. On the eighth night he showed up with his bundle.

"What you did was wrong!" Hershel told Ruth in front of them all. "You shamed me in the eyes of my father and my older brothers by walking out and taking my sons—"

132

"But I didn't leave you," Ruth responded in a conciliatory fashion. "I just went first and waited for you to follow."

"But it was for me to go first."

"Then why didn't you?" she snapped.

"It was wrong of you," he said again but not quite as vehemently. "I'm still the head of my family. It was for me to make the decision as to when to go . . ."

For a moment it seemed as if Ruth was going to give a sharp retort but instead she said softly, "Of course it was for you to make the decision, Hershel. And I didn't doubt for a minute that you were going to make the right one. I just sort of helped you along by going first. Sort of a little *nudge* in the right direction." She smiled teasingly, making an effort to be charming which didn't come easily to her. Charm was not one of Ruth's strong points.

Hershel looked sheepishly around the room—at Dora and Yacob, at Eve and David. Obviously he wanted to accept Ruth's words as the peace offering they were meant to be. Eve nodded, smiling, encouraging. Finally he smiled at Ruth. "A nudge . . . yes. But not so little."

"Not so big either since it took you long enough to get here," Ruth said now with a touch of tartness. "What was your hurry?"

Hershel missed her sarcasm. "The hurry was Father. That he always called me names was one thing. *That* I could swallow. But that he called *you* a slut and a whore was another. I couldn't very well let him do that and do nothing about it, could I?"

"Oh, Hershel! Oh, Hershel!" Ruth cried out softly. Slowly she walked up to him and laid her head against his chest. "I'm glad you didn't let him call me bad names. Hershel, I'm glad you're here." Her voice broke on the last few words.

Awkwardly Hershel put his arms around her. It was then, with tears in her eyes, that Eve knew it was going to be all right between them. And most likely, sooner or later, she'd hear from Miriam and Hannah.

Dora opened the door, and called out, "It's Hannah and Miriam . . . without any bundles, but they're wearing their wigs and their fancy dresses!"

Elated that they had finally come calling, Eve came running with Ruth close behind her. But hurt that they hadn't come before, she said, "Who are these strangers, Ruth?"

Ruth looked them up and down. "I'm not sure who they are. But they're certainly very dressed up."

"So? Very funny," Hannah said. "But are we going to be standing out here all day or are we going to be asked in? This is a formal call, after all. The least we expect is a glass of tea . . ."

"Well, come in," Eve said. "But I don't know if you *deserve* a glass of tea. Perhaps you'll explain what took you so long."

Hannah waved a hand at her before she kissed her. "Now, Evele, you know we had to wait until things settled down. It would have made things difficult for Abraham and Shlomo if we came before . . . It was just a matter of time. Certainly we were going to come visit, sooner or later.''

"So, all right, already. Now it's sooner," Ruth said. "So how come we're being honored today?''

"You're being so honored because Chaim made us come . . . That's why you're being so honored.''

"How did he make you come?'' Eve asked.

"So tell them already," Miriam said, "so we can have our tea. I'm sure they have a little something to go along with it.''

Hannah took a deep breath before beginning. "After Hershel left the house to come here Chaim said that he was forbidding everyone who lived in his house ever to speak to anyone living in *this* house. Well, for me that did it! Remember, Eve, when we spoke of that moment that comes to all men and women? That moment when they won't stand one more push? Well, that moment came to me and I stood up and told Chaim that while we were staying with him because our husbands chose to, and we were staying with our husbands because it was our duty, it didn't mean that he could tell us how to live. I told Chaim that short of killing me he couldn't stop me from talking to whomever I wanted, and since I wasn't dead yet, I intended to come calling on you this very day!''

"Then I said I was going with her too," Miriam interjected. "And it all seemed easier to say things, things that were sitting here on my chest.'' She touched herself. "Like when he hit my Becky, knocking her down. So I told him about that too. I told him that if he ever laid a hand again on my girls I'd be leaving for good. It was a surprise to me that I could say a thing like that to Chaim . . .''

"Oh my!'' Eve's eyes sparkled. "And what did Chaim say to that?''

Hannah laughed. "That's the best part. Chaim turned to Abraham and asked him what he was going to do about me? What was he going to do about his big-mouthed wife? Well, it seemed then that Abraham's big moment had come too because he told Chaim that he couldn't, and wouldn't even if he could, tell me to whom I could talk, that I was a grown woman with a mind of my own, a mind that he, Abraham, respected.''

"Oh Hannah, how wonderful!''

"Then Shlomo spoke up too, didn't he Hannah? And he also told Chaim that I was a grown woman with a mind of my own . . .''

"And then—?'' Eve was leaning forward in anticipation.

"And what?'' Hannah asked innocently.

"Hannah, I warn you. If you don't hurry and tell me what Chaim did then, I'll explode.''

"He sat down! That's what he did. He sat down as if the wind had been knocked out of him. Then Abraham said to him, and I repeat loosely since I can't remember every word—''

"Yes? Go on!''

134

"Abraham said, 'Father, I've been meaning to talk with you and now seems as good a time as any. My youngest brother, David, went off to live by himself, to be independent of any man and to run his own business. Then my next youngest brother, Yacob, joined him. Also an independent man. And now Hershel. That leaves me, the oldest by many years without a home that's my own, a business or a kopeck of my own. That goes for Shlomo too. Now Father, I don't want to leave you to be alone and I speak for Shlomo too, and we won't. But at the same time, we must have an equal share of the profits. And we must be able to regard this house as our own too. That means you can't order our wives around either or speak to them in a manner that is not respectful, if you get my meaning . . .' "

Hannah paused dramatically and Eve tugged at her hand. "Go on!"

"Go on what?"

"Hannah, I warn you— What happened then? What did Chaim say?"

"He didn't! He didn't say one word. He just went off to bed. He didn't scream and rage and he didn't curse and he didn't say *no!* So, Evele, like those Americans you're so fond of, I think we've won the revolution!"

11.

Eve passed her eighteenth birthday. With the matter of Chaim and his reign of terror, as she referred to it, apparently settled, she looked forward to the birth of her baby and Dora's. The future really looked bright for the Family Markoff and for the children to come.

She left the manor house that day with an order for a third maternity dress. Not only was the Countess delighted with her gowns but she had also asked Eve to start work on a layette for her expected child. For the first time the Countess had offered Eve tea, a very lavish tea. Yes, things were going well, Eve reflected, far better than she had anticipated, and her anticipations were always high to start with. Even the business was going well. While the brothers weren't getting rich certainly, they were managing to do enough business to feed the household, pay the rent on their house, and have a few kopecks left over at the end of the week to divide up among the three families.

As she walked, Eve could see the peasants working in the fields now that the ice and snow was gone except for those places well hidden from the increasingly warming sun. When she neared that part in the road where the fort held sway overhead, Eve crossed over as had become her custom each time she walked home from the manor house. She did this each time since she had no idea of the exact day when the supply wagon made its monthly visit to the fort—she hadn't actually seen the wagon since that first time. She searched the ground each time she came by to see if anything had dropped from the wagon for her to discover. Today she saw nothing—not a potato, not a beet or cabbage, and she turned to go on. But then she glimpsed *something* in the ditch, something mostly covered by a bit of remaining snow slush, here where the icy drifts had mounted so high one could have imagined they reached almost to the heavens which had first strewn them. She clambered down to investigate further, forgetting that she'd soil her skirts badly. The second her fingertips touched the soft leather pouch her heart leaped then fluttered. . . .

"Three hundred rubles!" David repeated in awe. He had never even heard of such a sum, much less seen it. "But what? Where?"

"I can only imagine that it must have been the monthly pay for the soldiers quartered there—"

"And fell out of the wagon? Does that make sense to you?"

"It's the only answer I can come up with."

"But surely they know the money's missing? It's impossible that they don't!"

"Of course they had to realize it was missing when they didn't find it on the wagon, but the point is it must be missing a long time already. The pouch was all but covered with snow. And almost everywhere else the snow's been gone for two, three weeks already, which means the pouch must have been covered by the first snowfall and covered more deeply each time snow fell, six, even seven months ago. The search for the missing money must be over, forgotten by now."

"Maybe we'd better give it back, Eve . . ."

"No, we can't do that. First of all, they'd never believe we found it. They'd say that since we're crafty Jews, we managed somehow to steal it, but since all Jews are also cowardly, we became frightened and decided to give it back. No, David, we can't take that chance."

"No, I guess you're right. But what will we do with it? We can't spend it. If we spent three hundred rubles, *someone* would be bound to get suspicious."

"No, we won't spend it. Not yet, anyway, and not ever all at once. We'll keep it and spend it slowly. Or rather, dispense it slowly."

"What do you mean—*dispense?*"

"You won't laugh at me if I tell you something?"

He laughed right then and there. "I've learned *never* to laugh at you."

"David, I really think that money *was sent* for me to find."

"Really? And by whom was it sent, may I ask?"

"You *are* laughing at me and you haven't even heard me out. I don't say it was God specifically. But somehow that very first day, when I saw the wagon climbing the hill to the fort, it came to me that if I kept on searching the ground all around there, some day I'd find something truly wonderful. And now I have! David, I'm sure I was meant to find that money and with a purpose! Not for us to use for ourselves but whenever there's a good reason—to feed the hungry or if, say, there was an impoverished carpenter who had no tools. We could buy him some so he could make his living. Or maybe if it becomes necessary to grease an official's palm for whatever reason. Oh David, I'm sure of it! I was *meant* to find that money!"

He looked at her amused and bemused and wondered why he had been lucky enough to have found *her*. "Are you sure you're really Elijah Brodkin's daughter?"

She laughed. "Why? Who do you think I am?"

"I'm not sure. Some lovely princess from some mystical land. Or maybe just a beautiful, crazy Russian gypsy . . ."

"Ah, if I'm a beautiful princess then you're my beautiful prince. And if I'm a crazy, beautiful gypsy then you're my beautiful man. Come here and I'll tell your fortune and there will be no need to cross my palm with silver. For you, beautiful man of destiny, it's all for free."

This was the second time she had called him that—man of destiny. The first time, when she had sent him with the book of commentaries to settle the question of the needle in the cow's stomach, he had asked her then to explain the term and she had said it referred to a man who was predestined to make the world a better place. Now, hearing the words again, he *knew* that it was the other way around—this incredible magical girl was the one who had the great gift of making the world a better place to be, the very, very, best place to be, and it was his luck that he had found her.

A week later the Russian world was in an uproar. The Tsar Alexander II, the greatest reformer Russia had ever known, was dead—murdered! And who was responsible? Greedy ingrates not satisfied with the progressive reforms made in their behalf—workers, peasants, the always scheming malevolent Jews! What was needed was a return to harsher times and punitive measures.

Accordingly, in all the towns where Jews lived the shops and stalls were closed down by the Jews themselves as a precautionary step, and all those usually engaged in dealings with the gentiles stayed home behind locked doors and gave themselves over to prayer. They prayed not for Alexander's soul but for their own salvation, and waited for the bad time to pass.

But Slobodka was not one of the towns slated to be spared by divine intervention. The night came when they heard the hoofbeats of many Cossacks riding on many horses. There was nothing to do but huddle together for comfort, in bed and in corners, and mumble more prayers, this time praying only that the hoofbeats wouldn't falter and come to a halt at their door.

Through the windows they saw the night lit up by orange flames. Immediately David pulled on his boots.

"David!" Eve screamed. "What are you doing?"

"Somebody's house is on fire! Some miserable wretch needs help, not prayers!"

"No!" Eve wailed. "You can't help. Not tonight. Nobody can help tonight. I won't let you go!"

"But you said I was a man of destiny," he offered bitterly. "It's never been true. I've never been that but tonight I will be!"

"No, you won't! You'll just be dead! Dead! Our baby will be an orphan before it's born. And for what? What can one man do? One man against fifty Cossacks? A hundred Cossacks? They'll cut you down with their swords before you go twenty feet and you'll accomplish nothing!"

"I don't care! If I kill one Cossack before I die, it'll be worth it!"

"But how will you kill even one Cossack? You don't even have a weapon. What will you take? A kitchen knife? You'll never even get near enough to the Cossack that slices off your head to use that knife. Can't you see? It's not your night. Wait until it is, when at least you'll accomplish something by fighting back, even by dying. If you die tonight, you'll die for nothing." But not sure this time that her words would work, she threw herself against the door barring his way, calling out for Yacob and Hershel to hold him back forcibly.

When the night grew quiet again David went out with his brothers to find that it wasn't some family's house that had burned but the town's House of Worship. The demonstration had only been a minor punitive action, a warning. In the morning the townspeople went about congratulating each other for having had their collective lives spared and thanking God for His mercy. That their Temple had been destroyed? What was new about that? They would rebuild as they had for centuries.

"We'll give a few rubles from the three hundred toward rebuilding the synagogue," Eve told David. "Not more, or everyone will wonder where we got it."

"Give the money!" David said with so much venom it broke her heart. "Let them rebuild! But I won't enter it! I'm through with synagogues and prayers!"

"But David," Eve protested. "We have to go on having faith!"

"Why? And faith in whom? They call us the Chosen People. No! That's not true! *We* call *ourselves* the Chosen People and *they* call us *drek!* But what were we chosen for? You tell me, Eve. What did God choose us for?"

Oh, she had answers for him. Words, words from the Torah and the Talmud, words that wouldn't mean anything to him now. What answers could she herself give him from her heart? But her answers wouldn't mean anything to him. Not now. She had failed him. When she had first come to live with him she had promised him manhood if he stood up to his father. And he had—he had stood up to Chaim and gone off with her on his own. A man, certainly! But she had prevented him from standing up to *them*, the true oppressors who made Chaim a mere puddle in a raging flood. Had she stripped David of his manhood for all the time to come? He seemed to have lost faith in everything—in God, in himself, in his Jewishness, maybe even in her as well.

12.

Although Eve had always known deep in her heart that Russian life could never be sweetly peaceful, even golden, she had allowed herself to dream of it. But after the night of the pogrom, she could no longer even fantasize about it. If she permitted herself to daydream at all about a beautiful world, it was a fantasy that excluded the bitter reality of Russian life altogether. Still, life was to be lived to its fullest, and she was determined to be cheerfully optimistic even within the confines of Mother Russia as it truly existed. It was into this Russia, after all, that she would soon deliver her child. Early fall, a lovely time of year.

The late August day was hot and the road to the manor house dry and dusty. The only thing that refreshed Eve at all was the sight of the giant sunflowers blanketing the land. She had almost decided not to go to the Countess at all that day since she knew the trudge would be exhausting. But the Countess was even closer to giving birth than she herself, and since she had just finished the last of the tiny garments that made up the Countess's expected baby's layette, she had decided to make the special effort to deliver the baby clothes. Most likely the Countess would think to send her home in the carriage.

Over the months they had become friends, as friendly as a Squire's wife who was a Countess to boot and a humble Jewish seamstress could be. The Count was away frequently and the Countess was lonely with only her servants for company. There'd been a sound basis for a certain intimacy between them. They were both young and with child and with a penchant for fashion and laughter and stories. And they shared an interest in art and literature. The Countess was hungry for a little knowledgeable conversation, and Eve avid for the juicy and lengthy tales of a sophisticated world she had only read about—balls at the Tsar's palace, picturesque descriptions of Venice and Paris and St. Petersburg, of exotic people and grand revelries. Eve had soon realized that the first negative impression she had had of the Countess was erroneous, although there were *some* negative qualities, the worst of which was a shallowness, an unawareness of anything that didn't revolve around her and her immediate circle, which was more a natural consequence of her birth and subsequent station in life than of any real meanness. As for these less-than-attractive characteristics, was there really that much of a difference between those of the Squire's lady and the women Eve was more familiar with? Wasn't everyone only concerned with his own life and affairs?

140

Once in front of the manor house, Eve decided to throw caution to the wind and knocked on the front door. She was simply too tired to walk another step, to go all the way around to the back door. If that Truska scolded her, let her! That disagreeable wretch couldn't scold her too severely since Eve *had* earned certain privileges in the household. As a matter of fact, she planned on demanding liquid refreshment the moment she entered instead of waiting demurely to be asked.

Yes, it was Truska herself who came to the door, her round face red and perspiring, looking *especially* glum and cross—she who normally had an unpleasant cast to her expression. "Oh, it's you! Go away! The boy is ill!" She crossed herself. "He won't last the day."

"Constantin? Oh, my God, I'm so sorry! What is it?" Eve had become fond of the boy whom she had seen frequently on her visits.

Truska wrapped her hands around her throat in a dramatic gesture. "He's very sick. He can't breathe. The Doctor's been here day and night, but he left this morning. Now only the priest is here!" she said angrily as if somehow this was Eve's fault.

"I'll go . . . I'll leave this . . ." She held out the package. "Please . . . Tell the Countess how sorry I am. Tell her I'll pray for Constantin."

Truska grabbed the package, started to close the door. Then Eve heard the Countess's voice, frantic and high-pitched with hysteria. "Who's there, Truska?"

"It's only the Jewish seamstress, my lady. Don't concern yourself. I sent her away."

"Eve? Tell her to come in! I want to see her!"

Eve turned around. The Countess was in the doorway, her huge belly so extended it seemed she'd topple from its weight.

"Eve! It's my little boy. It's my Constantin!"

"I'm so sorry."

"He can't breathe! It's the diphtheria!"

Diphtheria! Eve's instinctive impulse was to run.

The Countess beckoned her in. Her hair was in complete disarray, her dressing gown soiled and rumpled. "I'm going mad! And my husband isn't here!"

Eve could only think of the contagion. *Diphtheria the killer!*

"Father Gregory came this morning but the doctor's gone!"

Eve knew she had to get away and quickly. She had to think of her own baby. The manor house wasn't a place for a Jewish girl, not with a priest in attendance, with the crosses and the icons, with death so close by. Who knew how these people would react if death arrived while she was present?

"I'd better go, Countess. I don't want to bother you at a time like this. I'll come back when little Constantin's better."

"I don't think he's going to get better, Eve," she said piteously. "Even the doctor's left. He said Constantin's in the hands of the Heavenly Father now . . . I've sent for my husband but who knows when he'll get here? I'm frightened. I'm going crazy! You must come in and stay with me. Talk to me! I have no

141

one here with me except Father Gregory and he's with Constantin. I can't go back in there, Eve, I can't. You must come in!''

No! I don't have to! It's not my place!

But she looked into the Countess Sophia's imploring eyes. They were wet and tortured and pleading, no longer the eyes of the haughty woman Eve had encountered on their first meeting. Now she was any ordinary woman, now she was only any anguished mother, helplessly watching her child slip away. She was only another human being in need of comfort. *Can I refuse her?* Would she refuse any one of her sisters-in-law? If God and death itself made no distinction between Countess Sophia and the Markoff women, could she? The Countess, who had offered her as much friendship as she was capable of, was now as much a hostage to the capriciousness of fate as the lowliest of peasants, as the most long-suffering Jew.

Eve stepped into the house.

''I can't go back in there, Eve . . . The poor baby . . . His throat's so swollen he can't breathe. He just lies there unmoving as if death had already come . . . His face is black . . .''

Black? The throat distended? An image formed in Eve's mind. Old ladies with scarves on their heads . . . a small child with a blackened face . . . an engorged throat. Motionless as if already dead.

Yes, she remembered. *But can I? If I make the attempt and the child dies, they'll point a finger at me. I know it! God, I know it as surely as I stand here! They'll accuse me of killing him! Even the Countess will!*

But how could she not?

''Truska! Get salt herring and vodka! Hurry!'' Eve commanded.

The woman was startled, hostile. ''Salt herring?''

''Yes! You must have some salt herring in the house.''

''Yes, of course. The servants eat it but what do you want with it?''

''Tell her to get it and the vodka!'' Eve told the Countess.

The Countess stared at Eve, turned to the servant. ''Don't stand there!'' she screamed. ''Run!''

Father Gregory was a huge man with a long black beard, towering and terrifying. ''He is going to God!'' he intoned and shielded the bedside from Eve.

The Countess heaved herself at him, forestalling interference. ''Let her be!''

The priest stepped back, continued to chant, acted as if they weren't there at all.

Eve tore off a piece of the herring, then thrust the rest of the fish at Truska. ''Tear it into pieces!'' Then she forced the dark-faced, comatose boy's mouth open and pushed the hunk of herring she had ripped off into his mouth and forced it down his throat with her fingers, following with the vodka, pouring it straight from the bottle into the mouth even as it spilled over the boy's face, everywhere. She did it again and again, first the herring, then the liquid, over and over again, a chunk of the salt fish, then the burning liquid, sticking her fingers in, jamming it all down.

"There's a ball there in his throat, membranes, mucus, pus, an accumulation not letting him breathe . . ."

Then the boy started choking, an explosion of choking. He choked and coughed and sputtered, startled back to life from the brine and the fiery liquid. He choked and coughed until it all erupted, streaming from his mouth—water, pus, blood, mucus. It all came spewing out and he breathed.

Two coachmen brought Eve home in the Count's carriage. She was already in the first stages of labor—her water had broken on the way. David shoved the coachmen aside. He didn't want them touching Eve. They had done enough. He and his brothers carried her into the house and into her bed. As Dora and Ruth undressed her, Yacob ran to fetch Hannah and Miriam.

David, sitting at the kitchen table, swore to his brothers that if God and the goyim had exchanged his baby's life, or his Eve's, for the Count's son, he'd make them pay—he'd make them all pay.

But several hours later Eve gave birth to her son, Yitzhak, apparently none the worse for his premature entrance into the world. The boy was named for David's mother Yetta whom he had never known.

The Count in his regimental uniform and with many medals spread across his chest came calling himself to inform Eve that the Countess Sophia had given birth to a girl who was to be called Alexandra Evangelina in Eve's honor. Eve was very pleased yet at the same time she couldn't help thinking how different a story it would have been had little Constantin not lived despite the same efforts on her part.

Proudly she showed the Count her son born on the night Constantin had rejoined the living. "The Countess will be pleased, Madam Markoff, when I tell her that Yitzhak Markoff is a fine, vigorous boy. She has told me to tell you that she looks forward with all her heart to seeing you soon, and of course, I, too, bear you eternal gratitude. We are both in your debt. But it isn't enough to voice gratitude; it behooves one to show it. My wife told me that you are a dealer in livestock, David Markoff, so I have used my influence to obtain a government contract for you, sir. You will supply horses and cattle for His Imperial Highness's forces. This means, of course, that you will be under his protection—"

Eve and David exchanged amazed looks. *Under the Tsar's protection! An official contract to supply the Tsar's army!*

"Also," the Squire continued, "since you'll need more property with room to keep the animals as you do business, it will be arranged for you to have a parcel of land large enough for this purpose."

Did he mean that they'd actually hold title to this land?

The idea was almost too enormous for David to grasp. He wished desperately that he could confer with Eve alone, to hear her thoughts on the matter. But the Count was already tapping his thigh with his crop impatiently, waiting to be showered with thanks and their gratitude so he could be off.

No, he couldn't wait to speak with Eve. The moment was now and the decision was his. All Eve had ever demanded of him was that he be a man.

He cleared his throat, found his voice. "We thank you, sir. We are overwhelmed, even astounded." He struggled to find the proper Russian words. "Isn't that so, Eve?"

She nodded her head, her eyes focused only on David. "Oh yes, Count, we thank you."

Under the Tsar's protection—what seductive words.

She heard David speak. "The fact of the matter, Squire, is that while your offer is very generous, we cannot accept . . ."

Now the Squire was astonished. *These people! Who would ever understand them? But of course, this husband's only a boy, in spite of that long yellow beard. He doesn't realize . . . She's only a girl but a very capable one, bright and sensible . . .*

He turned to Eve, "Madam?"

She was looking only at David and her pride was showing. *Oh David! The devil with the Tsar and his protection! I know you're my only security.*

"Yes, Squire, that is our decision . . ."

For moments the Squire's annoyance warred with his amusement at the ridiculous notion of having to talk these people into accepting what amounted to a prize of a lifetime, even for non-Jews. "May I ask why you're refusing? Is it possible that you don't have a full realization of what's being offered you? What it will mean to you and your family? Wealth, for one thing . . ."

Eve could no longer contain herself. "That's part of it, sir. We can't accept a reward for saving little Constantin's life. Saving a life is a reward in itself, a great privilege that's accorded very few people. It's a privilege that will reserve us a place in heaven—"

Jews! An impossible race, just as everyone said. A stiff-necked people!

"That's a very admirable attitude and all very well, but I think you're being foolhardy. Both of you are extremely young and with much to learn about the world. I suggest you take the advice of an older man, one better situated in life, shall we say? Never look a gift horse in the mouth and always grab with both hands all that's offered you."

David was embarrassed. Sheepishly he said, "I beg the Squire's pardon but you see, it's not so much a matter of accepting that which is being offered. It's more of what I'd be giving up. If I accepted your offer I'd be an employee of the Tsar and now I'm my own master and beholden to no man."

"I wonder if that's ever true, David Markoff, for any man. But so be it. All I can offer you then are my thanks and my eternal gratitude. *I*, you see, will always be beholden to Madam Markoff."

He held out his hand for Eve's, took it and brought it to his lips. Then he offered his hand to David. "There is one more small thing. I have instructions from the Countess to inquire which day would be most convenient for the two of you and your son to call. I've been told not to take my leave until an hour and day have been set so that she may send the carriage for you. . . ."

After the Squire left Eve turned to David, feeling the desire for him in all the parts of her body, the taste of desire even on her tongue. In all the time they had been married she had never felt it as strong. It was as if all of her was aching for him with an urgency . . . and they were all alone except for their son sleeping in his cradle.

Mutely she went to him. She looked into his eyes. Everything she was feeling she saw mirrored there. She put her arms around him, felt his desire for her in the tension of his body against hers.

He picked her up and carried her into their bedroom, at the same time whispering endearments in her ear. As he undressed her, her body arched and moved to help him, and then when she was completely undressed, it moved and arched to meet his.

Fleetingly she thought of the Law that forbids the communion of man and woman when a wife was nursing, the Law that proclaims a nursing mother unclean. That Law had to be written by man and not God, written by someone who knew nothing of the passion of the body, and neither of the spirit, and was wrong! She was sure that God in His heaven knew this moment was right!

13.

With the birth of her son and David's subsequent refusal to accept the Count's astonishing offer, Eve realized that not only had David truly matured into the man she had always dreamed of, but that both she and he had finally left childhood behind, and with it all innocence. With that leaving had come a true emergence of their adult love for one another, as demanding as it was strong, as demanding as life itself. The question Eve pondered was, did love, as life, demand too much? But even as she pondered, she knew the answer.

It was a strange autumn that year. While the days were exceedingly cold the snows were late in coming and the sun shone for a few hours almost every day, day in and day out, clear and crisp in a cloudless sky. Eve wondered if the unusual weather was a good omen or not. But whether it was or not, her son seemed to take his cue from the yellow disk in the sky; his nature was unusually sunny as he gurgled and cooed, content at Eve's breast.

When she wasn't nursing, Eve sewed endlessly. There was the special layette she had promised Dora whose time was drawing close, and there were the orders that kept flowing without interruption from the Countess—now a gown for herself, then a special tiny dress for the infant, Alexandra Evangelina, or a pinafore for the Countess's older daughter. Some weeks the Countess would send the carriage for Eve and then the coachman would wait while Eve readied herself and her son whom she had to take with her since he had to be nursed. Then she'd spend the day with the Countess, fitting a gown, discussing the next one. On those days when there was a finished article to be delivered and the carriage didn't arrive, Eve stayed at home with Yitzhak and sent Dora in her place. Dora didn't mind the long walk. The truth was she so adored going to the manor house, she would have walked twice as far since the Countess treated her as grandly as she treated Eve herself, setting out the loveliest tea.

Dora insisted on describing the teas in detail to Ruth each time anew although by this time Ruth knew them by heart. The Countess herself poured very black tea from a baroque silver teapot, Dora would relate, then dispensed lumps of sugar with ornate silver tongs, proffered cream so thick it coated the sides of the fancifully engraved pitcher. Or did she prefer lemon slices? Slices so thin as to be almost transparent. And the teacups—delicate as rose petals and decorated with painted flowers of the most beautiful hues—pink and mauve and lavender. There were tiny sandwiches, each one with a different filling and fashioned of bread that was marvelously white. Imagine—white bread! And the pastries and *petits fours* iced in many different colors, some even decorated with ribbons of chocolate!

"And what do you talk about with the Countess while you have this marvelous tea?" Ruth would ask, enjoying Dora's pleasure.

"Oh, many things. The weather. The children. Hers of course, since my child isn't born yet. But the Countess is so kind—she shares all her little secrets about raising children with me. For example, she told me that once in a while one must taste one's own milk to make sure it hasn't gone sour— You must do that too, Eve." And Eve assured her she would.

"It all sounds wonderful," Ruth would say and occasionally, her cheeks getting very pink, Dora would ask Ruth if she wanted to go in her place on those occasions when she herself was substituting for Eve. Both Ruth and Eve knew this offer was made in the spirit of highest sacrifice since these visits to the manor house were a highlight in Dora's simple life. But it was a sacrifice Ruth wouldn't have dreamed of allowing Dora to make even if she were interested in visiting the manor house, which she most definitely wasn't. Far from it!

Ruth had become consumed with her new passion—books! Once Eve had taught her the rudiments of reading, there had been no stopping her. She had practiced and labored while Eve sat with her helping and encouraging, and ultimately rejoicing with her, and now Ruth could scarcely wait for free minutes to get to a book. She was reading in Yiddish but Eve had promised that soon she'd also master Russian. And after Russian? Perhaps they'd even learn English together. All Ruth knew was that God had been very good to her when He had sent Eve. Even all the hours spent on so many endless chores—how good these hours were as she and Eve discussed and talked as they worked. Wonderful discussions. Talk of life and philosophy, of the world and history, of famous people, even religion. What possible attraction could the manor house hold for her compared with that?

"Oh, no!" she'd answer Dora. "Who has the time? I have the children to look after, if nothing else. And you might as well take advantage now before you have a dozen children to look after yourself."

And Dora would sigh with relief. Even after she had her baby, if and when Eve would send her in her place, she'd carry the child in her arms just to go there. She'd go even if the snow covered the ground as long as it wasn't actually falling. If it were falling, naturally she wouldn't expose a baby to that. Especially if it were a girl since girls were more delicate. Secretly she yearned for a girl but she wouldn't tell anyone that since Yacob wanted a son . . . *expected a son*. But since it wasn't snowing and she was yet to give birth, what could be more wonderful than drinking tea with the Countess?

"Now, if the Countess doesn't offer to send you home in her carriage you must be sure to leave long before it gets dark," Eve instructed Dora. "And you must be sure to leave in time to walk slowly and to rest when you get tired. It's good for you to walk since they say that some exertion provides for an easier delivery, but it's not good for you to get overtired. So promise me you'll leave early enough and you'll rest by the roadside when you tire. If you don't I'm not going to let you go.''

''I promise! I promise, Eve. I *want* to do everything that's good for the baby.'' She draped a shawl over her wig and then wrapped the ends around her throat. She wore a bearskin coat over the special maternity dress Eve had made for her; it was bright yellow as she had requested. ''How do I look?''

''Lovely. Lovely enough not only to visit the Countess but to visit a queen! But if the weather should change suddenly, if it looks nasty and the Countess doesn't offer you a ride home in the carriage—she doesn't think sometimes— you must ask for a ride home. You tell her that *I* said you should ask since your baby is due shortly.''

''I will. You mustn't worry about me so.'' Dora was almost out the door before she remembered the package she was to deliver, the reason for her going in the first place. She came back to get it, blew kisses at Eve, at Ruth, at baby Yitzhak in his cradle, at Gershon sucking his thumb. ''Don't let him suck his thumb, Ruth! The Countess says it will make his teeth grow in crooked.''

The weather *had* changed. The sun had disappeared only an hour or so after noon, leaving the day not only colder but particularly gray and bleak. It looked as if the snow would fall at any moment and the night would come early, and still there was no sign of Dora, either on foot or by carriage, no matter how many times they opened the door to look.

''But she promised she'd ask for a ride—'' Ruth said, trying to assuage the anxieties both she and Eve felt as the minutes crept by and the day grew darker. ''Surely at any minute now the Squire's carriage will arrive. Most likely it's that; knowing that she'd be riding, she waited until the last minute to leave. I'm sure that's it—''

''I wish I was so sure. And I wish the men would come home with the wagon so that we could go look for her.'' Then unable to bear the wait any longer Eve said, ''I think I'll walk down the road a bit . . .''

''No,'' Ruth protested. ''Before you know it, we'll have to go looking for you too.''

''I'll just go a little way; Yitzhak is still asleep.'' Eve put on a jacket, a coat, a layer of scarves and opened the door. Then they both saw her, Stasia, the old peasant woman who often came to the door to beg a bit of food. But this time she was holding out something herself—*something wrapped in Dora's bearskin coat!*

They both ran the few feet to meet her.

''Here—'' the old woman stretched out her arms. ''I brought you the little one. She's still breathing! I delivered her myself,'' she said, mournfully proud. ''See, I bit the cord— These old teeth are still good for something.'' She grimaced, showing three or four yellow stumps. ''And I've kept the little one warm.''

As if in a trance Ruth took the bundle of fur and flesh. She and Eve looked down at the infant still covered with the fluids of birth, its tiny face screwed up in displeasure at the world it had come into.

Eve tore her eyes away from the baby, looked piteously into the peasant woman's wrinkled face. "Dora? Where is she? She must be very cold without her coat, poor thing, very cold . . ." Her eyes begged to be told that it was indeed so, that Dora was cold and in need of warmth, that mere warmth would solve Dora's problems . . .

But the old woman shook her head. "She's cold but no coat will warm her . . ."

Eve's scream rent the cold, still air. "Where is she?"

"She's lying in the road. Near the fort."

"When did she go into labor? Were you there from the start?"

"Yes, I was hiding—"

"Hiding?" Eve screamed again. "Why were you hiding?"

The old woman shook her head. "It was two of them from the fort. Two crazy drunken sons of whores," she said without rancor. "When I saw what they were doing to her I had to hide or they would have killed me sure as not."

"Oh my God!" Ruth wailed. "Oh my God."

"Let her finish," Eve said, like a stone now.

"From her screaming I could tell the baby was coming—even as they were doing it to her, one after the other, may their accursed cocks wither and drop off, one after the other. After they were gone, I ran out to her. I could see the baby's head already . . . But I think she herself had already gone to the other world."

Oh, Dora! Dora! They've snuffed out your sweet light!

"Take Dora's daughter in the house, Ruth. She has to be cleaned. When I return I'll put her to the breast."

It was dark and still out on the road. The only sound that could be heard was the sudden cracking of a frozen limb of a black, bare tree, then a thud as it hit the ground. Dora's torn, blood-soaked, bright flower-yellow dress struck an incongruous note in the harsh dusk. Dora's yellow wig, lying two or three feet away—another absurdity, but no more so than the still innocent face resting on one cheek in the dirt, the skin luminously pale. Eve took off her layers of scarves and covered Dora, then seated herself down at the edge of the road to cradle Dora's head in her lap, her fingers smoothing the short silky threads of Dora's silvery, shining hair.

"Dora! Dora! How will we all live without you?"

She closed her eyes.

"Loheyn baal horahamim yastireh-hol beseser k'nofov leolomim, ve'itzror bitzror hahaymim es nishmosoh, Adonoy hoo nahalohsoh, vesohnuah besholom al mishkovoh venomar omain . . ." But saying the prayer in Hebrew did not satisfy her, it wasn't enough. Would anything be enough? She began again: "Oh God, full of compassion who dwellest on high, grant perfect rest beneath the sheltering wings of Thy divine presence among the holy pure who shine as the brightness of the firmament, to Dora who has gone to her eternal home."

She broke down as pictures flooded her mind. And words that still echoed, echoed. Dora running to help her serve the children despite Chaim's fierce glowering . . . Dora . . .

Dora, seeing the plum taffeta fabric that would make up her new dress: "I could die without ever having anything so beautiful again . . ." Was Dora dead before she brought forth her little girl? *Oh God, did Dora know that she had delivered beauty out of filth?*

Dora, talking of Chaim to her and the other women. "I'd rather *he* was angry with me than all of you. I'd die if all of you were mad at me."

But you've died, sweet Dora, and not one of us was ever mad at you.

Dora, when they were talking of going to Vilno to see the Wonder Rabbi. "If *you* go with me, Eve, I just know the miracle will happen."

Yes, you always trusted me and yet it was I who put you on this road to be defiled and murdered! I! I sent you to that selfish, thoughtless woman who I knew might neglect to offer you a ride home in her carriage. And who knows? Perhaps, unknowingly, I made some kind of a bargain with the devil when I saved that woman's son's life—a Russian devil's bargain which demanded your life for his. Perhaps, unwittingly, I signed this pact in blood . . . Yours . . .

Dora, arriving at the new house. "Eve! We're here!" As if "here" were heaven . . .

Yes, it was I who promised you heaven, a sanctuary. But somehow, I promised falsely.

"Our babies will be more brothers, or sisters, than cousins. Just as you and I are more sisters than sisters-in-law . . ."

Yes, you were my sister. And I so arrogantly planned to be my sister's keeper. So arrogantly I planned on making life for you the lovely tea party you thought it was. Oh, Dora, I tried! But I couldn't! Not here in this godforsaken land. I failed and it's such a bitter failure, it's so hard to go on . . . and your daughter. Oh, I'll try to take better care of her than I did you, Little Sister.

Eve bent her head to kiss the cold-as-death forehead and as she did, the snow that had waited all day to fall finally began to float down.

"I'm going now, Dora. I must feed your daughter from my breast. Babies come into the world so hungry and all we can do is try to feed them so that we can send them out into the world strong enough to bear it.

"We'll be back soon to retrieve what remains of you here on earth. Oh, Dora, my sweet Dora . . ." she began to sob now. "I only hope you're in a place where there will be lots of lovely tea parties . . ."

The flakes of snow were coming down more rapidly. Already Dora's cold form was thinly covered with it. Dora was not even to be spared this final indignity.

Eve got to her feet, almost falling, to look up into the charcoal sky divesting itself of its frigid burden. Slowly she raised her arm making a fist and shook it, shook it at the cold heavens. "Oh, you accursed Mother Russia! You're a devil! A witch! A blackhearted whore!"

14.

Right from the beginning, when Yitzhak was still very young, Eve realized that he was never going to be a good student as little Dorie was, as Ruth's sons were. Especially Gershon who seemed to excel at everything. And Hannah and Abraham's son, Joshua, was so good at his Hebrew studies it was decided he should go to the yeshiva for further study. But if she was frustrated at Yitzhak's seeming inaptitude for learning and obvious disinterest in any Judaic custom, she never showed it. The only times she openly displayed her vexation with him was on those occasions when he plainly disobeyed, slipping away from his studies to horse around in the village with those boys of a similar inclination. While David chastened his son for disobeying his mother, he told her in private, "Why upset yourself? You know you can lead a horse to water but you can't make him drink. I guess he's a chip off the Markoff block and not the Brodkin. You can't fight it, Eve, he's going to be the strong, brawny type, not the studious and brainy."

"I guess so. But the important thing is, he *is* a happy boy and so good-natured." Still, she tried to impress on him even when he was yet very young that the important thing to remember was who he was and what kind of a man he wanted to be when he was all grown up. Young as he was, Yitzhak already knew what kind of man that was—one that resembled his father. He was sure in his heart that was also the kind of man his mother wanted him to be.

One other thing Yitzhak grew up knowing—that it was his mother's dream to go to America as soon as possible. She often told him how life would be in America. It was always a happy kind of story. And he heard her say many times how terrible it was to waste all the days of their lives in a land of fear, repression and death. He didn't understand exactly what she was talking about, but he did understand that life in America wouldn't be the least like it was in Russia.

In the months following Dora's death Eve started to think of time and life in terms of years . . . would link events with the years in which they occurred.

She and David had been married in 1880 as the year was drawing to a close. 1881 was the year Yitzhak had been born, Dora had died, Dorie had come into the world. That was also the year she swore to herself that she and her family were going to America . . . as soon as possible.

In the beginning Eve had several reasons for not leaving immediately—reasons and obligations. There was her father whose health was worsening, day by day. And there was the secret cache of the three hundred rubles. She still felt those rubles had been entrusted to her keeping by a higher force, to be dispensed only under extraordinary circumstances. When those rubles were gone, only then could they themselves be gone. There was Dora's daughter to think of— Hadn't she vowed to an already dead Dora that she'd care for Dorie not as a niece but as if she were her own daughter? And there was Ruth who was experiencing a kind of rebirth, a cultural awakening. How could she abandon Ruth when there was a very strong possibility that if she and David left for America, Hershel's spirit of independence would falter? It was very possible that both Hershel and Yacob would go scurrying back to resume their former place under Chaim's thumb. Then, not only would Ruth end up in Chaim's household again, but little Dorie too . . .

What Eve hoped to do, given a little time, was to convince Yacob and Hershel to go to America with her and David and Yitzhak. There was no need to convince Ruth, she was already more than convinced. Ruth was in love with the idea of America, of sending her sons off to free schools. In fact, Ruth even daydreamed that she and Eve would also go off to school, arm in arm, to learn English and all about what it meant to be an American. It went without saying that Eve also hoped to convince Hannah and Abraham, Miriam and Shlomo, to join them too. Then, before she knew it, they were well into 1882, the year that Yacob went off to America and David became what Eve had always known him to be—truly a man of destiny. But she was no longer so sure that this was the role she wanted him to play.

It had taken the trauma of Dora's death for Yacob fully to appreciate her true worth, that splendor of spirit that had illuminated his life without his ever realizing it. In the months following her death he grew increasingly despondent, showed little interest in his baby daughter. Perhaps if Dorie had been a boy it would have been another story but as it was, he was almost indifferent. Then one morning, eight months after Dora's death and without giving any previous clue as to what he'd been thinking about, Yacob rose from his bed and announced he was going to America. The family was stunned. *When? Where? What? How long had he been thinking about this?*

"Ever since that letter came from Dora's brother inviting me . . ." Yacob answered airily almost as if it were a party he'd been invited to attend.

Following Dora's death Eve had written to this brother in America to tell him about his sister's demise and the birth of her daughter. Boris Levitz had responded, urging Yacob to come to America with Dora's child, promising that he and his family would be delighted to hug Dorie to their collective breasts and would help Yacob get a new start in life in New York. When the letter had first arrived, Eve could not but think of what a truly wonderful opportunity it would be for both Yacob and Dorie. And it didn't matter that she herself would miss her, that letting go of the baby would create a vacuum in her life as sharply felt as if her own son, Yitzhak, would be going off without her. Besides, it wouldn't be too long before they all joined Dorie in America themselves. She would force herself to be happy about Dorie going off before the rest of them. . . .

Then it became clear that Yacob had no intention of taking Dorie with him. He mumbled various excuses. Dorie was too little. She needed a woman's care. How would he be able to take care of her first on board the ship and then in America? And besides all that, he knew Eve looked on the child as her own daughter. Surely it would be a sin to part them. He said that he would send for her as soon as he got established in America. Undoubtedly, he declaimed, it would not be more than a few months before he became a millionaire in the Golden Land and then he'd be able to provide for Dorie as if she were a princess. Of course he would send money back to Slobodka for her keep as soon as he started earning a little something. At the same time he knew that David and Eve wouldn't begrudge a small baby a few mouthfuls. *After all, how much did she eat? How much could it cost to feed her?*

Eve realized that Yacob would probably never send for Dorie at all. She wasn't even sure that they would ever hear from him again. It had happened before with men who had gone off to America, supposedly to send for wives and children as soon as they had the money. These abandoned wives were left to live the lives of widows, except that they could never wed again according to Jewish Law. But the men, free of familiar eyes in America, took new wives, started new families, the past well forgotten. Wasn't that what America meant, after all? A new life, the miserable past wiped from memory?

While gratified and relieved that she was going to keep Dorie after all, Eve could not help feeling a little angry, resentful that Yacob could so easily leave Dora's darling daughter behind, not to mention all memory of Dora herself. She could not resist a taunt: "Perhaps without Dora's daughter with you, you won't find yourself so welcome at your brother-in-law's door. . . ."

Yacob shrugged. "When I tell them I have to have money before I can send for her, they'll be inclined to help me that much more," he said, smiling a little, causing Eve to wonder if all along she had misjudged Yacob, thinking him a bit of a dolt. Had he *always* been this sly, or was it the bitterness of Dora's death having its effect on him?

Yacob said he planned on going immediately. The very next day, or the day after that at the latest. He would get on the train in Kovno, travel east and sail from Hamburg. All he needed to know was how much money David and Hershel were prepared to pay him since he was relinquishing his share of the business.

They stared at him in disbelief. If he had asked them to *lend* him some money or even *give* him enough to see him off, but to offer to *sell* what had been given him in the first place—that was the act of an unconscionable man, a greedy *chozzer*.

"Under the circumstances I say give him nothing!" Ruth said in disgust.

"Five rubles?" Hershel offered.

"No," Eve said, sick at heart over his greediness, wanting him gone already. "He'll need at least twenty-five." She looked at David hard. *Surely this was*

*an extraordinary circumstance—to send a man off to America. It was justifiable
to take this money from their secret fund.*

"That sounds about right," Yacob hastened to say, a bit sheepish now. "I
have a few rubles saved up to pay for my passage but I've heard that they don't
let you into America without a little something in your pocket."

"Let me think about it," David said slowly, as if he were already lost in
thought. "Wait a few days and we'll see what we can spare."

After a couple of days David told Yacob that if he would leave on horseback,
and not on train, would wait until he was in Germany before he boarded a train,
and *swore* not to tell anyone beforehand that he was leaving, they would give
him *thirty-five rubles*.

At first Yacob doubted his own ears. Had David really said thirty-five rubles?
Then, for a couple of fleeting seconds he wondered where they had gotten thirty-
five rubles to give him. Then he speculated about David's sanity. Finally, he
hastily agreed to whatever terms David wanted. He would leave when David
told him to; he would go on horseback; he wouldn't tell anyone, not even
Abraham and Shlomo, that he was going.

"And not Father either . . ." David wasn't sure how deeply his father hated,
how much he could be trusted.

"I would do whatever you wanted me to without even a kopeck if it came
to that," Yacob assured David.

Later Eve said to David, "I'm not sure at all that Yacob *deserves* so much
money—thirty-five rubles."

"I have to make sure Yacob does exactly as I ask—that he doesn't take the
train and that he tells no one he's leaving. It's important that no one knows
afterward exactly *when* it was that he left—"

"Why, David?" she asked, growing frightened. "Why is it so important?"

"Because before Yacob leaves he's going to avenge Dora's death . . ."

Then Eve was thoroughly frightened. While it was she, perhaps, who mourned
Dora's death most, it was David who still brooded over the fact that there hadn't
even been a real attempt to find the Cossacks who had raped and murdered her.
Even the Squire's efforts to find the Cossacks by demanding a full investigation
by the Commander of the garrison hadn't helped when Stasia, the old woman
who was the only witness, had grown suddenly deaf, dumb and blind. And who
could blame her? The Cossacks would retaliate against a gentile informer as
well as a Jewish one, and it was certainly not part of life's great design for this
ignorant Polish peasant to play the heroic figure. The Governor-General who
came to town to look into things told the Squire that without a proper witness
there could be no investigation. Where would they even begin?

Eve shook her head at David. "Yacob? Avenge Dora's murder? No, David.
That's the farthest thing from Yacob's mind right now. All he wants to do now
is leave, to forget that there ever was a Slobodka. What is it you're planning?
Tell me!"

But David only smiled, repeated: "Yacob is going to avenge Dora's murder.

154

Then he's going to escape with part of the money from the fort, with the Cossacks' money. Now, isn't that poetic justice? Before you told me about this poetic justice I didn't know such a thing existed. But now I think it is a very beautiful thing."

Eve was terrified. "David! No!"

He placed a gentle finger on her lips. "Silence. You taught me that silence is sometimes golden, just as poetic justice is beautiful, just as you told me what it means to be a man of destiny. . . ."

"Oh, David," she moaned. "Whoever said I knew what I was talking about?"

The next Wednesday morning, well before dawn, Yacob left on horseback. When Hershel and David went about their rounds, staying that day closer to home where people were more apt to ask where Yacob was, they told whoever inquired that he was home with a fever. On Thursday morning Eve bought a medicine for that fever from the peasant woman, Sonia, who made her living brewing up remedies for various ailments. Eve even urged her to make it particularly foul-tasting since it was for her brother-in-law Yacob of whom she was not particularly fond, and the old crone assured Eve with an appreciative cackle that she would do just that. On Friday, Eve returned for a laxative and urged Sonia this time to make it both foul and especially strong, since she suspected that her brother-in-law was playing sicker than he really was just to get out of working, and the family hoped to blast him from his bed. Sonia cackled even louder and obliged.

It wasn't until Saturday morning, so early in the day that the Cossacks in the fort were still lying abed, that they were awakened by a bomb going off in their midst. While there were similar incidents happening all over Russia, this was the first time such a thing had happened in Slobodka. Shock, followed by utter confusion, prevailed and it wasn't until almost an hour later that three Cossacks were found mangled in death. Then the other Cossacks rode out in search of the bomb thrower. The Commander directed them to start with the Jews. "They're ungrateful revolutionaries, every last one of them. Besides, what peasant has the brains to make a bomb?"

By the time the Markoff family returned home from their Sabbath service at the rebuilt synagogue—David with them for the first time since the burning of the House of Worship over a year before—a group of the soldiers came riding up, snapping their whips in a white rage. During the initial questioning it was divulged that the entire family had been at services that morning worshiping God—except for Yacob, of course. The lout had been sick in bed for days already, leaving all the work to be done by his brothers.

The Cossacks stormed the house looking for Yacob, breaking chairs, crockery, whatever was within three feet of them as they strode. Of course Yacob was nowhere in the house. While some of the soldiers were sent to search the immediate vicinity outside, several of them were sent to the barn and the stable.

They came back and told their leader that while Yacob wasn't to be found, there were *two* horses.

"Son-of-a-bitch!" David raged. "We had *three* horses. Some thieving bastard stole one of our horses! But surely this doesn't mean that Yacob threw the— You can't suspect Yacob? He was sick; this morning he was too weak even to go to the outhouse . . . And what would Yacob know of a bomb? Between you and me, my brother barely knows how to wipe his own ass . . ."

"If that's the case where *is* your brother?"

David lifted his shoulders, perplexed, as bewildered as they.

A group of them went back to Yacob's room, tore it apart, even splintering the walls. Then the leader raised his sword to the unmade bed and with one slice opened up the mattress, and there, completely shocking to the Markoffs, were the bits and pieces of the ingredients of a bomb.

"Yacob! Unbelievable!"

"I would never believe it if I didn't see it with my own two eyes!"

"If anyone would have asked me I would say he didn't even know how to hold up his pants."

The Cossack turned to David. "Couldn't wipe his own behind, eh?" he said as if in triumph. He yelled to his men: "Send out the word! We'll find the son-of-a-whore Jew! He only has a couple of hours start on us!"

Not finding Yacob, the Commander of the fort was quite willing publicly to execute David and Hershel but the Squire interceded, vouched for their innocence. It was Eve, after all, who had saved his son's life, and it was *Polish* blood, not Russian, that had flowed in his ancestors' aristocratic blood—flowed and bled fruitlessly against the invading Russians only a century before.

Still, Eve anguished over the fact that three mothers' sons lay dead. "There were only two men who murdered Dora, and these three men all could have been completely innocent—"

"No, there are no innocent Cossacks. If it wasn't Dora they raped and murdered, then it was somebody else's wife, sister, daughter."

"But we can't be sure of that . . ."

"I am. And wasn't it you who told me that the Book says 'an eye for an eye'?"

Her emerald eyes were dark with tears. She was no longer so sure of all the words she had spoken so easily.

"And what about those American revolutionists you talk about so much? Didn't they have to kill British boys, some of them surely innocent of anything except doing what they were told, believing that they were fighting for their country's good? Was it wrong for the Americans to shed those boys' lives in order to gain their own freedom?"

Eve's eyes beseeched his helplessly. She no longer had ready answers.

David smiled sadly, with commiseration for her plight. "The problem with you, Eve," he said softly, "is that you have the brain of a revolutionary, even the spirit, but you'll never have the heart."

1883 was the year Eve gave birth to a son who endured for two hours and then declined to join the living. It was also the year that Ruth finally mastered the Russian language and at the same time, started teaching her own sons in earnest, even little Gershon, barely three. It was Yiddish she taught them, leaving the Hebrew to the *melamed*. "At least when it comes time for them to join the real world, they won't enter it entirely ignorant," she said with satisfaction.

When Eve asked her what she meant by the real world, Ruth didn't hesitate for a moment. "Why, America of course!"

Eve nodded and offered to teach the older boys some arithmetic, history and a little geography.

1884 was the year Chaim Markoff went to his reward as a result of an accident precipitated, one might say, by the nature of the man himself. Ruth was moved to comment: "He who lives by the sword shall die by the sword," which, while not exactly apt, still expressed a certain truth.

There was a swing in the yard of Chaim's house, affixed to a stalwart tree. The seat was a slab of wood attached to heavy rope and a child could go as far up into the sky as he could manage to propel himself at a rate of velocity according to his ability and daring. On the day he went to meet his Creator, Chaim returned from the Inn full of drink. He paused to watch Rochel and Rissa, Miriam's younger daughters, taking turns on the swing while a couple of older children stood on the sidelines watching, spurring them on, daring them to go ever higher, ever faster. Then Chaim joined in, relishing every opportunity these days to vent some of his rage and venom since he could no longer taunt his sons or their wives under the new regime of equality in his household. "Yellow-livered dregs of a miscarriage!" he screeched. "Higher! Faster! What are you afraid of, you spineless pieces of woman's dung? Get off that fucking swing and let a man show you how it's done, you worthless stinking gutless turds."

Pushing the lot of them aside, he stood up on the seat of the swing and propelled himself violently into the air as high as the treetops and screamed: "See, look at how it's done, you sniveling pieces of cows' manure." Then the ropes tore and Chaim went hurtling through the air, first upward to the sky, then down to the hard earth, breaking both his neck and broad back at the same time.

In his insignificant and ignoble death, Chaim left his family to wonder how it was they had feared him so in life, while Eve could not free herself of the black hatred she still harbored. Accordingly she decided that she couldn't attend his burial. At the same time she encouraged David to do so, and to join with his brothers in observing the period of mourning—to sit *shiva* with them for the proscribed eight days.

"I won't do it!" David told her. "I *don't* mourn father's passing! I *cannot* forgive him! And to sit there while everyone in town comes calling and starts telling and retelling all the stories about him is more than I can bear. Besides, since I no longer believe in God, I can no longer practice religious ritual."

"By not believing in God you don't stop being a Jew. You were born a Jew, you *are* a Jew by blood and culture. You can't deny that."

David smiled, a rarity for him of late. "A lot of good it would do me to deny it. The gentiles, if no one else, would call me a liar. Of course I'm still a Jew."

"Well, sitting *shiva* is a Jewish custom, part of our culture, not just a religious duty."

"I'll never understand you, Eve. Feeling as I do about father, you still want me to do this for him?"

"No, David. Nor for him. For you."

"Now what does that mean? For myself I'm to sit there pretending a grief I don't feel? To sit and cry?"

"No. You don't have to pretend and you don't have to cry. Unless it makes you feel better to. Sometimes I think people cry only because they feel bad about *not* feeling bad that the person is dead. Actually, David, the *shiva* is not so much for the dead but for the living—a time to put *everything* to rest. The past and the bad feelings if they exist. It's better for the one who's left. I think it just makes him a more whole person."

"So what you want is for me to forget all the bad things father did?"

"Not exactly. Look . . . Callers will come to pay their respects. Some will lie and say what a wonderful person Chaim was. And those who won't say *that* will probably find *something* good to say about him. Maybe someone will remember a funny incident in which Chaim was involved and everyone will laugh . . . in a good way. And that's not wrong. It's for the best. I'm sure that if you put your mind to it, even you can remember something good that happened between you and your father."

Even if I myself cannot. But then it's not important for me to do this. Chaim wasn't my father.

"Think, David! There must be one good memory."

"Well . . ." He thought for quite a few moments before he spoke. "Well, I *can* remember one time. I was a little boy. Maybe five or six. He sat me on a horse. My first time and I was terrified. The horse was so big and I was so small and so far from the ground. Father knew I was scared and he yelled as he always yelled. And because he yelled I was too scared *not* to stay up there on that horse. Then father slapped the horse on the backside and the horse reared and still I sat, held on for dear life and then the horse started to gallop, but I held on to the reins and managed to keep from falling off. When it was all over I knew I had passed some kind of a test and it was the most wonderful feeling, as if I had beaten the world, the world of a five-year-old boy anyway. Then father reached up to take me off and our eyes met and it was as if he *knew*, that once, what I was feeling, and it was as if that once he and I shared some kind of a wonderful secret. At that moment, he even respected me. I was only a little boy. It was a big thing to be respected by my father."

Eve's eyes glistened with tears.

"It's funny," David said. "I didn't even remember that until now."

"Oh David, don't you see? You *must* sit *shiva* with your brothers and tell that story. Maybe they'll laugh with you or maybe they'll even cry. But then one of them will share *his* one good memory of Chaim, and then another will. And one by one you'll all feel better. You'll all put the bad memories to rest. That's really what a mourning period should be—a time to let go."

He was only half-convinced. "You know? You're an incredible woman. After everything, you *do* want me to forgive him."

"Yes. For your own sake."

While he thought it over, she thought about the boy she had married. A boy, an immature boy, an innocent. An innocent with the special charm of innocence. And it was gone. He had changed into the strong man she desired, but not without a price. Still so young, he had become a brooding, embittered man who raged against the constrictions of life as a Jew under the Tsar and against his own people who allowed themselves to be sinned against; a man who despised the Christian world who called him Christ-killer, and who refused to believe in a God Who allowed His people to be persecuted and their temples defiled. He was an innocent who had become a bomb-thrower, whose bomb had killed. Oh, yes—he had to rid himself of some bitterness and rage or he would soon be a man she no longer recognized at all.

Now this man smiled at her. "I'll make a bargain with you. *You* tell me one good memory you have of my father and I'll do what you want—"

She looked at him in astonishment. For all her easy words to him she knew that no matter how hard she tried, she would come up with nothing.

"That's not fair, David," she cried out childishly. "He was your father; you lived with him all your life. I knew him so short a time really . . ." She turned away from him so that he couldn't look into her face for she was sure if he looked hard enough he would find the truth written there—that the most vivid memory of Chaim whom she wanted him to forgive, was the one when the father came to the son's home to defile the son's wife!

She heard David laugh softly. "Well, you've had a couple of minutes to think about it and you can't think of anything good to say about father, can you? Not one single good memory." He gently mocked her.

For a moment it crossed her mind to make up a memory, a story of Chaim doing, saying, something nice, something she would say she had forgotten to mention before. But she couldn't do it. It was enough that she was keeping from David the truth of Chaim's visit that afternoon when only the semipogrom of peasants had saved her from his savage attack. At best a lie of omission, at worst a white lie.

"No . . ." she said at last. "Not a single good memory. But I will make a deal with you. I had intended to stay away from his burial myself and not to attend the *shiva* either. But if you will go, I will go with you. . . ."

It was as she had imagined it would be. David told his brothers the story of his father and the first ride on a horse and the others were all surprised to hear the touching story. *This was Chaim? Unbelievable!* Then Abraham had a story to tell of when he and Shlomo were little boys, really too little to be of much use to Chaim in the day-to-day business.

Thursday was the big market day in town when all the farmers in all the surrounding villages brought to town anything they had to sell, be it ducks or potatoes. On the night before market day the farmers would assemble at the tavern to have a few drinks and exchange gossip, and this was a good time to pick up a tip or two about what these men had held back from market—superior animals that were desirable for the kosher trade, better sold privately than at the cheap trade of market day. But Chaim couldn't very well go around eavesdropping himself—it was beneath his dignity. After all, he wasn't a *kocker*, a small-timer who bought one goose there or a couple of chickens here. So he would send Abraham and Shlomo in first—to slip and sneak around and overhear what they could; small as they were, no one paid any attention to them. Then they would repeat to Chaim what they overheard. . . . This goy here was fattening up ten cows and would be selling them within the month, or that farmer there—the one with the brown cap—had a flock of geese he said he was bringing to market in a couple of weeks *if* he couldn't manage to sell them first at a good price. Then Chaim, easily the tallest and broadest man present, carrying a cane or his riding whip as a sign of his importance, would sit down and buy the potential seller a drink and before you knew it, he had tied up a deal, beating out all competitors.

This one time, he, Abraham, had crawled under a table, assuming a reclining position, clowning around, showing off for Shlomo, trying to make him laugh, and it was in this position he heard what he assumed was a farmer telling of three fat cows he wanted to unload. Quickly Abraham crawled out from under the table and informed Chaim but inadvertently identified *another* peasant—he hadn't actually seen who was doing the talking—as the potential seller of the cows. Chaim sat down, ordered drinks for himself and the proposed seller of the cows, and made the pitch in his best, overbearing manner. When it turned out the man was not only the wrong man but an accursed pig-farmer to boot, Abraham thought he would soon be a "dead one" for sure.

"I thought that father would kill me absolutely. But you know what he did? First he laughed so hard I thought he had gone out of his head, then he lifted me onto the table—and this is hard to believe—he ordered me a vodka, my very first, and he roared at me, 'Drink it down!' After I managed to do so, coughing out my brains, Father said, 'Now you're a man . . .' "

At first everyone had laughed when they heard how Abraham had made the wrong identification, but when he was finished telling the tale, they all looked at one another in astonishment as if to say: "Go know, he wasn't always so bad after all . . ."

Then Shlomo snickered and everyone looked at him expectantly, now eager to hear a story they had never heard or possibly had forgotten . . .

160

"Remember the time," Shlomo said, "on market day when we helped father buy a cow for only two rubles and then after he bought it—"

Hershel broke in with a whoop of laughter and Abraham nodded with a grin, "It was funny all right . . ."

Even the wives smiled in anticipation. "So tell us already," Hannah said. "We could use a good laugh."

"Well, as you know, it's a different story when we go buying on market day from what it is when we buy out in the country. When we call on a farmer on his property we behave very much like gentlemen. We offer a fair price and we make a fair deal since these farmers make up our regular trade. Even father behaved like a gentlemen on these occasions. He might have cursed under his breath but as long as the farmer acted in a polite fashion, that was all he would do. Sometimes he even sat down in the farmer's kitchen to have a piece of bread and a herring. Certainly he'd have a few vodkas with the farmer once a deal was made. You have to understand," he said, talking to Eve now, "that under these circumstances there's none of this Christ-killer business since they respected father, and now us, as men who won't be crapped on and also because they know we pay a good price, buying as we do for the kosher trade. Money, as you know, talks louder than a goy's natural hatred against all Jews."

"For God's sake, will you get on with the story?" Hershel demanded, cracking a walnut in his fist.

"If you don't interrupt that's exactly what I intend to do. But first I wanted to tell Eve here the difference between the way of doing business on the farm and the way it's done at the market." He turned back to Eve and spoke in a pointed fashion. "On market day anything goes. A farmer comes in from far away with a single cow and who knows if we'll ever see him again? And father never had much respect for a deal that involved only one cow or a few ducks or geese. That was for the *kockers*, he always said. Anyhow, on market day anything goes and father enjoyed the game more than the *kocker* profit. So this is the way it went. We accompanied father, but we would pretend we didn't know him. Father would walk around by himself until he spotted a peasant with a nice fat cow and he'd go and look her over. He would stand there maybe combing his beard with his fingers, maybe glowering a little, and then he might ask, 'How much do you want for this fine heifer?' Only of course his voice would be tinged with a little sarcasm so that the words *fine heifer* would come out more like *shtik drek*—a piece of dung. You know how father did that—"

The brothers nodded, smiling, eager for Shlomo to continue.

"And the farmer, getting nervous, might say: 'Eight rubles' but with a question mark at the end, hoping to get five . . .

"Then two of us would come strolling along not even looking at either the farmer or father. We would just talk among ourselves while we circled around the cow saying things like *Oy vey, what a wreck! Nothing but skin and bones.* Maybe we would run our hands over her flanks and shake our heads in despair, or look into the creature's eyes and wonder aloud if she was coming down with the hoof-and-mouth. We would walk away in disgust. Then father would clinch the deal on the spot and the farmer was lucky if he'd got four rubles after that.

"Only sometimes we would get carried away and we would poke the cow or give her a shove that would almost knock her over. We'd say: 'Look at that. She's so sick she can hardly stand.' Or maybe we'd give her a kick in a leg so she wobbled. But father didn't like when we did those things. He only wanted us to talk. When we'd push the cow around he yelled and cursed us later— 'Thickheads! Driveling idiots! You damage the merchandise. She won't be fit to sell to a kosher butcher. We'll be lucky to get a lousy ruble from the sausage makers!' "

Eve kept nodding her head, encouraging him to go on.

"But you know how boys are. The next few times we'd listen but gradually we would warm up again. Which brings us to the story at hand. This time I'm talking about, it was me and Hershel and Abraham and David. Four of us, so you can imagine! We worked the poor cow over proper. A shove in one flank then a shove in the other, a punch in this leg and a kick in the belly. By the time we walked off to let father finish the deal, the poor thing could hardly stand. Father ended up paying the farmer only two rubles. But get this! As he was leading her away, she drops dead! Right there in the middle of the marketplace, the cow falls down stone cold. Father let out such a scream you could hear him in Vilno!"

The brothers laughed raucously while Miriam protested: "*Oy!* A terrible thing to do to a poor cow—" But she couldn't help laughing either, her belly shaking like jelly.

"Go on . . ." Eve urged, eager to hear what Chaim did then.

"We're laughing now but let me tell you we weren't laughing then. When we saw that cow collapse what we did was run as fast as we could out of the marketplace. Even as we ran we could hear father screaming and cursing. We knew what we should have done then—picked up the carcass, thrown it in the wagon and taken her to a goyish butcher since they don't mind buying dead animals, but we were too afraid to face father. So we hid out for the rest of the day. As for father, he just walked away, left the dead cow lying there and headed for the tavern. When sundown was approaching we knew there was nothing to do but go find him, facing a similar fate to the cow herself.

"When we walked into the tavern father took a long look at us and roared to the tavern keeper, 'Drinks for my boys and keep them coming. They need it for their brains. They're the stupidest, fuckingest, thickest, most half-witted, idiotic, blithering, dim-witted, addlepated, nit-witted Litvaks in the whole province, not to mention the biggest assholes.' And then he started to laugh too. God, how he laughed!"

Now the brothers were quiet and Hershel said in wonder, "You know, I forgot that father could laugh like that. I forgot that he liked a joke as much as the next one. Of course he liked it better when the joke was on the next one.

Like the time he sold that herd of cattle to the army. Oh, how he laughed that day!''

"What happened? When was this?'' Eve leaned forward eagerly. This was a Chaim she had never known.

"Oh, maybe ten years ago,'' Hershel said. "David was just a boy. We used to keep cattle ourselves then—graze them on rented meadows, a meadow here, a meadow there, wherever we could find one. After the cattle were fattened up, we'd sell them to the army. But there was an outbreak of the hoof-and-mouth, and all over the countryside the cattle were dropping dead. One by one, our herds went. First one meadow, then the next. Finally we had only one herd left; the disease hadn't reached that particular meadow, but it was only a matter of time, father figured. So he called in the officer that did the buying and since by this time the army was desperate to get the meat, the deal was made quickly. Just as quickly the cattle were loaded onto the train. Even before father had a chance to count the money, the cattle dropped dead right there in the cars! But a deal was a deal and the dead cattle belonged to the Tsar! Oh, did father laugh!''

The brothers all laughed too but Eve was shocked. "You mean he *knew* he was selling the army cattle that might die . . .''

Hershel grinned. "Never mind *might*. He was figuring on it. . . .''

"But wasn't he afraid of them? That they'd be furious over being cheated and would retaliate?''

Hershel shook his head. "You have to understand something. Father was an uneducated man but he was no fool. He had the army figured correctly. If no one said anything about the deal, it was just a case of bad luck that the cattle died. They had bought healthy cows which *then* sickened and died. Bad luck, that's all. But if they made a stink and asked for their money back or tried to punish father, that would have been admitting he had put one over on them, that they had been fooled, that father was smart and they were stupid. The best thing for the army to do was to say and do nothing.''

Hershel's voice was filled with pride for Chaim, and even Eve felt a kind of grudging admiration for him in spite of herself. Chaim had beaten the Russian Army!

Then when the condolence callers came, the stories expanded . . . how there wasn't a Litvak living that could lift more weight than Chaim, make a more cunning deal, drink more vodka, glass for glass. There wasn't a Russky far or near that could touch him. Several men remembered how one night he had even drunk Stash, the crazy Polack of drinking renown, under the table in the tavern that was frequented by the peasants. The stories became more wonderful every day, more colorful, the exploits more extraordinary, the funny stories more hilarious until Chaim became better in death and bigger than life.

At the end of the eight days of mourning, Hannah dryly observed, "Go know! A hero no less . . .''

Abraham and Shlomo proposed to David and Hershel that with Chaim gone, there was no reason the two sets of brothers should remain in competition with each other. Better they should merge forces and have one big business rather than two small ones. The proposal was accepted and it was agreed that henceforth they would be known as the Brothers Markoff, Cattle Dealers. It was true they dealt in all kinds of livestock but the title "Cattle Dealers" said better what kind of men they were. And one thing they were not, as Chaim Markoff himself wasn't, were *kockers* . . .

Eve always recalled 1885 as the year Ruth, increasingly proficient in Russian, insisted on reading both Tolstoy and Dostoevski, becoming such a devotee that she often had to be reminded that there were other things that merited her attention.

Ruth was especially fascinated with Dostoevski's *Letters from the Under-world*. She and Eve spent wonderful hours arguing which was the more powerful and telling novel—that or *Crime and Punishment*, Eve's favorite. But once Ruth began *War and Peace* it was almost impossible to engage her attention. She would rise at four in the morning after burning the midnight oil until she finally completed it, several months later. Then she and Eve almost had their first real argument.

"My God!" Ruth raved. "I was born on Russian soil and here is this world I know nothing about . . ." She applauded it as the most marvelous, incredible, realistic novel. Eve was willing to grant her that it was a remarkable piece of work but she deplored what she considered a tremendous flaw—the depiction of Russian life as an idyll of the Russian landed gentry with a horrifying absence of almost any of the more terrible aspects of Russian existence.

"I would hardly call *that* realistic!"

Ruth moaned in disgust. "It's a story about people, whether they're landed gentry, Jews or peasants. Can't you just read a book for the sheer pleasure of it without always focusing on 'the terrible aspects of Russian existence?' Can't you enjoy just reading? You don't have to love each character. Look at how wonderfully Tolstoy shows a woman's thoughts. Anna in *Anna Karenina?* And Natasha in *War and Peace*. Don't you think Natasha is a wonderful heroine?"

"Heroine? You call Natasha a heroine? Sophia Lvovna Perovskaya is *my* idea of a real heroine!"

"Sophia Perovskaya? Who is she?"

"Just the woman who led the revolutionaries who assassinated the Tsar! *That's* a heroine!"

"Oh," Ruth said, uninterested. "We're talking about literature, Eve. Not revolution. Maybe what that Sophia did wasn't so wonderful. These revolutionaries killed Alexander the father and now Alexander the son is much worse."

Eve had to laugh. Things had certainly changed. When she and Ruth had first met, Ruth had been on the sour side and a pessimistic person. She herself had been the optimist. Now where was her own optimism? Lost somewhere along the way, much as Tolstoy's own optimistic view had been lost, too, since he had written *War and Peace*. But she didn't tell Ruth *that* because in spite of their argument over the merits of the book, she didn't want to mar Ruth's pleasure in it. Another time they'd discuss Tolstoy's recent conversion, both in life and literature; Tolstoy himself was no longer so enthralled with the gentry of Russia.

No matter how she and Ruth disagreed, Eve mused, how wonderful it was to have someone to discuss these things with. All her life she had never had a friend to talk to about books. She had taught David, as well as Ruth, to read Russian, but he wouldn't read any of the literature. All he would read were the newspapers, the pamphlets and magazines, anything of that sort he could lay his hands on. Much of it was illegally published and had to be smuggled into the countryside. The more he read of this material the more his internal anger against the authorities grew. Yes, David had changed as much as Ruth but in a completely different direction.

The House of Worship was set afire again that year. It wasn't an official act this time but the work of a few village peasants, both Russian and Polish, and all, of course, drunk. There *was* an official investigation and the Commander of the garrison issued an official verdict—it was impossible to discover the true culprits since the wretched bunch of liars were covering up for one another. There *was* an official apology. The Jewish community had the sympathy of the Christian populace. That same week Eve miscarried. David insisted on attributing that loss to the synagogue burning. But Eve, not wanting to feed David's bitterness, insisted it wasn't so. "It's God's will," she begged him to believe.

"God's will? You have a strange God!" he said caustically, coldly. He said no more, unwilling to upset her further, and voiced no objection when she contributed twenty rubles from the secret fund to help rebuild the House of Worship once again.

With that contribution the fund was down to less than half its original sum. Ten rubles had gone to help rebuild the House of Worship the first time it burned, thirty-five to Yacob, thirty-five toward tribute to the authorities from the Jewish community. Feifke the traveling musician was given five rubles when his fiddle had been broken by a group of unruly youths, and five rubles had been given as a dowry so that Hinda Balinkoff, the cobbler's daughter, could wed Pincus Berishl, a carpenter's apprentice. Ten rubles had been used to help send a peasant's son to Moscow when even the priest's efforts had failed to cure him of a strange crippling disease. (When Eve discovered that ten rubles was all the Squire himself had contributed, David had only laughed ironically.) Thirty or so rubles had been expended on provisions for various members of the community.

Soon the money would all be gone, Eve reflected, and she would be that much closer to leaving for America.

Late that year Miriam made an official call on Ruth and Eve. Although the women from the two Markoff households saw each other two or three times a week informally, Ruth and Eve knew that this call was a formal one since Miriam wore her best dress (one that Eve had made for her) and her wig. Eve was amused and asked Miriam why they were being so honored.

"You are being so honored because I want to know if you think that just because my girls are girls they should grow up ignorant?" she asked indignantly. "After all, all boys get some kind of an education. They learn Hebrew at the Talmud Torah. And Ruth's boys are learning more. Besides Hebrew, they know Yiddish, not to mention arithmetic and history. My girls—nothing! Hannah's —nothing. We, Hannah and I, are surprised at you, Eve, that you would so forget our girls. And you, Ruth, I thought that since you've become so smart yourself, you wouldn't be so ignorant anymore and still think my girls don't deserve to know a little something."

"I don't think that at all," Ruth said hastily, although Miriam's phrasing made her want to laugh.

"So, *nu?* Why are you being so selfish? Here you've been lucky enough to live with Eve and learn and now you're passing on what you know to your children without a thought for our children who haven't been so privileged."

Both Eve and Ruth refrained from pointing out that Hannah and Miriam had often been asked to join in when Eve had been teaching Ruth to read and write Yiddish, Hebrew and Russian. The truth was that after the first few lessons, when Eve had still been living in Chaim's house, both Hannah and Miriam had lacked the necessary dedication to sit down and apply themselves; they had lost interest. They had mostly remained content to ask Eve to tell them stories of a historical nature, to have her read to them, or occasionally discuss with them matters related to art and literature, although Hannah liked better to talk about the meaning of life.

What Ruth and Eve did say was that indeed they had been thoughtless, even selfish, and that Miriam was to send over her daughters the very next day to begin their lessons, accompanied by Hannah's daughters, naturally.

Miriam nodded. "We thought that was what you'd say. Hannah also said I was to inquire about her sons too. While they go to *heder,* she says you, Eve, told her it wasn't enough to know Hebrew, the Talmud and the Torah. That an educated person needs to know a living language, needs to know everything."

"That's true," Eve couldn't help smiling. "I did say that and I still believe it. Please, tell Hannah to send her boys over too. I'll teach them whatever I possibly can. But tell me one thing, Miriam. I just saw Hannah a couple of days ago. Why didn't she say anything to me herself?"

"To tell you the truth, she's a little put out with you. And Ruth too, for that matter."

"But why? What have we done?"

"It's more what you *haven't* done."

"Now what does that mean?" Ruth demanded in exasperation.

Miriam puffed herself up to deliver this last thrust. "You haven't moved back to our house. Hannah says that with Chaim gone to his rest, there's no reason all of you shouldn't since our house is so big and this one so small. And it goes without saying, I agree with her. After all, Eve, you did once say that we were all more than sisters-in-law. You said we were all sisters. Now, as Hannah says, sisters belong together if it's at all possible. And who would say it's not possible?''

After Miriam left, Ruth asked Eve: "What do you think? Do you think we should think about moving back into the old house?''

Eve looked around her cozy, pretty house that had taken so much effort, the place where she and David had really begun life as man and wife. "I don't think I want to do that, Ruth. I would hate to leave my little house. As a child I lived in my father's house; then as my brothers took over, it was their house. Then I married and lived in Chaim's house. But this home is really mine, mine and David's. And yours, of course. I don't think I can give it up.''

Ruth smiled a little. "You'd have to give it up, leave it to go to America, wouldn't you? And you've always said a home is only where the heart is—''

Eve laughed a little. "*Touché*, Ruth. And a first lesson in French for you. *Touché* means you've scored a point. It comes from the sport or the art, if you will, of fencing. When one fencer touches the other with the tip of his sword, he calls out, '*Touché*.' ''

"Wonderful!" Ruth clapped her hands. "When do we start the French lessons?''

Eve's laugh rang out in delight. Ruth was wonderful! Her desire for learning was an inspiration. If only Yitzhak and Dorie grew up with that insatiable desire, she would be happy.

"To tell you the truth, Ruth, I don't know all that much French myself, really only a smattering. And I've been thinking. Whatever spare time we have, we'd both do better to start learning English so that by the time we go to America—''

"—We'll *already* be speaking English," Ruth finished for her. "Why, we'll be regular Americans.''

Regular Americans . . . Ruth was a wonderful person, and that was a wonderful phrase!

"Let's get busy, Ruth. We have a lot to do.''

"This minute?''

"Yes. We're going to fix Yacob's room up into a classroom. What with Miriam's children and Hannah's, and your boys, and Dorie and Yitzhak almost ready to start their lessons, that's what we need. A schoolroom. And tomorrow—''

"Yes?" Ruth asked. Apparently they weren't moving.

"Tomorrow I'm going to Kovno to look for books to start the English lessons. You know what we must do, Ruth?''

Ruth grinned at her. "No. Tell me, what must we do?''

"We must try to talk David and Hershel into learning English with us so that when we get to America they'll be regular Americans too.''

"And what about the children?''

"Oh Ruth, you're right. But those poor children, which language do we teach them first? Yiddish, Russian, or English?"

"I guess we have to start with Yiddish. Or maybe Russian. But we should definitely get to the English. That's our language of the future, after all. And the children, Eve, aren't they the future too?"

Eve nodded. She was never to forget Ruth saying those words. The children *were* the future.

It was the following year that Eve's father suffered a stroke. Eve rushed to his bedside thinking that this would be the last time she would see his sweet face, feel his tender touch. But when Eve saw him, it was clear that while he was paralyzed, unable to move or even speak, her father was surviving the crippling attack. So old and so frail . . . surely it was a miracle.

Her brothers prayed, giving thanks to a merciful God who had spared their father's life, even as they complained about the burden of a totally paralyzed individual on their household.

"Bundle him up," Eve told them, "and then place him in my wagon very very carefully. I'm taking him home with me."

The brothers gazed at their sister with joyful relief. God had spared their father and that was a miracle, but Eve assuming the duty of caring for him was a miracle too. Even as they prepared their father for the trip they reassured Eve that she was doing the right thing—it truly was her obligation. She was far younger than their wives who would have had to care for the old man; younger, stronger and certainly she had much more energy. And he *was* Eve's father, after all, and not the wives'. It was only fitting, therefore, that she assume this burden.

Eve merely smiled at them. "I'm already taking him so there's no need to talk me into it and certainly no need to justify it. And he isn't a burden to me. I *want* to do this, and not out of a sense of duty."

The brothers stared at her quizzically. *Not out of a sense of duty? What else was there?*

"For me, this is truly a *mitzvah,* a good deed. But a good deed done with joy."

Now the brothers exchanged glances. The gall of this half sister, this female, lecturing *them* on the true meaning of a *mitzvah!* She was as arrogant as ever! She was incorrigible!

Eve was going to say more but she changed her mind. They were incapable of understanding her. They understood acting out of duty, duty emanating from obligation. They would never understand obligation emanating from mere love.

With her father requiring his own room, new living arrangements had to be instituted. Although she and David had originally partitioned the rooms of their house to accommodate five families, the two families had since expanded to take up all the space available, and now it would be difficult to go back to more cramped conditions. Therefore, Eve proposed to Ruth that they move their

168

schoolroom to the larger Markoff house, which would create no burden for Miriam and Hannah.

"It makes sense," Eve told Ruth. "Especially since we seem to be getting a new student almost every week." Ever since they had started teaching Hannah's and Miriam's children in addition to their own, they had been beseeched by other mothers in the town to take pity on their ignorant daughters and give them a little education too, not to mention their sons, who learned only Hebrew and didn't know how to read Russian at all. What with all the proclamations the authorities were issuing lately, one after the other, a person could be in serious trouble if he didn't know how to read at least a few Russian words, especially words such as *prohibited, forbidden,* and words like that in general.

"It makes sense," Ruth agreed. "They have the room."

Still, Eve sensed that Ruth was somehow disturbed, even displeased.

"What is it, Ruth? What's bothering you? That I've brought my father here? Are you concerned about the added work involved? I don't expect you to do any of the extra work, you know. I—"

"Don't talk. Don't say another word. After everything you've done for me, you insult me by thinking I'm afraid of the extra work of caring for your father. If anybody owes anybody anything, it is I who owe you everything. My God! You took us in, you gave us a happy home here, you've taught me and now I can teach my sons. You've made my life a joy; from dust, from nothing, a joy."

Eve smiled wistfully. "You don't seem extremely joyful to me. There *is* something bothering you. I can tell and I have to assume that it's my father living here—"

"All right. There *is* something. I know it's a terrible thing even to think about, much less to say, but with your father like this, we'll never be able to go to America . . . until he's dead!"

"So that's it. I should have realized—"

"It must have occurred to you—" Ruth began softly, but then her voice roughened with what amounted to anger. "What is it with you? Are you such a saint that you don't even think the same thoughts other people do? Here you've been dreaming of going to America for years already. As it was, you could have left your father to live out his life with your brothers. But now—now he's completely helpless and you've brought him here to live with you and you can never leave him until he dies and you don't even wish him dead? Or do you and you just can't admit it, even to yourself?"

At that Ruth started to cry almost hysterically, begging Eve to forgive her for her terrible words.

Eve hugged the tall, thin body. "Don't, Ruth, don't. There's nothing to forgive. When someone speaks from the heart those are words that never have to be forgiven. I know you're disappointed. But we'll still go to America, we'll get there—"

No, Ruth didn't really understand any better than her brothers did that she loved her father, and therefore it was no sacrifice when she fulfilled her obligation to him out of the love she bore him. And it didn't make her a saint. She *knew* she wasn't a saint. A saint didn't have to fight selfish and rebellious thoughts every day of her life as she did. . . .

Ruth blew her nose, wiped away her tears, sniffing as she did so. "And David? What does David have to say? I know he's as determined to go to America as we are. Does he feel bad that you've brought your father here? Is your father a burden to him?"

"No . . ."

"Ah, another saint!" Ruth said, trying to smile, throwing up her hands comically.

No, not another saint. Just my David. He understands about life and love and obligation. He understands that obligation is love and love is obligation. And if life is to be love, than life must be obligation too. . . .

"Well, Mrs. Saint, what are we waiting for? Shall we go over to Miriam's and Hannah's and tell them the good news—that they're to be the proprietresses of the Slobodka School for Poor Children?"

1887—that was the year Eve miscarried once again. It was also the year that every last remaining ruble of the three hundred rubles was expended. Five men—two Jews, two Poles and one Lithuanian nationalist—were caught printing seditious material in Kovno. They were locked up awaiting removal to Moscow for trial. David arranged with the Governor-General to accept 110 rubles for the men's release, but the printing press was destroyed. It was from their savings, their fund for America, that the money came to buy another press, which was kept hidden when not in use, in a hole dug in the stable, covered with straw and manure. Eve knew once again that Ruth was wrong. She a saint? Hardly. She scarcely knew which of the two—the spending of their America money or the danger of keeping the illicit press—caused her more pain.

She would lie awake in her bed or walk the kitchen floor, to and fro, back and forth, the knot of anxiety burning like a small fire in her chest, worrying over that press. But how could she stop David? How could she deny him the right to be what she had wanted him to be in the first place? The more he became that man, the more he changed, the more she loved him. And she wondered: was it possible that a love could grow too big? too enormous to bear?

She had bitter arguments over the press with Ruth.

"You're endangering all our lives by keeping that press here—"

"It's what David wants. I can't deny him."

"You must."

"I can't."

"Why can't you? If you refused to tolerate it, David would listen. Out of love, if for no other reason."

"That's why I can't ask him to remove it. Because he would do it only out of love. And if he did something that went against what he believed in, in the name of love, then what kind of love would that be?"

"A smart love. A clever love."

Eve laughed. "Oh Ruth, love can be many things but I doubt very much if it can be smart."

A smile began to curl around the edges of Ruth's mouth. "It should be . . ."

"Hannah's a very practical woman with a lot of common sense and she once said to me, 'Between what *should be* and what *is* there's a world of difference.' "

"*Oy vey* . . . I'm worried that we're all going to be caught and shot in our beds and she's quoting Hannah to me."

"You can move out, Ruth. You and Hershel and the boys can move in with the others. Hannah and Miriam would be very happy if you did that. And I'd understand. Really I would."

Ruth held up a hand as if to halt Eve's words. "Leave you and David alone with this?" Ruth shrugged, at a loss for a word strong enough to describe the enormity of the danger the press represented. "And what kind of a person would *I* be if I left you by yourself with this?"

Eve smiled. "A smart person maybe? A clever one?"

Ruth smiled back at her. "I can be many things but I doubt that I can be that smart."

Strangely enough, those times of the day when Eve tended to her father were a surcease from her hectic schedule, rather than an addition to the frenzy of activities that crowded the day. While she washed him, she sang softly to him, songs remembered from childhood. While she fed him, she talked to him, chattering away about Yitzhak, Dorie, telling him all about the school. And then there were those moments when she'd just sit by his bedside, holding his hand, making his paralysis-induced silence a shared thing. It was a time when daughter and father communed in spirit, very much refreshing Eve's own.

David asked Eve to write some of the material that would go into the pamphlets they were printing. He tried to keep his face expressionless when he said, "You're the most logical person since—"

Eve nodded, her eyes big in her face.

"It's a lot to ask—"

"No more than I've asked of you."

"More, much more."

"Oh, David!" She rushed into his arms. "Maybe that's what makes our love special. That we can, must, ask more of each other."

He held her close, ran his hands up and down her back smoothing the fabric mindlessly, but then he looked at the dress she was wearing. It was one of her old, pretty dresses, a bright yellow one, but not nearly as bright as it once had been.

"I didn't realize— You don't sew anymore. You haven't worn a new dress in a long time."

"Do you mind? There just doesn't seem to be time anymore. The children, the school, my father . . ."

171

"Mind? How could I mind? Besides, if anything, you're more beautiful than ever." He removed the pins from the huge bun she wore—she no longer had the time to arrange it as fancifully as she once had—and as the hair sprang loose and fell, his hands followed its course, past her breasts, her waist, her buttocks, even the backs of her knees.

Still, the very next day she started to work on a new dress—a taffeta, emerald green to match her eyes. That night when David came home her hair was as intricately arranged in a cascade of curls as it ever had been when they had first wed.

Ruth was furious when she learned that not only were they harboring the printing press in their own stable but now Eve was going to write the seditious material that emanated from it.

"I don't know what David is thinking of—to involve you further in this. You, the mother of his son! I thought he loved you so much, that he was crazy about you. Now I think he's merely crazy. How can he ask this of you?"

"He can ask it of me *only* because he does love me. And because he should expect no less of me. Since I married him, all I've ever told him is that we have to fight for what we want. We have to fight for what we think is right."

"Well, you've done that. You fought for all of us against Chaim and that took a lot of courage as far as I'm concerned."

"At the time, Ruth. At the time. But now when I look back it all seems ridiculously insignificant. I was only a child and Chaim an insignificant bully. But this, the printing press, this fight for a cause, this is history, Ruth. This is a fight for life itself. Oh yes, I was always full of brave words but now is the time when I have to use those brave words where it will really count, not just let them float on the air."

"But what about us? *Us!* We're supposed to go to America."

"We'll go, Ruth."

"But when? You're risking your life. Why can't you fight for causes in America? Why must you do it now? And for whom? For the Russian people who hate us? Your first duty is to yourself and your family!"

"But I'm doing this for myself and my family as well as for others. And the time must be now, because tomorrow may be too late."

"Too late for what?" Ruth asked dully. "To be dead?"

"I never told you before about a rabbi of ancient times, who is still regarded as one of the greatest teachers of all time. His name was Hillel and he was descended from King David. One of his most famous sayings goes this way: 'If I am not for myself, who is for me? And if I am for myself alone, what then am I? And if not now, then when?' "

There was a moment of silence while Ruth digested this. Then she said, "So, *nu? So he said* . . . So does that mean you have to risk your life or spend the rest of your years in Siberia? Besides, when did he live, this Hillel?"

"About two thousand years ago."

"You see? He didn't even know there *was* an America to go to . . . or that there was a Siberia to be sent to."

"Ah, but there were other considerations, of those times. In every generation there are special questions and special answers. There are always situations that try our souls."

"Now *that* I believe," Ruth shook her head up and down vigorously. "These are the times that try *my* soul. But if you have a book that tells of this Hillel, I'll read it. Then I'll tell you whether I believe he knew what he was talking about."

True to her word, the very next day she began to read about the renowned teacher. Several days later she told Eve, "So I believe him when he says, 'If not now, then when?' And what I have to say to you is, if we don't go to America now, then when?"

Eve burst out laughing. "Soon, Ruth, soon. Have faith."

Several weeks later—although she never said she forgave Eve for allowing the printing press and all it represented into their lives—Ruth suddenly pulled the scarf from her head to reveal a head of black curls that softened the angular face.

Eve couldn't believe her eyes. "Ruth, you've let your hair grow!"

"And why not? I understand that in America they're not so foolish as to think that to be a proper matron you have to have a shorn head. I decided that by the time we get to America, I'm going to walk around as beautiful as you!"

Eve understood that Ruth's new curls were a belief in the future, a symbol of her faith that they all would see the dawn of a newer, better day in America.

Then the years began running together. 1888, 1889.

Those were the years when the medical clinic was opened. It was never really planned but rather burst into being, evolving out of a series of circumstances.

First, there was Eve's reputation as a healer, beginning from the time she had saved the life of the Squire's son and the townspeople began showing up at her door with their afflicted, regardless of the ailment—a broken arm, an infected hand, a strange fever—as did the peasants from the surrounding villages. In vain Eve protested, pleading her lack of medical knowledge, but still they came. These were the simple and the impoverished, too poor or ignorant to think of going to a doctor, or those who would as soon think of going to consult with the Tsar as a physician. Eve couldn't turn them away. Rather, she pored over medical manuals and did what she could. She disinfected; dressed; lanced; let blood; applied oils, salves and poultices; bandaged; administered hot baths and snow baths; washed bodies with water or oils; massaged with vodka; rubbed and purged. She used David's and Hershel's brute strength to straighten a broken bone and applied splints. As for the fevered and the chilled, she put them to bed in her own house and took the sickest in the wagon to whatever doctors in Kovno she could prevail upon. When a seven-year-old girl who couldn't or wouldn't speak was brought to her, Eve suspected that the problem might be mental rather than physical and pressed a reluctant Ruth into service, having her work with the girl with books and pictures. It was possible that the girl learned to read before she ever spoke, but when she did finally utter those first few words, Ruth ran through the house screaming: "She talked! She talked! Eve, come here— You have to hear her speak! David! Hershel! Hurry!" After that she was as committed as Eve herself to their makeshift health service. Then she, as well as Eve, despaired over all those they were unable to help. "What we need around here is a real doctor!" she'd say when they were at a loss as to what to do.

When Elijah Brodkin didn't awaken one morning and was buried the next, Eve felt more than grief. She was aware of a tremendous void in her life, a void that all the other things in her life, all her other loved ones, couldn't fill. Talking to, reading to her father, just touching him, had been a source of sustenance to her and now his empty room constantly reminded her that she had lost more than her father; she had lost her past. Now there was *only* the future.

When Ruth caught Eve repeatedly staring into the empty room she finally said, "Look! We can bed down two or three of our children in here, giving us more living space, or we can use the room to attend to our sick customers. We've barely room now to turn around in the kitchen."

"Oh Ruth!" Eve threw her arms around her bone-thin sister-in-law. "I was thinking the very same thing."

"Well, we might as well do it since it seems we're not going any place tomorrow or the next day. Not with that printing press out there," Ruth couldn't resist adding, reminding Eve that they had planned on departing for America when Eve's father had passed on.

But Eve, excited now about fixing up the empty room as a clinic, didn't pause to remonstrate with her as she usually did in response to these statements. Instead she dashed into the room to take down the curtains, and Ruth followed to help her.

"This is as it should be, you know, Ruth. Putting the room to a wonderful purpose. It was just standing there empty, and as you know, nature abhors a vacuum."

Ruth sighed. "No, I didn't know. So, tell me already. Who was it who said that?"

Eve giggled. "I haven't the slightest idea."

It wasn't until after Eve lost the baby she'd been carrying and hoping to name after her father that the final requisite of a real clinic was fulfilled.

How different was Eve's reception at the home of Dr. Golov from the first time she'd gone there with Dora. This time, she was no sooner admitted to the waiting room than Ivan Golov came running out to greet her, to grab both her hands and lead her personally into his office.

"I thought I'd never see you again, Eva Markova!"

"Although I'm happy to see you, Dr. Golov, I wish it wasn't necessary. But I seem to have a problem."

"Yes?"

"I have one child and I've been hoping for more. But I don't seem to be able to hold a pregnancy."

"I see. Well, we'll have to see if there's anything that can be done to remedy that." But he appeared downcast.

"What is it, Dr. Golov? You don't sound . . . hopeful."

He smiled then, his very white teeth flashing in the dark-complected face. "I'm just disappointed—"

"Disappointed? I don't understand."

"I *was* hoping that you'd come simply to visit me just because you missed me," he said jocularly. "Or perhaps because you were in the market for a husband."

Eve's lips tightened. "You and I seem to have a problem understanding one another, doctor. Just as we did the last time we met. I am deadly serious, in need of your medical expertise, and you make jokes! And in very bad taste, too. We Jews don't make jokes about the possible loss of a loved one and I assure you, I love my husband *very much.*"

He sobered. "Of course you do. Fortunately for your husband. I never thought you would love in any other way. Forgive me."

It wasn't until later, after the examination, that Eve understood why the doctor had made his poorly put but well-intentioned joke. He had been trying to be cheerful in the face of what he had already suspected.

"I am truly sorry, Eva Markova, but there's nothing I can do for you. Sometimes a woman's body just isn't strong enough to hold on to a pregnancy. But your case isn't entirely hopeless. Sometimes nature takes a hand, does for itself what man can't. Your reproductive system might strengthen all by itself and surprise us all. I wish I could have helped—you, of all women, certainly. Some day we doctors will know more, won't have to rely so much on Mother Nature. Sometimes I get so depressed about the women I can't help I feel like giving up."

Eve tried to concentrate on his words rather than on her own disappointment. "But you can't give up. Think about all the women you *have* helped and can help in the future. Like Dora . . ." Her voice trailed off. She had written to tell him of Dora's death and Dorie's birth. She had wanted him to know that, at least, he had succeeded in helping to give a child life.

He pressed her hand in sympathy. "I'm sorry. I know how much you loved her."

His dark eyes were wet with commiseration. He *is* a caring person, Eve thought. Then she knew why she been inspired to come see him. Perhaps it had never been for herself at all. Perhaps deep in her heart she'd known that he couldn't help her and that her visit had been preordained for another purpose, an even more important purpose. So she told Dr. Golov how he could help her, and many, many others. Even as he already knew that he would do whatever she asked of him, he said, "And you'd have me come all the way from Vilno just to deliver babies in Slobodka?"

She was able to laugh at this because she already knew that he was going to do just what she wanted him to. "No, of course not just to deliver babies. Practically every woman in the countryside can midwife under ordinary circumstances. It's the difficult births I'm thinking of, and the difficult conceptions, and the women who are too sick inside even to think about having babies."

Thus it was decided that Dr. Golov would travel to Slobodka once a month to assist in the Clinic. More than that, he agreed to prevail upon other specialists to donate a few hours each month there as well.

"An eye doctor? Please," Eve begged. "We desperately need a doctor knowledgeable in the treatment of eyes."

He could not help but respond to her enthusiasm, pleased that for the moment anyway, she had pushed aside her own personal anguish. "And what about an ear specialist? Have you no need for a professor for the ears?"

"Oh yes! And the lungs too! Oh, Doctor Ivan Golov, God will bless you!"

He laughed. "Which one? Yours or mine?"

"Both. Or perhaps they really are one and the same. But I warn you. Mine may be a woman . . ." she teased.

He threw back his head and laughed heartily. "In that case, I'll gladly accept that possibility too."

He escorted Eve to the train station personally. As the train pulled out he watched and waited for it to vanish fron sight, speculating as to the reasons he was willing to travel all the way to Slobodka when all about, in his own city, everywhere, there were thousands of women who needed his help.

Eve gazed out the train window at the moving landscape, her thoughts lingering only briefly on her own disappointment. She had been prepared for that, prepared and resigned. It wasn't as if she didn't have both a natural son and a daughter of the heart, and she believed in counting one's blessings. It was the Clinic that absorbed her thoughts. She determined that she would name it for her father. If she couldn't honor his memory by naming a child after him, then all the people helped by the Clinic would honor his memory even more.

Honoring was certainly better than mourning. When her father died, she had gone to the House of Worship demanding to be permitted to recite the Kaddish, the mourner's prayer, along with the men, and to do it for the prescribed one year. She knew that women weren't ordinarily permitted to do this, but her deep grief and zeal impelled her to try and sway the men. But they had turned her away, had reminded her that she had brothers who were saying the Kaddish for her father, and that it was their place and not hers. She had been angry and bitter and had gone out into the fields to do there under the open sky what they hadn't allowed her to do in the synagogue. She had held out her arms to the heavens and shouted the words:

"O God, full of compassion who dwellest on high, grant perfect rest beneath the sheltering wings of Thy divine presence amongst the holy and pure who shine as the brightness of the firmament, to Elijah who has gone to his eternal home . . ." Still, she had been consumed with anger. More anger even than grief.

Now she left the train and started the long walk home. Through the center of Kovno, over the bridge, past the fields and the woods. Then she stopped, paused for a moment to look all around her at the sky, at the meadows. No, there was no more need to mourn her father and she didn't need a synagogue to recite the prayers for his soul. There was going to be a *real* clinic with real doctors and truly, God was everywhere. Even in Slobodka!

15.

As the Clinic flourished, Eve frequently wondered which was the more important—the idea or the individual. The more she thought about it, the more she wondered if the two would ever fit together, if the needs of one would reconcile with the needs of the other. Though she fought discouragement, gradually she became resigned to the realization that no matter how hard she and David and others like them strove to make Russia a better place to live, it was going to take more years than they all had, totaled up.

As the Clinic flourished, their school prospered as well. Eve thought it was Russia rushing, trying to catch up with the rest of the world, but whatever the reason, they were besieged with requests to let yet one more child into their classroom. There were requests even from the most downtrodden of peasants, the most ignoble of Jews—people who had never before even dreamed of the possibility of one of theirs reading and writing. Occasionally one of the peasants pointed out that he wanted it clearly understood that it was Russian his child was to learn and not the Yid stuff, not even aware in his ignorance that he was using a word that was offensive to the patrons whose largesse he was seeking.

"No more! No more!" Ruth protested. "And I don't care if the child is Jewish, Lithuanian or Polish. How many more can we make room for? Look at you!" she accused Eve. "You're worn out. Your dress is hanging on you! You're even thinner than I am. It's not enough that you run between here and the School all day long, but you stay up all night writing that garbage for those pamphlets of David's—"

"It's not garbage! How can you say such a thing?"

"Because all those words don't help. Not anything or anybody. It doesn't do any good. All it does is get people killed. Last week, over a hundred people were shot in Minsk. Striking workers were shot down in the street, stirred up by the same kind of garbage you write!"

"But Ruth! We have to keep trying. If one strike fails, the next might succeed. If we don't keep trying how will anything ever get better?"

"There's no use in *us* fighting over this. Let's stick to the matter at hand. I say: no more pupils. It would be different if we had more teachers. But as it is, there's only you and me. Hannah and Miriam are worthless."

"They help here in the Clinic."

"I'm talking about teaching."

"I've been thinking about that, and I think it's time we let some of the older children teach some of the beginners. Hannah's and Miriam's children are very good at the Hebrew lessons and your boys are good at everything. And Dorie's excellent with numbers. . . ."

There was a bit of an embarrassed silence over the exclusion of Yitzhak's name, but then Eve laughed. "Now if we had a class in horseback riding or even in lifting a horse from the ground, I could offer Yitzhak's services. Or maybe if we taught handwrestling or the sport of seeing how far one can spit . . . Well, at least he is a help to David. There's nothing Yitzhak would rather do than go out with his father rounding up livestock, unless it's hanging around the marketplace seeing what mischief he can get into there."

Ruth gave a perfunctory little laugh out of politeness but her thoughts had already moved on. "It's never going to be done with, is it? The pamphlets, the School, the Clinic. We're never going to be free, are we? We just get in deeper and deeper." She held up a hand to Eve who was about to speak. "No. Don't bother to correct me. Deeper and deeper. More pupils. More patients. More pamphlets. More people with their hands out. And you and David are never going to walk away from it—this grasping, greedy *need* that's consuming us all. You'll never leave. I can see it. You'll never leave and we'll be stuck here in this mudhole until we're all dead!"

"Ruth, no!"

"Yes! How will you ever walk away from it? When?"

"You'll see. There'll be others to take the torch from our hands and go on with it. Just as in the races in ancient Greece. Or as in battle. When one warrior drops the flag, someone else picks it up and goes forth."

Ruth snickered. "Yes. They pick up the banner from the *fallen*, the dead! And these torch bearers. Where will *they* come from? The Slobodka marketplace?"

"Listen, Ruth. The ones we teach today will teach others tomorrow. And the Clinic—when Dr. Gorkin died, didn't Dr. Shenko take his place? And the pamphlets. If we stopped printing today, tomorrow, in some other town others would write the same material, twenty others, thirty . . ."

"If that's the case, do it. Stop today. And let the others take over tomorrow."

When Eve didn't respond, Ruth smiled grimly. "See. You *can't* walk away from it. And if you could, *David* can't. So much for your fallen banners. And as for your Clinic, if you left tomorrow, how long do you think your Dr. Golov would carry his humanitarian torch? He comes here and brings the other doctors only because he's in love with you. If you're so smart, why don't you know that?"

"Ruth, that's a terrible thing to say!"

"Why? It's the truth. Didn't you tell me there's one thing that can never be denied and that's the truth?"

"But it's not a truth. It's only your guess and it's . . . ugly!"

"Ugly? You've also told me that beauty is only in the eye of the beholder."

"I'm sick and tired of being told *what I said!*"

"If that's the case, then you'd better stop saying. But the truth of it is that you can as soon stop saying as you can leave here and trust that there'll be others to pick up your banner, to carry your torch for you."

Eve wondered about the truth of what Ruth had said. Did Dr. Golov come to help at the Clinic only because he was in love with her? She fervently hoped that wasn't so. Would she ever be capable of leaving the School and the Clinic and the pamphlets to others? It was true that at first she had remained in Russia because of a certain set of obligations. Then, as that set of obligations dwindled away one by one, there had been new ones, new reasons to stay. Wouldn't there always be new ones, unless once and for all she did walk away? Then, *if* she herself were capable of walking away from these obligations, would David be?

It was in the fall of 1890 that David came home at a gallop. He rushed to the stable, dug up the printing press from under its pile of straw and manure, dismantled it and dropped the pieces in the river, one by one. Eve asked no questions until the last piece was gone.

"Yitzhak . . ." David blurted. "Yitzhak and two of his friends from the village. They printed up broadsheets! *Kill Alexander! Kill the Tsar!* I caught him at the bridge going to Kovno. He was actually going to drop them in the streets, just let them drift on the air!"

"Oh my God! Where is he? Is he all right?"

"Yes, he's all right. But he's in hiding now—from me! After I grabbed the broadsheets from him and while I was dropping them into the river, making sure they sank, he rode away, laughing! When I find him, I'm going to flay his hide!"

"But are you sure he's in the clear? That no one saw him with those leaflets? That he never dropped any of them?"

"They were in his saddlebag. And he said he had them all."

"Then why did you have to destroy the press?"

"Because I couldn't take a chance on all our lives. How can I be sure those louts from the village, Yitzhak's friends, didn't take some of the broadsheets with them? Or that Yitzhak himself didn't drop a few somewhere? You don't understand, Eve. To them, this was all a lark! A lark! Can I risk all our lives on witless children who'd do something like this for fun? For an adventure? When I find Yitzhak, I'm going to pound some sense into him, I can tell you that."

"Don't be too hard on him, David. He's only a child, for God's sake. I know he's big and strong. That's why you forget that he's only a boy and expect him to act and think like a man. And don't forget from whom he comes . . ." she teased, trying to banter David out of some of his rage. "After all, that wild Markoff blood isn't all his fault."

David was neither amused nor impressed.

"Printing up declamations that say 'kill the Tsar' isn't a boy's game, Eve.

And now we've lost the press because of his foolishness. If they'd caught him, they wouldn't have stopped to ask his age. He'd have been sent to Siberia along with the rest of us. If we don't teach him to assume responsibility for himself, not to mention others, then we've taught him nothing.''

"But David, we are teaching him. Don't you see? He's just trying to be you, doing the things you do because he wants to grow into the kind of man you are.''

"No, Eve, this time you're wrong. Yitzhak did this thing not because he wanted to do what I do but only because it was *fun*. And you, of all people, should know there isn't time for anybody to grow into anything. This is Russia in the year 1890 and you know what that means. It means there's no time for a Jew to be just a fun-loving boy.''

1891, 1892. The years of the Great Famine, and hunger was the order of the land. In the Markoff household, less emphasis was placed on teaching and more on the Clinic as physical maladies flourished in the wake of starvation. Livestock became almost unavailable as did the products of the field. Eve traveled, among other places, to the Squire's manor where there was no apparent dearth of food, to beg for provisions for the townspeople, for the villagers' children, for the patients of the Clinic. The Squire was unable ever to turn her away completely empty-handed and would have a few heads of cabbage, a half-sack of beets, a sack of potatoes placed in her wagon.

"I have my own people to think of—'' he murmured in apology for the small quantity, knowing she would be back the following week.

The Countess still offered her a lovely tea with pastries and tiny cakes and dainty finger sandwiches, chocolates decorated with walnut meats and candied raspberries. Eve drank the tea with the very thin translucent slices of lemon while she emptied the porcelain dishes of their offerings, sweeping all into her market bag, leaving not even one cherry tart or sugar cookie on a plate. When the Countess inclined her head at this breach of good manners, Eve only smiled. "You'd be surprised to see how a sweet can cheer the sickest of children.''

But then the Countess was gone.

"She's taken the children to St. Petersburg,'' the Squire explained. It seemed that there was a growing disquiet among the peasants, and the Countess feared for her own and her children's safety.

"And will you join her, Squire?''

"These are my people on my land that are hungry. I can't desert them.''

When Eve repeated this conversation to David, he laughed out loud, then said: "I'd say he's less worried about deserting his peasants than he is about coming back to find that these peasants had taken over his land.''

Eve looked at him, shocked. She had apportioned scant time of late to keeping up with what was going on in the outside world, immersed as she was in searching out food and in caring for the sick at the Clinic. It had been some time already since she had stopped writing the pamphlets intended to fan the sparks of revolt.

"Has it really reached this point, David? That the peasants would or could dare try to take over the Squire's land?"

"What's happened to you, Eve? Haven't you been reading any of the newspapers? There's something emerging out of this famine besides starvation. Something good! Those hunger pains in the belly are stimulating even the thickest of heads. Alexander had almost managed to squash all thoughts of rebellion and dissension with his persecutions and edicts, but now—now it's breaking out all over again! And Russian socialists are no longer preaching just land reform—"

"Oh?" Eve asked wearily. "What are they preaching instead?"

"Marxism! Total Marxism! The peasants and workers taking over the State *completely*."

Eve shrugged. She was too worn in body and spirit these days to be impressed with those who preached and talked and discussed instead of *doing*. "Marxism is a philosophy, David. Something for intellectuals to debate about—mind exercises. What can it possibly mean to women who see their children dying while they squat in the fields gathering rotted potatoes into their aprons?"

David laughed softly, sadly. "What has happened to that girl I stood under the wedding canopy with? That firebrand who told me it was more important to feed the mind and the spirit than the stomach? Where has she gone? That girl who said freedom was all?"

"She's grown up, David. Grown up to realize that there is no Utopia. That's what Marxism is all about, really. A promise of a classless Utopian society. When I said it was more important to feed the mind than the stomach, it was the words of a foolish, self-important, thoughtless child. Now that I'm a mother I know one thing. You have to fill your children's stomachs first so that they can *live*. Then maybe they'll be able to find a Utopia in their future. But not here, David, never here. Maybe Russia, like the potatoes the women claw out of the ground, is too far gone, too rotted to be tasted of ever again."

Sorrowfully, David pressed Eve's body to his. He mourned for that bright, fiery girl who had grown into this wise, strong woman, disillusioned by times and circumstances even stronger than she herself. Even as he loved this woman more than the girl she had been, he also yearned for that girl with her burning, shining enthusiasm for life, yearned for that *girl* more for Eve's own sake than for his own. In America, she might be that girl again.

He buried his face in her breasts and murmured into them. "Oh, Eve, why don't we just give it all up now? Not wait any longer. Why don't we just go to America now? Right away?"

But now it was she who smiled sadly. "No, you'd be doing it for me and I can't let you do that. You see, I know who *you* are now, David. If I'm no longer the girl you married, you're not the boy I stood under the *chupah* with either. Now you're the man of destiny who wouldn't be able to forgive himself if he walked away from this deathwatch we're keeping over Russia. No, you and I have to see it to its bitter end."

182

He lifted his face from her bosom. "But you, Eve, you keep moving ahead of me. Once this would have been what you really wanted and now it is no longer. I tried to grow into the kind of man you wanted me to be when you were a girl and now that I'm here, your heart's desire is elsewhere. You've moved on without me— Oh, Eve, wait for me!"

"Oh, David, David!" She kissed him—his throat, his cheeks, his lips, almost in desperation. "I would always wait for you, always, whenever, wherever. But David, I have the feeling *you've* passed *me*. Oh, David, if that is the case you'll have to wait for me. You will, won't you?"

"Whenever, wherever. We'll always wait for each other."

1892, 1893. Cholera swept the country like an evil wind in the wake of that terrible storm, the Famine, but it was much more democratic, claiming its victims from all levels of Russian society—gentry and peasants, gentiles and Jews, Poles as well as Lithuanians and Russians. Many fell, most succumbed.

These days there was little mention in either Markoff household of escape to America. That was for daydreaming and there was no time for dreams or even talk of dreams. There was only the business of caring for the sick, the business of trying to stay alive, the business of the rites of death.

There was the boiling. Everything that was part and parcel of living was boiled. They spent all their time away from nursing the ill or burying the dead, boiling. They carried in the water in the huge pots kept especially for this purpose and they boiled everything they touched, everything they ate. The clothes and the sheets; the towels and the dishes. They boiled the chickens and the beef and even the herrings. They boiled the vegetables and the fruit. A child caught eating an unboiled plum or cherry was severely punished. What they couldn't boil, they disinfected. Every stick of furniture in the house, the floors and the walls. They warred on any fly daring to enter within, poured lye on the feces of the animals without. Still many fell and most succumbed.

Terrified eyes watched for the terrible symptoms—the colicky stomach pains, the looseness of the bowels, the copious rice-water stools, the vomiting, the headaches and the mental depression, followed quickly by a general collapse. This collapse was accompanied by a great thirst and the growing cramps in the hands and feet. The skin turned blue, cold and wrinkled; the voice grew husky while the pulse could hardly be detected at all.

Miriam's Becky fell ill and recovered, but then Hannah's Golda, recently wed and with child, sickened. Hannah never left her daughter's bedside as she kept feeling for the fading pulse, wetting the dry lips, forcing barley water into the resisting mouth, applying cups to the chest. When nothing seemed to work or quicken the heartbeat, she scolded Golda, first yelling then beseeching— "Golda, you listen to me! Goldie, listen to your mother! You've got to get better. Your mother wants you to get better! Goldie, you were always a good girl. Listen to your mother!" In answer, Golda first aborted the child inside her,

183

then died, whispering thickly at the last, "Mama . . ." from between cracked lips. They had to tear the girl from Hannah's arms.

Weeks later, Hannah said to Eve, "Remember that first night when we all sat down at the table with Chaim. You sat down first and then we all came over to the table, one by one. Later that night Golda said that when you first sat down, she was terribly frightened for you. She said she was scared Chaim would hit you, but then when Dora, may she rest in peace, came over to help you and then, Ruth, well, Golda said she was happy for you. But then she said that, at *that* moment, she was happy for *herself* too. Strange, she was only a little girl. She was a sweet girl, my Golda. Such a sweet girl . . ."

"A sweet girl . . ." Eve repeated, realizing that Hannah was still recalling all the days of Golda's short life. Day by day. Hour by hour. Word by word. She knew that forever and a day, Hannah would never stop recalling. Even in a land where death was a daily given, Hannah would never stop recalling, dipping into the recesses of her broken heart for a nearly forgotten word.

The very old succumbed first, and then the young. Ruth's Aaron died so swiftly Ruth had almost no time to steel herself, to brace herself with the defensive bitterness she screamed to the heavens afterwards, at the graveside and during the mourning period immediately after. But even this postmortem bitterness offered no comfort.

Then she herself fell victim to the plague and again her bitterness didn't help. Not even the bile-filled words she mouthed as she took her angry leave of the world of which she had despaired— "The worst of all is to die in this godforsaken mudhole," she croaked.

"No!" Eve shrieked in protest. "Oh, God, no!" She clutched Ruth's lifeless body to her breast, clung to her friend in death as Hannah had clung to her daughter. But in the end she had to yield in the presence of Hershel's wailing, Ruth's three remaining sons' sobbing as they too clutched, holding on to Ruth's blue and wrinkled hands. Eve knew that her own grief had to retreat before theirs. *And her guilt* . . . It was she who had kept Ruth in "this godforsaken mudhole" to die of its plague, no matter how hard Ruth had pleaded to escape to a better and sweeter place.

"She's gone to a better place," Eve mumbled to Hershel and the boys. "She's with God now, and with Aaron," she told them, only hoping that it was really so.

Then she went out into the yard where night was falling and she looked up into the gray-black sky searching for solace for herself. Once again she intoned the ancient words that were becoming more and more familiar to her, year by year and day by day:

"Loheyn baal horahamim yastireh-hol beseser k'nofov leolomim, ve'itzror hahayim es nishmosh, Adonoy hoo nahalohsoh, yesohnuah besholom al miskovoh veomar omain. . . .

"O God, full of compassion who dwellest on high, grant perfect rest beneath

184

the sheltering wings of Thy divine presence among the holy and pure who shine as the brightness of the firmament, to Ruth who has gone to her eternal home. . . ."

But reciting the prayer didn't help. She could forgive God for calling Ruth but she could not forgive herself for keeping Ruth here in this misbegotten Mother Russia to be so cruelly taken. Spring was almost at hand and the land was black and wet and soggy with the melting snows. Not able to bear her guilt, stronger than even her grief, Eve flung herself to the ground to wallow in Ruth's forsaken mudhole.

David found her lying there, her skirt and blouse soaked with the wet dirt, face and hair bespattered with the soil, clutching handfuls of the sodden dank earth within her fists. "My poor girl, my poor sweetheart," he murmured helplessly. Tears rolling down his face, he stooped, picked her up, held her body close to his, covering himself with her mud, rocking back and forth, and he, too, began to intone the Kaddish, the mourner's prayer, although he hadn't prayed in years. Eve knew that this was his way of helping her atone, of sharing her guilt.

There was a new edict that the bodies of the cholera dead were to be cremated instead of buried. This was an additional burden to the Jews, a violation of their ancient law that their dead were to be committed only to the earth. "There won't even be a grave to visit . . ." Hershel wept as the acrid smoke crept upward to the sky.

"No," Eve allowed, "but instead, you'll be able to feel Ruth all around you, looking down on you always from up there—" She indicated the heavens by lifting her head. She thought of Shelley's words—"heaven's ebon vault." But she knew these words would hold no beauty, no comfort for Hershel. "That way, she'll be there for you no matter where you are."

In the weeks that followed, Ruth was there for Eve too, everywhere. She couldn't stop thinking of all the things she had said, even as Hannah had thought of every word her Golda had uttered, every deed she had ever performed.

Ruth, unveiling her crop of newly grown curls, laughing, saying, "I decided that by the time we get to America, I'm going to walk around as beautiful as you."

Oh Ruth, you'll never see America now. But beautiful? Oh yes, beautiful, and it didn't matter if you wore curls or if your hair was shorn. It was your beautiful spirit that kept me going so many times when I thought surely I was too weary to go on.

Ruth, so determined to go to America, deploring everything that stood in their way, and still the one who had suggested using Eve's dead father's room for an official Clinic, knowing full well that the Clinic would only be another obstacle to their leaving. And why had she done this? Because she wanted to fill the void formed in her, Eve's, heart created by her father's passing. *Oh, a loving, giving Ruth . . .*

And a courageous one. When the printing press had first come into their lives Ruth had worried about the danger the press represented to their families. But when Eve had told Ruth that she would understand if Ruth and her family went to live with the other Markoffs, Ruth had replied: "And what kind of a person would I be then if I left you by yourself with this danger?"

Oh, I know what kind of a person you were, Ruth. Not only scaldingly honest but valiant. And loyal. As true a friend as I have ever known. Or will ever know. I will miss your tart tongue but loving heart, your satirical view of life that was tempered by your wonderful humor. Oh, we cried together, you and I, but oh, how we laughed too!

The images of Ruth kept appearing before Eve's eyes; her words kept re-echoing in her ears. Eve could not run away from them.

Ruth, enthusiastic, falling in love with literature. Reading *War and Peace,* rising at four in the morning after being up to midnight to read it. Raving over the novel's Natasha—"Don't you think Natasha is a wonderful heroine?"

No, you were the heroine, Ruth. Working day and night—teaching, nursing, toiling and sacrificing even as you pretended to complain. Natasha?—a toy woman, a doll, a vain, indulged and self-indulged girl-child. You, Ruth, were a flesh-and-blood woman. Real. With a dream. Of being a free and educated woman in America—your boys, American school boys.

The vision of Ruth and her voice followed Eve no matter where she went, what she did.

Ruth, saying to her when they first started teaching their children, "I guess we should start with Yiddish but we should definitely get to the English right away. That's our language of the future. And the children—they're the future . . ."

Oh yes, Ruth, English was supposed to be the language of our future. And our children, yours and mine, they are the future, yes . . .

The truth was, much as it hurt to admit it, that she had cheated Ruth of her rightful future and now it no longer mattered whether she had been right or wrong in delaying the family's departure for the New World; right or wrong in deciding which obligations had deserved precedence; in choosing her priorities. There was only one thing that mattered now—what she could do to make up for having failed Ruth in her lifetime. And she had the answer to that; she could see to it that Ruth's boys, along with her own Yitzhak and Dorie, realized *their* future in America. For them, at least, the dream could still come true. This time she would not be put off. This time there would be no delay.

Without a word to anyone, Eve began to solidify her plans. She began with making lists—those possessions they would take, those they would leave, those things they would try to sell. Then, a list of names of people to be consulted and contemplated as to the possibility of taking over the responsibility of the Clinic; a list of those who could possibly assume leadership of the School, with a subsidiary list of those who could teach what. Too, she compiled a roster of possible buyers for the Markoff Brothers' Livestock business, *if* Hannah and

Miriam and their families decided to make the trip into the future with them. Finally there was a summary of their assets. Soon, she would be able to surprise them all, including David, with a complete set of plans.

She was counting on David's acquiesence, his fervent willingness to go along with her decision. Hadn't they sworn to wait for one another, whenever and wherever? Of course that vow had been only a figure of speech, rather a vow of allegiance, meaning that one would go along with the other wherever it was that either of their hearts led. David would understand that her decision had been made with a heartfelt urgency and with a rightness to it that could not be denied. It was, after all, a matter of trust.

But before she could announce her plan, to tell David of her desire to leave while the season was still summer, David moved first, and past her. Or perhaps, as she would think about it later, it was time and circumstance, even destiny, that propelled them all into a situation that left no room for personal desires.

Eve was out in the yard hanging up the wash—all the articles of clothing she had just boiled, even though the epidemic had waned. For as long as she still passed her days in Russia, she was incapable of *not boiling*. It had become habit, as natural as breathing. More than habit; in the wake of death, it had become compulsion. It was late afternoon on a particularly hot day, and her thin dress clung to her body in the humid heat. When she straightened for a moment to wipe the perspiration from her brow, she saw David riding in from the west. Quickly she shielded her eyes, then squinted them. Silhouetted against the setting sun, David appeared to be enveloped in flames. Her heart pounded as she rushed to the gate to meet him. Then she saw that he was not enveloped in flames at all but apparently drenched in blood. "David!" she screamed.

He jumped off his horse and she realized that it wasn't *his* blood; there was no wound. She almost swooned in her overwhelming gratitude to a merciful God. She rushed to throw her arms around him, forgetting or perhaps not even realizing that in doing so she would taint her yellow dress with the blood that covered him.

David tried to push her away but he was too late and her dress was blemished. "Into the house!" he ordered. "Quickly!"

They ran, hand in hand, and as she did Eve wondered whose blood it was that streaked her dress, soaked David's shirt and breeches, caked his face and soiled his hands. But there was no time for questions.

"Take off your dress!" David commanded. "We'll have to burn it too." Just before he began to strip himself of his shirt, he threw some other articles of clothing that he had been carrying on the floor. Eve hadn't even noticed that he had been carrying them but now she saw what they were—the blouse and breeches of a Cossack!

"David?"

"We'll talk later!" He threw his own shirt and breeches into the fire where the pots of water for the washing still boiled. Wordlessly, she handed him her dress and he threw that in too. Glancing at her in her white petticoat and chemise, he told her to go put on another dress and to bring him another shirt and pants. "We might be having unexpected company! And I'll need a basin of water to wash up. Quickly, Eve!"

"Yes, but here— You'd better throw these in the fire first!" She picked up the pieces of the Cossack uniform with only her fingertips. The cloth was already stiffening with the drying blood.

"No! We're washing those!" He grabbed for the uniform, intending to throw the two pieces into one of the pots of boiling water.

"No!" she cried out instinctively, not knowing if she meant for him not to wash the uniform, or not to throw it into the boiling water if he wanted the blood stains out. Between stiff lips, she said, "If you want to get rid of blood stains, you use cold water, not hot."

As they dried the uniform before the fire, David spoke in a low voice, constantly looking through the window for any sign of an alien visitor, or one of the family coming home: "I had no choice, you understand. I was on my way home from the meeting in Barkan's cellar. I was already crossing the bridge when I realized this Cossack was following me! I didn't even have time to think or plan. All I knew was that he must have been following me ever since I left the meeting, that he even guessed what kind of a meeting it had been. All I could think of was that he would follow me home and that we would all be denounced—you and me and Hershel. Maybe even Abraham and Shlomo. And maybe all the men of the organization. I knew there was only one thing to be done. So, as I came off the bridge, I hid in the stand of trees. When he came riding off, I rode out and—"

"With what?"

"My stiletto."

"And what did you do with the body? Just leave it there?"

"No. I buried it where they'll never find it."

"And his horse?"

"I considered taking it here, painting it as the gypsies do—but I decided it was too risky a business."

"But what will they think when they find his horse?"

"I hope the gypsies will get it first. If not, they'll know its rider is missing anyway. They'll already be searching for him. When they don't find him they'll assume he has deserted . . . They desert all the time."

"But if they can't discover the body but assume the man deserted with or without his horse, and we've burned your bloodied clothes and my dress, then why, in God's name, are we saving the only remaining and most incriminating evidence of all—the uniform?" She pleaded with her voice and her eyes but she already knew the answer. Dear God, she already knew the answer. "Why, David? Oh why?"

His eyes answered hers, blue-black and burning like hot coals. "But you already know the answer to that, don't you Eve? If certain tasks become necessary, if certain actions must be taken, can you think of *any* disguise that might be more effective? Eve! Eve! Just think of the possibilities!''

She helped him bury the uniform in the stable where once the printing press had been hidden, covering the hole with forkfuls of straw and piles of manure, thinking of nothing *but* David's possibilities and her own, now, impossibilities. But mostly, she was afraid. David's organization, a group of National Socialists, were not men whose work was carried on in violence. Rather, they were men who used the word, vocal and written, and who planned strikes, not killings . . . But times were changing in Russia; every year there were more men joining the legion of protestors, there were more groups and organizations, there were more strikes leading to uprisings, more acts of rebellion. What more enticing inducement could exist to move from one form of protest to another than an almost foolproof disguise, the uniform of the enemy?

So once again her own desires had to be put aside, their urgency diminished by the times and circumstances, and maybe destiny. Still, Eve wondered what would have happened if she had made her announcement that they were all leaving for America *yesterday* . . . Would the Cossack uniform have gone into the fire as well as her dress and David's shirt and breeches? Now she would never know.

16.

In the year 1894 Yitzhak was *bar mitzvah* and according to Hebrew tradition, became a man. David kissed him on both cheeks and admonished him to be the kind of man that would make his mother proud. Eve, slightly embarrassed at how Yitzhak had stumbled in his reading from the Torah, nevertheless hugged him in a manner that suggested she was very, very proud of him. At least Yitzhak felt that she was.

There was a great celebration in their house that evening. There were many images that would linger in the *bar mitzvah* boy's mind for a long time—his father leaning down to kiss his mother whose face was turned up to his with the lovelight shining. And his mother, in a beautiful new dress, blue with deep folds and touches of lace at the neck and wrist—flushed and laughing. There was lots of wine and vodka and wonderful things to eat. All his friends and cousins were there, joking and singing. There was even dancing, as much as there was room for in the small house. The potato pancakes kept coming from the oven in endless layers, and the windows were etched with lovely frost trees from the deep cold outside and all the warmth within. Yitzhak drank enough to get a little tipsy and all the guests laughed and proclaimed him, "a true Markoff."

A hush fell over the party when the Squire arrived. Everyone present knew of Eve Markoff's friendship with the Squire, knew the story of how she had saved the Squire's son's life when he was at death's door. Still, who would have thought that he would actually attend the *bar mitzvah* celebration? Under the circumstances, the Count stayed only a little while but long enough to sample the refreshments, to clink a glass of vodka with David, to pay his compliments to Eve. He kissed her hand and then kissed Yitzhak on both cheeks and presented him with thirteen rubles, one for each of his years. After the Squire left it took a few minutes before the party regained its high festive air. Yitzhak's friends looked at him with awe. Thirteen rubles and a kiss on each cheek from the Count!

Through a kind of haze Yitzhak heard his mother whisper in his ear: "Now that you are a man the important thing for you to remember always is who you are and from whom you come." But he was only thirteen years old, and it would take many, many years before he would really understand the meaning of his mother's words.

That same year, Alexander III died in Livadia at the age of fifty. It was said that he had always been a robust man but that his strength had been sapped by his fear of revolutionaries surrounding him on all sides, and that he ended his days hiding behind a coterie of agents of the police. Eve was hopeful that the "leaden coffin lid" of Alexander's reign, as it was described in the illegal newspapers, might in some way be alleviated by Nicholas, the son who succeeded his father. David scoffed at this possibility; as it turned out, he was right and Eve foolishly optimistic. When the delegates of the oppressed asked of the new Tsar "that the voice of the people be heard," his answer was not reassuring. "Let all know that I intend to defend the principle of autocracy as unswervingly as did my father."

Eve and David were constantly debating as to what form "revolt" should take. Agrarian? Economic? Political? Violent or peaceful? Strike or riot? Legal or subversive? But no one ever held to a particular position. Each one of them could be on either side of the fence on any particular day, depending on the latest incident in Moscow or St. Petersburg. The truth was they enjoyed their debates, even when "discussion" occasionally became "argument." When it came to "doing" they were always as one and the "discussion-arguments" were only part of the tapestry that made up the fabric of their daily lives, interwoven with the essentials—the making of their living, the more or less secret activities directed toward making the country a better place to live, the Clinic, the School.

Eve was constantly sewing as ordinary life went on amidst the turmoil of a troubled land. Much to Miriam's relief, her pretty daughters, each with a pleasing roundness to them, were married, one by one, and Eve was asked to make each one a new wedding dress and the essentials of a trousseau. There were always squabbles to be settled as Rochel complained that Rebecca's wedding dress had been more elegant, or Rissa cried that Rochel's wedding nightdress had been prettier. Eve would add more lace to the one, more ribbon to the other. Then, when the babies started coming, Eve went to work on the layettes. When Rena lamented that her baby would have only hand-me-downs, Eve had to be sure that that wasn't the case.

Hershel's oldest son, Daniel, went off to Moscow to become a lawyer. Daniel had always excelled in Russian and when he expressed the wish to study law so that he might help those accused Jews who were almost always without representation in the courts, Eve was delighted. Hershel, on the other hand, went to pieces and screamed that it was impossible. *A Jewish lawyer?* They'd tear him to pieces. Better he should be a dealer in livestock too. At least the Markoffs were making a good living. Better Daniel should stay at home and not attract any attention to himself. Besides, they'd never let him become a lawyer in the first place. Did they want Jewish lawyers shooting off their mouths in the second place?

Daniel appealed to Eve who appealed to Hershel. "This is the way it's supposed to be," she told her brother-in-law. "First Ruth learned and then she taught her children and they learned. Now they have to take the knowledge they have and go forth with it, out into the world to try and make it a better place. Oh Hershel, Ruth must be laughing up there in heaven!"

Hershel shook his head helplessly. "Even you wouldn't say Ruth was exactly what you would call a laugher. She might be pleased but she's not laughing. Maybe, at most, she's smiling a little." If anyone could resist Eve it certainly wasn't he. After Ruth died, how would he have managed without her? She was like a mother to his boys. "But even so, how will we manage this? Who will even allow Daniel to study?"

"Oh, we'll manage," Eve assured Hershel. "We'll grease a palm here and there . . . And with the Squire's good intervention . . ."

David had to laugh at this. Ruffling Eve's hair affectionately, he teased: "One of these days the Squire's going to tire of you. One of these days he's going to say, 'Enough, Jewess! Enough of your demands!' "

"Oh, I don't think so," Eve dimpled at him. "By now we're old friends. Old friends and good ones."

"It still beats me how you can ask him for favors on one hand and berate him on the other for not sharing his land with his peasants."

"He loves it when I argue with him. He says it's the only form of recreation he has these days, what with the Countess living in St. Petersburg with the children. Anyhow, our little arguments have helped. He *is* a better Squire than most. He *has* instituted some reforms. He's old and change comes hard for him."

David's mood changed abruptly. "Hard? Nothing is as hard as life at the bottom of the world. And for every squire at the top there are millions on the bottom."

But the Squire did exert his influence on Daniel's behalf, and Eve did pay off a few officials, and it was done. The day Daniel left for Moscow, Eve ran outside and exulted to the heavens, "Are you watching, Ruth? It's not America but we're not doing so badly, are we?"

In the year 1895, they hung a picture of the Tsar and the Tsarina, the Princess Alix of Hesse, known as the Empress Aleksandra Feodorovna, on the wall. Since this was not choice but edict, Nicholas II and his bride gazed down from the walls of every home in all Russia, no matter how grand or humble.

In the June of 1896, there was a strike of 30,000 workers in St. Petersburg, which seemed like a miracle to David and Eve. They tried to share their enthusiasm with Yitzhak but he wasn't even vaguely interested. Ever since his thirteenth birthday he was no longer made to study anything since his parents had decided that education by force accomplished nothing. Still, it did seem like a bit of irony to Eve that of all the Markoff children, her son was the one least interested in anything outside of his boyish amusements. He did help David in the business since he loved animals, and he loved riding around the countryside on his horse, but other than that he wasn't even curious about his father's "other activities." He knew only vaguely that there was a Cossack uniform his father would dig up occasionally to aid in the escape of some political prisoner or other or something of that nature. If and when he thought about it at all, it seemed to him that there should have been something more exciting to do with it, something that was more fun, like throwing a bomb. Sometimes he'd overhear a conversation concerning an act of terrorism and he'd think *that* sounded like fun.

Occasionally David would get exasperated with him as he did when it got back to him that Yitzhak had been seen drinking with a bunch of Cossacks at the tavern, then going outside with one of the Cossacks' swords, mounting a Cossack's horse and riding through town, flashing the sword over his head in wide and wild flourishes. Eve always defended him. "He's only fifteen. He'll mature. He's sweet and he's good. Those are the important qualities."

Although no one would ever dare to use the word in front of her, Eve knew he was often called that *shaygets,* the word for a male gentile, by the townspeople because with his blue eyes, yellow hair and snub nose he resembled the Russian or Polish peasantry, especially since he was already as tall as his father, and as burly. She believed that his appearance and his great strength—he was already known for the feat of lifting a horse from the ground to well over his head— created a kind of bias against him, as well as his good nature and his hearty laugh, qualities usually taken as a sign of the fool by those who spent all the time of their lives at the very serious business of just eking out an existence. Eve was convinced that time would show exactly what kind of man her son was—a good one.

That same year a pamphlet appeared that greatly interested all the Markoffs. It was entitled "The Jewish State" and was written by one Theodor Herzl. It proposed the establishment of a Jewish state in the land of Palestine. For weeks the families talked about it, almost *argued* about it, since Eve and David, while agreeing in principle that a homeland *should* be established for all the Jews of the world who were never truly citizens of the lands where they were born and lived, still dreamed of America, and most of the other Markoffs, inspired by Hannah, declared themselves fervent Zionists.

David understood that many Jews would be drawn to the idea of their own country, but what puzzled him was how strongly and how quickly the other members of his family embraced Zionism. "You'd think they were thinking about all this for years now."

Eve smiled. "They have, or at least Hannah has. And through her, Abraham and their children have, as well as Miriam and Shlomo and their children."

"I had no idea. When was it that Hannah started thinking about Palestine?"

"A long time ago. It was the first year we were married, when I thought the most important thing in life was to be free of your father. When that was my idea of independence." Eve laughed a little, remembering . . . "We were talking about being free and I said to Hannah that in America even Jews could be free. And she asked me about Palestine, asked me if I didn't think that a Jew would be better off in his own land, the land of Israel. So even as I thought only of America, the idea of Israel caught hold in her heart and apparently never let go. Even as I dreamed, she dreamed . . . We dreamed of different places."

David put his arms around her. They hadn't even talked about America of late, not since the Cossack uniform had come into their lives, almost a living presence. "I'm sorry," he murmured now, kissing the top of her head. "I've kept your dream from coming true."

"Oh, no, David. The two of us together is the dream. The two of us and Yitzhak and Dorie. And we'll get there yet. I know it!"

In 1897 the whole family went to the railway station in Kovno to see Gershon off to Germany. Gershon wanted to be a doctor and since the study of medicine in Russia was, for him, an impossibility, Eve enlisted the aid of Ivan Golov. Between them they made the necessary arrangements. Almost nothing could have pleased Eve more. By helping Gershon fulfill his dream, she was fulfilling what she felt was her obligation to her dear, departed Ruth. She whispered to David, "I'd like to think Ruth is watching this moment and saying, 'Okay, Eve, so we didn't get to America. But we didn't do so bad after all. At least all that milk from my breasts and all that teaching didn't go for nothing! My Gershon will be a doctor! Who would have ever dreamed of such a thing?' "

All the Markoffs were excited, laughing one minute and crying the next as they kissed Gershon goodbye. Only Yitzhak was subdued as he watched Gershon kiss his mother, heard him say, "I'll make you proud of me, Aunt Eve," and heard his mother say, "But I'm already proud of you, Gershon, as proud as can be." Then he heard Gershon say, "When I'm a doctor I'm going to come back to work in your Clinic." His mother answered, "Where you work, Gershoniu, is not as important as that you help wherever it is you're needed. Just be the best doctor you can be, the best kind of Jew, the best man you can possibly be. More than that not even your mother could have wished for."

For maybe the first time in his life Yitzhak felt his eyes burning hotly with unshed tears as his heart was pierced with pain. All his life his mother had looked at him with love, but never with the wet-eyed pride she was now bestowing on Gershon. At that moment he vowed to himself that he would do something to make his mother as proud of him as she was of his cousin—even as proud as she was of his father.

The following year a stranger came to town. He was known under only one name—Korchek. No one knew anything about him except that he came from Moscow. He was dark-skinned, dark-eyed, wore a small, pointed beard and seemed to have a lot of money, often standing treat to the young men who hung around the tavern. Yitzhak's friend Sasha Polinski made his acquaintance before Yitzhak since he was at the tavern more frequently than Yitzhak, who worked during the daylight hours with his father. When Sasha started to go to evening meetings in Kovno that were organized by Korchek, Yitzhak went along since

Sasha and he were close friends. (While Yitzhak always bested him at arm-wrestling, Sasha usually won the distance peeing contests. His stream was always a perfect arc.) That was how Yitzhak became a member of the Social Revolutionaries, formerly known as the People's Will party, which he didn't know anything about. All he knew was that the Social Revolutionaries stood for two things—agrarian revolution and terrorism. He scarcely knew what agrarian revolution meant but the word terrorism made his blood run hot and his pulse beat fast. Only a real hero, strong, powerful and truly brave, could be a terrorist and who in the whole, wide world of Russia wouldn't be proud of a strong, brave hero?

Eve awoke that late spring morning with a heaviness of spirit and at first couldn't even reason why. It was her favorite time of year when all signs of winter gloom, threatening skies and melting snows were finally gone and the humid heat of summer had not yet set in; a time when the yellow sunflowers she dearly loved covered the land and filled her heart with their golden color. It was a time to be especially savored because it was a season so brief.

Then she remembered about the investigation. A gentile boy, the four-year-old son of a peasant, had disappeared. At first scant attention had been paid by the authorities. After all, it was only a peasant's whelp and each year any number of brats were almost expected to vanish, most likely stolen by the gypsies. It was a given of Russian life in the provinces, and who could keep track? So many fair-skinned little ones running loose and so many dark-skinned gypsies slinking through the nights. Besides, the damned peasants always had a few more children than they could feed and the gypsies would sell the child to people who *wanted* a child and could feed it. Then, suddenly, the situation had changed and for some reason of their own the authorities had become very interested, and the Governor-General himself was coming to town to head the investigation.

The Squire had come calling to discuss the situation with Eve, to warn her. "There's talk that the boy wasn't stolen by gypsies at all but by the Jews. Stolen and slain for his blood for your matzohs."

Eve had merely nodded, not bothering to say that the boy had disappeared *after* the Passover season when the matzohs had been made. She didn't bother to remonstrate at all. She and the Squire both knew that some kind of story had to be fabricated, that it was once more time for a demonstration against the Jews, those supposed purveyors of sedition and rebellion, those eternal scapegoats upon whose backs all Russia's problems were to be laid.

"I can be of little help to you this time, my dear friend. I'm already called the *Jew-lover* in certain circles. In very powerful circles. My word no longer counts for anything. *They* trust no one these days, most especially a Polish count who has actually given away some of his land to his peasants. And I'm old."

Eve nodded. She saw that it was so. The Squire had already been along in years when she had first met him. Now he was quite ancient, frail and wizened, his soldierly bearing gone.

195

"I'm leaving for good. I'm going to spend my remaining days in St. Petersburg with my family. I'm leaving the land in charge of an overseer. When my son is old enough, perhaps he'll come back and take it over . . . assuming he wants to . . . assuming that there will be anything left. Who knows what the future holds?" His gaze grew vacant and his voice trailed off.

"But that is another story and you, you have your own problems, my dear Eve, my dear friend." His eyes filled with tears and Eve tried to smile at him so that he wouldn't be quite so sad.

That conversation had taken place a week earlier, and Eve realized that this was the day the Governor-General was due to arrive in Kovno. All Slobodka was frightened, talked of nothing else.

She turned to David still asleep beside her, wanting to discuss the situation with him once again. Perhaps just talking about it would alleviate some of the anxiety tearing at her heart. But his face was so sweet and gentle in repose she couldn't think of awakening him to such harsh reality. Rather, she smoothed the yellow hair back from his fine brow and as his eyes opened he immediately smiled at her.

"Is it time to get up and go to work already?" he asked her.

"No. Not yet. There's a little time left before that. There's just time enough for me to tell you I love you and if you hurry, there's time enough for you to tell me that you love me back."

His arms reached out for her and as she nestled against his chest, she murmured dreamily, "You know what I would like?"

"No. Tell me, sweet Eve."

"Once, just once, I'd like to make love in the open fields, surrounded by and covered by and hidden in the sunflowers, our bodies warming in the sun . . ."

Just before he covered her lips with his, before he covered her body with his, he whispered, "Living with you *has been* making love in the sunflowers, so warm under the sun."

She prepared breakfast while David washed and dressed himself, preparing for the day's work. Hershel came into the kitchen all dressed for work. Eve forced herself to be cheerful with him in spite of the feeling of dread that was with her still.

"Good morning, Hershel. The sun's not quite up yet but it looks as if it's going to be a really lovely day. Sit down and have your breakfast."

She turned back to the stove as Hershel sat down, saying, "Today's not so good. Today's the day the Governor-General is coming. God knows what will happen."

David came in. "Where's Yitzhak? Isn't he up yet? You'd better go wake him, Eve. We have a long ride today."

Eve went to see if Yitzhak was up and dressing, or still asleep. Usually she had to rouse him. But she found his bed empty, the bedspread undisturbed. Yitzhak, who had still been out when she and David had gone to bed the night before, had never come home at all!

196

"David!" She ran back to the kitchen. "He's not here—"

"Has his bed been slept in?"

"No . . ."

Their eyes locked in mutual apprehension. When David finally spoke his tone was deliberately angry. "Well, he's been out raising hell with those bummy friends of his again. He's probably somewhere sleeping off a gutful of liquor. But he knew we had a long day's work today. He's totally irresponsible. Other than that, there's nothing to concern yourself about, Eve. But I'll tell you one thing—I'm going to come down hard on him."

But still the premonition of doom clutched Eve's heart again. She only hoped that David's words were true, that Yitzhak was somewhere sleeping off a night of carousal. "Are you going to wait for him? Aren't you going to look for him?"

"Certainly not. We're all going out today—Abraham, Shlomo . . . We can't sit around waiting for an irresponsible boy who refuses to act like a man. But when I get hold of him, I'm going to—"

"Take it easy," Hershel interjected. "Calm yourself, David. He *is* only seventeen. Just sowing a few wild oats. It's not so terrible. Remember how we were at seventeen? We were a pretty wild bunch, David . . ." Hershel gave a little laugh, but he avoided looking at Eve. He was embarrassed for her and for David too. Yitzhak was their only son, their only child, and while he was a nice boy and so cheerful, clearly he was never going to amount to anything, while his three boys—well, they were certainly sons to be proud of; Daniel studying to be a lawyer and Gershon going to be a doctor. And Asher, smart enough to be teaching others while he was writing all kinds of things himself. A writer, of all things! How Ruth would have loved that! "It's not terrible," he said again.

"Hershel's right, David. You're making too big a fuss. Yitzhak is just high-spirited, full of fun." There was no point in telling David that she had a premonition of *something*—exactly what, she couldn't even say. Yet at the same time she didn't want David to be angry with Yitzhak if that was all there was to it, that he had spent the night horsing around with his friends.

David appeared to be partially mollified, unwilling to upset Eve with any further talk. He had never really discussed with her that he suspected Yitzhak, along with his no-account friends, of consorting with that Korchek bunch for whom he had no use at all. They were terrorists more for the thrill of violence than for any ideological reason and in the end, they always caused more trouble than good. He has warned Yitzhak against them, but Yitzhak, good-natured oaf that he was, had only laughed. Yes, he was a damned fool, his son Yitzhak. A sweet, innocent fool who didn't know that the Korcheks of the world exploited people like him for their own ends; that in their own way they were as dangerous as the Cossack who torched a poor soul's home or a tyrannical Tsar who didn't give a damn about his people.

David and Eve kissed goodbye, each smiling reassuringly at the other, both keeping their misgivings to themselves. Eve stepped out the door to watch David ride off, smiling broadly as he turned astride his horse to wave to her. Then she went back into the kitchen to begin the tasks of the day.

Dorie came into the kitchen, half-dressed, her young face still flushed with sleep. Yet, she sensed something. "What is it, Aunt Eve? What's wrong?"

Eve kissed her. "Wrong? What would be wrong on a beautiful day like this?"

Dorie, sweet and barely sixteen. What would she know of premonitions that stole their way into your heart in the middle of the night and gripped like a vise? A feeling of dread that froze the spirit. . . .

"Sit down, Dorie, and have your breakfast. Then we'll wake Asher. I want you both to go over to the schoolroom early today." She tried to think of a good reason to give Dorie. "I want you and Asher to go over all our books and make a list of the ones we'll need copies of. And I thought maybe you'd make up a list of new books, too, that the two of you think would be useful."

She knew Asher and Dorie. Making up a list of books they'd like to see on the schoolroom shelves would be a challenge to them, one they'd enjoy. It would easily occupy them all day, which was exactly what she wanted. She needed to be alone in the house to wait for Yitzhak to come home.

Eve was out in the yard hanging the wash to dry in the sun, constantly looking up and down the road for a sign of anything unusual, her eyes alert for the sight of Yitzhak, when a thought struck her. As she resisted it, it only grew stronger. She left the basket of wet clothes sitting on the ground while she walked around the back of the house to the stable. She dashed quickly inside and closed the gate behind her. Working furiously with the pitchfork she cleared away the layers of straw that covered the hole where the Cossack uniform was hidden. Then casting aside the pitchfork, she used a shovel to dig out the manure . . . until she saw that she was right! The uniform was gone! *Yitzhak! Oh, Yitzhak! Oh, dear God, what has he done?*

As she stared into the empty void wondering what to do next, as if indeed there was anything to be done at all, the stable gate flew open. Her heart felt as if it had stopped beating. She saw a Cossack—tall, broad, towering—and it wasn't until her eyes adjusted to the sunlight streaming through the open gate that she saw that it was no Cossack but her son. It was Yitzhak!

He was breathing hard, grinning. "Mother! I've done it!" He laughed as if the world were his, as if he himself had conquered it.

"Oh, Yitzhak, what is it you've done?"

"I've killed the Governor-General! Because of this uniform I was the only one who could get close enough."

"But why, Yitzhak, why?"

The broad, proud smile slipped from Yitzhak's face. How was it that his mother didn't understand the importance of what he had done? "Because he *was* the Governor-General! He was going to head up an investigation . . ."

Eve gazed at him with a mixture of sorrow and dismay. Yitzhak would never be able to understand that he had accomplished nothing with his act, that now the investigation wouldn't stop at all but intensify until many innocent people might pay for this one senseless act of violence.

But they were losing valuable time. "Quick! There's no time for talk! Get out of the uniform! I'll get your other things."

When she came back with his clothes, she handed them to him and picked up the uniform and ran again to the stable gate.

"Mother! Where are you going with the uniform? Put it back in the hole!"

"No! We can't take the chance of keeping it. We have to burn it! Put on your clothes and get into the hole!"

"Me?" He was perplexed. "Why?"

"Do as I say! Hurry!"

After she'd watched the uniform burn, she raked over its ashes and returned to the stables. Yitzhak was crouching in the hole as she had directed. "I'm going to cover you up—I'll leave you just enough space to breathe. No matter what, even if you think you can't bear the stench another second, you must stay hidden until I tell you the coast is clear, that all danger is past."

She worked as fast as she could covering the manure with the straw, then tethering David's horse in such a fashion that he stood directly over the hole. Subsequently he'd cover the straw with fresh manure.

Finally, trying not to retch from the stink, wiping the perspiration from her brow with her soiled skirts, she closed her eyes and willed herself to composure, or rather, the appearance of composure. Once she left the stable, she faltered again, fell to the ground, was sick, retching again and again until she was completely drained. Then she rose and went inside the house. She had to pull herself together, clean herself up so that she could face whoever showed up at the door . . . and to wait for David to come home so they could plan what to do.

She was in the yard wearing a fresh green dress, the red hair combed out and falling loose, blazing in the sun, when the soldiers came. They spoke to her not at all when she indignantly demanded what it was they wanted, merely shoved her out of their way roughly as they marched into the house and proceeded to tear it apart, even smashing through the walls and pulling up the floor boards. Then they went to the barn and repeated the procedure and her heart rose up into her mouth and she almost choked on it. It would be only a few minutes now before they attacked the stable.

What do they know? Do they know it's Yitzhak they're searching for, or is this only a random search? Are they simply going from house to house to house just seeing whom they can flush out?

My God! She had committed a dreadful mistake by hiding Yitzhak in the hole! If they found him now they'd know he was the culprit even if they didn't know before. Who else would be hiding under a pile of excrement but the guiltiest of men?

She watched them leave the barn and turn toward the stable. Her knees started to buckle and she felt herself swooning. Oh, she wanted to do just that!

To fall in the dirt, claw the ground, beat her chest and lament to the skies! But she couldn't. She had to steel herself and remain where she was. Not fall, not run after them into the stable as they tore it apart. She had to stand exactly where she was until they came out with . . . or please, God . . . without her son.

Oh, why hadn't she told Yitzhak to get back on his horse and ride? Ride and ride until his horse collapsed, then keep on going until his feet no longer supported him, then crawl on his hands and knees until he could board the first ship he came to that was sailing for freedom and America. Then, later, they could have followed him—she and Dorie and David. And they could all have been free and alive and safe . . .

Now, it was too late.

Not able to bear the suspense any longer, she turned toward the stable to see them leaving, the building half-demolished, but *without* Yitzhak! They hadn't found him! Oh, dear God, they hadn't found him!

Still, they didn't speak one word to her. They mounted their horses and rode off, out of sight! They were gone. Now all she had to do was wait for David to come home.

Then the Squire's carriage came clattering down the road going so fast it barely held the road. The horses came to a halt in front of her house and the coachman helped the Squire out. The old man was shaking in his distress. "I was ready to leave for St. Petersburg but I had to come warn you . . . They know, Eve, they know."

Eve's hands flew to her throat. "What do you mean—they know? *What* do they know? They've already been here and found *nothing! Nobody!* I tell you they've been here and found nothing and now they're gone!"

"Oh, my dear, they'll be back! They've probably gone to search the surrounding area, the woods. You see, they *know* it was your David in a Cossack uniform who killed the Governor-General!"

David? David! They assumed that the assassin in the uniform was David!

She started to say that David had been away, out in the country, working. But what did it matter who they assumed it was? Yitzhak? David? What did that matter?

"How do they know?"

"Someone followed the Cossack who was the assassin back here. He saw him enter. He didn't see him come out again. Then this informer went back to Kovno to spread the word."

She scratched at the cloth of the Squire's coat with both hands. "Who? Who was it?"

"Oh, my poor friend, my dear friend, does it matter? All that matters is that they know. They're scouring the countryside but they'll be back."

Eve sank to her knees. No, it didn't matter. It didn't even matter who they thought it was, David or Yitzhak. The Squire was right. They would be back.

She began to wail, softly at first, rocking to and fro on her knees, keening, as women had done for centuries.

The Squire watched her, wringing his hands helplessly, the tears running down his withered cheeks. He turned back to his carriage, to his driver for assistance in getting back in. "I had to warn you, but I can't do anything else . . . I'm powerless to help you. But, Eve, I must tell you. If David escapes, they say they'll take twenty Jews instead; they'll burn down the entire town."

She heard the carriage ride away and she beat the ground with her fists. She looked up into the sky, shook her fists. "God, it's not fair! Not fair!" Even as she knew that her words were the words of a helpless child.

She needed David! *Yes! David! David will know what to do!* David would be home any minute. Between them they'd figure out what to do.

She got to her feet. She would go meet him. She walked to the fence, opened it, closed it behind her and crossed the road to the open field to wait for David to come home.

She saw him from the distance, riding toward her, his yellow curls blowing as he rode. Then he jumped down from his horse and took her in his arms. Yes, it was her David, her David. And yes, they had made love in the sunflowers, had been warmed by the sun. . . .

PART TWO

Jennie

1898—1900

17.

Yitzhak boarded ship in Hamburg, his ticket entitling him to third-class accommodations, better known as steerage. He could have bought a second-class ticket since he wasn't without funds—his mother had handed him a small leather bag with many rubles when she had kissed him goodbye. But Yitzhak was unaware of the distinction between steerage and second-class and the man at the ticket office never inquired as to what kind of quarters he desired. Rather, he took one look at Yitzhak, filthy and frazzled after the long journey in the saddle and on foot, and assumed he was third-class material.

Yitzhak was without any possessions except for the clothes on his back, which were by this time in a ragged and deteriorated state. In contrast, his fellow passengers were loaded down with their treasures—bundles of pillows and down comforters, brass candlesticks, even samovars, and with changes of clothing packed in straw suitcases or stuffed into pillow cases. The Orthodox Jews—those men with long beards and broad-brimmed hats, the women bewigged or with scarves covering their heads—even toted sacks of whatever foods could last a few days so they wouldn't have to eat the nonkosher food that was included in the price of the ticket. Yitzhak had had such a sack of provisions when he had started out on his journey—dried salami, a few loaves of hard bread, a hunk of cheese, even some salted herrings, onions and cucumbers—anything that his mother could throw into the sack quickly. Naturally, these supplies had been totally depleted long before he reached Hamburg.

The passengers were led to their quarters—wooden bunks one on top of the other, three bunks high. And there they were, in the belly of the ship—Jews and gentiles, Russians and Poles, Germans, Hungarians, Rumanians and Slavs of all kinds, thrown together as they never had been in life before. They were shown the buckets for their slops and instructed how to empty them—over the rail and never against the wind. (It would serve as a source of raw humor for the trip's duration whenever someone forgot the latter admonition.) It would only occur to Yitzhak later in life, much later, that he and his fellow passengers constituted the very dregs of humanity assembled in the bowels of a seagoing torture chamber.

Lines were quickly drawn. The Jews huddled with Jews, the gentiles with gentiles, and within those boundaries: Germans with Germans, Russians with Russians, and so on, although most of the passengers spoke more than one·

language, a necessity of the times. Of course, those who traveled together as a family stayed together to share, if nothing else, their common misery.

Yitzhak lay awake that first night consumed by a variety of emotions. One part of him was very excited—it was the highest adventure to be on his own bound for the Golden Land of which he had heard all his life. But part of him was already homesick and he yearned for the sight of those he loved and had left in Slobodka. He thought of his mother in one of her pretty dresses lighting the Sabbath candles, of his father riding home in the receding sun, rushing into the house to kiss his mother, she with her face uplifted to receive the kiss. He thought of his cousin Dorie with her pale blond braids falling down her back, blushing as she set the table while he himself teased her affectionately about her casting sidelong glances at their cousin Joshua. He thought of how the fire leaped in the hearth and cast its golden glow on all of them as they sat down to eat— his Uncle Hershel, Asher, Dorie, his mother and father. Or perhaps it was some holiday meal and all the aunts and uncles were there with their children. . . .

He couldn't sleep. All around him were those special sounds of the night in the pitch-black hole—restless turnings; hacking, sneezing and coughing; retching and moaning; sighs and cries and whispers. Disturbed by these sounds in the long night Yitzhak decided to get up and go on deck. It was, after all, his first time on the seas and he wanted to breathe in the fresh clean air instead of the fetid odors of packed humanity at its least attractive level. He wanted to peer into the black waters where he'd be able perhaps to visualize the life that awaited him in America.

He put on his boots and tiptoed over to the doors, though it was unlikely that many slept. But the doors wouldn't open! The patrons of the steerage class were actually locked in for the night! A great rage rose within him. He hurled himself against the doors again and again, first with his right shoulder and then with his left, alternating in a near-frenzy. He was Yitzhak Markoff, famed for his size and his strength, from a family famed for their strength and their courage. No one dared lock him in! But the doors were of iron, not wood, and while they groaned and even clanked from the assault of his bulk, they did not yield.

"Crazy man," an old man complained from his hard bunk. "Don't fight what's clearly stronger than you. Go to sleep and let us other poor souls sleep."

So Yitzhak lay down again and was subject to the strangest of sensations. For the first time in his seventeen years he wanted to bawl. He wanted to curl his body up into a ball and cry himself to sleep. But at the same time he knew he couldn't do that. He was Yitzhak Markoff, a hero and a man, not a boy. Hadn't he single-handedly killed the Governor-General? Hadn't his father kissed him when he was *bar mitzvah* and bidden him to be the kind of man who would make his mother proud? And hadn't his mother herself whispered to him that very same night: "Now that you are a man, the important thing is always to remember who you are and from whom you come"?

He had to remember that he came from Markoffs and that they were a strong breed and brave. They weren't babies who whined and cried in the night. And his mother—not even a man—was known for her strength of character and fearless spirit. Even she wouldn't have cried in the desolate and lonely night.

He comforted himself with visions of how life would be in America. How he would make his way and prosper. How he would do wonderful deeds. Maybe he'd even become famous for something, although he didn't know what that would be. But he envisioned how when his mother and father and Dorie, and even Uncle Hershel and Asher, Gershon and Daniel, and maybe Uncle Abraham and Aunt Hannah and Uncle Shlomo and Aunt Miriam and all their children came to America, they would be overwhelmed with pride over what he had accomplished. They'd be as proud of him as his father and mother must have been over his feat of killing the Governor-General.

There was one thing that marred this picture. When he had left Slobodka his mother hadn't said to him as she had said to his cousin Gershon: "Be the best kind of Jew, the best kind of man you can possibly be. More than that not even your mother could wish for." But then he comforted himself: he had left in such a hurry there hadn't been time for his mother to say much of anything except to wish him Godspeed. And her eyes had been wet as she kissed him goodbye, just as they had been wet with pride when she had kissed Gershon goodbye.

Finally he fell asleep, vowing to himself that's what he would be—the kind of man who would make his mother proud. For that matter, the kind of man who would make his father proud too.

In the morning he felt much better. Breakfast was served at long wooden tables where everyone sat together. While only about half the passengers ate, there already being a prevalence of seasickness (although it was summer and the seas were fairly calm), he ate copious amounts of porridge and boiled potatoes, beans and buckwheat groats and drank huge amounts of tea to wash it all down. Then he bolted for the upper deck where the air was fresh and the sun was shining.

On deck, as below, those of a feather flocked together. He looked around for a congenial group to join and this didn't necessarily mean his fellow Russian or Polish Jews but rather those of a similarity of personality and age, just as in Slobodka where he had been friends with Jews and gentiles alike so long as they enjoyed a good laugh and a good time. Almost immediately Yitzhak spotted a group of young men pitching coins, an activity he excelled in, and drifted over to watch them play. He quickly ascertained that the language they spoke was neither Russian nor Polish but it had a familiar flavor all the same. He deduced that it was German since he remembered his mother saying that the Yiddish language had evolved from the German.

Soon he was catching a word here and there even though the German accent was different from the Yiddish, and he was pleased with himelf. He was probably good at languages, he thought, just as his mother was. He also remembered his mother saying that in Germany the Jews often spoke German rather than Yiddish as they did in most countries where they lived. He reasoned that these fellows weren't Jews—they wore no beards and not one of them had his head covered.

Also, if they were Jews, at least a couple of them would have had their heads buried in a prayer book or would be trading opinions on this or that point since most Jews were likely to do this. In Slobodka, his father's family, the Markoffs, were the only Jews noted as men who would rather fight than discuss. His own father had been one of those, he had been told, before he had married his mother.

At first the group ignored Yitzhak as boys will when they already have their own gang and have no need of an outsider. But when he reached into his pocket and took out a few kopecks (careful not to dip into his bag of rubles) and jingled them about, they looked at him and indicated he should toss one. After Yitzhak had won a few rounds and let them win a few, it looked as if they were getting on. They understood a few words he said, as he understood a few words they said. Soon they were even teaching him a few words of German. They said the word a few times and Yitzhak repeated it until he got it right. There *was* a great deal of laughing at Yitzhak's expense but it was all of a good nature. By the time they were ready to go below for the noonday meal, they were all friends.

The midday meal consisted of potatoes and beans, just as at breakfast, but in addition there was rice and onions and dried herring—all items of food which were not *bad,* but not particularly appetizing either. But when great bowls of aromatic cabbage cooked with sausages were brought out and the Jews at the table turned up their noses, Yitzhak's friends dug in with relish, while he looked on with an almost unbearable envy. Although he had been present on occasion when his peasant friends had partaken of pork, he had never been tempted to taste it before since he had lived in a house where the table groaned under all kinds of appetizing foods, with meat and fowl in plentiful supply. But now with the prospect of a diet consisting only of beans and onions and a little herring thrown in for the next couple of weeks at the very least, his mouth watered painfully.

Yitzhak's friends urged him to have a sausage or two, their mouths full of now agonizingly appealing *fleisch,* but he resisted. While a Jew might under extraordinary circumstance be forgiven a little goyish fish or chicken, even a bit of beef, he'd surely burn in hell for eating pig. But by the time the evening meal was served, burning in hell in some impossible-to-conceive future seemed much preferable to suffering the tortures of denial in the present, and Yitzhak tasted of the forbidden food and found it delicious. So delicious that, after waiting a moment or two to see if he were going to be struck dead after all, he shamelessly gorged himself. At the same time he dismissed from his mind the image of his mother delicately frowning at his sinfulness. (He knew his father would most probably be more forgiving of this particular infraction of the Law.) As for the elderly Jews sitting at the table, he simply ignored their dire looks and loud sounds of disgust.

On the second day of the voyage the meals were not quite as bountiful as the day before, and Yitzhak learned a few more German words. He also played cards with his new friends, a pastime he hadn't indulged in frequently before since he had preferred a more physical type of entertainment. As a result he lost all his loose kopecks and was forced to dip into his pouch of money several times until he had reduced the sum total by several rubles. Now he knew this was something his father would have frowned upon. He would have said something about a fool and his money being soon parted. Yitzhak was more ashamed of playing the fool than upset over the loss of the money. The money had less reality for him than being a fool did since he had never really *needed* money before. So concerned was he over this loss of face, he lay awake all that night thinking what he could do to remedy the situation. And the solution came to him.

The next day he challenged his German friends, one or all, to an arm wrestle, with side wagers. The first to accept the challenge was the fellow Yitzhak liked the most—Hans. It took him just one second to put Hans's arm down. The rest of them were surprised but not astounded since Hans was the smallest of their group. The next one to take up his challenge was Franz, who was bigger than Hans. Yitzhak put his arm down almost as quickly. By the time he went through the bunch, each young man increasingly burlier and stronger than the one preceding, he had not only recouped his losses but was several marks richer. To his astonishment, he was also no longer just the friendly outsider but an admired pal, truly one of them.

The next day Yitzhak became more than just a pal; he achieved the status of something nearer to a hero, someone the boys were *proud* to call a friend. One of the passengers who had observed the hand wrestling was a hefty German Jew who had been to America before. He came up and congratulated Yitzhak on his prowess, felt his bicep and said, in a mixture of Yiddish and German so that everyone could understand, that in America Yitzhak could be a prize fighter, a boxer. The word "boxer" was not one any of the boys were familiar with. As for *prize fighter,* Yitzhak knew what a prize was and what the word *fighting* meant, as he knew what wrestling and brawling, kicking and shoving and punching meant, but the combination of the two? No.

The older man said he would show them what he meant. Taking the classic stance of the "boxer" he threw Yitzhak a right fist to the belly before Yitzhak even knew what he was up to. The blow knocked the wind out of him for a second, coming as it did as a surprise, but he quickly recovered, feeling he was made to look like an oaf. Also he knew a wise guy when he saw one, since they were not without them in Slobodka. They must have had wise guys in Germany too since Yitzhak's chums looked at him expectantly, waiting to see how he was going to respond.

"Oh, you mean like this?" Yitzhak asked as he went into a crouch, at the same time imitating the fellow's formal boxer stance. Before the words were out of his mouth and before the wise guy knew what hit him, Yitzhak threw him an uppercut to the jaw that laid him out unconscious.

Yitzhak's friends went crazy with delight. There was nothing like seeing a wise guy bested, especially when the winner was one of your own. They poured a bucket of water over the wiseacre. When he came to, they hooted and jeered him, asking him if maybe he wanted to manage Yitzhak's career as a prize fighter when they got to America.

That night the friends celebrated when Heinz pulled a bottle of schnapps from his sack. They all howled with pleasure and pounded Heinz on the back for his foresight in packing the bottle. They passed the schnapps back and forth among them until the bottle was empty and then they all sang. The songs were German ones but somehow Yitzhak managed to sing along, humming to fill in the gaps as all linked arms and swayed side to side, comrades one and all. The next day, still full of pride, the boys went among the passengers, challenging the lively ones either to arm wrestle with Yitzhak, or "prize fight." But among all the miserable crew, they couldn't find a single taker.

By the sixth or seventh day Yitzhak barely thought of the family back in Slobodka since he was having too good a time to be homesick. He was arm wrestling, playing cards, pitching coins, staging peeing contests which involved seeing whose stream could clear the deck rail. He and his friends even played leapfrog. At the same time that they were playing childish games they were flirting with all the girls, or at least those who weren't under their parents' watchful eyes or too refined to respond to the callow young men's uncouth ways.

On the eighth day at sea Yitzhak shaved off his beard, using a dirty pane of glass as a mirror. To rationalize doing this, Yitzhak told himself that it was the only thing to do since it was next to impossible to wash in the steerage quarters and it was no secret that at least half the passengers were infested with lice. Even his mother, he felt, would have applauded his good common sense. Of course what he was doing in removing the blond beard, which distinguished all the Markoff men, was making himself look more like his companions since he felt that, with it, he stuck out like a sore thumb. He did leave a good-sized mustache, not in the way of moral compromise, but because without his beard, he looked so much younger. The mustache compensated for that; it gave him more dash.

Still, Yitzhak was not without some twinges of guilt. He couldn't think of one Jew back in Slobodka who didn't wear a beard as soon as he was man enough to grow one, if one didn't count Moishe Grodnik who had lost all his hair due to a strange illness. But he consoled himself. He wasn't the only Jew on ship who would land in America without this symbol of his Jewish manhood. As the days passed, more and more of the Jews emerged barefaced, just as more and more indulged in the forbidden pork. Perhaps this was due to the fact that the longer they were at sea, the more deplorable the food served became. As one Jew declaimed, "Is it any worse to eat pork than it is to eat maggots?"

It was a long journey. Maybe sixteen days, but Yitzhak lost count. Even as his fellow passengers sickened and a few even died, he was having too good a time to mark off the days. Still, he was neither blind nor deaf. At night particularly, the moaning and the groaning, the sighing and the weeping, like some chorus of lost souls, was enough to sadden the heart of the most hardened, especially when typhoid fever became a fellow traveler.

The day the ship sailed into harbor was a beautiful day. Not even the most miserable of the immigrants could deny this. They crowded the deck, even the ill, yearning for the sight of the famous Statue of Liberty with her torch held high. His mother had, on occasion, recited the lady's plea, Yitzhak recalled: "Give me your tired, your poor, your huddled masses yearning to breathe free . . ." He remembered how tears would fill his mother's eyes as she repeated the words, just as tears now filled the eyes of many of the huddled masses on deck, sick as they were, and as tired and as poor.

But where was she? the passengers demanded of each other. Where was this Lady of Liberty they had all heard so much about? Weren't they at Ellis Island, New York? Their eyes desperately searched the skyline. The Lady was nowhere to be seen. Was it possible that they weren't in the United States of America after all? There were fresh outcries on deck as these troubled masses considered the frightening possibilities.

Hours later the passengers were informed that because of the typhoid fever in their midst, they weren't going to be allowed on Ellis Island but were going to be detained there, on Staten Island, which at least was also New York, the United States of America.

18.

Much of what actually occurred at the quarantine station in Staten Island Yitzhak would piece together months later, in hindsight. That certainly was true of most of the actual conversation. Later on he would berate himself for not paying a little attention when his mother and Dorie had been practicing their self-taught English on each other. As it was, only Otto of his group was familiar with any English since Otto's uncle, a seagoing man, had married a woman he had met at some port or other in one of the British Isles. Accordingly, it was through Otto that much of the "official" information was passed along to the rest of the group of boys.

Most of Yitzhak's time at Staten Island passed with him in a state of general confusion. Of course he would have been less confused if there had been "formal" interpreters as there were at Ellis Island. Still, there was a lot of "informal" Yiddish-English translation going on where the Jews huddled together, and he missed out by simply not being there, since he stayed exclusively in the company of his shipboard companions.

Ignorance, self-imposed or inadvertent, was certainly his sin. Later on he would figure out that in addition to the unofficial interpreting that must have been going on among the Jews, there must have been, too, an official from the Immigration Society that helped green Jews without an American affiliation such as a relative or friend "relocate"—find a place to live within the Jewish community, and in many cases, a way to make a living. Since Yitzhak didn't know at the time of the existence of such a person he didn't know to look for him. Certainly that official wouldn't have known where to find *him*, even if he knew of Yitzhak's existence. Would he have dreamed of finding a proper Jewish boy of seventeen years playing blindman's bluff with a bunch of loutish German youths? Surely not, since the Jews all stuck together, praying and demanding of God why they had been brought to this frightening prison of a place. *Simply to test their faith?*

Still, later, it would remain problematical whether even knowing of this representative of the Immigration Society's presence on the Island, Yitzhak would have sought him out. It would be years until Yitzhak would fully understand what had happened to change the course of his life to an extent that was beyond imagination. Ultimately he would see that landing in Staten Island instead of Ellis Island was only one circumstance out of several that combined to alter this course. He would realize later that most of what occurred was the result of both his ignorance and his foolishness. Of course, a certain malicious humor on the part of others was also responsible. And too, some of what happened could only be attributed to what Americans would call Lady Luck, or the cast of the dice.

Yitzhak's friends, still waiting for their medical clearance and eventually tiring of their self-amusements, finally discussed among themselves their plans for the future. It had never occurred to them, until boredom set in, to talk of anything at all serious. Even now it was done with a certain flippancy, almost as if it were a matter of scant consequence, unlike the other immigrants to whom the future was a matter of frantic concern, even of life and death.

Only Franz of that German contingent planned to stay in New York. He was going to live with his uncle in a place called Yorkville and serve as apprentice to Uncle Helmut, who was a master baker. "At least I won't go hungry," Franz smiled, patting his already protruding belly.

The others were going to Milwaukee, Wisconsin; St. Paul, Minnesota; Galveston, Texas; Chicago, Illinois. Strange-sounding names of strange places. Even repeating them carefully didn't help Yitzhak pronounce them correctly. They simply wouldn't roll off his tongue. He was amazed that his friends were going to such places. In Slobodka, he had never heard of anyone going to any place in America other than New York.

"At least I won't go thirsty," Hans said, laughing. He was the one going to Milwaukee. While he wouldn't be living with his aunt and uncle but in a rooming house, he was going to work in the brewery where his uncle worked. His uncle had promised to find him a job there. The others laughed, wishing *they* would be the ones with the luck to go to work in a brewery.

Of the group only Otto had no definite place in mind since he had neither relative nor friend in America. He had left Germany rather hastily where, he hinted, he had killed a man in a drunken brawl in a waterfront bar. But Otto didn't seem overly concerned by his lack of a destination. After all, he did know some English. He figured that once he was released from the Staten Island quarantine station he'd simply strike out and see where fortune took him. But he wouldn't mind being a butcher, he said. "At least, then, you always eat. Why, I bet a man could live the rest of his life just eating wurst with a little kraut thrown in for good measure, providing he always had a few beers to wash it all down."

"Come with me to Milwaukee," Hans offered. "I'm willing to wager my uncle will get you a job in the brewery too. At least, you'll have your few beers."

Otto considered this, inclining his head from side to side. "Why not?"

"We have to take a train there. It's many miles from New York, maybe a thousand," Hans told him.

"Then I guess it's out," Otto chuckled. "I haven't got but a few marks to my name."

213

"In that case you'd better come with me," Franz said. "Since Yorkville is in New York, how much can it cost to get there? Maybe my Uncle Helmut even knows a butcher you can work for."

"Why not?" Otto said again. It didn't make a whit of difference to him. "Where are you headed for, Yitzhak?"

"I have a name and address of someone who is a kind of relative—"

As he had been ready to leave and his mother had given him the pouch of rubles, she had told him that inside the pouch was also the address of Boris Levitz, the brother-in-law of his Uncle Yacob, Dorie's father, who had gone to America some fifteen years before. While they had never heard from him again, Eve was sure that the brother-in-law would be able to direct Yitzhak to Yacob, and she hoped that Yacob would look out for him as she and David had looked out for Dorie—as if she had been their own child.

When Yitzhak emptied the pouch of all his money, the piece of paper wasn't there. When had he lost it? he wondered. Or where, for that matter? It had never occurred to him to look *for* it or *at* it in all this time, since he had been content in the knowledge that it was there.

The boys doubled over in laughter. They thought it was hilariously funny that he had lost the name and address of the one person in America who could help him. They laughed so hard it was contagious and it was only a few seconds before Yitzhak joined in with them. His predicament didn't seem too dire. Surely a man who had left home a hero, who had actually killed the Governor-General, could find his Uncle Yacob if he put his mind to it. He had a vague notion that it would be as simple as walking the streets asking whatever Jew he came across where to find him. As simple as it would have been to walk around Slobodka and ask where to find the family Markoff.

And that's what he would do. Since his Uncle Yacob was in New York, he would simply ask, through Otto, how to get to New York from Staten Island, then catch a ride in a wagon since he didn't have a horse. If he couldn't do that he would walk until he came to New York and then he would start asking. Getting from Staten Island to New York must be like getting from Kovno to Slobodka.

"And what trade will you take up in America?" one of the boys asked.

"Are you going to be a rabbi?" Heinz snickered, and they all laughed again as if being a rabbi was something terribly funny.

"Oh no," Yitzhak answered in all seriousness. "I'm not very good at books. But I have a trade. I'm a cattle dealer."

"You stupid son of a Jewish bitch!" Heinz sneered. "You *can't* be a cattle dealer in New York. Everyone with one bit of a brain knows they don't have cattle in New York!"

Yitzhak was on him in a second, had him wrestled to the ground in another, and pounding his head against the filthy floor in a third. Heinz begged to be let up. "I didn't mean to insult you," he said, "but everyone knows the place for cattle is in the West."

West? Yitzhak had never heard of the West. "Where is it, this West?"

"It's in Texas," Heinz told him, and the others nodded. If Heinz was on his way to Galveston, Texas, who should know better than he?

The period of quarantine was finally over and the immigrants, at last, were being processed. As the line of dispirited and frightened people shuffled toward the big desk where two bored-looking officials questioned, wrote and stamped, even the lighthearted German boys grew somewhat apprehensive.

"Are they speaking only English?" Hans asked Otto, who stood in front of his small contingent since he would be the one to act as interpreter.

"Yes, of course," Otto answered authoritatively. "What else would they speak?"

"A little German, maybe?" Heinz offered.

"No!" Otto was suddenly not as confident as he had appeared earlier when still some distance from the ominous desk.

"Maybe Yiddish?" Yitzhak suggested.

"No, you lummox! Do they look like Jews to you? They're Americans. Plain Americans."

Yitzhak shrugged. They could be Americans of Russian or Polish background. "Maybe they speak some Polish or Russian?"

Otto was extremely nervous now. "No! Don't you see? As each group comes up, they find one person in the bunch who speaks some English and that's the way it's done. All of you are lucky you have me," he assured them. "If you didn't, you'd really be in trouble. Those two are *real* Americans. That's why they can't speak any other language but English."

What did Otto mean by *real* Americans? Yitzhak wondered. His mother had told him that in America everyone came from somewhere else since the country was so new. His mother had said that the only *real* Americans were the Indians, who had been there when . . . when . . . Yitzhak tried to remember who it was who had discovered America and found the Indians already living there, but he couldn't. Still, he said, "My mother, who has studied American history, says there are no real Americans except for Indians who have red faces. These men don't have red skin."

"The Indians don't live in New York," Heinz said, proud of his knowledge. "They live out West!"

"What does your mother know anyway?" Otto said with derision. "She's only a yiddle, a dumb yiddle from some pesthole in Russia."

Yitzhak jumped out of line to wrap his hands around Otto's neck and squeezed and squeezed until Otto's eyes began to pop.

"Hey, Frank!" one of the "Real Americans" sitting at the desk drawled laconically to his partner. "Our krauts are getting out of hand here—" He rose from his chair and growled: "Hey, cut it out, you heinies, or you're going to go to the back of the line again!"

Yitzhak only understood that the official was upset. He let go of Otto's neck and Otto's hands went to his throat, rubbing it. "You stupid son-of-a-bitch

Jew! Now you've got us all in trouble! Now we probably won't even get into America."

The rest of the youths glared at Yitzhak except for Hans who thought of Yitzhak as a special friend. They weren't even *in* America yet but already they were in trouble with the authorities. And it was Yitzhak's fault.

Still, the Real Americans didn't seem all that distressed by the fighting. They were talking to each other and smiling, apparently making jokes.

Actually, the two officials were bored stiff, weary of these dregs of humanity they had to deal with, day-in, day-out, the bedraggled, filthy steerage bunch with their impossible names. At least the last crew before this one had had fairly decent names a man could spell and pronounce: Reilly, Dugan, Jameson . . .

They went through the German boys one by one, making fun of them, their names, their beer bellies, even the cities they came from. Finally, they came to Yitzhak, "Ah, here he is—the strongman who chokes people. What's your name, Strongman?"

Yitzhak smiled uncertainly.

"Your name, *dummkopf!*" Otto yelled. "They want to know your name."

"Yitzhak Markoff."

One official nudged the other. "Did you get that, Frank? Yitzhak Markoff! Our strongman here is a yid."

"I don't know, Mike. He don't look like no Yitzhak Markoff to me. Not even a beard."

"No beard and no cap, not even one of those yarmulkes like the other sheenies. And he likes to fight. If you ask me, he looks more like a Stash. Where do you come from?" he asked Yitzhak.

Yitzhak looked to Otto for a translation but Otto played dumb. Why should he help this lousy Jew who had tried to choke him? But the official called Mike told him, "Tell your friend we want to know where he comes from."

"They want to know the city you come from, stupid."

Yitzhak started to lunge at Otto again but thought better of it. "Slobodka. Near Kovno."

"Did you get that, Mike? He's a Sasha."

"Oh, he could still be a Stash . . ."

"True, but his kraut buddy speaks to him in *Goiman*. And he looks *Goiman*. And that smile. A real smiling Dutchman if ever I saw one. I say he's a heinie."

"If that's the case, then he should have a proper heinie name. What do you say?"

"Let's find out first if he has a sponsor here." He turned to Otto. "Does he have anyone here who's assuming responsibility for him?"

Otto sneered. "Who'd assume responsibility for a lousy yid?"

"It's not nice to talk about your friend like that, kraut. Does he or don't he have a sponsor?"

Otto was sullen now. Because of Yitzhak he'd been reprimanded. "He has an uncle someplace, but he has to go looking for him."

216

"No sponsor. Very well. Tell your friend here that we're going to give him a real American name."

Otto repeated this information to Yitzhak and Yitzhak nodded. This must be the way it's done, he thought.

"Hey, Mike, since his name is Markoff why don't we just make it Marx? Now that's a good kraut name."

"Not bad. But this boy is a wonderful fellow. And very important looking. How about we put one of those *vons* in there, before the Marx. Von Marx . . ."

They broke into laughter.

"*Wunderbar!* And how about a first name?"

"Heinz, for Heinie?"

"Naw, that's his friend's name. We want something original. How about Siegfried?"

"Nah, we don't want to do that to him. That sounds too Jewish." They started laughing again while all the boys stood around wondering what was going on. Even Otto, who understood many of the words, didn't know what was so funny.

"How about Wilhelm?"

"Very *gut!* That's what it will be—Wilhelm von Marx. A wonderful name. He could even be a baron with a name like that!" He wrote it down and stamped the paper. "There you are, Wilhelm, old chap. A real American name."

Yitzhak took the paper and gazed at it uncomprehendingly. The others crowded around and looked at Yitzhak's paper in amazement. *Wilhelm von Marx was a real American name?* Hans was impressed. "In Germany only very important people have a *von* in their names," he told Yitzhak and Yitzhak was pleased. A wide grin spread across his face.

Soon they were all laughing—the officials, the German youths and Yitzhak as well. All but Otto who sneered. The stupid son-of-a-bitch didn't even know what had happened to him. He didn't even know what kind of a name he had. He didn't even know that officially he had lost the right to be Yitzhak Markoff ever again for as long as he was in America.

19.

Before leaving the quarantine station the boys traded in their money for American dollars. Right before his eyes, Yitzhak saw his fortune dwindle by half; it seemed two rubles were only worth, more or less, one dollar. Here he had thought he had come to America—*di goldeneh medina,* the golden land—to make his fortune, and here he was already impoverished! He saw Hans staring at his American dollars in a state of bewilderment too! He too had handed over many more marks. Then they looked at each other in their mutual state of shock before they started to laugh at themselves and at each other. Well, they'd have to start all over and make a new fortune!

They stepped out into the light of the day, and that too was a shock after the dark of the cavernous building they had just left. Yitzhak blinked, then looked around. There was a fence with a crowd of people standing behind it and there was an air of expectancy emanating from this crowd. Yitzhak realized that these were the friends and relatives of those immigrants who were being met, and then as these fortunates passed through the gate to the "outside," there was a great embracing, a pounding of backs, exuberant kissing, shouts of joy and recognition.

Suddenly, Yitzhak was filled with a tremendous sense of loss, a feeling of envy that stuck in his throat and made him want to cry. And when had he cried? Never. Not even when he had ridden away from Slobodka forever, even as the tears coursed down his mother's cheeks.

He wondered where these friends and relatives had come from. How had they known to be here on this particular day of release? Who had summoned them? How had they been reached? If only his Uncle Yacob, whom he had never known, could have stepped out from that crowd of welcomers to pound him on the back, to embrace him, to ask a multitude of questions all at once about Dorie, Yacob's own daughter, about Yitzhak's parents, about all those loved ones at home . . . Yitzhak wondered if he would have recognized his Uncle Yacob, or Yacob him. Most probably. They were both Markoffs and everyone said all the Markoff men looked alike. Of course Markoff was no longer his name and he no longer had his beard. But then Yitzhak reassured himself: he still looked like a Markoff even without the beard. He was determined to find his Uncle Yacob even if it took him all day and the next.

He turned to Hans. "Well, what do we do next?"

"We'll wait for Otto and the others to come back. They've gone to find out how to get to New York, the real New York."

They waited and waited until it became clear that Otto and the others were *not* coming back; revenge, most likely, on Otto's part, and a joke on the part of the others. They'd been left to fend for themselves without a word of English between them. For a moment or two they looked at each other bewildered, but then they broke out into laughter again. They were young; they were strong; and so far anyway, they had each other. Besides, they—the officials—wouldn't allow them to hang around without any notion as to where to go or what to do. Would they? Even if there wasn't an official interpreter, they must have some kind of provisions made for cases like theirs. They must!

Hans spotted an official at the gate. He was looking at the pieces of paper others were thrusting at him and then gesturing, pointing. Hans dug his own piece of paper out of his pocket with his uncle's name and address and showed it to the uniformed gentleman who glanced at it quickly and uttered a few words, one or two of which were in German. At the same time he pointed—"Ferry-boat."

"Ferryboat," Hans said to Yitzhak. "Ferryboat," Yitzhak repeated to Hans. It was their very first English word!

They passed through the last gate that separated them from the new world! Finally, they were really in America! They looked at each other, grinning widely, and then they started to run. They just ran without even knowing where they were running. When they slowed down to catch their breath, they looked around for the ferryboat that would take them to the real New York where Hans would find his train to Milwaukee, and Yitzhak—his Uncle Yacob.

When they stepped off the ferryboat and walked a few blocks east, it was truly another world, as different from Staten Island as the new land was from the old. There were hundreds of people, maybe thousands, scurrying about, and great blasts of noise. There were vehicles pulled by horses which were called streetcars, and the streets were one great marketplace with vendors hawking their merchandise in loud bellows amidst organ-grinders, men playing accordions and fiddles with their hats outstretched, and boys playing a game of "one o'cat," which involved a ball and a bat. And the buildings—ten, twenty stories into the sky, one next to the other with only a dark alley between.

The two boys were overwhelmed and confused. Hans sighted a policeman and wanted to ask him where his train station could be found but Yitzhak wouldn't allow him to do this. *Never ask a policeman anything.* In Slobodka, the general rule had been to stay as far away as possible from anyone in a uniform. Although his mother had always said that the authorities in America were on the side of the people, Yitzhak wasn't sure this was true. After all, his Mother had never been to America. It was just possible she was wrong.

Besides, all around him were literally hundreds of Jews he could speak to, ask questions of. One thing about Jews was that one could always distinguish them from the others while Hans might have trouble telling a German from a

Pole, a Russian or even an Englishman. Yitzhak assured Hans that when the time came for him to go he himself would ask a Jew about the train that would take him to his uncle. In the meantime, he would try to find out where it was that his own uncle, Yacob, was located.

He went up to those Jews with long beards and broadbrimmed hats, one after the other, inquiring if they knew one Yacob Markoff. They gazed at him in amazement. *Who was this greenhorn who looked like a goy and spoke Yiddish with a Litvak accent sprinkled heavily with German besides?* When Yitzhak introduced himself with the name he was barely acquainted with himself—Wilhelm von Marx, they looked at him as if he were crazy and tried to move away from him, muttering ". . . *meshuge* . . ." Those who answered him at all told him they had never heard of a Yacob Markoff. Someone knew a Markoff in a place called Brooklyn, which had just become part of New York City, but his first name was Morris. Another knew an Israel Markoff who lived over on Division Street, wherever that was, but no one knew of a Yacob Markoff or where he could be found. Then it dawned on Yitzhak that if they had given *him* a new name, an American name, then it was quite possible they had also given his Uncle Yacob a new name too when he had arrived in the country.

All in all, it was quite possible that Yacob Markoff as such no longer existed and that he, Yitzhak, who also no longer existed under that name, was on a hopeless quest. Once he had accepted the futility of looking for his uncle, Yitzhak discovered that he was hungry, and he and Hans decided to get something to eat. And what a choice they had with carts all about them laden with goodies of all sorts, and saloons (called taverns at home) and restaurants in abundance. It was a veritable feast of gustatory delights. All they had to do was make their choice. First they had a sausage piled high with sauerkraut and slathered with mustard—a touch of the familiar—and then they went into one of the small shops and had coffee and cakes sprinkled with nuts and sugar. Then, sighting a saloon displaying a sign with a stein of beer with a big five on it, they quickly ducked inside to have a draught to wash it all down. They paid their five cents and discovered a lunch, *free* with the cost of the beer! There were hard-boiled eggs, slabs of various cold meats slapped between thick slices of bread and great hunks of cheese. They gorged themselves; Yitzhak alone devoured six hard-boiled eggs, until the bartender threw them dirty looks. Then, chortling, they ran outside and spotted two young boys coming out of a place called an "Ice-cream Parlor." The boys were licking with obvious relish at something white and creamy. It looked irresistible and they dashed inside to buy some of whatever it was for themselves. Coming out of the parlor with their own paper cones and tasting of the substance which was icy cold and melted on the tongue in a pool of delicious sweetness, they stopped walking and stood in one place until they finished off their cones in a state of bliss. All around them the hordes, intent on their pursuit of daily life in the city, streamed past them, jostling, pushing, completely disregarding their existence.

They alternately walked and ran without a thought to where they were headed, stopping frequently for a taste of this or that, washing it down with a foamy brew. They looked into the store windows full of incredible things, watched women hanging up their wash in funny little cages outside their windows, goggled in astonishment at the "El," a contraption that seemed something like a cross between a train and a caravan of wagons attached one to another, and which ran with an astonishing amount of noise high up, higher than the rooftops, almost as if it were a train in the sky. An amazing place, this America!

"Do you think possibly that's the train that goes to Milwaukee? Like that? High in the sky?" Hans asked Yitzhak.

Yitzhak shrugged. Anything was possible in America, it seemed. "Don't worry," he assured Hans. "When the time comes, we'll find out." In the meantime, he was reluctant to give up Hans's companionship . . . his only friend in this strange land. He already knew that this New York City was going to be a lonely place without him.

Even when night fell the streets were still filled with life, another characteristic of the city that amazed Yitzhak. Even the children still screamed and laughed and played their games. Vendors still proclaimed the virtues of their goods and couples walked hand in hand, arm in arm, while the heat of the day quivered in the humid air about them. America was a land of street people, Yitzhak concluded, unlike at home where people were happy to be home, safe, behind their own doors at night and if the men went out at all, they headed directly for the local tavern or inn.

He and Hans had walked all day without having any idea as to where they were. But they were tired. When they came to a park with benches, an oasis of green in the treeless city, they were glad to sit down and wonder where they would spend the night. Observing men dressed very much like themselves sprawled out on the benches, asleep, they decided to do the same, catch a few winks where they could. So they shared the bench since it was the only one unoccupied, their heads on opposite ends.

Yitzhak didn't know how long he'd been asleep when he awoke to a rapping on the soles of his boots. He opened his eyes to see a policeman standing over him, with a club in hand. Quickly alert, Yitzhak was prepared to defend himself, to do whatever was necessary not to fall victim to the dreaded uniform's club.

As he warily sat up, the officer spoke and his tone, while not exactly friendly, wasn't harsh either. The words he spoke were English, but with a musical lilt to them. (Later, Yitzhak would learn that it was an Irishman's brogue.) Then when Yitzhak muttered a few Yiddish words under his breath, the policeman answered with a few Yiddish words of his own; Yitzhak was not surprised— even the Russian policemen and the Cossacks knew some Yiddish.

Yitzhak understood that the policeman wanted Hans and him to come along, that he was going to provide them with a place to sleep indoors. At first Hans protested, but reluctantly he agreed to go along at Yitzhak's urging. Once at the police station, they were led to a large cell where men slept on a dirty concrete floor without even the thinnest of straw mattresses. The policeman pointed to a

221

space on the floor that was unoccupied, then closed the cell door and locked it. When they heard the lock click in place, the friends glanced at each other in dismay. Had Yitzhak misunderstood? Was it possible they had come to this new land to find freedom and instead had found a country where they jailed you for such an innocent act as sleeping on a bench? And for how long? Yitzhak cursed himself for a fool. Better he should have resisted, then fled.

But in the morning, very early, the cell door was unlocked and the men were given hot but very bad coffee in tin cups with rolls that were only slightly stale, and shown the front door. They were free to leave after all! One way or another, no matter how crude the accommodations, the fact was that they had been shown an act of kindness in a strange country, in a city full of strangers.

Still, when Hans asked Yitzhak if he wanted to come along with him to Milwaukee to work in the brewery too, Yitzhak did not hesitate a second. "Come," he said. "Let's find out where this railroad station is."

20.

The journey to Milwaukee was a revelation to Yitzhak, an awe-inspiring one. As the train ate up the miles and the scene through the window changed endlessly, he was overwhelmed by the size of the country that was now his, and by the disparities in the magnificent terrain. While he'd been aware that Russia was a big country, occupying a huge part of the world's space, he'd known this only because he'd been *told* this. The reality of its size had been a concept he never fully understood since he had never traveled very far from his tiny corner of the whole. But now, right before his very eyes, he was seeing a big America in all its green glory and magnitude, and was moved by its magnificence, even sobered by it; for him an unusual state of affairs. Every now and then, like a flash of lightning gone before he could really seize hold, he sensed what the future could hold for him in the new land. For a few seconds he actually felt destiny within his grasp, but then the sensation slipped away, eluding him. He never quite got a stranglehold on it. But for those few seconds he caught a glimpse of what his mother must have possessed and passed on to his father—that sense of destiny and the knowledge that man could mold it to his purpose if he only dared to try.

But these thoughts were few and far between. There were other things that drew Yitzhak's attention and concentration—the amusements of the present, playing cards with Hans, fooling around with the German-speaking girls on the train, talking to all the other people who spoke German. (As luck had it, there was a preponderance of recent German immigrants in his carriage.) They all seemed to like him and so in turn, he was drawn to them, pleased to bask in their admiration.

The two young men were ill-prepared for their lengthy journey since it had never occurred to them to buy food to last them their trip. All they had to eat between them was a bag of assorted cheap candies they had bought in the railway station just before departure. But it wasn't long before the other passengers, more foresighted than they, were sharing their provisions with them, especially the younger women who thought the two boys very handsome. They seemed especially to like the taller and much more muscular of the two, that Wilhelm. They loved his mustache. "And those blue eyes. They're darker than cornflowers. They're more the color of bachelor buttons . . . Don't you think?"

223

"And what a flirt! Don't you think he's a flirt? The other one, that Hans; he's a whole lot shyer . . ."

But the young girls weren't the only ones on the train who shared with them. The older people did too. They smiled fondly at the boys as they would have at their own sons. These were boys no one would have minded having for sons . . . Nice boys, with a sweetness to them. And the others, the families, the ones with children who seemed never to stop eating, shared too, even though they didn't have as much to share what with the children. They particularly liked the one called Willy because he played with the children, tickling them, teasing them in a gentle way and showing them tricks with coins and a handkerchief that made them gasp in wonderment. A really nice boy, they thought, even if he spoke a terrible German with very bad grammar. And a peculiar accent . . . One woman said she had heard a Jew talking that way, with that accent, but another woman told her that he couldn't be a Jew since everyone knew that German Jews only spoke German and good German at that. It was decided, since it wasn't polite to ask, that either he came from some very small village where they didn't have a school, or maybe from Switzerland where they couldn't make up their minds what language they spoke—Italian, French or German. Or maybe he was a German boy who had gone to live in Poland, or a Polish boy who had gone to live in Germany before he ended up in America. "Does it matter?" another party was heard from. "He's nice and nice-looking. He reminds me of my cousin Heinrich who everyone said was the nicest-looking boy in Munich . . ."

Every now and then the train stopped in a fairly large station where there were vendors selling sandwiches, mostly cheese and ham, and Hans and Wilhelm dashed off to buy almost every sandwich available since they were ravenously hungry. And too, they wanted to share with those passengers who had so generously shared with them. Sometimes these vendors had bottles of colored liquid, green and orange and red, for sale. These beverages were incredibly sweet since they were nothing more than sugar and water. Sometimes they had small bottles of milk for sale too, nowhere as sweet and frequently sour, having already gone "off." Even so, Hans and Wilhelm bought the milk when it was available since they were country boys accustomed to drinking milk, even sour milk, in prodigious quantities back home, and hadn't had a drop of it since they had left the old country many weeks before. It was almost as if they were starved for it. Perhaps it was the boys' spirit in their men's bodies crying out for the drink of their youth.

Yet, the first time Wilhelm drank the milk along with his ham and cheese sandwich, it didn't go down easily. While he had taken quickly enough to eating the forbidden meat on shipboard, the mixing of meat with dairy—a religious taboo but not one as serious as that of eating pork—was much harder for his stomach to accept. It was as if his moral consciousness were centered somewhere in his digestion rather than in his brain. But as the journey wore on, he made the adjustment. By the time he would reach his destination, he would no longer become nauseated just by the mixing of the two, the *flayshedig* and the *milchedig*, although years later, he'd be hard put to say he ever *enjoyed* the combination, childhood habits dying hard.

On the other hand, giving up his mother tongue came much easier. It was a much more gradual process. During the first few days on shipboard, he spoke a combination of German and Yiddish with the Yiddish prevailing. As the voyage progressed he moved on to *more* German words and fewer Yiddish ones. During the train trip, he spoke even less Yiddish and then only when he spoke to Hans. He didn't even know he was doing this. It was completely unconscious. Then he started sprinkling his speech with the few English words he had begun to pick up. If anyone had mentioned to him that he was doing this—speaking less Yiddish and a lot more German with a bit of English—he would have shrugged. It was, as far as he knew, just the way of things. Besides, his mother would certainly have wanted him to learn English; she had always believed that it was good for Jews to learn the language of the land they lived in, for she explained it meant that they had found a home that was truly their own.

But Wilhelm didn't think about any of this just as he didn't think about what his father would say about a young man who gave up his true name without a question or care. Or what his mother would say about his drinking milk while he ate meat, and pork to boot. Or what either one of them would say about his making a place for himself in a community where no Hebraic prayer could be heard, not even a good Jewish joke.

The truth was, at this point he barely thought about his mother and father at all. All he could think of was the excitement of his adventure. Oh, he intended to write to them and he surely would . . . as soon as he was settled, as soon as he had a chance, as soon as he had a place where he could sit down at a table or desk and pick up a pencil or a pen and put it to paper . . . He would write to them and tell them that he wasn't in New York after all, that he had never found either Uncle Yacob's brother-in-law or Uncle Yacob himself. He would write that he had a good friend named Hans and that he was living in Milwaukee, Wisconsin, where there was a big brewery and that he himself was going to make his livelihood helping to brew the beer. And . . . well, he would think of other things to write about when the time came. After all, how many things were there to say?

Hans's Uncle Rudy took one look at Willy, felt his bicep, muttered, "*Ach!*" and nodded his head in approval, his chins waggling. Without a doubt, the brewmeisters would be glad to put him to work. "They can use a boy like you, Willy. A man who can pick up a barrel of beer like it was a pile of eiderdown and *smiles* while he's doing it . . ." Uncle Rudy laughed heartily as if he'd made an extremely funny joke.

Hans laughed as if he too thought it was comical, as did Rudy's wife, Ursula.

225

Rudy's son, Eric, who worked at the brewery too, laughed and so did Rudy's plump daughter, Emma. Everybody was laughing so Willy joined in as they all gathered around the table to eat.

If Willy's taste had been more refined or his knowledge of the culinary arts more extensive, he would have realized that the food on the Husseldorf table, while prodigious, was not very good. Basically, it was overcooked and greasy. Even if he had recognized it as something less than fine cooking, it wouldn't have mattered; his appetite was huge and the time since he'd eaten a homecooked meal, or a real meal of any kind, extensive. Even if the food was overspiced and the meat exceptionally fatty, there was pitcher after pitcher of dark, foamy beer to wash everything down until a man was not only sated but content as a well-fed baby.

To begin, there was *Hühnerleberpastete*, a kind of liver pâté liberally mixed with *Grieben*. Now there was a dish that reminded him of home. How he had loved the chopped chicken livers his mother had prepared! She too had mixed in lots of the golden fat cracklings that everyone regarded as a treat. He wasn't crazy about the *Ochsenmaulsalat*—the salad made from the meat of an ox's mouth—but he wolfed it down anyway. He liked the *saure Sülze*, the jellied meat sausage made from calves' and pigs' feet, much better although he surely wouldn't have if he'd known that the feet of the pig were involved. Kosher dietary laws aside, he wouldn't have found the idea very appetizing. And he really relished the cold roast of lamb that was white with solidified fat. He didn't mind fat and he ate no fewer than six of the *Fleischknödel*, the delicious plump pork dumplings that accompanied the roast.

He lost count of how many steins of beer he drank; it must have been several at the very least. They all ate a lot and guzzled down much beer, including Ursula and Emma. They ate, drank and laughed heartily. The Husseldorfs were great laughers, Willy decided, and found that reassuring. They were acting as nice to him as they were to Hans, he mused, warm and welcoming. Particularly amiable were the looks he was getting from Emma. While this pleased him— he *was* flattered—at the same time he was not enticed. When it came to girls, amiability wasn't enough. He liked his girls pretty and Emma with her blotchy complexion and broad, snoutlike nose, did not meet his standards. Still, he smiled back at her. He couldn't do otherwise with all the Husseldorfs so nice to him.

By the time they were drinking large mugs of dark rich coffee and eating the *Apfelküchel* served with mounds of sweetened whipped cream, everyone was very relaxed as well as stuffed and flushed. Rudy Husseldorf leaned back in his chair expansively, picked at his teeth with a gold toothpick as he pointed a fat finger at Willy. "Tell me," he said, "how is it that a big strong boy like yourself with a fine German name speaks such a broken German and with a funny accent?"

Willy blinked, taken aback. He thought he was speaking very good German and had actually been proud of himself over what he viewed as an accomplishment.

226

"Well, I'm *not* German!" he blurted out defensively, perplexed as to why Hans's Uncle Rudy would say he had a good German name when it was actually an American name.

"Then if you're not German," Uncle Rudy said reasonably, "why do you have a German name?"

"But my name was given to me at the immigration station when we landed. The officials there said I should have an American name, that my own sounded too foreign for America."

"They said Wilhelm von Marx was an American name?" Rudy Husseldorf sputtered in disbelief.

"Well, that's what Otto said they said. He was the only one of us who understood what they were saying."

Uncle Rudy's sputtering turned to laughter as he spewed bits of *Apfelküchel* into the air. "That name is no more American than Husseldorf. The only real American names are the English ones. What happened was that they played a big joke on you," and he laughed so hard he started to cough and choke and his face turned crimson red. The others couldn't help but join in. It *was* a funny joke!

Rudy Husseldorf wiped his eyes with a red kerchief. "Well, no real harm done. It's a good name to have if you're going to be working at the brewery. So, tell us, what's your real name, Willy?"

"Yitzhak Markoff."

"Ah!" he said and glanced quickly at his wife with an expressive eyebrow. "A Jewish name, a Russian-Jewish name?"

"Yes sir."

"Well, you should do well in America, Yitzhak-Willy. Here, like in Germany, all Jews do well. They are very good with money. Everyone knows that." He chuckled. "I'll have to tell them to watch out for you at the brewery or before they know it, you'll own the damned place!" The others laughed again in appreciation, and Willy laughed along again although he wasn't exactly sure what the joke was.

He was well liked at the brewery for his unfailingly cheerful nature and his willingness to laugh even when the joke was on him, which it frequently was while he was new at the job. But more, he was respected for his size and strength; his ability to lift a filled barrel as if it were a feather; and because this ability also rendered him capable of doing twice the work of anyone else, with few exceptions. There were always those quite willing to loaf a bit while Willy, who never tired or flagged, covered for them by doing more than his share. Only once was he reprimanded by the foreman and even then it was only a slight reprimand and jocularly presented. It was when Willy made a suggestion. Although he himself didn't mind hoisting the barrels to his shoulder and carrying them, even running with them, it still would be easier and probably faster, he said, to *roll* the barrels of beer from the place where they were filled to the platform where they were loaded onto wagons to be sent to their destinations.

227

"That's very clever of you, Willy," the foreman smiled, "but I don't think your fellow workers would like that very much since there wouldn't be as much work to do and then they might lose their jobs. Especially when the fellow who cost them their jobs was a fellow almost right off the boat who got his job because somebody else spoke up for *him*. Maybe you'd best keep your ideas to yourself."

Then the foreman said to another man in a low voice but loud enough for Willy to hear, "Leave it to a Jew to think up things that will cost other men their jobs, just like back in Germany." This made almost no impression on Willy other than the fact that it was clear Hans's uncle had repeated the story of how he had lost his real name, which made him look like a fool. It would be the last time he would tell that story to anyone since the last thing he wanted was to appear foolish. The next time it occurred to him to make a suggestion, he would think twice before he acted.

Willy lived no less insular an existence in Milwaukee than he had in Slobodka. The days, weeks and subsequently months of his life were spent almost entirely in the company of his fellow workers. He and Hans shared a room in a boarding house (and a hall bathroom with the rest of the floor's occupants) where the clientele consisted, probably by circumstance and not by design, wholly of single men who also worked in the brewery.

Included in the price of their room were three meals a day. Breakfast and dinner (which was served at five-thirty on the dot and not a second later) were eaten in the communal dining room. The noonday meal was a packed lunch consisting inevitably of four thick meat sandwiches on white bread, with a different filling for each of the six days of the workweek. On Mondays it was ham, on Tuesdays liverwurst, blutwurst on Wednesdays, roast pork on Thursdays, bratwurst on Fridays and headcheese on Saturdays, and was then repeated without variation on the following Monday. (One stein of beer per man was provided free of charge by the brewery to wash down the men's lunch. More, experience had proven, made the men too boisterous and unruly to do a proper afternoon's work.)

Then, after their labors and the early dinner, Willy and Hans embarked on an evening's entertainment in the company of the same men with whom they worked, visiting local saloons and brothels with a frequency that would have threatened the health of older and less robust men. On Saturday evenings they enjoyed the same type of entertainment they had the rest of the week except that the Saturday night diversion lasted into the early morning hours, ending up perhaps in some strange bed. Occasionally the routine varied—a beer garden instead of a saloon, a "fairly decent" young woman's company instead of the more or less faceless women of the whorehouses with whom Willy was very popular since he was better-looking than most and noted for his "size."

Sunday dinners were always at Uncle Rudy's house regardless of all the other many Sunday activities—concerts in the park which were heavy on the drums and the brass, and lots of picnics, all kinds of picnics sponsored by the brewery and all of Uncle Rudy's many German-American societies. There were parades and celebrations and festivals in the beer gardens, and finally there was the Turnverein, that institution founded in Germany to further physical education, which the German-Americans still held dear to their hearts.

Once exposed to the Turnverein whose many activities took up weekday nights as well as weekends, Willy became very much involved. Most attractive to him were the wrestling and weight lifting competitions. At first the other contenders made great fun of Willy as a possible threat to their prowess. While he was tall and, one might even say, well built, with muscular arms, where was his bulk? They themselves were men of enormous proportions with great beer bellies and tremendous girth, thick necks, legs like trunks of aged trees, bulging chests. They had heard how Willy ran with barrels of beer but what of it? How, in a wrestling match, could he even get a hold on them? He was a joke!

The more intense their mocking, the more intense was their downfall when he outlifted every one of them, pinned the most ferocious giant of them all to the ground in a matter of seconds. After they got over their initial humiliation, they too became part of the amazed audiences who wondered where his strength came from. And what was he to say? *I am Yitzhak Markoff of the Slobodka Markoffs, men famed for their fearlessness and their legendary strength.* He said nothing; he laughed.

But soon he had to remove himself from the competitions since no one was willing to pit himself against him. So, rather, he gave exhibitions and the members of the Turnverein turned out in crowds to watch him break chains, lift not mere dumbbells and barbells but weights that were brought in on special conveyances since not even four men could carry them—great boulders and huge slabs of granite. Even a horse was led into the hall one night so that Willy could do his old Slobodka stunt of elevating the horse over his head. At this, the crowd assumed his strength lay in his arms. Another time, he went outside the hall to the rail line that led to the brewery, and the crowd followed. A flat car was brought out and filled with bricks and Willy crawled underneath and lifted the whole thing several inches from the ground. The crowd went wild, sure now that his strength was in his back.

Then one night Willy performed a stunt that brought down the house and thoroughly confused everyone. He had two men lie down on the floor separated from each other by four or five feet. Then he knelt down between them, tying the ends of a length of rope around the waist of each man, after which he affixed a comblike device of iron to the middle of the rope and plunged it into his mass of curls. Clasping his hands together over his head the better to show he wasn't using his arms, he rose from his kneeling position and stood up straight and tall, the two men dangling on either side of him like two hunks of beef tied around the middle. Now everyone asked each other: "Where does the strength come from? His head? His *hair?*"

Willy only laughed.

All in all, after several months of living in Milwaukee, there were two major realities in Willy's life, one of which he was unaware, the other of which he was . . . uncomfortably so.

Without being familiar with the word or even conscious of its meaning, Wilhelm von Marx had become thoroughly *assimilated* into one stratum of American life of the period. Having lived solely within the perimeter of a society composed of only German-speaking immigrants (with the exception of a few whores he visited from time to time), he now spoke a German that could have fooled most, although he still would have been hard put to read a few words or write them. But he got along very well without this and what was more, he was thoroughly accepted, admired and even loved by a few in the circle in which he moved.

The second reality was one even the most oblivious of men couldn't ignore: Emma Husseldorf had marked him for her own and her family was quite willing that this be so since they aided and abetted her whenever and wherever possible. Emma always sat next to him at Sunday dinners, and afterward they were left conspicuously alone in the parlor. She was also hustled into a rowboat with him when there was a picnic, pushed into his arms when there was a polka, and thrust upon him as a companion for an evening at the Turnverein when there was a lecture that didn't interest him in the slightest to begin with—

"Why?" he demanded of Hans when he felt the situation was getting out of hand. "Why do they want me?"

"Why not? Emma is in love with you."

"But Uncle Rudy? And Aunt Ursula? Why are they so willing?"

"Why not? They like you."

Yes, he knew they liked him. He was even pleased that they did. But like him for a husband for their daughter? It was ridiculous. More, it was frightening to him. "I'm not even eighteen yet . . ."

"So what?" Hans replied, partly earnest, partly teasing. "They don't mind that. Uncle Rudy himself was only eighteen when he married Aunt Ursula. Besides, they think you'll make a wonderful husband."

"Me?" Even though *he* was pleased with himself he couldn't imagine why they would consider him a good prospect for a husband. "Why would they think that?"

"Why not? You're big and strong and good-looking. Maybe not the biggest and the best-looking but certainly the strongest. They put a lot of store by that. They're thinking of all the *Kinder* you and Emma will have—big, strong, yellow-haired *Kinder*." Hans was laughing now, with affection, but still he was glad it was Willy's freedom that was at stake here and not his own. "And don't forget you're a good worker too. You'll make a steady living."

"But I'm a Jew, a different religion. And they . . . you . . . are Catholics."

Hans shrugged. "They don't care so much about that. For one, you're not one of those crazy Jews that wear those things on their heads or have a long beard. The way you look they hardly think of you as a Jew. And besides, they're not so devout themselves. At least, Uncle Rudy isn't. He doesn't even go to church every Sunday with Aunt Ursula. In Germany people frequently marry Jews. Uncle Rudy says that sometimes he thinks there's hardly a family in Germany without a *little* Jewish blood.''

"But you don't understand," Willy said desperately. "Where I come from, in Slobodka, it's a terrible thing for a Jew to marry a . . . gentile. It's like . . . to the other Jews it's like you're dead. A rabbi would soon as cut off his tongue as marry a Jew to a goy.''

"But you're not in Slobodka," Hans laughed again, still teasing. "Here in Milwaukee the priest will gladly do it, marry you to Emma. Why I'll bet you a week's wages that you and Emma will have the biggest church wedding in Milwaukee, maybe in all Wisconsin.''

Willy suddenly realized that while Hans was fooling around, he was not far off the mark. Even in the villages surrounding Slobodka there had been a few weddings of Jews to Catholics. The priests had been more than willing to take a Jew into their fold—a *geshmott*, a turncoat Jew.

Yes, there'd been *geshmott* Jews even back in Slobodka. He could remember Aunt Hannah saying that it was better to burn in Gehenna, which the Talmud described as a dark place filled with the fumes of sulfur and everlasting flames, than to be a convert. Or was it that she had said a convert could only end up burning in Gehenna?

But it didn't matter which of the two it was. For the first time in months, after having thought of Aunt Hannah, Willy thought of his mother and father. What would they think of this situation? Would they already think of him as a lost soul? His father, even though having given up going to synagogue himself, had still remained as fervent a Jew as one could think of. So he might think badly of him. Now, his mother, more compassionate than most, with an understanding of the human heart, had always said that charity was a basic tenet of Judaism, and that included charity of the spirit, so she would undoubtedly speak and act charitably toward him. But what would she really think and feel about him? After all, she had charged him: "Always remember who you are and from whom you come . . ." And she had said to his cousin, "Be the best man you can possibly be, the best Jew . . ."

He knew what the answer was. His parents wouldn't sit *shiva* for him as if he were dead, but on the other hand they wouldn't be proud of him either. His father would most likely be ashamed; his mother's heart would most likely be broken.

Willy made three vows that day. One was that no matter how hard the Husseldorfs pushed, he wouldn't get in any deeper with Emma, to whom he had never been the tiniest bit attracted. Second, he'd enroll in a night-school class to learn English well. That would most certainly please his mother. As it was, she'd be disappointed to learn that he'd been in America for almost a year and still knew so little English. And third, he'd sit down that very night, or at

231

the very least the coming weekend, to write that first letter to his family that he had put off for so long. Why had he, when it had been at the back of his mind nagging at him? Perhaps because it was so painful a thing to tell them how it was that he was no longer Yitzhak Markoff. Besides, it seemed that he never found the time necessary to accomplish this monumental task. Writing a letter in itself, without the additional burden of disclosing such distressing information, seemed an overwhelming undertaking. He had never written a letter in his life. Still, how wonderful it would be to get a letter from home in return, telling him all the latest news. His mother and father sending him their love all the way from Slobodka to Milwaukee, Wisconsin, U.S.A.

21.

Yitzhak didn't write that letter home either that night or the following night, or on the weekend either. His spirit was willing but the flesh was weak. Rather he did what he usually did—seeing how much beer he could drink before his fellow-revelers fell on their faces, or he himself threw up, or fell into a stupor. Chug-a-lugging beer after beer was not one of those competitions at which he was likely to win any prizes since the lads he drank with had more of an aptitude for it. Besides, beer was not really his drink. Vodka was the drink of the Markoffs, he told himself in consolation for his shortcomings as a beer drinker. If he'd been drinking vodka he would, of course, do much better. Even if the drink was plain schnapps instead of the filling beer he would do much better.

As to his vow to enroll in one of the night-school classes to learn English, he tried. He went down to the neighborhood school to sign up only to learn that the present class was already three weeks old. The teacher, a pretty young woman with a determined manner, insisted he join the class anyway, promising to give him a bit of extra help so that he could catch up with the rest of the class. But he desisted. It would have been hard enough for him to sit there and keep up, but to try and catch up? No, he would just wait for the next class to begin.

He asked one question before he left. "How long do you think it will take before I know English well enough?"

She smiled softly. "I have to answer your question with another, Mr. von Marx. No, with *two* others. 'What is long?' and 'What is well enough?' "

He didn't answer since he had no idea of how to answer. She probably didn't expect to be answered, Yitzhak thought. He wondered if this Miss Steuben was one of those German-Americans with a touch of Jewish blood. Jews, he knew, answered questions with other questions, especially those questions which had no answers.

He found something appealing about Miss Steuben and it was not her prettiness especially. He thought it was perhaps her gentleness of manner which he detected under the determined way about her. And her willingness to help, plus her obvious intelligence. Perhaps it was because those qualities reminded him of his mother although Miss Steuben didn't at all resemble his mother physically. Whatever it was that he liked about Miss Steuben, he went away cursing the fates that had put him in the path of Emma Husseldorf instead of the teacher.

Well, he had vowed to put Emma out of his life in one way or another. As

233

for Miss Steuben, he would see her again since he'd be back when the new class started. That wasn't exactly what happened but fate did take its turn in helping him remove himself from Emma's vicinity.

Generally speaking, there was no problem between labor and management at the Brewery. While it wasn't the policy of the owners to consult the workers as to how the company was to be run, there was a general understanding between the workers and the management that the children and other relatives of their employees would get preference when there was a job to be filled. That was certainly the case with Rudy Husseldorf, who had worked at the Brewery practically from the first day he had set foot on American soil. There hadn't been a question of this when it was time for Rudy's son Eric to go to work there, or when Rudy's nephew, Hans, needed a job. Hadn't they even hired Hans's friend, Willy von Marx, since Rudy's request was enough of a recommendation?

That's the way things were run around the Stutts Brewery. All the workers were regarded as family, and the Stutts knew the workers felt the same way about them. Didn't they pay the highest wages in the area? Didn't they pay the hospital bills when a man was hurt at work? And wasn't there a ham for every table on Easter Sunday and a plump turkey at Christmas?

When a head bookkeeper was needed in the office, there was a slight disruption of the usual hiring policy. A good bookkeeper was nearly as important as a good *Braumeister* and it took years of experience to qualify for either. And so, when Dieter Muller's oldest girl, whom he had even sent to a special school to learn how to keep books since she was an especially homely girl who would have trouble finding a husband, was turned down in favor of one Jacob Pulitzer, a German Jew who had kept the books for a world-famous munitions maker in the old country, it created a situation that was the talk of the brewery for days on end, even weeks.

The owners explained to Dieter Muller that the position demanded a man of experience and Dieter himself had to admit that his daughter had none. Besides, she was a woman and would marry soon enough and then what? Then she had to stay home and pretty soon, the *Kinder* would come along. (Dieter did not interrupt to say that it was quite possible his daughter would never get a husband, for his wife would never have forgiven him if he said that to Herman Stutt, he with his pretty, spoiled daughters.) And besides, was it fair to give a good job like that to a girl when men had families to support? It was admirable that Dieter had educated his daughter, but *bookkeeping?* Didn't Dieter know that women had no head for figures? "Church, kitchen and children . . ." they admonished him. Those were the only rightful interests for women. They also reminded him that times were bad and if they all wanted to keep their jobs and earn their living they needed someone pretty slick to keep track of where all the money was going.

Having all this explained to him, Dieter only nodded and grunted and went away not angry with the Stutts who were, after all, concerned about all of them keeping their jobs. No, it was that Pulitzer's fault, that little conniving, slimy *Itzig* who had convinced the Stutts that it was only his superior bookkeeping that would keep them all out of the poorhouse in times like these. It was he, the Jew, who had managed to take over just like the Jews always did wherever they went. It was the same back in the old country.

All the Muller relatives who worked in the factory, even those only related by marriage, were equally outraged. Poor Hilda . . . As if she didn't have enough troubles with that *schrecklich* face of hers, being done out of her position by that outsider of a Jew. And Dieter Muller's friends were also indignant, and worried. Once you let one of them in, there was no stopping them. Before anyone knew it, even their sons wouldn't be able to get a job sweeping up the floors. All the jobs would be sucked up by the *Itzigs*. They had always had the best of both worlds. They were allowed to keep their Christ-killing ways and at the same time they were respected and rich, while good Germans had to kill themselves just to get a piece of bread.

Jacob Pulitzer, a quiet, unimposing figure of a man who wore a pince-nez, a relatively short beard that was pointed and well trimmed, and who came to work bareheaded, was reviled in every corner of the brewery. Willy heard him called every derogatory term in the German vocabulary—a *Schwanz*, an *Affenarsch*, a *Scheissdreck*. None of this affected Willy. These were only words that were used in day-to-day conversation at the brewery. Besides, what did Jacob Pulitzer mean to him? He was as far removed from him as he was from the president of the United States. If the men wanted to call him a fucking asshole, what did he care? For that matter, Dieter Muller and his *miesskeit* of a daughter meant nothing to him either.

Even as the name-calling began to subside and the talk around the brewery turned to other things, Ludwig Shummel, one of the young men from the boarding house, did a particularly cruel imitation of the bookkeeper, aping a Jew praying. "How's this for the dirty *Jude?*" he crowed.

At the time, Ludwig and Willy were passing barrels of beer, one to the other. The other men laughed uproariously—that Ludwig was a card. But something clicked in Willy's head, almost like the cocking of a trigger. Dirty word name-calling was one thing, *this* was another. A mental image of his mother came to Willy—her head covered, saying the blessing over the Sabbath candles. Raising the barrel he was holding, a hand on each end, he tossed it, missing Ludwig Shummel by only an inch. The keg fell to the floor with a crash, its slats splintering open, and the beer foamed out in a spreading pool.

The men, jumping out of the way, were startled, confounded. *What had gotten into Willy?*

"You crazy son-of-a-bitch!" Ludwig yelled as Willy brought up a right to his jaw and Ludwig sank to the ground unconscious. When he didn't come to right away, and had to be taken to the hospital, the men argued which of the two had rendered him senseless—hitting his head on the concrete or the uppercut itself.

Willy was discharged immediately. What had possessed him? He could have and probably would have killed Ludwig if he hadn't missed with the beer barrel. But Willy laughed with disdain. "You stupid assholes! If I wanted to hit him with the keg of beer I damn well would have! And if I had killed him, he wouldn't have been the first!"

When he walked outside that spring morning, leaving the brewery behind him for good, he was jubilant. The air was fresh and sweet, and God, how sick he was of the stink of the place . . . He hadn't realized before how repugnant the smell of beer really was.

Willy went to work for the railroad on the outskirts of town. He was a country boy and didn't want to be cooped up all day again. Since he had to be near his new place of work he found a new rooming house. While he and Hans and even Uncle Rudy had had a good laugh over Ludwig being sent to the hospital, the experience had been a somewhat sobering one for him. He more or less severed all his ties with the brewery, which included Uncle Rudy and his daughter Emma. He still saw Hans from time to time, but the railroad was a brand new world and he was ready for new friends and new experiences.

He was getting a fresh start, yet it didn't occur to him to change his name back. Wilhelm von Marx was the legal designation on his papers, and less than a year away from the constrictions of Russian life, Willy still had an innate wariness of getting involved with anything official. But he did plan on making some changes in his life. For one thing he would start saving some of his money. His mother always had a little nest egg salted away for a rainy day—a *knippel*. She had said it was for those times of special need. Of course, in Russia, those times of special need were more often than not. Here in the land of opportunity the situation couldn't be as bad. In his own case, he had been fired one day and had a new job the next. Yes, it was a wonderful country just as his mother had always said, and he was going to write home and tell them so that very week. They were most likely wondering what had happened to him. For all they knew, he could have fallen off the ship coming to America and drowned in the Atlantic Ocean.

But then, getting involved in the new job, he forgot all about it again as he discovered, amazingly enough, not everyone spoke German even though the place he worked was barely twenty miles from the brewery. The man who had hired him did speak German but the foreman spoke English and addressed the German workers through an intermediary. The foreman's English was tinged with the same musical lilt Willy remembered the policeman in New York using. He learned soon enough that it was the Irishman's brogue. Gradually, and at last, he was learning English and even a few words of other languages: Swedish, Hungarian, even French. And he had a chance to use a little of the Russian and Polish he was already beginning to forget. The truth was, he had already been thinking in German almost exclusively.

Here again, as in the brewery, Willy was immensely popular with one and all. The bosses were impressed with the ease with which Willy wielded the pick and the axe and the shovel, moving boulders as if they were pebbles. They were equally pleased with his energy and zeal. Laboring in the humid heat of summer was nothing to Willy, so grateful was he to be out in the sunshine with the smell of the grass and wildflowers all around him. (Soon enough it would be winter, although he had lived through one Wisconsin winter and next to a Russian winter it was almost as if nothing.)

The other workers liked him as well as the bosses did. He drank beer with the Germans, whiskey with the Irishmen and vodka with the Russians, Poles and Swedes. He laughed hard at their jokes and didn't jeer at the tallest of their stories, and he knew how to handle himself physically. That quality was the one, perhaps, that made the largest impact since they were all what one might call a roughneck crew. There was the time when Peter Jurgenson, a giant of a man maybe six-and-a-half feet tall and slow to anger but once aroused, deadly, was stung by a jab of Johnny Flynn's sarcastic tongue. Johnny was only a bantam and when Jurgenson picked him up ready to hurl him, Willy felt compelled to step in until Jurgenson cooled down. He crouched down, wrapped his arms around Peter's legs while Peter himself had Johnny up in the air, then lifted them both two or three feet off the ground. Jurgenson, unused to being picked up by another man, was so astonished that he dropped Johnny Flynn, but much more gently than if he had thrown him. He and Willy then helped Johnny to right himself. After that, Flynn was much more careful with his remarks, or at least where he directed them, and Peter invited Willy to go fishing with him the coming Sunday.

But everything comes to an end. When fall came, the railroad asked Willy if he wanted to go to St. Paul, Minnesota, where they were adding a feeder line. Although somewhat reluctant, Willy felt compelled to go since they were making him a foreman. And wasn't that what America was all about, getting ahead and making more money? He felt he couldn't refuse since he wanted his family back in Slobodka to be proud of him.

St. Paul, Minnesota, wasn't that much different from Milwaukee as far as Willy could see, nor were the men he worked with different from those on the railroad back there. He lived in the same kind of rooming house, only this time he didn't socialize with the men who lived there as much as he had before. In his new position as foreman he found it unwise to go out drinking with the same men who would be working under him the next day. Sometimes he wished he had never accepted the foreman's job; he had less fun now, and much more responsibility.

With more free time in his evenings he decided once again to enroll in the night school for immigrants who wanted to learn English. But it was well into the fall by now and once again the class was already well under way. So again he didn't enroll and went out that night all by himself to get drunk. He didn't need the class, he told himself; he was beginning to speak what he felt was a good English and he was learning more every day. Just as in Milwaukee, the

237

workers on the railroad were of many nationalities, with Swedes and Germans in the majority, but the English-speaking Irishmen were a close second, and he made it his business to converse with them extensively. The reading and the writing would come later.

Still, when he went down to the bank to open his bank account—he had begun to save two or three dollars a week—he was dismayed to find that while it was called the German Immigrants First National, everything was written in English. (He didn't stop to consider that he wouldn't have been able to read anything even if the written language had been German.) But the German clerks explained everything to him and he took home a bankbook which he could look at. At least he could understand the numbers that were written on the pages. Numbers were the same in any language.

Nevertheless, a certain melancholy had set in. Perhaps, Willy thought, he had been keeping too much to himself. When one Sunday during breakfast he was invited by one of the boarders to come to the local Turnverein that afternoon—there was an exhibition of gymnastics—he quickly accepted the invitation. It would be an opportunity to meet some girls if nothing else, and maybe he would offer to do one of his lifting stunts.

He went for a walk after breakfast to explore some of the city. But it was a gray, raw day, and he decided to go back to his room and practice some sleight-of-hand instead. He'd do that for a while and then after Sunday dinner, it would be time to go to the Turnverein. By the time he got back to his room he had lost all desire to practice his tricks and he lay down heavily on his bed and stared at the ceiling. Clearly he was restless, a condition heretofore unknown to him. Maybe it was that he was homesick. All week he'd been thinking about his family back home, wondering what it was they were doing. Suddenly, he sat up! Right now he was going to write that letter home. Immediately! And he had a lot to say, a lot to write. He'd tell them about how he spoke English, how he was working on the railroad, not as an ordinary laborer but as a foreman. He'd write that he was making *ten* dollars a week, which was like twenty rubles in Slobodka, and that he even had a savings account!

For thirty minutes or so he paced back and forth in the small room as he thought of all the things he could write about. Then realizing that he didn't even have a scrap of paper to write on, much less a pencil or pen and ink, he ran downstairs to see if his landlady had a sheet of paper and an envelope for him.

"Writing home to the old country? To the parents? Very *gut*. Here, take *two* pieces of paper in case you make a mistake."

He ran up the stairs, excited now over the prospect of what he was about to do. How happy they'd be when they received his letter! Probably all the neighbors would come over to hear his mother read it to them. Certainly his relatives would come, to hear all the news from America.

He began to write but the pen felt funny in his hands, stiff, clumsy. Within a few seconds he had ink all over his fingers. He got up gratefully, relieved by the opportunity to go to the basin of water and wash his hands, then dry them slowly. He sat down again and after a couple of minutes of effort he managed a single Hebrew character. It was over five years since he had last read or written, ever since he had become *bar mitzvah* and had refused to take any more lessons. He began to form another character then threw down the pen. It was hopeless! How was he going to write a whole letter in Yiddish when he couldn't rightly remember the alphabet? He had never been any good at it. And he certainly couldn't write the letter in Hebrew. Nobody wrote letters in Hebrew. It was a language you prayed in and recited without really understanding it. Even so, it would still be the same alphabet one used for Yiddish.

No, he had forgotten everything, everything. As for the Yiddish words tumbling through his brain, he could hardly distinguish them from the German anymore. As for the little Russian he'd known, enough to read the signs posted by the authorities, but never really enough to write, he had forgotten that too. Besides, for him to write Russian, the Greek alphabet, was really too much to expect.

If only he had written that first letter home when he had gotten off the boat.

He lay down on the bed, severely depressed now. Then he jumped up. There *was* a solution! He would simply find someone to write the letter for him, as they did in Slobodka. Whenever an illiterate person needed something to be written, he would go to a scribe to do it for him. They often came to his mother, and she'd write a letter for them in Yiddish or even in Russian.

Yes, that's what he would do. He would find a Jewish person to write the letter for him, but where would he find this person? It had to be where Jews lived. There must be a Jewish section in St. Paul, he thought, and when he found it, he'd ask around. His Yiddish had to be still good enough for that.

As far as Willy could make out, the Jewish section of St. Paul was not much different from the rest of the city. It did, however, appear different from the Jewish part of New York City that he had seen briefly. Aside from the fact that New York City was so much more crowded and the buildings so much taller, New York's Lower East Side also exuded a vitality and a gaiety that seemed missing here. Except for those Jews with long gaberdines and broadbrimmed hats, and the shops with their signs in Yiddish—"Fresh-killed Chickens," "Suits Tailor-Made," "Soda Water 3¢ a glass," he might not have known where he was. At the same time, when he realized that he had actually read the signs in Yiddish, his heart pounded wildly with pleasure. *He hadn't forgotten everything after all!*

He stopped an old man with a long gray beard and explained in a combination of German and halting Yiddish that he needed a letter written for him. The old man backed off from him as if he were crazy so Willy tried another man, this one a little younger. But this one didn't answer him either. His suspicious look seemed to say: *What did this burly shaygets want with a Jew anyway? To beat him up?* He hurried away.

But a woman sweeping the sidewalk listened to him, understood finally what

239

it was he wanted and told him in a combination of English and Yiddish that there was a young woman, Jennie Metzsky, the daughter of the rabbi, who wrote letters for five cents each. "She's a lovely young lady who's very educated. She could write a letter for you in English, no less Yiddish or Polish. She lives there, down the street," the woman pointed. "The brown house with the big flight of stairs up from the street. On the second floor."

When Jennie Metzsky opened the door, Willy was startled into silence. The woman had said, "a lovely young lady . . ." but he had taken those words loosely, interpreting them as meaning that she was a *nice* girl, a ladylike girl, the way older women tended to describe a girl who was even ugly but who had good manners and gentle ways. But Jennie Metzsky was truly lovely in face and form. Her coloring was so different from the blond hair and blue eyes of the girls and women he had met almost exclusively in the past year or so. The long black hair, eyes the color of a midnight sky, skin like ivory. He had not seen skin like that since he had left Russia. In America, everyone seemed to have red skin, pink skin, a ruddiness, *rotbruchig* . . .

When he didn't speak, Jennie Metzsky smiled faintly. "Yes?" She waited for him to tell her what it was he wanted.

He had planned to speak in Yiddish, as much Yiddish as he was capable of, but he was so shaken by the young woman's presence that the words came tumbling out in a mixture of German and Yiddish with a few English words tossed in as if for good measure.

"I'm sorry but it's not quite clear. Is it a letter written in German or in Yiddish that you wish? I don't write German although I do understand it a little."

She spoke first in Yiddish then repeated it all again in English—a perfect English, as far as he could tell. It was entirely without a trace of a European accent and it must have been perfect because she herself was perfection.

"Yiddish," he blurted. "I want it in Yiddish."

"Very well. Will you come in, please?" She stood aside and he entered into a kitchen. There was a round table draped with a cloth in the middle of the room. Beyond the kitchen he could see a small room, and beyond that, one more. Everything was meticulously clean, almost painfully so, and almost bare of furniture. But the linoleum floor sparkled with wax and the curtains at the window were white and starched. She herself wore a starched dress, cotton, although the season called for something heavier. Over it she wore a shawl for warmth.

"Please be seated," she said in English and removed the cloth from the table, brought out paper, pen and ink.

"You can talk Yiddish to me if you like," he assured her. "While I've forgotten how to write in Yiddish, I still understand. I mean, if you're more comfortable speaking Yiddish, that is—"

"It makes no difference. I'm equally comfortable speaking Yiddish or English."

"You speak a wonderful English. I can tell even though . . ." his voice trailed off.

"Well, I've been in America a long time. I came when I was a little girl."

"How old are you?" he asked eagerly, speaking in English now.

"Eighteen."

"Me too," he said, delighted. "Actually I'm almost eighteen and a half . . ."

"Well, I just turned eighteen. Where in Germany do you come from?"

"Oh, I'm not German," he said quickly.

"But you spoke a mixture of German and Yiddish at first—" She laughed. "A kind of German, anyway . . ."

"Yes," he sighed. He was ashamed but he would have to tell this Jennie Metzsky the whole story of how he had lost his true identity. If she were only to write his letter for him and he would leave and never see her again, he wouldn't have to. But under the circumstances, since he had no intention of going away and never seeing her again, there was no way of avoiding the truth.

"I was born Yitzhak Markoff in Slobodka . . ." he began. By the time he was finished telling her how he had been renamed by the men at Staten Island, aided and abetted by Otto, there were tears in her eyes.

"People can be so cruel," she said.

"Yes," he agreed, gratified by her tears and at the same time subdued both by her refinement and his own state of enchantment.

Then she gave a little laugh. "But the joke is on them, in a way. Marx is both German *and* Jewish . . ."

"It is?" He was astonished. "How do you know? Are you a German Jew?"

"Oh no. We come from Poland . . . Warsaw."

"Then how do you know?"

She smiled, shrugged. "It's just one of those things one knows . . ."

"*I* didn't know it . . ." His face flamed and he felt stupid, inadequate.

"Well, *they* didn't know it either." She wanted to make him feel better. "Some people know some things and other people know other things."

"Yes, that's true. I probably know some things other people don't know." He didn't want to appear such a fool in front of this obviously knowledgeable girl.

"I'm sure you do," she said quickly.

A feeling of warmth enveloped him, something he hadn't felt since leaving Slobodka. Jennie Metzsky was not only beautiful and smart, she was also very, very nice. Nice in a way that his mother was.

"I'll make some tea," she offered. "We can drink it as we compose your letter. Would you like some tea?"

He had gotten into the habit of drinking coffee since living in America. "I'll have coffee, if it's no trouble."

Her face reddened. "I'm afraid we don't have any coffee. It's very expensive and—"

He cursed himself for an oaf. She had offered him tea. Why did he have to ask for coffee? Now he had made her feel bad. "As a matter of fact," he said, "I really prefer tea. It's just that in America one thinks one has to drink coffee to be a real American . . ."

She was relieved. "That's true," she said, putting the kettle up to boil on the stove. "People often do what they think is expected of them rather than what they really want to do. I do it myself but my father *never* does."

"Never?"

"No. Never. He does what he knows is right and never wavers."

Willy laughed. "My father tries to do what he thinks is right, too, but sometimes my mother talks him into doing what *she* thinks is right . . ."

"Well, you use the word *thinks*. Perhaps that's the difference. You see, my father always *knows* he's right. He never doubts his own righteousness."

Willy was impressed. To know that one is right all the time, never to doubt, was a big thing.

Jenny sighed. "But then again my mother died. Perhaps if she were alive she, like your mother, could have changed his mind sometimes."

"When did your mother die? Where?"

"In Warsaw."

"What did she die of?"

"My grandmother, my mother's mother, claimed she died of starvation."

"How was that?"

"Grandmother said she simply didn't have anything to eat. She said that whatever food there was she gave to my father and me. You see, in Warsaw there were many rabbis, almost one on every street. Each rabbi would have his own little congregation that he would conduct services for, or that would come to him for a divorce or to get a judgment. Wasn't it like that in Slobodka? For instance, if a housewife was suspicious of a chicken, if she suspected it might not be kosher for any reason, then she would go to the rabbi and tell him the problem. Then he would make a decision—kosher or not kosher. The rabbis that were more reasonable were more popular. The people were poor. They *wanted* the chicken to be kosher. But my father was always very strict in his interpretations about what was kosher or not. Or about any Law. He wasn't popular, and as a result, had no following at all. So he hardly made any money. That's what my grandmother told me . . ."

"And what did your father say to that?"

"Nothing. He never spoke to her. He wouldn't allow me to speak to her. He said she was beneath contempt. Soon after that, we came to America."

She set his cup of tea down in front of him. As she did so he could smell her natural perfume and his head whirled so that he could hardly think. Finally he said, "You came to St. Paul?"

She took a sip of her tea. "No. At first we lived in New York. On Rivington Street. But there were as many rabbis there as in Warsaw. Father couldn't get a congregation."

"How did you live?"

"He made a little money tutoring boys for their *bar mitzvah*. But then the Relocation Society asked him to come here, to St. Paul. There were Jews here and no rabbi. So we did and here we are." She smiled at him, looking at him from under her lashes, but with an innocence, not consciously coquettish.

His heart fluttered and he had difficulty remembering what they were talking about. "So do they like him here? The people in his congregation?"

"Sometimes there are quarrels. But he's the only rabbi here."

"And he makes a living?"

She shrugged. "The people here are poor too. He gets twelve dollars a month and then so much for every child he teaches in the Hebrew school. Fifty cents each."

"How many children are there?"

"It varies. Ten, twelve, fifteen. Sometimes there have been more. But sometimes the people can't pay anything."

He figured in his head rapidly. "But how can you live?"

"I give English lessons and I teach some of the women how to read in Yiddish. And I write letters . . ." She blushed. "I get five cents a letter."

He blushed then. "I'll give you ten cents. A quarter—"

"Please . . . No . . . Oh, my goodness, we never started your letter and it's late. My father will be home soon. I try not to do anything when he's home. It disturbs his concentration. He reads and studies when he's home. He doesn't like it when people are here—"

"But he knows you write letters and give lessons, after all. He knows you make some money, doesn't he?"

"Yes, he knows but he doesn't think about it. He scarcely even knows what he eats. He thinks only about the Torah and God. We must hurry and write your letter before he comes home."

Willy didn't want to leave, and he had a feeling that Jennie didn't want him to leave either. But he had an idea. "Why don't I go now and come back another time? Tomorrow. Then we can write the letter and not have to hurry." At least he would have an excuse to see her again.

"Tomorrow? But tomorrow is Monday. Don't you work tomorrow?"

"I'm through early. We start at five in the morning. I'm through at three-thirty in the afternoon. I could be here a little after that. And your father?"

"Oh, he's at the synagogue then. After three he teaches in the Hebrew school when the children are out of the regular school. He teaches to six, usually . . ."

Willy was overjoyed. "You see? It comes out just right. We can write my letter and we won't disturb your father."

She nodded her head and smiled at him shyly.

It was already starting to get dark when Willy left the Metzsky apartment, but he was so exhilarated he hardly noticed. He had intended to hire a cab to take him back to the boarding house but he forgot even to look for one. Rather, he ran through the streets without even realizing he was running.

22.

Willy had never been in love before. There had been girls who had caught his eye before, girls he had tried to kiss and once having kissed them, had tried to go further and further until the girl either submitted or put him firmly in his place. Once put in his place, he never tried to force himself upon her. If it wasn't *that* girl, it would be another, and it didn't matter that much to him. But that night as he lay in his bed he didn't even attempt to deny to himself what had happened—he had fallen in love! He had fallen in love with Jennie Metzsky, the daughter of the St. Paul Rabbi.

He had intended to go to the Metzsky apartment straight from work so that he'd get there, at the latest, a little past four o'clock. But at the last minute he was embarrassed to go there unshaven and unwashed so he rushed back to his boarding house, washed and shaved with water that was ice cold, changed his clothes, then ran out into the street to hail a cab. As he was about to climb the flight of stairs leading to the Metzsky house he spotted a little bakery hidden in an alley. It occurred to him to get something there to go along with their tea, assuming she would make tea for them again. Well, he'd assume that she would and if not, then the cake would serve as a present from him to her.

Staring at the baker's assortment in the case, he couldn't make up his mind. What would she like? A fruit tart? A piece of strudel? The little buns with raisins and nuts? Or those sprinkled with sugar? Perhaps some cookies? Unable to choose, he took two fruit tarts, a piece of the strudel, a few assorted buns.

Breathless, he knocked on her door and Jennie threw it open. "It's you!" she cried. "It's almost five o'clock. I thought you weren't coming anymore!"

"Oh, if I wasn't going to come I would certainly have come to tell you that—"

They both laughed at this ludicrous statement and he handed her the bag of cakes. She made a little expression of surprise. "Oh, you shouldn't have," she said, flustered, and he could tell she was pleased. There were round spots of color on each cheek.

"The tea's ready. I put the kettle on at four . . ."

"I went home to clean up . . ."

"But you didn't have to . . ."

"I wanted to . . . I didn't want to come messy." He sat down at the table. "But now it's late."

She put the cakes on a plate and set it in the middle of the table. "We'll start the letter today and if we don't finish it—"

"I'll come back tomorrow."

She didn't look at him. "Yes."

The next morning he shaved before going to work and took a change of clothes with him. Even stopping to buy some chocolates he was there a little after four. But there was someone else there, a woman who needed a letter written in Polish.

Jennie was formal with him in front of the woman. "Won't you please sit down and wait, Mr. von Marx?"

He sat and fidgeted as he waited for them to be done. He was furious with the woman for taking up *his* precious time. He watched as Jenny wrote. How little her hand was, how white and delicate. All of her was delicate, delicate and so lovely.

Finally the woman left and he thrust the sack of chocolates at Jennie. "You mustn't," she said, choosing one and offering him one. "You brought cakes yesterday. You shouldn't spend so much money." He watched her bite into the candy with her small white even teeth, with fascination. How delicately she did even that . . .

"I make a lot of money," he assured her. "I'm even saving three dollars a week in a bank!"

"Really? That's a fortune. My father and I are trying to save some money too, although he hardly realizes how hard it is. We're saving up to go to Palestine."

"Palestine? But why do you want to go to Palestine? When are you going?" His heart was filled with terror.

She laughed. "Not for a long time. The most I manage to save is twenty, twenty-five cents a week. And even then only by stinting on— Well, we won't be able to go for a long time, two, three years."

He was partially mollified. Two, three years was a long time. An eternity. Anything could happen in that time. Maybe, even . . .

She blushed, almost as if she could read his thoughts. "Shall we have tea first or finish the letter?" They had barely started the letter the day before.

"Tea," he said and sat down while she went to get the kettle. "But why do you want to go to Palestine? America is such a wonderful place. I'm already a foreman on the railroad and have a bank account and no one bothers me. My mother talked of nothing else for years."

"Oh, it's not I who wants to go. I mean, I don't know for sure if *I* want to go at all; but my father does. He's determined." She put out a plate with a few of the cakes from the day before.

"But why? Here in St. Paul he's finally a rabbi with a congregation and he has a Hebrew school to teach—I bet in Palestine they have more rabbis than they need. I bet they have nothing but rabbis there." He took a cake and wolfed it down without even realizing what he was doing.

245

She shook her head. "You don't understand. Being a rabbi isn't what's so important to Father. It's the Torah—to read it over and over, to know it by heart, to feel it, to breathe it . . . To him it's life itself and not only this life either, but the life to come. To my father, it's the Hereafter that's all important. Here, he says, we live among infidels, heretics, unbelievers who have already lost the Hereafter. Here, he says, Jews are as good as goyim. They work on Saturdays, they go around with their heads uncovered and their beards cut off . . ."

She flushed in sudden embarrassment. Willy grimaced. "If I didn't work Saturdays, I wouldn't be able to work for the railroad. Even in the brewery we had to work Saturdays . . ." he mumbled.

She smiled a sad smile. "You see. You're talking about practical matters like being able to work and earning money, and to my father practical matters are of no importance. To him there's only true adherence and complete observance. There's no room for compromise."

Willy hadn't ever thought about any of this before. But memories of conversations between his mother and Aunt Hannah came back to him. "But how does he know it will be better in Palestine? The Turks are in charge there," he said in a tone that implied he was telling her something she might not know. "So how can it be good for Jews there?"

She shook her head helplessly. "That doesn't matter to Father either. Palestine is the land of Israel, part of the Covenant God made with Moses . . . It's the Promised Land."

Willy's head ached with anxiety. He was deeply confused. Hadn't his mother called America the Promised Land? And who would know better than his mother? But maybe he remembered wrong . . . Had she only said that America was the Golden Land? "But what about the Turks?"

Jennie gave a small distressed laugh. "You just don't understand. For Father, since they don't believe in the true God, they're as nothing. For him, they simply don't exist."

Willy's face reflected his confusion and his misery. He was in love for the first time in his life and as luck would have it, the object of his love's father was a man for whom thousands, maybe millions, of people were invisible.

Jennie must have had an inkling of what he was feeling for she smiled at him sweetly in commiseration, put out her hand and caressed his for a moment before she realized what she was doing and quickly withdrew it.

Still, she *had* done it. For Willy the moment was so exquisite that the joy of it stayed with him as he took his leave, as he spent the evening lying on his bed reliving the moment, and all the next day as he toiled along with all the men who, for Rabbi Metzsky, didn't exist. For the time being he even forgot that he himself could be decidedly counted among them.

The next afternoon they finally finished writing the letter to Slobodka. Although he had fully intended to do so before he started the letter, at the last minute Willy couldn't bring himself to divulge either his new name or the fact that he was living his life as a non-Jew, albeit without such intent. Jennie urged him to bare his soul, pleading with him that an evasion of the truth would only lead to more misunderstandings which would become harder and harder to resolve with the passage of time. She was sure his parents would both understand and forgive him.

"Would your father understand or forgive?" Willy countered.

Jennie's cheeks pinked. She had to admit that he wouldn't . . . neither understand nor forgive. But in turn she asked Willy if his parents were as totally unbending as her father, almost using the word fanatical before she caught herself.

"My mother might understand and she would undoubtedly forgive me. But she would be so disappointed. Very disappointed and sad besides. As to my father—" He shook his head, saying nothing. How could he explain to Jennie that while his father wouldn't likely fault him for living the life of a nonobserver, he most probably wouldn't be able to understand how a man could give up his name and his identity as a Jew, without being less of a man for doing so. To David Markoff, what his son had done would probably be the same thing as giving up his honor, much less his manhood. Even as he couldn't bring himself to tell his parents the truth, he couldn't bring himself to say this to Jennie. *Dishonorable, less than manly?* Words he didn't want her possibly to associate with him in any way. So far, he hadn't so much as held her hand, but that was as it should be. She was a high-minded person, a girl of culture and refinement, and it was most important to him that she admire him as he did her, and that she respect him, even look up to him as his mother did his father.

Finally signing his name to the letter, there was still another problem to be dealt with. There had to be an address given so that his parents could write back to him. How could he give the address of his boarding house where he lived as Wilhelm von Marx when his parents would write to Yitzhak Markoff? His landlady would give the letter back to the postman on the spot. And he couldn't direct his parents to write to Yitzhak Markoff in care of Wilhelm von Marx, or to Wilhelm von Marx in the care of Yitzhak Markoff, for that matter. While his parents would attribute such *care-of* business to the peculiarities of life in America, his landlady would undoubtedly question him extensively. Was he keeping a secret boarder of his own in her house? And what kind of a strange name was Yitzhak Markoff?

It was Jennie who came up with a solution. "I'll put down Yitzhak Markoff in care of Rabbi Metzsky and give *our* address. That will take care of everything."

Willy was overwhelmed. It meant only one thing to him—that she expected to keep on seeing him. Otherwise how would she be able to give him the letter from Slobodka when it arrived? He could see in his mind's eye the two of them poring over it together, discussing the homey news . . . He would have to sort everyone out for her— Tell how come his cousin Dorie was more like a sister to him. And how his cousin Asher, his Uncle Hershel's son, helped his mother in the school while he wrote stories about peasants and squires and the Jews of

Slobodka. Then, she would most likely want to hear all about the School and probably about Aunt Miriam's daughters, whom they had married and how many babies each of them had. In his mind, he conjured up all kinds of continuing intimacies.

Then a fancied image of Jennie's father, with a long black beard and the burning black eyes of the zealot interfered with this comforting vision. "But your father!" he cried. "What will he think, say, when a letter arrives here for a Yitzhak Markoff he has never heard of?"

"But Father doesn't even know a mailman exists. We hardly ever get a letter, for one thing. Even if he acknowledged there was such a person as a mailman he would have no idea of when he comes. Believe me, he knows more about when the Messiah is coming than any postman."

So it was done, the envelope was sealed, and Willy was gratified on more than one count. Now that Jennie was aiding him, even abetting him in his act of duplicity about his identity, there was a bond of intimacy binding them closer.

Still, when it was time for him to leave, he panicked. He had seen her Sunday, Monday, Tuesday and Wednesday—four days in a row—and his visits had already become the focus of his life, what he waited for through the evening and the night and the whole workday. Now the letter was done and he wouldn't have an excuse to come more than, say, once a week for just a visit . . . or to see if his letter had been answered. Besides, he couldn't expect an answer before at least three months had passed.

But she gives lessons! In English and in Yiddish! He could ask her to teach him to write in Yiddish so that next time he could write a letter to his family by himself. No! That wasn't good enough. He *had* once written in that alphabet if not perfectly, at least well enough so that it wouldn't take too many lessons to relearn it. Learning to read and write English would take much longer. It was a whole new alphabet to learn. He would ask, even demand, that she teach him English!

"Tomorrow!" he blurted. "Tomorrow I want to start English lessons. I'll pay twenty-five cents a lesson. Naturally, I'll want a lesson every day . . ." he said as if expecting an argument of some kind.

But to his surprise and relief, her face lit up at his words. "I was thinking the same thing myself," she said. "Oh, not that you should pay so much money, that's far too much, but that you really should learn to read and write English. And that we should begin tomorrow . . ." She lowered her lashes and then opened her eyes wide. He stood there at the door so happy that he was almost paralyzed. All he could do was smile at her and watch her smile back at him. In fact he could swear he saw sheer joy shining from those black eyes.

"Tomorrow . . ." he said, and for the first time thought about how it would feel to hold her slim body against him.

"Tomorrow . . ." she answered softly and then his body actually ached to crush hers against his.

Willy could barely wait for quitting time. His eagerness to see Jennie again had begun just moments after she had closed her door on him the day before. He planned to bring her flowers today. He had no idea what kind—he'd talk this over with the florist. It was late fall and the only flowers available were those specially raised in heated glass houses, he knew, and therefore very costly. But he didn't care. He planned on buying a large bouquet, a very large bouquet, so that when he handed it to her she would be excited and overwhelmed, flustered and enchanted. So much so that he'd be able to take her in his arms and kiss her and she wouldn't resist. He had thought of nothing else but kissing her since they had parted last evening.

All day long he went over it in his mind. He'd wash and change his shirt in five minutes after the workday was done. Then he'd run to where the streetcar began its route. He'd get off where he'd seen this shop with beautiful flowers in the window. He'd buy the bouquet in another five minutes, then jump on another streetcar if it happened to come along, or he'd go to the big hotel on the corner where cabs waited, the horses stamping their feet impatiently as if eager to get moving. If all went well, he'd be there only a few minutes past four. Maybe he'd even take a few minutes more to stop at the bakery in the alley, too. He'd get a few of those fancy little cakes with the French name that Jennie liked so much.

But when quitting time finally came, he couldn't find his clean shirt. Had it been misplaced accidentally or somehow mysteriously disappeared? He strongly suspected it had been hidden by some of the men as some kind of a stupid joke. After searching for it fruitlessly for ten minutes, he swore aloud that he'd kill the culprits when he found out who they were, but by this time most of the men were gone and the ones left looked at him blankly, clearly not the fools responsible.

By the time he got to the streetcar stop it was obvious he had missed one by seconds because he waited and waited. Finally he started to run and walk in spurts. After he had covered nearly a mile, one finally came along and he jumped on only to get off after a few blocks because he spotted the florist shop. But as it turned out, there wasn't a single flower to be had!

"How can this be?" he thundered at the florist. "Every time I've ridden past I've seen flowers in the window."

"The wagon from the greenhouse broke down today and there was no delivery. And flowers are in scarce supply this time of year anyway. But we have plants," the proprietor offered enthusiastically. "Take a plant instead. Who's the person you were going to give the flowers to? A sweetheart? Flowers die but a plant lives forever. She'll remember you three months from now."

Willy looked over the selection of plants, bewildered. None of them seemed as beautiful and romantic as a big bouquet of flowers with their wonderful smells and colors.

"Here—take this one. A snake plant," the shop owner urged. "Very hardy. It will never die, just like your sweetheart's love for you. And see how pretty the pot is."

Willy cast a doubtful eye on the sparse foliage. It hardly seemed the right thing to have a first kiss over, but it was late and getting later every second. "I'll take it."

The florist wrapped a piece of green butcher paper around it and Willy dashed out of the shop to the hotel. He quickly saw that there wasn't a single cab waiting. Every other time he had seen not one but *several*. He cursed his luck and broke into a run. He couldn't waste any more time waiting for another streetcar or hunting down a cab. He passed a jeweler's with a giant clock in the window. Going on four-thirty already! He'd have less than an hour with her. He would skip the bakery. The plant all by itself would have to do.

Twenty minutes later he bounded up the stairs, taking them two steps at a time. Jennie was standing in her open doorway. "Where were you? I was so worried. I thought something must be wrong . . ."

Now that he was finally here and saw how upset she was over his lateness, how impatient she seemed to be to see him, and looking so lovely in a wine-colored dress besides, all his own tension and anxiety melted away, leaving him spent but incredibly happy. "No, nothing's wrong. Everything *seemed* to go wrong today but it wasn't anything serious." He grinned at her. "Everything is wonderful!"

As soon as she closed the door after them he thrust the plant at her. "Here—" Startled, Jennie took it but the wrapping slipped and the plant fell to the floor, the pot smashing into pieces.

"Oh, no!" She knelt down to the shards and scattered soil and began to cry.

He fell to his knees too, dismayed and upset by her tears. "It's nothing. Don't cry. We'll pick up the pieces." He realized that she was overwrought by the wait, that it wasn't just dropping the plant that made her cry. He was very disappointed himself. He had pictured them kissing over the bouquet and now here she was, crying over dirt and broken pottery.

"My beautiful plant—"

"I'll get you another."

"No . . . The plant itself is fine. See—" She held it up. "I can plant it in something else. I have a pretty bowl I can use—" She tried to smile at him through her tears. "It will be as good as new."

"Yes . . ." his fingers traced the tears on ivory cheekbones, gently pushed back delicate wisps of ebony hair. He felt a great surge of tenderness within him. "You mustn't cry," he whispered.

"No," she whispered back. Her face was very close to his, uplifted, and he had only to move his head an inch or two so that their mouths met, brushed, then brushed again. Her lips were incredibly soft, incredibly sweet, and he wanted to brush them again with his, but she said, "Oh . . ." and looked away in confusion.

She began to gather up the broken bits of pottery in the florist's green paper and he helped her. Then she swept all the soil together and deposited it in the bowl she'd brought out and tamped it around the plant with her fingers. He took her fingers in his hand and put them to his lips while they looked into each other's eyes.

For a few seconds he brushed the fingertips back and forth against his mouth, while they both stood motionless, trancelike.

Then she sighed. "It's late. You'd better go. My father will be home any minute—"

He didn't argue. He had no desire to meet her father. It was the last thing in the world he wanted at this moment.

"I'll be back tomorrow and I'll be sure to be on time—"

"No, not tomorrow."

It was as if he had received a hard fist to the belly. "Why not? Do you have someone else coming for a lesson tomorrow?"

"No. I've been giving all my other lessons in the early afternoon so that when you—But tomorrow is *Friday*. And it gets dark early . . . *Shabbes!*"

Yes, of course. He had forgotten. When the sun went down it was the beginning of the Sabbath. They would be eating early so her father could go to the synagogue for the evening services.

"Do *you* go to *shul* too on Friday nights?"

"No."

"Then I'll come after . . . after your father leaves."

"Oh no!"

"Why not?"

"Because after Father leaves I have to read and pray. I couldn't possibly not—"

"But who would know?"

She shook her head. "I couldn't," she said firmly, leaving no room for argument. "You must go now. I'll see you Sunday. Sunday, you can come early. Father gives Hebrew lessons all day . . ."

Sunday was two days away. It seemed like an eternity. "Saturday," he said.

"Saturday I'm in the synagogue."

"Saturday night then." Saturday night was a special night for everyone, Christian and Jew alike. They had frequently had parties in Slobodka after sundown, after the Sabbath was done. "We can even go out. To a concert or a music hall. To—"

"That's impossible. I never go out."

"Never?"

"Never . . . like that. Sometimes there are weddings or *bar mitzvah* parties I attend with my father. Otherwise, I'm here with him. He would never allow me to go out—"

"But why?" He was beside himself. "Why not? You're old enough. Why,

251

here in America everyone goes out. I see them everywhere . . . Couples. To-gether. Men and women. Boys and girls. Even Jewish girls . . ."

"Not the Rabbi's daughter. Even among our congregation there are very few young men Father considers suitable for me to— Occasionally, very rarely, he allows one of them to come calling on Saturday night and then he usually ends up quizzing them all evening."

"Quizzing them on what?"

"Their knowledge of the Talmud. On different interpretations. But we can't talk now. You must go!"

Wending his way home, Willy felt less the eager suitor and more like a whipped dog. He tried to console himself by reliving their kiss . . . Or had it really been two kisses? There *had* been a split second before he had brushed her lips the second time.

When he arrived at his boarding house, he found that dinner had been in progress for at least a half hour. He had been late for dinner all that week and as he eyed the unappetizing remains on the table, the men began their teasing about where he had been and why he was late again. Already depressed and dispirited about not seeing Jennie for the next two days, he ignored them while he thought about what to eat. The last of the roast pork was obviously cold, squatting grimly in its own congealed fat. The dumplings accompanying the pork were as limp and deflated as little pillows which had lost their stuffing. The potatoes, bloated with the water in which they had been boiled were also unappealing, as were the string beans, coated with bacon drippings that had solidified. There were also peas, shrunken and deformed, which resembled hard little pellets more than they did a vegetable. If he had had an appetite when he had first sat down it was surely gone. Then when Kruger, the burly bruiser sitting on his right, downed a glass of milk with his last bite of pork, Willy's stomach turned over in revulsion. He could almost picture the bits of white pork fat floating on the milky liquid in Kruger's round stomach.

He poured himself a glass of beer from the pitcher, thinking he wouldn't eat at all.

"What's the matter, Willy? Lost your appetite? Is that what comes from getting your little tippie wet?"

There were chuckles and snickers from the others while Willy forced himself to smile.

"Why shouldn't he get his tippie wet? He's got a pole and *she's* got a hole."

The men hooted raucously at this and Willy's smile disappeared at this reference to a "she."

"I bet she's not only got a hole but likes it stuffed with a thick sausage and hard-boiled eggs."

This quip brought huge laughs, but Willy's face began to lose its color.

"She must be a pretty juicy little pigeon for Willy to let his dinner grow cold."

This statement was mild in itself and mildly received, but then Kruger cracked, "I'd say she must be too hot a sow for Willy to let his own porker grow cold . . ."

At this, Willy grabbed hold of Kruger's beefy left hand with his own right and squeezed, and squeezed. The men grew quiet as Kruger's hand turned red, then scarlet, then the color of plums, and then a deep purple, his face growing whiter by the second until he gasped, "Enough!" and Willy let go. The hand was swollen to one-and-a-half times its normal size and Kruger held it with his other hand as if it were broken.

The landlady, bringing in the dessert, muttered, "*Ach . . .* barbarians!" and the men jeered Kruger unmercifully until he ran from the table.

The men urged Willy to go out drinking with them—it had been a long time since he had last joined them—but Willy shook his head and went up to his room. Still, he was very restless. He lay down on the bed and got up, lay down again, then jumped up. Finally, he decided to go along with the boys.

After an hour or so at the saloon, someone suggested they go down to the Red Peacock, a brothel with crystal chandeliers and completely wallpapered in red, and where the women only wore red—red petticoats, Merry Widow corselettes, negligees, gowns. For this fanciful innovation the men paid twice what they did in the ordinary cathouses. The color red seemed to fire the clientele's imaginations as well as excite their physical desire.

While Willy had been to the Red Peacock on several occasions and had been as beguiled as any of his companions, he had no interest in going there that evening. For one thing, he would feel not only disloyal to Jennie but also unworthy of her—to go from her chaste lips to the sullied arms of those ladies of joy who had lain with so many men . . . How would he be able to face Jennie on Sunday? If, God forbid, she ever found where he had spent the night, what would she say or do? What would she think of him? Most likely she'd find him so repulsive that she wouldn't be able to look at him ever again even if she wanted to, which of course, she wouldn't. Besides, the thought of going to the Red Peacock didn't even arouse him, brought no response at all from his loins.

He'd go back to his room and let his friends take their base pleasures with the equally base women of the Red Peacock. He'd simply lie on his bed and think of Jennie, he decided. He'd think about the delicacy of her features, the musical quality in her voice. He'd think of how sweetly she laughed and how prettily she smiled. The more he thought about this the more depressed he grew. A hell of a lot of fun that would be. All he'd probably be able to think about would be how she refused to see him until Sunday. She could have allowed him to come to the apartment on Friday night after her father was gone . . . Or even on Saturday afternoon when the services were over and her father adjourned to the studyhouse with those members of his congregation who were similarly inclined. But no! She'd chosen to do what her father thought she should do, had chosen to do what she thought was the proper thing instead of worrying about him and how he felt. She didn't care about seeing him! She probably didn't give a damn about him at all!

253

He went with the boys to the Red Peacock. But once there, looking at the women in their various stages of undress, he still couldn't work up any enthusiasm. For the first time he found the whores—scarlet undergarments and all—unattractive, even repulsive. They were either too skinny or too fleshy, their breasts too pendulous or too voluptuous, their behinds too large or too flat. This one had a too large mole, that one was ridiculous with too perfectly round rouged circles on each cheek. Their mouths were too thickly coated with grease and the eyebrows too thick or too penciled. Even the pores of their skin were too visible underneath the caking powder. And their overblown aggressive manner was offensive rather than stimulating.

One of the women who called herself D'Arcy plumped herself down in his lap and laughingly ground her buttocks against his loins and the spread lips of her mound against his groin while she threw her arms around his neck and wetly kissed him, her tongue fighting to enter his mouth. But he resisted, finding her repugnant. His disinterest was a challenge to her and she took his hand and placed it inside her negligee, rubbing it back and forth so that he could better feel the twin bulging hills of flesh. "Like that, honey?"

When still he didn't respond, she opened the dressing gown and lifted one large, pointy-tipped breast and forced the nipple into his mouth. "Take a suck of the titty, sweetie. It never fails . . . Suck, suck, oh, I'm getting so hot . . . you're making me so hot I'm on fire . . ."

He spat the nipple out.

Temper rising, she felt for his penis and finding it still flaccid, seized it through the cloth of his trousers and worked it up and down and around and around. Then, fearful that he might ejaculate right then and there, she stopped and whispered, "Upstairs, sweetie, and let me wrap my lips around that big cock . . . Mmm . . . I just bet you've got one big enough to choke a horse . . ."

Willy got to his feet abruptly, depositing the startled harlot on the floor and ran from the room while the rejected daughter of joy screamed after him: "You cockless auntie, lousy faggot, go home to your mama and tell her she's got a frigging pansy for a son."

Back in his own room, Willy wondered if there was something wrong with him. It was the first time he could remember that his organ hadn't responded to the occasion. But then, thinking about it, he realized what had happened. The symbol of his manhood had, like himself, matured, and was becoming more choosy about where it took its pleasure.

He laughed a little sourly and lay down on the bed more depressed than ever, worrying about his situation. Where was it all going to lead? How was it all going to end? Exhausted from his thoughts and his worries, he fell asleep in his clothes. An hour later, he was awakened from a dream of Jennie. Even though he was alone, he was overcome with embarrassment. He felt so foolish, like an inexperienced, callow youth . . . And he was ashamed for himself and for Jennie, who, even if not in actuality, had still been violated by his male lust. At least he *thought* it was she whom he had violated—he couldn't be sure since the female form he had ravaged in the dream had been faceless, no more than a gossamer creature rather than a flesh-and-blood woman. Only the undeniable emission stiffening his trousers bore witness to any reality.

He moved from shame and embarrassment to chagrin and then to something closely resembling anger. He felt cheated by the shadowy quality of his dream. If only he'd really seen the lovely image's face, looked into *her* dark eyes, felt *her* long black hair brushing his chest, *her* fingers tracing circles on his back, had known that his lips were kissing *her* lips, sucking *her* breasts, that it really was *her* thighs lying supplicant under his . . . Then he could have been satisfied and sated, then he wouldn't feel so sad and empty . . .

23.

Willy awoke that Friday morning with a fresh resolve. He was going to become a person worthy of Jennie Metzsky. Instead of spending the next two evenings in acts of debauchery, or even in innocent but frivolous pursuit of pleasure which would leave him no better off than he was to begin with, he was going to spend the time improving himself. By Sunday when he'd see Jennie again, he'd already be a better person.

Toward that end, on his way home from work that night he stopped off to buy a book—a simple child's primer. Each page had a large, colorful picture on it with one word printed below in large block letters. When he bought the book he had no expectation of reading the words because even though he now used many English words in daily conversation, he still hadn't the slightest idea of how these words would look in print. What he intended was merely to copy the word over and over so that when Jennie told him what the letters were and how they sounded, he'd be able to surprise her by writing them, amazing her with his accuracy and his intelligence.

After dinner he went straight to his room and sat down with a pencil, a notebook and the primer. He opened the book and stared at the first page. It was seconds before he realized that he could read the word! The picture was of an apple—a word he knew very well in English, one he had used not once but many times! The word printed underneath the apple had to be the English word for it. He turned the page quickly. A picture of a ball. And he knew the word for that. The next page—a picture of a cat! What fool didn't know the English word for cat?

Sunday afternoon he tore up the stairs to the Metzsky apartment and in his eagerness almost beat the door down with his pounding. How proud Jennie would be when he showed her how many words he could actually read! But it was Willy who was amazed when Jennie threw the door open wide and threw her arms around his neck. "I was so worried you weren't coming! I was afraid you were angry with me—"

Willy was so startled at this reception he dropped the packages he was carrying—the primer and notebook, the box of chocolates. They stared at each other breathlessly for seconds before they both bent down at the same time to pick up the packages and bumped heads. Then they laughed and picked up the fallen articles and closed the door on the outside world.

"I could never *not* come," he whispered.

"And I could never not want you to come," she whispered back. And he kissed her, but this time it was more than a mere brushing of the lips.

The next few weeks were the happiest Willy had ever known. The time he and Jennie spent together was more or less divided between the English lessons and the conversation of two young people getting to know each other intimately, lovingly. Plus, of course, the kissing and embracing, the tenderly whispered endearments, which began when he first entered the apartment and ended when he left. On Thursdays, when they were so acutely aware of not seeing each other again until Sunday, the embraces and endearments intensified. Still, Willy didn't urge her to let him come Friday evenings or late Saturday afternoons since that would lead to mention of her father, raising a specter he wanted to avoid. Talking about her father, considering his presence, meant allowing disturbing thoughts, even frightening images, into the private paradise they shared for a little while, five times a week. He chose doing with only the five times rather than allowing discordant notes to threaten their heavenly time together. And that also included any thoughts of the future. Didn't everyone always say the future would take care of itself?

All that mattered for the present was that he was madly in love with Jennie and she with him. He knew this because she had told him so, and she was not a young woman who would ever tell a lie.

Willy was learning English rapidly, spurred on by his desire to be someone of whom Jennie would be proud. At first he had been taken aback when Jennie explained to him that mere recognition of words such as *apple* and *ball* and *cat*—with the visual aid of pictures—was not really reading. It was only that—recognition—and not much more. To begin with, these words represented only the simplest of nouns, and reading was so much more. There were all kinds of things he'd have to learn before he could really read, write, or for that matter, speak English properly. He assured her that he wanted to learn everything—reading, writing and speaking properly. He had to, in order to be worthy of her.

"What I would really like is to speak English like you do—without an accent."

"I don't know if I can teach you to do that," Jennie said doubtfully. "I think, maybe you'd need a special teacher, one who specialized in such things."

"*You* speak without an accent . . ."

"But I came here when I was only eight. That probably makes the difference."

"Won't you even try to help me get rid of my accent?"

"Of course I'll try. But we have so little time together—"

He wanted to say, "We'll have the rest of our lives together . . ." but he was afraid. For one thing, his Aunt Miriam would have said that that was tempting fate. For another, he didn't want to bring up the future with all its possible problems. Rather, he wanted them to go on just as they were, in an almost dreamlike existence where no one else existed but the two of them.

In addition to the lessons and the kissing, there was also teatime when they just talked and laughed and learned new things about each other. Inevitably the time came when Willy told Jennie how it happened that he had come to America, how he'd been a member of an organization that fought against the tyranny of Tsarist Russia, that he'd been a fighter for the oppressed, how he had killed the Governor-General, and how his mother had first buried him in the hole covered by straw and manure, than dug him out and sent him off to America. . . .

At first, Jennie was shocked to learn that he had killed a man. Her upbringing had been such that she couldn't conceive of an act of such incredible violence under any circumstances. And she couldn't imagine a world where Jews weren't as passive as her father and people like him. Not to mention her innate gentleness. It took her some minutes to digest this information before she looked at him with awe! Why, he was David fighting Goliath, a true hero! That's what she called him, gazing at him with dark, shining eyes. He thought he could die happily at that moment looking into those black pools of admiration.

But then her eyes clouded over. "Your poor mother!" she cried. "How terrible it must have been for her to send you off to America not knowing if she'd ever see you again. How she must have cried after you were gone!"

He protested. "Oh no! Mother was happy. She was thrilled that I was going to America at last. That had always been her dream. She said I would go first and then they'd all follow in my footsteps. In *my* footsteps . . ." he repeated proudly.

But the light in Jennie's eyes dimmed at the word "footsteps" and his own eyes lost their enthusiastic glow. They both couldn't help but think where his footsteps had taken him, down such an alien road, and how neither his mother nor his father would ever be able to follow him down that road, much less want to.

Willy realized that he would have to do something about the course his life had taken in America so that not only his mother and father would take pride in it but Jennie would too, would find him as heroic in his new life as she thought him in the old. One of these days, soon, he'd do just that. But for the present, all he could think of was the time he and Jennie spent together.

He told her all about his family, leaving no one out—the aunts, the uncles, the cousins. Most of all, he talked about his parents, telling her all the stories he himself had been told over the years—the exciting tale of how his mother had been claimed as a Markoff bride, how it took some time before she had accepted, then come fiercely to love his father. He related how his mother had rebelled against the tyranny of his grandfather and how she had won out, staking out a rightful place for herself and for her Markoff sisters-in-law as well. He told Jennie about the School and the Clinic and how everyone in that part of the world respected Eve, even the village priest and the Squire.

Jennie was full of admiration. "Oh, she sounds wonderful!"

"She is . . . But she'll be coming to America one of these days and then you'll see for yourself. You'll love her just as everyone in Slobodka does. As for my father, I think you'll like him too."

He told her all about the printing press and then went on to tell things about his father that he had never even thought about before, certainly never put into words. He said that his father was in many ways an angry man—angry with the Tsar for being insensitive to the needs of his people, both Jew and gentile. And angry with the gentiles for the crimes they perpetrated against the Jews, fellow human beings. But at the same time he was angry with the Jews for their acceptance of their role as scapegoats. "That's what Father called them—the scapegoats of the universe. And he was angry with God for allowing them to be the scapegoats. He stopped going to synagogue because of this anger. Yet, he's basically a gentle man. He hardly ever loses his temper as his father did. My grandfather Chaim was famous for his terrible temper. The more I think about it, the more I see that Father is really full of love. For me and for my mother, of course, but for everyone else too. Mother says the real reason he was so mad at God was because it hurt him to see how people suffered so. And he fights back, he keeps fighting back, in his own way. I must admit that I used to get mad at *his* way. I wanted him to be a terrorist, you see, because I thought that was exciting, that being a terrorist was more heroic than printing up pamphlets and trying to organize peaceful strikes—that sort of thing. He told me that on the few occasions that he perpetrated acts of violence, he tried to be sure in his own heart that these acts were both sensible and just. He told me to be sure to do only those things that brought about real good and to make sure that the cause was just. Mother says that while Father might not always love God, that he gets angry with Him, he *always* loves justice . . ."

"Oh, Yitzhak! How lucky you are to have a father like that . . ." They looked at each other in astonishment and laughed. Without thinking she had suddenly called him by his real name, the name given him at birth by a mother and father proud to be the parents of such a wonderful boy. It must have been the stories he was telling her, the stories she was so avid to hear. But oh, how good it sounded to his ears, that name he hadn't heard in so long a time.

He told her about the bottomless herring barrel. "There was a porch in back of our house where food was stored, and a barrel always stood there, full of herrings pickled in brine. Sometimes, when times were especially hard, or the winter especially long, those herrings were all we had to eat. Mother would say to me or to one of my cousins, 'Go get a few herring out of the barrel, but be sure not to look inside to see how many are left.' She told us that as long as no one ever looked to see how many there were left, the barrel would never be empty."

Jennie was fascinated. "And—"

"And no one ever saw the bottom of that barrel."

She was incredulous. "You mean it was never empty?"

"Never. No matter who came to our door looking for something to eat, he never went away hungry. There was always the herring barrel. I can't tell you how good they tasted! A herring or two with a boiled potato . . . Now I think that maybe there's no better dish."

"Wait a minute. It's hard to believe that all of you, all the children, never *once* peeked inside."

"Of course we didn't. If Mother said not to look, no one ever dreamed of looking. And when she said the barrel would never be empty, no one ever doubted—"

For a minute, Jennie just sat there as if in a trance, thinking. Then she nodded her head. "It was faith. In God. That He would provide."

Willy laughed. "No. It was faith, all right, but not in God, in Mother."

Again she stared at him in silence, then looked away as if she were upset.

He was perplexed. Why had the story distressed her? It was a wonderful story, and true. Then he thought that she was upset about her own mother dying of starvation. She was probably thinking about that, about how her father, with all his unswerving faith in God and in his own righteousness, had let her mother starve to death. That's what she herself had more or less told him.

When she turned back he saw her eyes filled with tears and he ached for her, tried to think of something to say that would make her feel better. He took her hand and covered it with kisses and then he saw that her teary eyes were also filled with commiseration. With pity! To his amazement she said, "My poor Yitzhak!"

He was amazed. "Why do you say, poor Yitzhak?" he asked softly.

"To have lived as the son of such a mother and father and to live the way you do now . . . It's terribly sad."

"Sad?" he asked, uncomprehending.

"Oh yes, terribly sad. Don't you realize, Yitzhak, what you've done, wittingly or not? You've given up your birthright."

He stiffened. "I don't know what you mean."

"Oh, I think you do, Yitzhak Markoff. You've surrendered your wonderful heritage, and for what? What do you have now that can possibly compensate for what you have lost? Oh, Yitzhak, what will become of you?"

He did then what only a few minutes before he would have thought impossible. He put on his coat and left the Metzsky apartment without another word to the girl whom he loved, the girl who meant everything in the world to him.

For the next week Willy followed a strictly ordered regime. He rose each morning to drink several cups of black coffee, mechanically munched on two or three hard rolls, eschewing the lumpy porridge, the hard-fried eggs (whereas in the past he had been known to consume six, eight, even ten), the thickly cut slabs of bacon marbled with fat, the heavily salted and spiced sausages. It was his stomach not his head that dictated the rejection, his head only tried to ignore

260

the noise and clowning of his fellow boarders, pretending they weren't there at all. He went to work and issued cold, clipped directions to the men under him, where before his tone had been cheerful and friendly. For lunch, he ate four cold meat sandwiches but without thinking about it, sitting by himself away from the others. He also emptied a pint of vodka, a practice strictly forbidden by the company. Although he made no attempt to hide the bottle, no one made any remarks about it since the others had gotten the message that he was not in the mood for talking and was not about to tolerate any wisecracks or comments either. Once he emphasized this point by picking up an axe and driving it into the ground with a vengeance, providing a kind of barrier between himself and the others. At quitting time, he walked back to the boarding house instead of taking the streetcar, hoping to tire himself sufficiently so that he could collapse on his bed, black out and awaken in the morning to live out the next day in exactly the same manner.

Toward this end, he stopped to buy a quart of vodka every evening on his way home, which he began drinking halfway there. Bypassing the dining room completely, he climbed the stairs to his room and lay down on the bed, tipping the bottle of colorless liquid into his mouth every two or three minutes. But it didn't work. Even after he'd finished the vodka, he was nowhere ready to fall into the stupor he craved. Rather, by this time, he was no longer able to stave off the thoughts he had been pushing away all day.

He hardly knew which caused him more excruciating pain—his longing for Jennie or the contemplation of what she had said to him. Both these subjects took turns crowding his brain until he thought he couldn't bear it and maybe he would go mad. And if madness meant the wiping out of his consciousness, all the torment, he was just as willing.

The things she had said to him—that he had lost his birthright, that he had surrendered his heritage—how those words stung! Seared! How they tore at his insides! And how much contempt for him they revealed! How could she have said these things to him, she whom he had thought the kindest of persons, the sweetest, the gentlest, the most tender and dearest? He had thought her the most admirable person he had ever known, next to his parents. He never would have believed it possible that she, the very model of what a woman should be, could be so cruel. And to him, of all people! He who had admired her, worshiped her, revered her, held her in such high esteem that he wouldn't even allow himself to contemplate going farther than those innocent kisses and embraces that led only to the most painful frustration. But he had been willing to endure it, so highly had he regarded her. And for what? So that she could lash out at him so bitterly, so harshly? He'd been a fool! He should have realized what she was—a Delilah tempting him even as she hid behind her piety, her refinement, her shield of innocence . . . What he should have done was take her by force, throw her down on the floor and take her, rather than listen to her mealymouthed pretenses of purity. Or he should have dragged her by that beautiful long hair into the bedroom beyond the kitchen and deposited her on the bed, ripped her high-necked modest bodice from neck to waist, exposing her breasts to his view. No, he hadn't even let himself think of such things before. Oh no, such thoughts were too vile for his virtuous goddess! But it was he who had been the innocent . . .

He should have possessed each breast in turn. First, with his hands, and then with his mouth until she grew so aroused that she would abandon all her false pretenses and beg him to go on, to explore her body further with his kisses, to direct his manhood ever lower on her quivering body until he had completely penetrated her and transformed her from a protesting girl to a lustful woman as wanton as any tart! *That* was what she deserved! *That* was what she probably wanted even as she pretended to be so pure, even as she repeated her father's narrow-minded hypocritical mouthings.

But he was unable to keep that vision of her alive. Instead, he buried his face in the pillow, his entire being racked with feelings and images far from carnal. He could see her in his mind's eye, in the dim light of the oil lamp, her lashes casting shadows on her cheekbones as she so earnestly instructed him. Then he saw her laughing gaily at herself as she bit into a third chocolate, protesting that she really shouldn't, knowing that her naughty sweet tooth might even entice her into tasting a fourth. He saw her gazing at him with admiration as he told her how one of the workers had managed to get himself pinned under a caboose that day; even as men from several gangs were joining forces to get the fellow out, he, all by himself, quickly and simply tilted the caboose sufficiently to free the fellow. Then he remembered how, as he read from a long passage without a second's hesitation or a mispronounced word, she positively glowed with satisfaction and approval. And there was the time her eyes shone with perfect understanding as he described the unique pleasure of mounting a horse everyone said was too wild to be broken and riding out into the day, his body as one with the steed's, and both of them as one with the wind, the land and the whole world . . .

Oh Jennie, my darling Jennie!

How he missed her! How he yearned to see her, touch her, even her little finger, hear her voice so sweet and clear . . . He soaked the pillow with his tears, past embarrassment, past shame, past caring.

By the end of the week Willy admitted to himself that if Jennie's words had been biting, even cruel, they were also true. He hadn't forfeited his birthright by simply having had his name changed by insensitive clowns; rather, he had done it all by himself when he had fallen so quickly and so easily into the life of a non-Jew. As for his heritage, he *had* denied it, not by word, but by deed. He had done it when he had allowed himself to forget his mother's admonition: ". . . never forget who you are and from whom you come." He had forgotten and quickly, without rhyme or reason, too easily. He added another word that Jennie had omitted—betrayal. He had betrayed everyone—his ancestors, his mother and father, most of all, himself.

Somehow, just as Eve had always been able to sense such things, she must

262

have sensed what he had done, what kind of life he was leading; sensed and grown ashamed, even angry. Otherwise, where was her letter in answer to his? It had been three months and no answer had come. She and his father, not to mention the others, had obviously decided to turn their backs on him as surely as he had on them.

And he deserved that even as he deserved Jennie's contempt and disdain. He was completely alone in the world now, without parents, without a sweetheart, without even a friend. Even his companions and fellow workers, who meant nothing to him but who liked and admired him, liked and admired him as Wilhelm von Marx, not as Yitzhak Markoff.

By Saturday night Willy missed Jennie so much he thought of killing himself. What did he have to live for, anyway? He had no future. And if he had one at all, it was so bleak and dismal as to be worth nothing. A future without the joy and sweetness of Jennie Metzsky was like an eternity in hell.

By the time Sunday morning dawned Willy was exhausted from not having slept all night, but he had a plan. He would redeem himself and at the same time make Jennie Metzsky his own. He'd go to the Metzsky apartment that afternoon and dressed as a gentleman, not a common railroad worker. He would be very formal with her for even though they had been sweethearts, they no longer were. And also because she had no respect for him at present. Not that he could blame her.

Yes, he'd be very formal, pleasant but distant, and he'd say that he'd come to inquire if the letter from Slobodka had possibly arrived. He would keep acting as if they had never been sweethearts. Then he would politely request that she continue giving him his lessons in English. She would most likely say yes. Then he would say that in addition to the English, he would also like to refamiliarize himself with the Hebrew language and the study of the Talmud and the Torah. Undoubtedly, she'd agree. Then as he made progress, he'd write another letter to his parents. In Hebrew. Then they'd be able to see that he was not only still a Jew, but a practicing one. By that time he would have already started to win Jennie back since she would realize that his intentions and goals were not only proper but to be admired. Then she would not only love him but respect him as well. Once he was knowledgeable in the Talmud and the Torah he could begin attending Rabbi Metzsky's services and only then ask if he could call on the Rabbi's daughter. By that time, he'd even be able to withstand Rabbi Metzsky's quizzes. So much so, that he'd not only be acceptable to the Rabbi's daughter, but to the Rabbi himself. Then they would name the first baby after Jennie's mother if it was a girl, and if it was a boy—well, perhaps they'd name it after his grandfather, Chaim Markoff. Even if he hadn't been a very likable man, it probably would please his father.

Willy was dressed and ready to leave by ten o'clock but he wasn't sure how early he could arrive at the Metzsky apartment. He wasn't sure when Rabbi Metzsky would be gone. The last thing he wanted at this stage was to run into him! But he was too worked up merely to sit and wait around. He'd just start out, then he could take his time. He'd stroll leisurely. It would take him an hour-and-a-half at least, maybe even two hours if he took his time. And he'd stop to buy Jennie a little present, if he found a store open. Well, if he didn't find a store on his way, there'd be stores open in Jennie's neighborhood. Sunday was an ordinary day there. He'd think about what to buy her as he strolled there, taking his time.

He started out forcing himself to walk slowly, taking small steps instead of his usual strides. One street, another. His heart was pounding harder from the effort of restraining himself from running than it would have if he had raced all the way there. What he really wanted was to take flying leaps through the air.

Despite himself, his pace increased steadily. He forgot to look for an open store, forgot to look into the shop windows for an idea of what he could buy her—a scarf, a bottle of cologne, maybe a book. From small steps he went to a jaunty saunter, then to a brisk stride and soon he was running, more or less out of control, his speed accelerating.

Before he knew it, he was there . . . on Jennie's street! He didn't even know the time! How long had it taken him to get there? Was it possible Rabbi Metzsky was still at home? What time, he wondered, did the Hebrew school classes begin on Sundays? And the gift for Jennie! He'd go buy the present—He looked around wildly for the right store—a dry-goods store for a scarf, a bookstore for a book. What kind of store sold cologne? *No, he wouldn't buy a present!* A young man gave his sweetheart gifts, but they were no longer sweethearts. He was paying her a formal, businesslike call. First, he was going to inquire if his letter had arrived, and then he was going to discuss his lessons.

He'd wait in the alley for a while, watching the front door of the apartment house to see if Rabbi Metzsky came out. But he hadn't ever seen Jennie's father! How would he be able to tell? Even if a man with a long beard emerged, could he be sure it was he? How many men with long beards lived in the apartment house? Two? five? more?

He waited in the alley anyway, keeping his eye on the door, trying to calm himself, practicing what he'd say when Jennie opened her door to him. Would she be formal too? Or cold? Would she be friendly, as he himself planned to be? Friendly, but still formal. Or would she be friendly but distant? Or maybe she'd pretend she didn't know him, would pretend that she had already forgotten him. Maybe she'd even have another young man there, giving him both lessons and tea! The idea took hold and he grew frantic. If there was a young man there, one with a covered head and a beard or even one without a hat and a beard, he'd kill him! He'd pick him up with one hand, open the door with the other and hurl him down the stairs, head first; that's what he would do!

Now, he was unable to contain himself. He ran from the alley and up the stoop, taking the stairs two, three at a time until he was at her door. He pounded on it until it flew open and there stood Jennie, one hand to her mouth and the other holding her heart. Before he could open his mouth she reached out, pulled him inside and slammed the door shut. "Oh Yitzhak!" she cried and threw her arms around him. "I thought I'd never see you again . . . I was frantic. I never meant to hurt you, to accuse you—I was just distressed for you . . . I—"

"I know, I know . . ." he mumbled. "I was such a fool . . ." She was clutching him to her so tightly he couldn't even think. "I went mad. I've been crazy all week."

When she didn't release him, his arms went about her as tightly as hers were about him. His senses reeled as she continued to press against him so feverishly his body forgot what it was supposed to remember, that this was his Jennie, pure and innocent, and that it couldn't respond. He tried to remember, tried even to push her away. Fuzzily, even as their lips clung pressing ever harder, too, he thought that if they parted for a second, separated their bodies and their lips, they would be able to catch their breaths and have a chance to think. . . .

Desperately, he pulled his head away from her open, seeking mouth, wanting to look into her eyes, to warn her . . . But her eyes were closed and her mouth still open, her breath coming in great short gasps and he gave up his own struggle. His own eyes closed, his head bent to hers again and his mouth moved over hers hotly.

Mouths clinging, arms not letting go, they moved into the small room beyond the kitchen where he had never been. Blindly their bodies found the daybed and then softly, she cried out. . . .

Afterwards, he was afraid; afraid that she would cry and not be able to stop, afraid she'd be angry and order him from the house, afraid she wouldn't be angry but repentant and tell him she could never see him again. Or, she'd feel guilty and in her own guilt, turn on him, hating him.

But incredibly she didn't cry and wasn't angry and she certainly didn't order him from the house. Rather, she just smiled at him shyly. His heart sang. Still, he apologized. But she wouldn't accept his apology, insisted that she herself was at least equally responsible. He was astounded. He couldn't believe his luck. She was so decent, so beautiful, so sweet, so smart and so fair. Still, that didn't assuage his own feelings of guilt. He was the man, after all, and it had been up to him to protect her from his male lust and passion, from the demands of both their bodies. She probably hadn't even known what was inevitable, bound to happen, what the fervent kissing and tight embraces would lead to. She had led such a sheltered life, more sheltered surely than even the most sheltered. She had never had a sweetheart before, had never gone walking with a boy much less sat with one in a park, or at a concert like most American couples. She hadn't even been alone with a young man in her own house without her father present in the room. Who could be less experienced than she? Clearly, he was to blame and he alone.

"We'll get married right away," he blurted, eager to assume his responsibility and then said it again, but this time jubilantly, realizing that it had all happened for the best, that even the weakness of his body was going to make his dream come true. Now, they wouldn't have to worry about Rabbi Metzsky's approval. Getting married was the only decent thing to do. Suddenly, the future held out only visions of glory. They'd get married, get their own apartment, have babies, make love every night. . . .

He was astonished to see the smile fade from Jennie's lips. "That's impossible," she said, pushing back the hair from her face nervously.

"But why? We've been together like a husband and wife . . ."

Now she was distraught. "And what am I to tell my father? That I'm marrying somebody called Wilhelm von Marx? He'd sit *shiva* for me, that's what he'd do, just as if I were dead . . ."

He saw immediately that she was right. That was exactly what her father would do. And he couldn't urge her in her state. He understood her distress. Making love had been beautiful. Rabbi Metzsky praying for her soul in death was not.

"What shall we do then?" he asked.

"About what? About loving one another?"

His heart rejoiced. *She* had said it—that they loved one another. "Oh, I do! I love you, Jennie, with all my heart and soul. I meant, what will we do about our future?"

The smile appeared on her face again and she kissed him. "We'll go on loving each other until the end of time. . . ."

She said it lightly enough but to him they were the most beautiful words he had ever heard. "But what will we do about your father? About getting married?"

"I have a plan. I've been thinking about that all week when I was so desperate, worrying about whether I'd ever see you again. We'll turn you back again, from Wilhelm von Marx to Yitzhak Markoff!"

It was the same plan as his own. He was going to study Hebrew and the Talmud and the Torah. He would become not only a Jew again but a learned one, and pious, a Jew of whom even Rabbi Metzsky would have to approve.

He was elated and yet still puzzled that their lovemaking hadn't disturbed Jennie at all. Stumbling over the words, he asked her about this and she seemed genuinely surprised. "But we love each other. What can be wrong about expressing our love?"

He found the simplicity of it exquisite. She was truly wonderful. He laughed with joy. "We love each other—" he repeated. So what could be wrong about that?

Then she giggled and lowered her lashes coquettishly. "And besides, the Scriptures are full of men and women making love and not being married to one another either . . ."

Then they both laughed so hard until they were helpless with it, and then they started kissing all over again.

They attempted to adhere to a strict schedule wherein most of their time together was apportioned to the business of study and only a small part to lovemaking and frivolity. They told themselves that the sooner Willy learned what he had to learn in order to be thoroughly acceptable to Jennie's father, the sooner they'd be able to begin their idyllic life together, without guilt and fear of discovery. Actually, they didn't share these two emotions equally since Jennie was more plagued by the fear of being found out before they had Willy ready, and he was more filled with guilt. To him, each time they made love it was as if he were luring her, his wonderful angel and paragon of virtue, from her proper path of righteousness for the first time. But even so, even with the feelings of guilt and fear and their avowed dedication to a program of conscientious study, they still couldn't help but fall into each other's arms the second the door closed on the outside world, their magnetism for each other being stronger than any commitment to study or pang of conscience or fear.

Still, that late Thursday afternoon when Rabbi Metzsky came home early due to a tail end of winter snowstorm that emptied his classroom, they were not in each other's arms but sitting at the kitchen table more or less innocently with their heads over a book. Just the same, Willy watched Jennie's face pale as she jumped up the moment her father entered.

"Father! Is anything wrong?" she asked in Yiddish.

He answered her curtly, his eyes averted from Willy, who nonetheless stood up quickly, almost knocking over his chair in his haste.

Jennie looked from one to the other. Finally she blurted, "Father, this is . . . Wilhelm von Marx . . . whom I've been teaching—"

"How do you do, sir . . . Rabbi . . ." Willy was rattled even as he towered over the gnomelike figure whose beard reached down to almost his middle. The Rabbi was so gloweringly self-possessed while Willy felt like an awkward school-boy whose knuckles were soon to be severely rapped.

But the Rabbi didn't acknowledge Willy's words, much less his existence with a word, a nod nor even a scowling glance. He walked through the kitchen and through the curtains that separated that room from the two others beyond. "Tea!" he barked as he disappeared from sight. "Hot tea!"

Jennie rushed to the stove. "You'd better go—"

"Why? We weren't doing anything but sitting there—"

"Go, please. I'll see you Sunday," she whispered.

Reluctantly, he put on his coat and cap, his scarf and gloves. "I'll be back tomorrow night. We have to talk."

"No . . . Sunday, please."

Slowly, he walked down the steps and out into the street. He felt anger; more, he felt ridiculous. He had killed an enemy of the people, had licked men ten times as threatening, twenty times, as that little bit of a man and here he was running. . . .

It was dark and the snow was coming down in a heavy blanket. It had only started to fall a little before he had left work but there was already an accumulation of several inches. There was no use looking for a horse and carriage, or waiting for a streetcar. He had had enough experience with snowstorms in St. Paul to know better. He chuckled sourly. His mother would be surprised to learn that the Russian winters had nothing on the Minnesota winters. He hunched into the gusts of icy moisture. The Minnesota winter had nothing on his state of mind.

"But I don't understand why you introduced me as Wilhelm von Marx. Why didn't you give him my name as Yitzhak Markoff? Then at least he would have known I was a Jew . . ."

Jennie's eyes widened and her mouth opened in surprise. Then she smiled a little, shaking her head from side to side. "You still don't understand. As Wilhelm von Marx you're nothing to him. An unbeliever, a zero, someone who doesn't even exist. But if I introduced you as Yitzhak Markoff who sat there without a beard, and before the Scriptures with his head uncovered, he would know who you were all right. He'd know that you were a Jewish infidel, a heretic. Then he'd point a finger at you, damning you for all time to come as a curse on all Jews all the way back to Abraham! He'd denounce you as a lost soul, one who hadn't only lost this world but, what's worse, the one to come. . . ."

"But then I could have come back as a penitent, a lost soul who finds his way back, and your father could have been the one to redeem my soul. Then, he'd—"

Jennie shook her head. "No. To some Jews a penitent can even be a holy man, but not to Father. A repentant Jew who had once lost his faith would be forever flawed in his eyes, always suspect."

Willy sighed. "Well, since you've already introduced me as von Marx, there's no use even talking about it. Now I'll have to let him think I want to convert to Judaism. But since he'll be the one to convert me, he might even begin to like me . . ."

Jennie broke into laughter at this. The preposterous idea that her father might like him because he converted him was so funny she couldn't help herself. She shook her head at him again. "The rabbis in Germany don't mind converts. They even welcome them as the Catholics do Jews who join their fold. But the Jewish orthodoxy isn't looking for converts. Why, the orthodox rabbis are required to make three separate efforts to discourage gentiles from converting. And those are the *ordinary* orthodox rabbis—"

"Meaning what?"

She laughed again. "Meaning my father wouldn't even talk to them in the first place, much less *three* times."

Willy stared at her with disbelief, even anger. First she dismissed every solution to their problem he offered as impossible. Nothing, it seemed, would satisfy this fanatic of a father. And to top it all, she *laughed! How could she laugh?* "All right then, if nothing's going to work, you tell me what we're going to do—"

Now she merely smiled. "Nothing. For now. You see, in a way, Father's attitude toward gentiles—that they don't exist—is very helpful to us. He never even looked at you. He never saw you. Oh, he didn't like your being here, but he knows I give lessons. But since he didn't see you he won't even remember your being here, much less your face or your name. Then, when we present you as Yitzhak Markoff, a beautifully learned man . . ." She put both her hands on his shoulders. ". . . With your beautiful yellow beard . . ." She kissed him quickly on his chin, "and with a yarmulke on your beautiful yellow curls . . ." She ruffled his hair. "Why, then he'll love you as much as I do!"

They both laughed at the ridiculous notion, the very idea of Rabbi Metzsky *loving* him.

"Then, do you know what he'll do next?"

"No, tell me." Although he adored the proper, decorous side of her, he couldn't resist her when she was laughing and carefree, even silly.

"Why, he'll probably shower you with kisses, like this—" She showed him exactly what she meant, and he was reassured. How could he not be?

Despite Jennie's lighthearted words that day, they became much more conscious of Rabbi Metzsky's comings and goings, kept a much more watchful eye on the clock, tried to anticipate any possible change in the order of the Rabbi's day. At the same time, they stepped up the pace of Willy's Hebrew lessons, drilling him more and indulging in playfulness less.

Even as Willy's familiarity with the Talmud and the Torah intensified and his mastery of Hebrew grew more complete, he noticed an increasing nervousness in Jennie. She was as sweet as ever, as demure and compliant, and when they made love as passionate, but there was a change in her. He couldn't put his finger on it exactly. Perhaps it was that she laughed less than before. There definitely was a somberness about her now. She even burst into tears unaccountably. Somehow, Willy sensed that their time was running out. They'd have to reveal his existence as a suitor and as a learned, observant Jew very, very soon.

He started examining his face every few days as he shaved before going to work, speculating as to how he'd look with a beard again. It had been almost two years . . . Then one morning he put the razor down. It was time to stop shaving. He wondered how long it would be before he had a beard of a decent length.

It was a Friday and he decided not to go to work that day. Instead, he'd go buy a skullcap and a prayer shawl in one of the stores in Jennie's neighborhood before they closed early for the Sabbath.

Carrying the articles wrapped in brown paper, he stationed himself in the alley, waiting endlessly for Rabbi Metzsky to come out the front door on his way to the synagogue. He was going to surprise Jennie and what a surprise it would be! For one, he had never seen her on a Friday before. When she saw him with the prayer shawl draped across his shoulders and the yarmulke on his head, she'd probably weep with joy.

He tore open the wrapping paper. He couldn't wait another second. Filled with exhilaration, he put the shawl on and then the yarmulke . . . tentatively. Somehow, it didn't sit right. Maybe it was his hair. Probably, he needed a haircut.

Finally he saw Rabbi Metzsky emerge, walk to the corner and turn left. The synagogue, Willy knew, was two streets up from the corner. He had gone there several days before just to see how long it took to make the walk from the Metzsky house. As soon as the Rabbi disappeared from view Willy came out of his hiding spot. He ran up the stairs, unable to wait another second to surprise Jennie. The yarmulke fell off and he stopped to pick it up and put it back on. He knocked on the door. She'd wonder who it was, never dreaming it would be he on a Friday night.

As soon as she saw him grinning at her she broke into tears but laughing at the same time. He laughed too, exuberantly. He picked her up off the floor even as he pushed the door closed with his foot. The skullcap fell off again as he carried her through the curtains into the bedroom beyond. This time he didn't bother to pick it up. He laid her down on the bed and the prayer shawl slipped off his shoulders and fell to the floor. Neither of them took notice.

It was only moments later, or so it seemed, that there was a passionate outcry. It was neither Jennie's nor his. Then immediately after, there was another scream and this time it *was* Jennie's. He jumped up. Rabbi Metzsky stood in the curtained doorway clutching his beard with one hand and beating his chest with the other, his fist clenched. He was wailing to God. It was the most tortured lament Willy had ever heard. As the Rabbi turned and ran out of the apartment, leaving the door wide open, Willy could still hear his cries as he stumbled down the stairs. Then, he could only hear Jennie wailing. . . .

She wouldn't even listen to him, to his pleas that she pack a few things and leave with him right then and there. They'd go to a hotel and in the morning they'd find out where they could be married quickly. Then they'd come back and tell her father that they were man and wife and what could he do then? Either accept them as man and wife and Yitzhak as a penitent or send them both away. But that was highly unlikely since her father needed Jennie more than she needed him. Without her, her father had nobody. But she had him, Willy. Or was it Yitzhak? He no longer could distinguish between the two.

She continued to cry, seemingly unable to stop. She covered her ears with her hands so that she couldn't hear his pleading. She told him to go. She told him she'd see him on Sunday. She was hysterical. And she wouldn't listen to him. She screamed at him to leave until finally, he did, although he *knew* it was the wrong thing for him to do. But he didn't seem to have any other choice.

He had no intention of waiting until Sunday to see her and find out what had happened between her and her father. Therefore he didn't go to work that Saturday either and waited once again in the alley for the Rabbi to leave, and was ashamed of himself for doing so. It was a cowardly act, he knew, but he was afraid of seeing the Rabbi, of confronting him. Afraid lest the Rabbi say something so provocative that he, Yitzhak Markoff, would kill him. Or maybe it would be Wilhelm von Marx that would kill him. He was sick of them both, Wilhelm *and* Yitzhak. He only wanted to take his beloved Jennie away and leave them all behind—Willy, Yitzhak and Rabbi Metzsky.

He waited for what seemed hours. Had the Rabbi stayed away at the synagogue the whole night through, praying for Jennie's lost soul? He had to be sure. He'd walk down the street and around the corner to the synagogue to see if the Rabbi was there. He'd have to go inside. Without thinking, he felt his head. He couldn't go inside the synagogue bareheaded. But he had his cap on, his head would be covered. Still, they'd look at him strangely, wondering what he was doing in their midst on *Shabbes* . . . But what did it matter how they looked at him?

But he was wrong. No one even glanced at him. He stood in the entrance way of the synagogue and the backs of the worshipers were facing him, swaying back and forth as they recited their chants, filling the room with the strange and mysterious music. On either side the women sat, curtained off, separated from the men but equally immersed in the magic of the Sabbath.

The atmosphere was redolent of an aroma that came back to him, flooding his nostrils and his senses. It was a blend of burning tallow combined with a hint of miracles and dreamy visions of heaven . . .

For a moment Willy's own body swayed. Overwhelming memories, a sudden dizziness . . . Then he saw Rabbi Metzsky leading his congregation and Willy's spine stiffened as he watched the Rabbi rock to and fro, eyes closed in sublime supplication.

He turned on his heel and left. Jennie was home alone . . .

At first she wouldn't even open the door to him but when he yelled that he'd break it down, she opened it a crack. "I can't let you in . . . I promised I wouldn't ever see you again . . ." She was crying.

He shoved it open, almost knocking her down. He could see that she hadn't slept at all. She was wearing the same dress she had worn the night before and it was hanging on her now, limp and dispirited, as if she had lost ten pounds overnight. Her eyes were bloodshot, her ivory skin sallow. She hadn't even brushed her hair, he thought, as if this was the worst portent of bad things to come.

"You can't stay . . ." she managed to say through her sobs.

He sat down at the table and ordered her to sit too. She fell into the chair but didn't stop crying.

"What happened after I left?"

"After a few hours, Father returned."

"And—" he prompted her. She didn't answer. "What did he say?"

As the tears rolled down her cheeks she gave him an odd, sickly kind of smile. "That day . . . when I introduced you to him . . . He said he knew who you were immediately . . ."

"What do you mean—he knew who I was?"

"He said he recognized you at once as a Jew who had lost Paradise . . ."

Her words frightened him. He was afraid now that he had lost not Paradise but Jennie. "How could he know anything?" he scoffed bitterly. "He didn't even look at me. Is he such a holy man that he can see out of the sides of his head?"

"He said that you might fool others but one son of Abraham always knows another, especially one who has sold his birthright. He said that—"

He cut her off by slamming his fist on the table. He didn't want to hear any more of what Rabbi Metzsky said. He was sick to death of him. What he really wanted was for Rabbi Metzsky to disappear off the face of the earth. Still, he asked, "Did you tell him I'm prepared to do anything he asks? Anything he wants? Did you tell him I'd go to his damned synagogue morning, noon and night, if that's what he wants?" he shouted.

She began to cry even harder. "I told him everything. But it's no use, Yitzhak. No use . . . He said if I married you I'd be selling my birthright too . . . He'd sit *shiva* for me!"

"But it's all right if you're a fallen woman who's made love to the devil? That he can forgive you? Is that what you're saying?"

When she only sobbed louder he stood up and shouted, "Pack your things. Or don't pack your things. But we're leaving right now. Together!"

She shook her head. "No, Yitzhak! I can't. I can't go against him . . ." There was a finality to her words.

He threw himself down in the chair again. Was it possible she really meant not to see him again? He couldn't believe it. He reached out his hand for hers but she snatched hers away as if his touch would burn her or sully her further. "But you said you loved me," he whispered harshly. "I believed you . . . I didn't think you could ever lie . . ."

"Oh, Yitzhak, I do love you. I love you more than anything, but—"

"But you love your father more . . . Is that it?"

When she didn't answer he screamed at her, "But you love him more? That crazy narrow-minded bastard? You love him more?"

"No! No! But I have to honor him. I can't go against him! Oh, Yitzhak, don't you see? It was always too late for us. It was already too late for us that first day we met. Maybe it was too late for us when we were born. Maybe it was written even then that we weren't meant for each other."

"I'm sick of hearing that mumbo jumbo. If you love me, you'll come away with me—" He got up, knocking his chair over, and pulled her out of her chair. She felt like a limp rag doll. He took her hand in his hands and forced her lips to his. They were warm, as he knew they would be, and unresisting, but they weren't responsive either. He kissed her again, this time with a brutal fervor, mashing his mouth into hers until he could feel her teeth. But even as her lips finally began to move under his, he looked into her opened black eyes and saw the hopelessness there. He let her go, even pushed her away and back down into her chair.

"All these months you've deceived your father, and that was all right. You even laughed about it. And now that you've been found out, you've become the holy daughter that can't defy her father. And as for him, he'd rather have you a—" he broke off, searching for a word. "He'd rather have you a whore—"

She gasped and he began again, "He'd rather have you a whore than a woman married to a man who loves you, who loves you enough to be any damned thing you two hypocrites want him to be—"

She threw her head down on the table and slammed it against the wood again and again, then cradled it in her arms, moaning softly.

He looked around the room slowly. It was all over. For a second he thought of tearing the room apart, of smashing every stick of furniture in it, every glass and cup. Then he looked at the girl whom he loved, crying so quietly now, and he turned and left the apartment. Rabbi Metzsky had been right about him. He was a Jew who had lost his Paradise.

PART THREE

ANNE

1900—1901

24.

For a week Willy did nothing except lie on his bed, going over everything in his mind again and again. Sometimes he would get up, go to the window and look out. It was late spring in St. Paul, and here and there he saw a tree spreading its boughs with their new spring-green leaves much as the birds returning from the South spread their wings. But even that sight didn't revive his spirit. He was too filled with bitterness.

He was not quite nineteen and he felt that his life was behind him. He had lost not only Paradise but all hope. He had fallen in love with a girl whom he had admired as much as he had loved her. He had respected her. In fact, he had often thought how much she resembled his mother. Not physically of course, but in so many other ways. Jennie was smart and bright as his mother was, and possessed of the same sweet compassion and ladylike demeanor and high character. Or so he had assumed. But now he knew he had been wrong about the latter. His mother would never have given up her true love because of the hypocritical rantings of a religious fanatic. His mother, he was convinced, would have done what she knew was right, would have fought for what she believed in. Hadn't she done just that for all the years of her life?

Jennie was flawed, blemished by her father's terrible, merciless God. What kind of a God was He, anyway? A cruel God who promised two poor souls an eternity of hell as punishment for their sin of loving one another. Well, to hell with them all—Jennie, her father, all the believers in a punitive God! If that was their Judaism, they could keep it!

Then he thought about his mother. She and his father were not blameless either. They too were hypocrites. Hadn't they packed him off to America only to forget about him? They had turned their backs on him, abandoned him no less than Jennie had. He never would have believed such a thing was possible. He never would have believed that they wouldn't even answer his letter. It was as if he no longer existed for them. Even if they had somehow found out that he had turned into Wilhelm von Marx, where was their faith? Surely they could have given him a chance to explain, to make things right before they washed their hands of him. What kind of love had they shown him?

Well, he could live without them, too. He had . . . for nearly two years already. . . .

Then he thought of the time that had elapsed since he had set foot on American

277

soil. What had he accomplished except for getting his heart broken, trading Yitzhak for Wilhelm? He was heartily sick of him too—Wilhelm von Marx! A ridiculous name for an American. What was he but an oaf and a fool, a guzzler of beer, a crony of other oafs and fools who spent their lives making crude jokes and indulging themselves in vulgar pursuits and pleasures?

Well, he was through with Wilhelm von Marx as much as he was through with Yitzhak Markoff! As much as he was through with the railroad! He realized at that moment that he disliked working for the railroad even as much as he disliked working for the brewery.

Oh, he yearned for the old life in Slobodka when little things had brought him so much joy . . . a time and place where he had been happy. He yearned to ride a horse again down open roads and through the wildflowers. He yearned to smell the sweet air of country fields as he played with his dog, Wolf. He even yearned to be forking hay with his cousin Dorie, singing cheerful songs about children bathing in the river, bittersweet ballads about love. . . .

He didn't realize that what he really yearned for was a return to childhood days when life had been simple, when he had believed in the faithfulness of his mother and father, in dogs and horses and laughter, even in himself. What he really yearned for was a return to innocence.

But he knew that it was time for him to leave St. Paul. There was nothing left for him here. He was a cattle dealer and he'd go where there were cattle to deal in, country air to breathe, horses to ride. He'd been told that there were countless herds of cattle in Texas. He remembered the name of a town in Texas . . . One of the German boys from the ship had been headed there. Galveston. He'd go to Galveston, Texas, the American West, and he'd go there as a real American with a real American name.

He had learned enough to know that many real American surnames had a "son" tacked on after an American first name such as Jackson, son of Jack. Or Johnson, son of John. Jameson, son of James. He'd be Markson. James Markson. A touch of the truth without the bitter aftertaste. What name could be more simple, more American?

He was no longer so ignorant. Even if he had lost his youth and his hope, he had gained a certain knowledge of how things were done in America. If one wanted to have his name changed officially, all he had to do was go to a court and request it. That's what he'd do as soon as he got settled in Texas. And he would become a real citizen too. His English was good, thanks to his lost love, and after a while he'd find a teacher who would help him lose his accent. He had no intention of remaining *any* kind of foreigner for long.

He went to the bank first to withdraw his fortune. It was quite a bit since he had been saving carefully for the last few months, building a nest egg for what he had assumed was his future as a husband. Now he would have a few dollars to get started in the cattle-dealing business.

He went down to the railroad office to tell them he was quitting and to pick up the two weeks' salary that was due him. He was told he'd have to come back the following week on Friday—payday. When he told them that he'd no longer be in St. Paul, that he was leaving the very next day, they asked him for a forwarding address where they'd mail the money to him. He was stymied until the paymaster told him they could send a money order to whatever city he named, in care of General Delivery. Then he told them to send the money order to Galveston, Texas, to James Markson.

The paymaster nodded. "Okay, Wilhelm. Or is it Jimmy then, me lad?"

Then, he couldn't help himself. He went to the Metzsky apartment to instruct Miss Jennie Metzsky that just in case a letter arrived for Yitzhak Markoff, which was highly unlikely, to send it on to James Markson in care of General Delivery, Galveston, Texas.

Who knew what he was thinking? What he really had in mind? Did he secretly hope that she had changed hers? That she'd throw her arms around him as she had done in the past, so fervently and gloriously? That she'd tell him she wanted to go with him to Galveston or wherever, to the ends of the earth?

He would never know. The Metzsky apartment was empty. Jennie was gone, disappeared, vanished . . . He inquired of the neighbors. They didn't know anything. The Rabbi, they said, had never been a man one just talked to about the ordinary things of life. He was closemouthed. As for the daughter, they hadn't even seen her the last few days. A lovely girl . . .

One of the neighbors who spoke English fairly well seemed kindly disposed and he scribbled down on a piece of paper—Yitzhak Markoff in care of James Markson in care of General Delivery, Galveston, Texas. "Just in case you should see Miss Metzsky, give her this please . . ." The woman smiled, shrugged. "Why not?"

He went down to the synagogue and tried to get some information out of the *shammes*, the caretaker. But he wouldn't talk to James Markson at all. James Markson was a stranger, a gentile stranger, and if the *shammes* could help it, he never spoke to that kind at all.

Landing in Galveston, a bustling port city at the eastern end of Galveston Island, which sat smack in the blue waters of the Gulf of Mexico two miles off the mainland of Texas, James Markson was forced to laugh at himself, a very caustic laugh. God, he was a fool! No wonder no one wanted anything to do with him. Not his family and not Jennie Metzsky. And he couldn't blame them. He had done it again! Once burned, an innocent. Twice burned, an idiot! First he had come to America as a Jew named Markoff intending to make a life for himself in New York City and had ended up as someone named Wilhelm von Marx, a gentile working in a brewery in Milwaukee and stupid enough to think that he could go back to being what he had been; stupid enough to have fallen in love with a cowardly, faithless woman. And now, going West to be a cattle dealer, to feel once more the joy of having a horse under him, to feel the wind and the sky and the open country all around him as he rode out on the open plains, he had landed in a busy, waterfront city which most likely had never even seen a cow! *Where would it graze?* And the only horses here most likely were those hitched to ice wagons. . . .

It was all a huge joke. On him!

Well, he'd hang around until his money came through from the railroad, then go where the cattle were. Only, this time, he'd make sure he went to the right place. Nobody had told him about Texas—that it was such a huge place. Maybe it was as big as all Russia. That's what happened when a man was ignorant. It wasn't even enough to speak English well. There was so goddamned much to know and to understand. A man could live a lifetime and spend all his time reading and learning and still know only a teacup's worth of the vast sea of knowledge. How he'd wasted his years dodging learning when his mother had tried to entice him to the world of books and education . . . But he didn't want to think about that or about his mother either. That part of his life was over and he'd do better to get on with it and forget the past.

He took a room on the south side that fronted on the Gulf, rather than on the north side fronting Galveston Bay, only by chance. The Galveston harbor stretched across the north side where ships from all over the world came to deposit their wares and take away the products of Texas—cotton and grain, sugar and rice, tin and other ores. On the south side was the seawall, below which spread the thirty-mile-long beach of white sand, blue water, and a boardwalk with its attractions—casinos and pavilions. He decided he liked the south side best so for once it seemed that he had made the right choice.

Every day he checked with the Post Office to see if his money from the railroad had come. When it hadn't, day after day, he wasn't all that disappointed. He was almost relieved. He had a chance to think, to walk, to inhale the essence of Galveston. It was truly a foreign place to him, different from anything he had ever known. The summer days on the Gulf were not those of the intensely humid heat he had known in Slobodka or in Milwaukee or St. Paul. Rather they were pleasantly warm and fanned with a breeze coming off the water, and with a tranquility about them. Even at the harbor with the ships coming in and out, with the hurly-burly of loading and unloading, there wasn't the same discordant electricity in the air he had felt during his brief time in New York City or even Milwaukee. Walking through the heart of town along the wide white boulevard of Broadway, which bisected Galveston, was an interesting, revealing experience. Here were stately mansions the likes of which he had never seen, and level with the earth. On most of the other streets, the houses were raised, reached only by a flight of stairs, since stormy weather brought rising tides that could wreak havoc with their watery turbulence. Here on Broadway, he guessed, the rising waters didn't dare swell to such heights, to touch the residences of the rich. Here, in Galveston, James took ironic note—irony being one of his newer characteristics—it paid to be rich just like anywhere else, whether it was Slobodka, Milwaukee or St. Paul. . . .

He walked the city's eight square miles, seeing everything there was to be seen, exploring, beguiled with everything—the profusion of magnolia, oleanders, palm trees, flowers and trees he had never seen before. Even the poorer sections of town, with the dirt streets and clapboard houses, were fascinating to him. In St. Paul and Milwaukee he had never seen a black man's neighborhood. He had seen very few of the black men altogether. Here, they were very much in evidence, especially on the docks.

Idly, he speculated as to where he'd fit in if . . . *just if* . . . he decided to stay on in Galveston. Shipping? On the docks? He could certainly lift bales of cotton and sacks of grain if that's what he wanted. But did he want? He didn't think so. That wasn't what he came west for, was it? Clearly he wasn't cut out for boatbuilding or repairing docks since he had no knowledge of either. He knew nothing about grain elevators or machine shops, cotton compressors or chemical plants, none of which appealed to him, anyway. There was also a nail and wire plant, a tin smelter and a meat-processing plant, all unattractive to him. What he wanted was to be out in the air. Perhaps he could be a fisherman since he liked the beach area best. Walking along the sandy stretches he experienced a feeling of serenity he hadn't felt since he had been a really young boy. Vaguely he recalled a summer day, falling asleep in his father's wagon, dozing ever so lightly, then awakening to the lazy buzzing of a few bottle flies . . .

There on the beach, gazing out at the water, watching the children building sand castles, he felt a release of the tension of the past months. But all the dreamy speculation was nonsense, he rebuked himself. As soon as his money from the railroad arrived, he would be off—to the central part of the state, or maybe to the Panhandle to the north, where he'd find cattle to deal in and horses to ride . . .

But the day his money came he already knew that he couldn't leave. He had given his new name and the city of Galveston to the Metzsky's neighbor, and if he left Galveston what then? Although he expected nothing, expected never to hear from her. In fact, he didn't even want to hear from her again, the fainthearted Miss Metzsky. Still, he had to know for sure, didn't he? One way or the other? Whether or not she'd try to contact him? That was supposing, of course, that she would come back and get his message, and would therefore know where to reach him. Most probably, if he ever did get a letter from her, he wouldn't even answer it.

When the clerk at the post office handed James his envelope, he looked at it speculatively. "I see you're a railroad man. Well, if you're looking for work, the Southern-Pacific is hiring on the mainland where the tracks end . . ."

"But that's only loading and unloading, not laying track, which is what I did. I was a foreman—"

The clerk shrugged. "I hear tell they're planning on building some kind of a bridge, a causeway they call it, from the mainland to here. Then they'll probably be laying track right on the causeway straight into Galveston City. It makes sense that if you went to work for them now, you'd be first in line for a real good job once they start laying the new track. Well, suit yourself, brother. Looks to me like you'd make a real good yard hand.''

"I thank you," James said. "I'll give it some thought." Why should he bother explaining to this stranger that he had hardly come to Galveston to load and unload railroad cars.

"You do that. Pay's real good. Twenty-five cents an hour for white men and twenty cents for niggers . . . Them's good wages for just using your back.''

James thanked him again. He couldn't help but laugh to himself. That was a good one on his mother. She was forever telling everyone that America was the land of the free with equal opportunity for all. He wondered what she'd have to say about white men and black men getting different wages for doing the same work. Most likely, she'd look up the president of the company and lecture him about his peasants. Then, if that didn't help, she'd probably have his father printing up leaflets and trying to get all the workers to strike for the sake of the black men. Fat chance! But at least here it was highly unlikely they'd be sent to Siberia for their efforts.

But what did it all matter to him, anyway? He wasn't about to go to work for the railroad to tote drums of oil or whatever. He had already done that kind of work and it seemed pretty clear that if he wanted to better himself, he should try using his head for a change, instead of his back. Still, he had to get some kind of work if he was going to stay in Galveston for a while. So far, he had no idea of just what. . . .

He was feeling restless that night but not in the mood for a saloon or a dance hall, one of the places where for the price of a drink you could squeeze up to a girl. He wandered down to the beach to walk along the water; he sighted the lights of the Pavilion about a half mile in the distance. There, he knew, was dancing, the kind of dancing where you brought your own girl to whirl around to the music of a real band. Suddenly, he was lonely, terribly lonely. He had barely spoken to another person since he had arrived.

He went inside the Pavilion. There was a mood of festivity, a big crowd, since people came to Galveston for the summer months to enjoy the sand, the water and the carnival-like attractions of the beachfront. He watched the couples dancing, their arms around each other, the men with their chins on the women's heads dipping and swaying, and he turned away to the long silvery bar for a drink.

"A vodka," he said to the bartender.

The bartender laughed. "We got four kinds of drinks here and vodka isn't one of them, friend. We got bourbon and beer and gin and schnapps. Name your poison.''

"Bourbon."

"Neat or branch?"

Since he didn't know what branch meant, he said "neat." He downed it and watched a girl, a very pretty girl with very red lips in a white dress with stones on it that sparkled, join the musicians on the bandstand to sing. The girl, more than the couples dancing together, made him feel even lonelier than before.

He ran out of the Pavilion into the stream of people strolling along the walk, laughing and eating ice cream. There was a row of stalls, all with open doors, and in front of each a barker shouted the attractions to be found inside. Delilah, the Snake Lady; Egypt, the Belly Dancer and her three Egyptian sisters; various games of chance. He didn't stop until he got to the last stall, three times the size of the others. The barker, a middle-aged man with a ruff of white hair, dressed colorfully in blue pants and a green shirt, urged: "Come on in, folks. For only ten cents, one thin dime, you get to see the Black Threat take on all contenders. Step right up, the doors will be closing in five minutes. Don't miss the thrill of a lifetime!"

Curious, James peeked inside. There was a kind of ring set up, a wooden platform with ropes posted all around. Standing in the middle like some Nubian prince, mighty arms folded across his chest, was a tall black man, his head shaved clean as a cannonball, and stripped to the waist. Even to James, he appeared threatening. To one side sat three blond youths, obviously Texas farmboys, big-boned and stripped to the waist as well, but not one of them looking nearly as ominous as the Black Threat. He guessed that these were the "contenders." In a circle around the ring there were some fifty chairs for the paying audience, only half of them occupied.

"Come on in, Sonny," the barker said, spotting him. "Only ten cents to see the thrill of a lifetime. We'll be closing the doors any minute. What's a mere dime for the thrill of a lifetime?"

Why not? James thought. He hadn't anything better to do and he *was* intrigued. He strongly suspected that the Black Threat was going to make short work of the farm hands.

He forked over his dime and the promoter looked him over speculatively. "You're a big, strong-looking boy, Sonny. Ever done any wrassling?"

"Some . . ."

"Where?"

"Here and there . . ."

"Maybe instead of being one of the audience you'd like to take your chances with the Black Threat."

James took another look at the man in the middle of the ring. Why not? he thought. "Maybe . . ."

"You got five bucks?"

"I have. What do I need it for?"

"To be a contender. To wrassle the Black Threat you got to put up five bucks."

"And what do I get if I beat him?"

"Hmmm . . ." the man scratched his head. "A natural enough question. Twenty-five bucks."

"Did those three fellows there put up five dollars?"

"Naturally. Of course. What do you think? That they get the chance of a lifetime to win twenty-five dollars without putting up anything?"

"What are the rules?" He was no longer the fool he used to be. He knew enough to ask about the rules of the game.

"Two pins out of three. No holds barred. But of course you're expected to act like a sport, like a gentleman. No gouging out the eyes or things like that."

"I don't gouge out eyes," James said, handing over the five dollars.

He went inside and removed his shirt, taking a chair next to the three Texans. They looked him over, gave him tentative smiles, but no one spoke. They sat there for at least another half hour or so silently while the man in the green shirt and blue pants kept threatening to lock the doors on possible spectators at any second.

Finally, the chairs filled up, the doors were closed as promised, and the barker got into the middle of the ring to introduce Jack Johnson, the black scourge of Texas. "And here, ladies and gentlemen, are the contenders, the gentlemen who will attempt to defeat the undefeatable."

One by one the country boys went up to be flattened in about two minutes. One minute of scuffling about, the other minute for the actual pinnings. Watching, James saw that this would probably be his fate too unless he took care of Johnson in the very first seconds. When it came his turn, no sooner did the bell ring than he made a dive for Johnson's legs, lifted him from the floor and then over his head, whereupon he spun around for a few seconds and tossed him out of the ring and flat on his back. It took several minutes before Johnson was revived.

James went over and shook his defeated opponent's hand, apologized for rendering him unconscious. Johnson smiled weakly. "It's okay, friend, I don't want to be no wrassler, anyway. Boxing's my game."

James got his twenty-five dollars and the entrepreneur, introducing himself as Joe Hyman, shook his hand. "I never expected to be paying out this twenty-five smackers. Come back and see me tomorrow morning. What's your name?"

"James Markson . . ."

"Jimmy Markson? What the hell kind of name is that for a Litvak? Come back and see me tomorrow, Litvak Jimmy. We'll have ourselves a talk. Now get the hell out of here before you ruin my night for good."

"So how would you like to go to work for me?" Joe Hyman asked.

"Wrestling? Like the Black Threat?"

Joe Hyman laughed. "No. You tossed Jack out of the ring last night but I still don't think you're a wrassler. What you are is a strongman."

James was doubtful. "I don't think so. That's not what I had in mind when I came here. The *last* thing I had in mind . . ."

"So what? It's only for the rest of the summer. So in a few weeks we clean up and you make a fortune. You get half the receipts."

James smiled faintly. "What's a fortune?"

Joe Hyman laughed again. "Who the hell knows? A strongman act will be a strong draw. Wrassling? No big thing—half of Texas wrassles. But feats of strength? They'll eat it up. Now, what can you do by way of being a strongman?'' he asked as if it were all settled.

"Anything. In Slobodka, I lifted a horse over my head. By the way, how did you know I was a Litvak? Nobody else I ever met in America guessed.''

"That's because you never ran into a *Landsmann* before. I'm from Kiev myself and I always recognize a Litvak accent when I hear one. It's like a third ear.''

"So how is it you don't have an accent? You talk like a real American . . .''

"Well, for one thing I came here over thirty years ago when I was a *boychik* like yourself. That's a lot of years. Then when I got here, I hitched up with an actress, an English actress, Shakespeare, if you'll believe it. She knew how to get rid of an accent. She gave me lessons until I was speaking like a native, good as an Apache . . .'' and he slapped his knee in enjoyment at his own joke.

James didn't get the joke but his interest was aroused. He wanted to speak like Joe Hyman did, without a foreign accent. "Hitched up?'' he asked. "Does that mean married?''

"In my case it did . . .''

"Do you think she could give me lessons? Would she?''

Joe Hyman chuckled. "Hitched means married, *boychik,* but it don't say for how long. Me and the English bimbo parted company a long time ago. To tell the truth, she was a good speech teacher but a terrible actress. And besides, she didn't draw flies. We barely took in a dime. But if you want to lose your accent, that's what I'd advise you to do. Find yourself an actress, but for Christ's sake, don't marry her unless she's good. Or at the least, a decent lay.''

They worked out a routine. "No lifting horses or stunts like that. That *looks* too hard,'' Joe said. "We want to grab the suckers, the contenders. They'd be afraid even to attempt a lift like that. We want stunts that are impressive but not impressive enough to scare them away. Or at the most, *one* spectacular stunt to pull them in.''

They decided that James would change his act every few shows in order to keep pulling in the crowds. He'd break chains with his hands, his teeth and his chest. He'd do his hair lift, his back lift, his chair lift and his stove lift. He'd twist nails with his fingers and throw them into the audience. As they were talking Joe Hyman grew so excited, he said to hell with it—they'd bring in the goddamn horse and lift it too! And they'd get hold of a twenty-ton fire engine and let Litvak Jim pull it down the boardwalk with twenty men on top for good measure! He'd be the talk of the town and they'd even come from Houston to see him . . . from the whole damn countryside. . . .

"Will you charge twenty-five cents admission? You said wrestling wasn't as good a draw and you charge a dime for that—''

"No, Sonny boy, we keep it a dime. I'd rather see them lined up two hundred deep trying to get in than frightened away by the price. Anyhow, the admission is just to pay the overhead. The real money is getting them *finifs* from suckers thinking they're going to match you and win the prize. And I got a feeling no one—not one Texas cowboy—is going to top Litvak Jim."

"One second! You're not thinking of calling me by that name—Litvak Jim, are you?"

"Well, as a matter of fact, I was. You got some objection, *boychik?*"

"Yes."

"Can I ask what it is?"

"It's not dignified."

Joe laughed. "So it's dignity you want. Well, all right, how does the Masked Marvel suit you? We'll put an eye mask on you, get you some fancy longjohns and we'll pull them in by the droves."

James had to laugh. He liked Joe Hyman. He couldn't help it. The Masked Marvel it would be.

"Tell me, *boychik,* how did you end up with a monicker like James Markson?"

"It's a long story . . ."

Joe nodded sympathetically. "I know from long stories. But how about I call you Jamie since James is kind of formal and somehow, Jim doesn't really suit you."

Jamie put out his hand to shake on it. Jamie it would be.

25.

Joe Hyman was right. The Masked Marvel turned out to be such a big draw that Jamie was putting money away in his bank account every week. It wasn't only the summer people and the citizens of Galveston City who lined up to see him perform; they came from all over Galveston Island as well as from Houston and all the outlying areas. He was written up in the newspapers, a local celebrity. As Joe said, the rednecks came crawling out of the woodwork like so many *vontzen,* bedbugs, to challenge him. There was no end of suckers (also Joe's word) willing to put up a five-dollar bill on the chance of matching or even beating him. Although no one even came close, Jamie worried about it happening. Not Joe. "You can't win 'em all, *boychik.* If you think you can, you're a fool."

Jamie could count on Joe for a bit of advice to cover any situation. When women of all types and ages showed up after each show asking to feel his muscles, Joe wasn't at all surprised. But he was critical when Jamie made late appointments with some of these ladies for almost every night of the week. Joe commented drily, "Just because they're pitching, it don't mean you always have to be there catching. The man who can't let a few get away is trifling with nature. Didn't your father ever teach you to throw a few back?"

With the summer drawing to a close and the beach season nearly over, Joe worked on Jamie to move on with him. He said he was thinking of heading for Florida as soon as the hurricane season there was over. "But Florida is the least of it. There's a fortune to be made out there. Chicago. Atlantic City. Coney Island. We'll grow your hair long and call you Samson the Great instead of the Masked Marvel. Or how do you like Hercules the Iron Man? What do you say, *boychik?* We'll make you a sensation. Who knows? Maybe we'll go to Europe too. To Paris, even. You'll be an international attraction. Come along with me," Joe urged. "Where is it written, after all, that you got to stay in Galveston? What are you, after all, a cowboy? An Indian? What do you want to do? End up on the docks lifting bales of cotton for a couple of bucks a day when you can be a real star?"

"I can't go with you, Joe."

"Why not?"

How could he explain to Joe that going around the world as a kind of freak attraction wasn't what he had in mind as a future? That this would be fine for

287

Yitzhak Markoff, or even for Wilhelm von Marx, but wasn't at all right for James Markson . . .

"I can't, Joe."

"All right. If you can't, you can't."

But Joe was so downcast, Jamie knew that it wasn't his moneymaking ability only that made Joe Hyman so reluctant to part company with him. Jamie sensed that Joe felt for him what he himself felt for Joe—affection, even a kind of love. If he himself was the son Joe had never had, then Joe was the replacement for the father who had turned his back on him, the father who hadn't even cared enough to write.

"So tell me, Jamie, what are you going to do with yourself?"

"Thanks to you, Joe, I have quite a bit of money in the bank. Enough to go into some kind of business for myself."

"And what business would that be?"

"I'm not sure. I have to think about it."

Joe gave him a last bit of advice—this time about finding the right teacher to help eliminate Jamie's accent. "In every town there's always a well-educated girl who will be glad to help you. You'll find her in some kind of theatrical group, maybe a glee club. Maybe a teacher who gives elocution lessons. There's always one who's lonely and eager to teach a handsome young man with your qualities." He winked. "But watch out. That kind will kill you in bed, or else they'll marry you."

Joe Hyman was due to leave Galveston the ninth of September, and on the night of the seventh, a very hot and humid night, Jamie and Joe did their last show together. After the show they went to have a few drinks, a farewell celebration. It was well into the eighth before Jamie got to bed, and he slept late the following morning. For one thing, he was in a state of depression about his only friend leaving, and he slept to dodge that depression. When he awoke it was raining, but no more than a shower, and there was a nice breeze coming in through the open window. He went back to sleep, enjoying the drop in temperature.

An hour later he awoke to the sound of wind rustling around his room and the rain blowing in, in gusts. He shut the window, pulled on his pants and boots, threw on a shirt and went downstairs, intending to go down to the beach to enjoy the break in the weather, to feel the strong breeze blow through his hair and the mist upon his skin; to watch the waves roll in and break upon the white sand.

The landlady was shuttering all the windows. "Did you close your shutters, Mr. Markson? There's a storm coming up. A big storm. If you were thinking of going out, you'd better change your mind real quick."

"I don't mind a little rain. I was going to take a walk on the beach."

She laughed. "I know you're the Masked Marvel but you're no match for a hurricane, and that's what it looks like is brewing out there."

"A hurricane?" He was unbelieving. "It's just a little rain and wind blowing

288

up—'' He had heard about hurricanes, but this? These Texans should see a Russian blizzard. "This is nothing—''

"Wait till you see them winds blowing over fifty, sixty miles an hour. They've been known to blow over a hundred. Come here,'' she called him over to the window. "See those clouds—''

There was a thickening of clouds, low in the sky. "That's a sign that it's no ordinary storm. I saw clouds like that a few years back when I was in a house that blew away just like that—'' She snapped her fingers. "Well, I have to see to my shutters.'' She wagged a finger at him. "Now don't you be stubborn. You stay inside! Listen to somebody that's older and has had a little experience!''

As soon as she left the room, Jamie went to the front door. When he opened it, it was like magic! The rain stopped just like that! The wind became no more than a breeze again and the clouds parted and the sun shone out of a piece of blue sky!

Why, the storm had passed! It was all over, already! He went down the flight of stairs to the street which was nearly deserted. There were a few stragglers. A woman running through the streets, pulling three children of various sizes along with her. Here and there were men pounding nails into boards, covering windows.

Then, in a second, the wind picked up, changed from a breeze to gusts and the rain came down harder. He had to admit that there was something strange going on. The wind was crazy, blowing first in that direction, then in the other. The rain came down in squalls, a burst, then a lessening, then an outpouring. Then there was a bolt of lightning that ripped across the sky and with it a virtual blanket of rain, so dense he couldn't see through it. Another bolt of lightning and there were objects flying through the air. He couldn't see exactly what they were; the density of the rain was too intense.

Joe! Joe was sleeping in his little room behind the stall. Did he know enough to get out of the way of the hurricane? He had to get down to the beach and make sure that Joe had gotten out of there safely.

It was impossible to see at all now. He stumbled over what felt like a body. Then for a moment the rain lessened and he made out what he had tripped over. It was the woman he had seen dragging the three children, but now there were only two! They were lying under their mother as she cowered in the street. She looked up at him and screamed, "My baby! I lost her!''

Wildly, he looked around. He couldn't see the child anywhere. He got down on his knees and yelled into her ear over the roar of the storm, "Get on my back and wrap your arms around my neck! I'll pick up the children!''

"I have to find my little girl,'' she wailed, not moving.

There was no time to argue with her so he scooped up all three of them in his arms, even as the woman fought him, staggered to his feet and made for the nearest building. But the wind kept changing course, pushing and pulling him, and the woman kept struggling within his grasp. "My baby, my little girl . . .''

"I'll go back for her," he said over and over, reaching the stairs finally, shouting as he climbed them, so the occupants of the house would open their door. But it was impossible for anyone to hear anything over the noise of the wind, the rain and the blasts of thunder. He heaved his back against the door, almost splintering it until someone came running and opened it.

He ran back into the streets, now seeing, now not, not knowing even where to look for a child no bigger than a flea. If he found her, would she still be alive? But then he saw her, a tiny bit of debris, pinned against a wall by a chance figuration of fallen boards that shielded her even as they held her fast. She was crying but she was alive. A feeling of exhilaration flooded him, ten times more exquisite than when he had killed the Governor-General!

When he finally got near the beach, he was alternately striding and wading as the water line reached his knees, then rose to his waist. Then he was floating as he lost footing. There was flotsam rushing past propelled by the charging waters—boards, railings, pilings, an odd shoe, a doll, bodies. He wondered where they had come from; who had been out there on the beach today? The driving rains blurred the atmosphere and through the haze, he saw a wall of clouds, a moving mountain of waves, waves that appeared to be hundreds of feet high. He saw nature at the pinnacle of its power, stronger than a thousand like himself, stronger than a million Yitzhak Markoffs.

Another of the incessant bolts of lightning cracked across the all-enveloping sheet of clouds, and he saw, realized, that everything was gone—the seawall, the boardwalk, the Pavilion, all the stalls . . . everything gone.

Joe!

By dawn, the clouds had broken, the water had drawn back into the sea, and a brilliant sun shone upon dark blue waters, laced and fretted with silvery foam. The estimate of the dead was between five and six thousand, mostly by drowning. Jamie Markson went down to the beaches again after having worked through the night, pulling, lifting and heaving, trying to beat the hurricane by wresting some of its victims back from the edge. But he never found Joe Hyman's body. If there was a God, Jamie thought, He had spared that little girl but He had also reached out to take back into His now gentle heavens his only friend in America.

The next day Jamie Markson bought a horse and wagon and went about collecting whatever he could find that was salvageable from the wreckage wrought by the storm. The people to whom the salvage belonged were glad to sell it to him. For one thing, most of the junkmen were stealing it, and the ones who did pay offered only half of what Jamie Markson was giving. Second, in a day's time word had spread how the Masked Marvel was one of the few who could be rightfully called heroes of the Galveston Hurricane of 1900.

With many wagonloads of salvage to dispose of, Jamie had two options; the first was to resell to one of the junkyards already in operation in Galveston; the second was to set himself up in his own yard. He was considering sites when he learned that he had a caller at his boarding house. His landlady came to summon him to her parlor. She was impressed and excited: "It's Mr. Karl Hess himself!"

Jamie recognized the name at once. Karl Hess was the owner of the biggest junkyard in Galveston, probably the biggest in that part of Texas. It was the one he most likely would have sold his salvage to if he hadn't decided to establish his own yard. "He's a very important man," the landlady gushed. "Some say he's the real owner of the Galveston First Savings and Loan."

To Jamie, Karl Hess looked more like a banker than a junkman. He was tall and portly, dressed in a proper business suit with a thick, gold watch chain draped across his vest, and his shoes were highly polished. With shoes like that, Jamie guessed, Mr. Hess most likely sat in an office and rarely ventured into the yard.

Karl Hess wasn't a smiling man. Solemnly, he shook hands with Jamie and didn't waste time in getting to the point of his visit. "I understand you have several loads of salvage to dispose of, Mr. Markson, and I also understand you're looking at property with a mind to going into business on your own—"

At this point, Jamie realized that the purpose of Mr. Hess's call was not to make him an offer for his junk. It was highly unlikely that a man of his importance, and dressed as he was, was in the habit of seeking out the scrap himself. *So he must have come to try and sell me a piece of property.* He interrupted, "If you're here to sell me a lot, Mr. Hess, I'll save you some time. I'm only looking to rent a yard. I'm not ready to buy. Besides, I'm not even sure I'll want to stay in the junk business. I'm just sort of trying it out—"

"Hear me out, Mr. Markson. I'm not in the real estate business. I'm in the scrap business and I'm here to make you a proposition."

He does want to buy my junk! Jamie almost laughed. It seemed incredible that a man of Hess's stature would actually call on him just to buy a few wagonloads of junk.

"And it's not just to make you an offer for your scrap. I'm proposing that instead of opening your own business, you come in with me. Galveston doesn't need another yard. Mine is the only large operation. The others are of no consequence. Ragpickers," he said with contempt.

"You mean you want to give me a job in exchange for my junk?"

For a moment, Jamie thought that Mr. Hess was actually going to smile, but it was no more than a twitch of his thick brush mustache. "No, not just a job, Mr. Markson. A share in the Hess yard—a five-percent share."

Jamie stared at him. Did this man take him for an idiot? Did he expect him to believe that for a pile of junk he was going to give him a five-percent piece of his lucrative business? *What's the catch?*

"Why would you want to do that, Mr. Hess? I don't even know anything about the junk business. Not really. It was just that I saw all this wreckage lying around after the hurricane and I needed to do something— Why would you be willing to give a stranger you don't know anything about a piece of your business?"

291

Although he spoke in a low tone, his anger was beginning to mount. This big shot thought he was talking to some fool, trying to put something over on him, though he couldn't figure out what it was.

"I'll explain it to you, James Markson. For one thing, I *do* know something about you. I know that you saved lives during the hurricane and that you put your own life at risk doing so. I know that you're courageous and tireless. All Galveston is impressed with you, not to mention their admiration for your feats of strength. And I've seen you perform, several times. You're strong and in perfect physical condition. Even more, when I watched you perform, accompanied by my wife and daughter, we were all impressed with your integrity."

"My integrity?" *What's the man talking about?*

"Yes. I'm a skeptical man and what I expected to see in your act was trickery and hocus-pocus. But I didn't find it. I found only a straightforward, honest presentation of your powers and saw that you gave your challengers every advantage, a fair shake.

"And I've learned through sources that you worked for the railroad in Milwaukee and in St. Paul, and that you were quickly made a foreman. That means two things to me—that you're a hard worker and have leadership qualities. So, sir, in summing up, I find you brave and courageous, and of high character, physically strong and in excellent condition besides being willing to work hard and assume command. As for the fundamentals of the waste business, I'm sure you'll pick them up in short time."

Jamie's anger at being taken for a fool had quickly subsided as Karl Hess enumerated all the qualities that made him desirable, but there was one question still unanswered as far as he was concerned. Before he could ask that question, Karl Hess held up his hand. "You're wondering why I haven't simply offered you a job instead of part of my business. I'll explain because I want to be completely candid. I'm sixty-one years old and I have only one child—a daughter. In other words, I don't have a son to take into my business. But since I've built it myself from nothing I care very deeply about it. At the same time, I'm expanding and I need someone to share the responsibilities with me, a man I can trust completely. Five percent is little enough to get that man. While I don't want to extend false hopes, I want you to understand that I need a man who will be able to take over the business completely at some point in the future."

He took the watch from his fob pocket and looked at it pointedly. "What do you say, Mr. Markson?"

Mr. Hess was not a likable man, Jamie thought, but he seemed to be frank and straightforward. And five percent of the biggest junkyard in the city was more of an opportunity than he had ever thought possible. After all, he wasn't even twenty! How could he turn down such an opportunity? *What do I have to lose?*

He put out his hand and Karl Hess said, "Be at my office tomorrow morning at seven. I'll have a contract ready. And be sure to bring those wagonloads of scrap with you." Jamie looked quickly to see if there was a smile on Mr. Hess's face at these words, or even one in his eyes. There wasn't.

The Hess Salvage Company took up one square block and was as orderly as a junkyard could possibly be. The office was spare and meticulous. As soon as Jamie walked in, Mr. Hess handed him a contract. "How well do you read?"

"Pretty well." That was one thing he could thank Jennie for . . .

"Good. You can read your contract over immediately. I will leave you alone for a half hour. If you have any questions, I'll be in the yard. When you're ready to sign, I suggest that unless you've had your name legally changed to Markson, you sign it Wilhelm von Marx."

Jamie was flabbergasted until he remembered that Mr. Hess knew that he had worked for the railroad so he would know under what name he had worked. And he had probably learned about the railroad from the post office. *A thorough man.* He wondered if Mr. Hess also knew that his name had been Markoff before it was von Marx. Well, he wasn't about to ask him. Anyway, that was highly unlikely. He couldn't have possibly traced him back to Staten Island. . . .

"Have you had your name changed legally to Markson?"

"No, not yet."

"I'll have my lawyer start those proceedings for you . . . that is, if you wish—"

"Yes, sir."

"Good. May I ask why you decided to change your name from von Marx to Markson?"

"I wanted to be a real American . . ." Jamie mumbled.

"Good. Admirable. I too wanted to be a real American when I came from Germany so I shortened my name from Hessmeister."

Jamie was astonished. Mr. Hess spoke an English that sounded perfect to his ears. "I thought you must be American-born. You haven't any accent at all."

"Of course not. I saw to it that I lost it and I suggest you do the same. You speak English surprisingly well. Your grammar is good but to speak English perfectly, you have to get rid of the German accent. You should see to it soon."

"Yes, I intend to."

"Excellent. Now I'll leave you to your contract."

Jamie began to read. The contract was made out to James Markson, also known as Wilhelm von Marx. Jamie smiled. Karl Hess was a very thorough man and, obviously, a smart one. Only a fool would deny that. But he wasn't as smart as Joe Hyman. Joe had known the difference between a German accent and a Litvak one.

Mr. Hess returned precisely a half hour later, quickly checked Jamie's signature on the contract and suggested that he walk around the yard and get the feel of things. Jamie did exactly this, walked around for an hour observing the secondhand clothes dealers bringing in their loads, the rag-and-bone men with theirs, the junk dealers with mixed loads of bottles and metal. Everything was weighed and the men were paid their few coins. Then, the workers would go through it all—separating the bottles from the metal, the tin from the iron, the wheat from the chaff. The bottles were washed before they were smashed, a sledgehammer was taken to the iron. Without even thinking much about it, Jamie picked up a sledgehammer and went to work.

He was at it for about an hour when Karl Hess called him into the office. "I didn't take you into my business to wield a sledgehammer. I have men to do that for fifteen cents an hour."

Jamie flushed at the reprimand. If Hess didn't want him for physical labor, why had he stressed his strength and physical condition as one of the reasons he wanted him in the business in the first place? "I want you to observe all phases of our operation. Here, we have the files," he pointed to some file cabinets, "of to whom we sell and from whom we buy."

"I just saw from whom you buy—all those wagons pulling up to the weighing counter."

For the first time Jamie saw his new partner laugh. "Those are the ragpickers, the penny-ante peddlers. If I counted on them, do you think I'd be where I am today? We buy from every large shop in the city, from every factory, from the docks, from the refineries, every industry in Galveston City. We send out our own wagons twice a week. The heart of the salvage business is the buying and the selling, not the things in between. All that must be done as efficiently as possible, of course, but buying and selling is what the salvage business is all about."

Jamie chuckled. "Just like when you're a cattle dealer. You don't care about the in-between business of raising the cows—just the buying and selling."

Karl Hess glanced at him sharply. "What's this about the cattle business?"

"I headed for Texas in the first place because I wanted to deal in cattle," Jamie confided. "Buying and selling. But when I arrived in Galveston, I realized I had come to the wrong place for the cattle—" He laughed, inviting Karl Hess to laugh with him at the preposterousness of the situation.

But Hess didn't laugh. Instead, he asked rather sternly, "You mean you came to Galveston City and didn't know it was a port city?"

"No." Jamie laughed again, but not as heartily.

"Did you realize how close you were to Houston?"

"Yes, but what of it? Houston's a large city and a port too. They certainly aren't grazing cattle there."

"Didn't you ever look a few miles *beyond* Houston? There are plains there, Mr. Markson! Endless miles of plains with grazing cattle. Where did you think those men came from, who challenged you when you were the Masked Marvel? They were mostly cowboys, I'm sure."

"I thought they were just boys, farmboys mostly." His smile faded along with his voice.

Once again, he thought, he had looked no farther than his nose, had just accepted and gone along with whatever destiny or fate or whatever offered him. As a result, here he was—a junkman instead of a cattle dealer.

Well, at least he was a junkman with a part of the business and from now on, he vowed, he wasn't going to take just what was handed to him. From now on, he would make his own destiny!

He looked up to see Karl Hess looking at him curiously. He wondered what Hess was thinking. Was he thinking that James Markson was a damned fool, after all? That he simply lay down and took whatever was handed to him? Well, if that was what he was thinking, he would find out differently. He would find out that he had chosen well when he picked him for a partner. He'd find out that Jamie Markson was a man who knew what he wanted and went after it.

26.

Jamie was invited to Sunday dinner at the Hess home for one o'clock, on the dot. "We always eat at one on Sundays, on the dot, right after church," Karl Hess had told him.

He rented a fancy rig and driver, feeling it was warranted—his first social engagement in Galveston and his first excursion into the world as part owner of a thriving enterprise. As the horses cantered down Broadway where the Hesses lived, the wide, white street lined with oleanders of different colors, Jamie was deeply impressed. There were magnificent houses on this boulevard. Mansions! Even palaces!

He was disappointed when the rig stopped before a house that was clearly less than magnificent—a large, white-shingled house with gingerbread and a cupola. He should have known better, he told himself. He should have known that Karl Hess would live in a house less ostentatious than the others. As he went up the few steps to the front door, he thought that when he became rich he'd have one of the others. One of the large and stately mansions of limestone, or perhaps one with columns and a large veranda.

Mr. Hess came to answer the door himself. Right behind him were two women, one older and one younger. Jamie was introduced. Mrs. Hess didn't smile; Miss Anne Hess did. Mrs. Hess wore a dark dress of nondescript design; the daughter—a pale gray dress with a jabot of white lace and a matching flounce of lace at the wrists. A plain dress, more or less, but not unfeminine. She wore a coronet of blond braids and a pleasant expression on her face, which was neither pretty nor unpretty. She was neither slender nor plump. She appeared a woman to Jamie, rather than a girl. She might have been a maiden and he assumed she was, but the correct word for her, he thought, would be spinster. But the entrance hall was very dark. Heavy dark velvet draperies covered the two, tall narrow windows on either side of the heavy front door. Perhaps he was mistaken and she wasn't as old as he assumed.

Mr. Hess took out his gold watch, glanced at it quickly, put it back into his vest pocket. "Shall we eat?" It was a rhetorical question. It was two minutes past one.

They went directly to the dining room. Jamie guessed that the whole house was kept dark for as they passed the parlor he could only make out shapes of large, overstuffed chairs and sofas. The dining room was somewhat lighter.

Here, lace panels covered the windows, allowing a bit more light into the room. The table, covered by a lace cloth, was set with heavy, ornate silver and crystal that sparkled. But it was the only thing in the room that did; the chairs flanking the table were heavily carved and upholstered in a deep brown plush material, and the sideboard and china closet were massive pieces of dark wood.

Karl Hess took his seat at the head of the table, Mrs. Hess at the foot. Mr. Hess indicated that Jamie was to sit in the chair exactly in the center of the table, directly across from Anne Hess. Here in this room with the benefit of some daylight Jamie could see that Anne Hess had passed her thirtieth birthday, give or take a year or two.

Mrs. Hess rang a little silver bell and a woman, dressed in a black uniform and wearing a white apron, came in with a tray. On it were two cut-glass pitchers, one filled with milk, the other with water. She proceeded to fill the two goblets at each setting from the pitchers before putting them down on the sideboard. Jamie looked at the glass of milk before him and sighed inwardly.

"We are abstainers," Karl Hess explained unnecessarily.

Jamie sighed again. He would have appreciated a large shot of bourbon at this moment. Anne Hess smiled at him from across the table, guessing perhaps what he was thinking.

Karl Hess folded his hands, cast his eyes down and began to recite a blessing. Jamie flushed, uncertain of what to do. He had had dinner every Sunday at Uncle Rudy's house in Milwaukee, but they had never said grace. They hadn't been regular churchgoers, of course, and they certainly hadn't been abstainers. Right at that very moment Jamie thought of how good a foaming stein of Milwaukee brew would taste and his mouth actually watered. He would have gladly settled for a mug of good Texan brew.

He heard Mr. Hess say, "Amen," followed by Mrs. Hess, and then Anne. He looked up to see all three looking at him expectantly. *What the hell! Amen* was the same in any language, any religion. "Amen," he mumbled, half waiting for a bolt of lightning to come crashing through the roof and strike him dead.

Nothing happened. Mrs. Hess said to the waiting servant, "You may bring in the fruit compote, Anna," and dinner commenced.

As soon as Jamie had seen the pitcher of milk, he had assumed he would be served the same kind of meal as at Uncle Rudy's—hearty German dishes that, while heavy and even greasy, were both stomach-filling and soul-satisfying. But the food served at the Hesses was neither. It was plain, it was dry, and for the most part overcooked. Even the mashed potatoes were dry, tasteless and as white as chalk. Fleetingly, Jamie recalled his mother's mashed potatoes nearly golden in color, flecked with crispy bits of rendered chicken fat when served with meat, or yellow and smooth with butter and creamy with milk when served with dairy dishes. Thinking about it, he was momentarily overwhelmed with longing and regret, even as he knew it wasn't just golden mashed potatoes he yearned for.

As he cut into a thin, parched lamb chop he realized that he would rather be at the boarding house than here in this somber room with these somber people. The daughter, Anne, wasn't as grim as her parents; there was an air of hopeful expectancy about her; still . . . He glanced up quickly, even guiltily, to see if anyone was looking at him, possibly reading his mind. But all he saw was Anne with a kind of half smile on her lips and the stern countenances of Mr. and Mrs. Hess.

He turned back to his lamb chop, marveling that it could be so tough and so thin at the same time. At least, at the boarding house, he'd be drinking beer, he mused, enjoying the Sunday specialty of chicken-fried steak, fried potatoes, beaten biscuits and lots of cream gravy. At least, the other diners would be talking, laughing. Here, the meal was consumed in silence, each mouthful thoroughly chewed and thoughtfully swallowed. His own mouth was so dry he gulped water after each swallow. When Anna, the servant, refilled his water glass for the second time, Mrs. Hess finally spoke to him. "You don't drink milk?" she asked as if this were a sign of deficient character.

"Sometimes," he mumbled. Nothing, at that moment, could make him take a swallow of the milk. Not even Mrs. Hess's frown.

It wasn't until the coffee had been served that Karl Hess leaned back in his chair a bit and began to talk in a conversational tone. Jamie was hoping he'd reach for a cigar so that he himself could bring out the pack of cigarettes he had in his pocket. Ordinarily he hardly smoked, but at that moment he was longing to light up and take deep drags in order to better pass the time until he could leave. But of course, Mr. Hess didn't smoke. Certainly not in this room, with the windows shut so tight. There wasn't a spare breath of fresh air.

To Jamie's surprise Mr. Hess did not talk about business at all. He seemed only concerned with one topic—the city of Galveston and its future. He was obviously very much involved in civic affairs, as behooved one of the city's leading businessmen. First, he discussed the Strand District, the city's financial center, which, he claimed, had the potential to be "The Wall Street of the Southwest." Jamie nodded even though he had never heard of Wall Street at all, had no idea of its significance or its location. At the same time, he made a mental note to find out.

Mr. Hess was also concerned about the causeway, still in its planning stages, which would connect Galveston City with the mainland. Until that was built, thus bringing the railroads into the city, they couldn't even hope to keep up with Houston, especially now that the bridges between the mainland and the City had been washed away by the hurricane.

Jamie could see that Karl Hess felt deeply about Galveston, was fiercely competitive, bitter almost, toward Houston, which was easily becoming the larger and more important of the two cities. "When I first arrived in Galveston, the population of both cities was almost the same. Now, they have nearly 45,000 people while we have a little more than half that."

"It must be the petroleum—"

Hess looked at him sharply. "Yes, what about the petroleum?"

Jamie knew only what he had happened to overhear one night in a saloon when two men were arguing about where the petroleum being refined in Houston originated. "The oil—most of it comes from outside of Texas right now, from Louisiana. But the refining is still done in Houston. That must be a big boost to them." Jamie was careful to skirt that which he didn't know. He saw Karl Hess glance quickly at his wife; Hess seemed impressed with his knowledge.

Still, Hess said, "Our main problem is with the men who run our city. They're stupid, shortsighted. Houston has fully developed her harbor and here, we're always lagging behind."

"Yes, you're right." Again Jamie was careful to repeat only what he had heard other people say. "All the harbors in Texas have to be deepened if they are to be major ports. The shallow tidewaters of the Gulf—"

Karl Hess leaned forward. "I didn't realize you had such a good grasp of the situation. That's good. That's excellent. A smart businessman always gets involved in the running of a city. He has to understand what its major problems are. We'll have to see that you get involved."

Involved? What was Karl Hess thinking of? He barely knew anything about the salvage business and here, Hess was talking about involving him in city affairs and problems! Older men than he, and those certainly more knowledgeable, weren't doing such a hot job, according to Hess and he wanted *him,* young and ignorant, to get involved. Being a partner of Karl Hess's was far more complicated than he had bargained for.

How was he going to be able to do this? It was impossible. He knew nothing! It was an impossible situation! Of course his mother used to say, "Oh, Yitzhak, *all* things are possible!" whenever he complained that he couldn't do something. And to his mother, they were. Everyone had always said that Eve Markoff accomplished the impossible.

"Well, I would think that since they have to almost rebuild the whole city, what with the damage caused by the flooding and all, one of the most important things would be to build a new seawall that would rise several feet above the highest waterline marked by the storm. Then, on top of that seawall, they could put up a new hotel, a pavilion, all kinds of shops for the summer people and all kinds of different attractions."

Jamie saw Hess throw his wife a look that clearly said, "See, I've chosen wisely." To Jamie he said, "You know about such things, Mr. Markson? About seawalls and waterlines?"

"No, sir. Not really. But it makes sense, doesn't it? My mother always said that anything is possible if a person puts his mind to it. And that in the end the answer is always simple. That usually it's only a matter of common sense."

"Your mother sounds like a clever woman."

"Yes." He hadn't intended to speak of his mother.

"And your mother has a clever son in you. It's in the blood. Blood always tells."

Hess rose and indicated that they would adjourn to the parlor. "Anne will play the piano for us. She plays very well. Whom do you like? Wagner? Brahms? Beethoven? Anne knows them all. She's very clever too.''

After Anne had been playing the piano awhile Jamie began thinking about taking his leave. He considered simply rising, shaking hands with Karl Hess, thanking Mrs. Hess for a wonderful dinner, thanking Anne for her wonderful music, and going. But was it that simple? Was he supposed to stay until he was dismissed, one way or another? He had the feeling that he was expected to stay until Mr. Hess indicated that it was time for him to leave. He felt as if he'd been there for hours already. Uncertain about what to do, he sat and tried to display a pleasant expression on his face, hoping to show that he was enjoying the music.

When Anne had been playing for exactly one hour, Mr. and Mrs. Hess rose from their chairs in unison. "It's time for our Sunday afternoon nap," Karl Hess said, and Jamie leaped to his feet. He was convinced that Mr. Hess was indicating that it was time for him to go and he was both relieved and grateful. "Yes, I must be going."

But Mr. Hess said, "Nonsense. You must stay a while. I'm sure you two young people have lots to say to one another with us old folks out of the way." Mrs. Hess frowned but Karl Hess chuckled a bit and Jamie responded with a little smile. It was the first attempt at humor that he had heard from his new partner.

He sat down again and Anne rose from the piano stool and sat down next to him on the dark red, plush sofa. For lack of something else to say, Jamie observed that Anne was a very pretty name.

She had a most peculiar laugh—one high squeaky note emanating from her throat. "My name was Anna but Father changed it to Anne when he shortened our name to Hess. Our servant girl, Anna, had just come to work for us straight off the boat, as they say, and Father didn't think it would do for both of us to have the same name."

"Yes, I see." He wondered what he could say to her next. "You play the piano very well."

"I've been playing since I was a little girl. I play the violin and the flute too. Father believes a girl should be accomplished. He always says that one teaches sons how to get on in life and daughters how to do nice things, such as playing the piano, painting pictures, crocheting, petit point and gros point—needlework, you know."

Jamie immediately pictured his mother sewing, forever sewing—shirts, dresses, infant clothes for his cousins' babies. "My mother does needlework."

She issued that high squeaky note again. "Really? I think that's amazing!"

"Amazing?" He smiled uncertainly at her, unsure of her meaning. "Why is that amazing?"

"That your mother and I *both* do needlework? I think that's truly amazing. Really a remarkable coincidence. I mean, both of us doing the same thing like that?"

Close as they were now, Jamie saw why Anne appeared to have a perpetual half smile. It was because her teeth protruded. Not a lot, but enough to keep her mouth open a little.

He wondered when he could properly leave. Did he have to stay until Karl Hess came downstairs again and hinted that it was time for him to go? "I'd better go—" he told Anne.

"Oh no! Father will be so disappointed if you leave now. Without saying goodbye to him. Mother too, of course."

Karl Hess didn't come downstairs again until six-thirty, and then it occurred to Jamie that he might be pressed into staying for supper. Horrified at this possibility, he jumped up and blurted out: "I've been having such a good time, I nearly forgot— I have a seven o'clock appointment!" Fortune was kind to him—Karl Hess didn't inquire with whom his appointment was.

By the time he got back to the boarding house Jamie had made up his mind to give his family one more chance. He would write them another letter. The truth was, being in the cheerless Hess household all afternoon made him think of the warmth of his old home across the world.

He owed his family one more chance to respond to him, he told himself. Why, it was very possible that the first letter had gotten lost. He didn't know why he hadn't thought of that before. He'd give a return address of Y. Markoff in care of J. Markson and he didn't give a damn what his landlady thought. He'd write the letter in English since his mother would be able to read it and would be pleased to see how well he had mastered the language. He'd tell them all about how well he was doing in America.

The next morning Karl Hess told Jamie how much Anne had enjoyed talking with him. She had said that she thought him very intelligent. Jamie thought back to their conversation. For the life of him he couldn't imagine what he had said that could have been even vaguely construed as intelligent. Girls just liked to say these things—if one could call Anne Hess a girl.

"Now," Hess said, "—about getting you on the City Commission . . ."

"The City Commission?" Jamie was startled, bewildered. Surely Mr. Hess was pulling his leg. They'd talked around the subject but he had thought it was nothing more than idle talk. Now he could see Mr. Hess was dead serious. "But I don't know anything about being on a Commission. I wouldn't know what to do. And why would they want me?"

"You leave all that to me. They'll want you."

"But if I got on the Commission what would I do?"

"For one thing you'll offer your ideas on building a seawall to guard the city from flooding when the next hurricane hits. You'll tell them your ideas about the boulevard above the wall—the shops, the hotel, the attractions. And then you'll head the committee to push the development. Once the work begins, why, you'll be the one in charge. Now, don't worry about it. I'll see to it that you have enough time to devote to it. I told you there's more to being a businessman than just business. Before you know it, you'll be a young man of importance. A man who'll play a big part in the future of Galveston. Now, have you given any more thought to what I said about ridding your speech of that accent? If you're going to be a big man in this city you're going to have to do it at once!''

Jamie remembered Joe Hyman's advice about finding an actress, perhaps a young woman in a local theater group who would be happy to be of assistance. He told Mr. Hess this, leaving Joe Hyman's name out of it.

Karl Hess's face turned red. "A ridiculous notion. Some floozie with rouged cheeks? Now, let me give you some advice. When there's a job to be done, always seek out a professional. There's an elocution teacher, a Miss Janus, with much experience. She used to give Anne lessons how to recite with the proper dramatic inflections. Anne's enunciation and accent have always been perfect, needless to say.''

Before the week was out, Jamie had his first lesson with Miss Janus, and he gathered why Karl Hess had wanted her rather than some young thing Jamie might have found for himself, some young thing who might be flighty, even racy. Miss Janus not only spoke English precisely without even a trace of a regional accent, she also shaped each vowel and consonant in a highly visible manner as she conversed. She was also very plain with a longish pointed nose, and somewhere in her forties. Mr. Hess probably thought that a pretty young woman might possibly prove to be a distraction from the lessons at hand.

Jamie's life was a busy one. He worked at the junkyard from six to six, mostly buying and selling since Karl Hess wished to take advantage of his public image as hero of the Great Flood. People liked him because they admired him, and therefore liked doing business with him. Sunday afternoons he spent at the Hesses' and two evenings a week he took his speech lessons with Miss Janus. Two evenings a week, sometimes three, he had his committee meetings since he was not only involved in the building of the seawall, but also in construction of the causeway that, once completed, would link Galveston City with the mainland. He was also involved with the Deepwater Commission whose concern was the improvement of the harbor.

Sometimes when he went to bed, he'd think about his life. He'd ask himself if he was truly happy. Happiness, his mother had told him, was mostly a contentment of the heart. If that was true, then he wasn't happy because he certainly wasn't content. For one, there was the matter of his Sunday afternoons which were growing more and more burdensome. Then, there was the increasing pressure to attend church services with the Hesses since Karl Hess believed that no man could be a leading citizen, the man at the helm, without also being a churchgoer. He certainly couldn't be an atheist, Karl Hess declaimed menacingly. An atheist was an abomination, and the citizenry of Galveston would never suffer an atheist as a civic leader. Jamie didn't tell him that he wasn't even sure that he wanted to be a leader; that mostly he just wanted to be a successful busi-

302

nessman. Instead he did some homework and came back with a label for what he was—an agnostic. "I do not deny God, sir. I only deny the possibility of knowing him. Therefore, in all conscience, I cannot attend church service."

Karl Hess narrowed his eyes within the puffiness of his upper and lower lids. He didn't believe Jamie for a minute, but for the time being he would have to accept his position.

Still, Jamie was plagued with the question of what to do about Anne Hess. The situation was becoming intolerable. The Sunday dinners seemed to be growing shorter and shorter with each week. It was as if they were all being propelled through the meals on a huge wind rushing through the dining room in order that the elder Hesses could retire that much more quickly upstairs or, of late, disappear through the front door. The Sunday naps, it seemed, had given way to Sunday constitutionals, and if not constitutionals, drives in their rig, or concerts, even receptions at private homes, although Mrs. Hess was not a convivial woman, hardly a type for socializing. She had no store of small talk, being given more to frowns, leaving most of the conversation to her husband.

Anne, on the other hand, was devoted to chatter. Once her parents took their leave, she prattled on without cease. She discussed everything that was of no interest to Jamie endlessly, as if she had been wound up like a mechanical toy and couldn't stop even if she wanted to. She offered him bits of useless information on all manner of topics. *Did he know that there were sixty different classified varieties of oleanders represented in Galveston?* "That's why we're called the Oleander City." *And did he know that Galveston was once the headquarters of Jean Laffite, the pirate?* "That's why we're often referred to as the Treasure Isle." *Did he know that there were 5,280 feet in a mile?*

He didn't know and he didn't care. All he knew and cared about was that from the moment he entered the Hess house, her blue eyes never left his eyes, beseeching him. He wondered how blue eyes could be so bovine. He had never seen a blue-eyed cow. Sometimes he thought of black eyes, as shining and deep as the sea at night and he was shot through with pain until, with great concentration, he eradicated those eyes from his mind. Black eyes, shiny and deep, were *faithless* eyes, as faithless as green eyes. It had been a long time already since he had written a second letter home without getting an answer. It clearly was a case of out of sight, out of mind.

Then, one afternoon, after the Hesses had vanished out the front door, making sure to note that since they were attending a reception that day, they wouldn't be back much before seven, Anne, in a much prettier, more formfitting dress than usual—actually the first time she was wearing a dress with a hint of décolletage—departed from her usual repertoire of small talk. They were in the parlor, Jamie sitting in one of the deep armchairs rather than on the sofa where Anne could plump herself down beside him, steeling himself for the tedious hours to come, when Anne threw herself to her knees before him.

"You must wonder why I've never married—"

"No," he mumbled. "Not at all . . ."

"Oh yes, you have. I've seen the question in your eyes."

She was wrong. He had no questions at all regarding her except how he was going to extricate himself from her without threatening his position at the junkyard. He had signed the contract with Karl Hess without, as they said, reading all the small print. He had no doubt that he could be thrown out at any time on Hess's whim.

"I've had suitors, you know. Lots of men, rich important men, wanted to marry me."

He could see she was in a state of extreme agitation, almost distraught. "I'm sure of it," he hastened to say.

"It's my father, you see. He said that none of these men, even though rich and important, was good enough for me, that I should wait, wait for someone who was truly worthy of me, a man who was of the highest character."

He didn't know what to say to that. "He was right, of course."

"Then you agree?"

"Certainly."

She was somewhat mollified, her apparent anxiety somewhat dissipated. She smiled at him. "Good. I didn't—I didn't want you to think that I was undesirable, that . . ." the cowlike blue eyes entreated. "You don't think that, do you?" her voice rose again, a note of hysteria creeping in.

"Of course not."

"Oh!" she breathed. "I'm so relieved to hear you say that— You *do* think I'm desirable?"

"Of course." He knew he was being led into a trap of admission. He knew it, but how could he say otherwise?

Since she was kneeling, only her upper body was free to throw itself across his thighs, her head nestling in his groin. He was so startled he almost jumped up, which would have thrown her to the floor. But she pulled herself up, got to her feet and stood over him so that he had to look up to her.

"Oh why? why?" she breathed excitedly. "Why didn't you say something before?"

"I—"

She sat down on his lap this time, throwing her arms around him. "Were you afraid I'd reject you?" she whispered. "Is that it?"

He shook his head not knowing even what he was saying "no" to. She pulled back a little, so that she could better look into his eyes. "I wouldn't, you know. I wouldn't ever reject you. I want you as much as you want me."

With that said, she rose and walked over to the couch, laid herself down, closed her eyes, wriggling around until her skirt and petticoat were well up around her waist. He couldn't believe his eyes! She was not wearing underdrawers! Even as he set about unbuttoning her bodice almost mechanically, he couldn't help but realize that Anne Hess had known exactly where their conversation would take them. He had been skillfully seduced.

As it turned out, it was his week for being seduced.

304

When he went for his lesson that Tuesday night, Miss Janus admitted him into her parlor wearing a Japanese kimono. It was scarlet, embroidered with gold dragons, and even before she allowed it to fall open he suspected that she was wearing nothing at all underneath.

Her body was not attractive. Her breasts were small but not perky, as small breasts often were; hers were little more than fleshless flaps. Her ribs stood out while her buttocks were flat and flabby at the same time. Her legs were both skinny and knobby. Still, he was aroused, almost a perverse arousal. He knew he would take her and enjoy it.

She was like an animal, starved, even ravenous, and he relished her savagery. As she reached out for him, her tongue darted out of her mouth into his like a snake's, thin and long and strong. It went everywhere—into his mouth and out again. It licked his ears, his throat, his belly, it washed his thighs. She bit him—his tongue, his bottom lip, his neck, his shoulder, the cheek of his behind—with sharp little teeth. Her elastic lips, as flexible as they were when shaping the sounds of speech, wrapped themselves around his mouth, his chin, his breasts, his phallus . . .

When he finally entered her, she screamed like a coyote and raked his back with her fingernails, her legs enclosing him like a vise. Then, when she had finished shuddering so violently, so convulsively, she was at him again like a tiger—licking, kissing, biting, scratching, finally throwing herself down again but this time on her belly, raising her buttocks in the air. The blood rushed to his head. No woman before had ever offered him her rear cavity.

When he left, he was already looking forward to Thursday when he was due to return.

27.

If he had stopped to think about it, Jamie most likely would have figured out what would eventually come to pass. It was inevitable, as inevitable as spring following winter. But he was very busy that spring of 1901, busier than he had ever been in his life. He never did stop to think about it. It sneaked up on him as so many things in his life had.

It was Sunday afternoon and he arrived in his new carriage to take Sunday dinner with the Hesses, which was, of course, the same intolerable routine that was followed every Sunday afternoon. As always, dinner would be served precisely at one, or at the very latest five minutes past the hour. The time didn't vary and the menu, barely. On the sideboard would be the invariable two pitchers of milk and water. On the large silver serving platter would be one of the three meat courses, which were served on a rotating basis—lamb (in the form of thin chops or a roast leg); roast chicken (always between five and six pounds); or a roast fresh ham. Why, deep in the heart of Texas, there never was a cut of beef was beyond Jamie's understanding. Then after dinner, the Hesses were off and Anne and he would copulate, usually in her blue and white chaste bedroom.

But that Sunday afternoon, the usual was not to be.

Anna, the servant woman, admitted him, took his hat. Then, thin, disapproving lips barely moving, she told him that the Hesses awaited him in the parlor. Mrs. Hess, sitting stiffly upright in one of the dark red overstuffed chairs, wore her habitual frown. Karl Hess, pacing back and forth, seemed angry, particularly forbidding. Anne was crumpled on the sofa, crying softly. Seeing him, Karl Hess pointed a thick finger: "There you are, you rotter! You scoundrel! You ungrateful snake in the grass! I took you in, into my business and into my home, treated you like a son, and how did you repay me? By ruining our innocent little girl, by taking advantage of her!"

Jamie cast a quick look at Anne, sobbing louder now. *She's betrayed us, me, by telling them!* He was furious with her. God, but she was a sniveling bitch! First she had tricked him into fucking her and now she had informed on him! Or had the Hesses just guessed what was going on and forced an admission from her? Well, they were more to blame than he. Right from the start they had thrown the two of them together. *They've been pushing her at me! They've left us alone on purpose! What did they expect to happen?*

But he knew the answer to that. They had expected him to fall in love with her, or at least to stoke his greed sufficiently for him to propose marriage. But their plan had gone awry. Instead of his proposing, their virtuous little girl had seduced him.

He wanted to shout that she was ten years older than he and hardly the little innocent they thought she was. But how could he do that? Especially in the face of Karl Hess's formidable wrath? For one, he'd look like a terrible fool and second, he'd be compounding his supposed sin by sounding like an unchivalrous bastard.

Then the solution came to him. He'd apologize to them all. He'd beg their forgiveness on his knees. He'd swear that if they found it in their hearts to forgive him, he'd never darken their home again. At the same time, he would try to atone for the unforgivable by working his fingers to the bone for them. He would promise to break his back in the service of their business. It went without saying that he would never attempt to see Anne again. He'd say that he didn't deserve to see her again; that he wasn't fit even to clean her shoes much less kiss her feet. Then, they, with true Christian charity, would forgive him and allow him to remain in the salvage business. At the same time he would be spared Anne's bovine presence forever! That alone would be worth everything! Even the groveling . . .

Even as Jamie was working himself up to utter those degrading but ultimately rewarding words, he heard Karl Hess say, "And now that Anne is pregnant with your child, you're going to do the right thing by her or by God, I'll have you horsewhipped right in the middle of Broadway! I'll have you tarred and feathered! I'll make you wish you were never born! I'll destroy you!"

Jamie, his face white as the proverbial sheet, stiffly informed Mr. Hess that it wasn't necessary to threaten him, especially since he wasn't frightened by threats and was prepared to do the right thing by a pregnant Anne. He would never even think to do otherwise. That in spite of what Mr. Hess thought of him, James Markson was a man of honor.

The moment he said this, Mr. Hess's furious scowl vanished, although Mrs. Hess's grimace did not. Immediately Hess rushed over to him and seized his hand and pumped it vigorously. "Of course you're a man of honor. I always knew it was so. If I had thought otherwise, would I have treated you like a son in the first place? Of course not! It was just that I was so overwrought to discover that you two naughty children couldn't wait, that your passion for each other was so overwhelming, so powerful that you—"

Mrs. Hess coughed and her husband caught himself up quickly. He took out a white handkerchief and blew his nose. "That you two were so much in love that you forgot yourselves . . ."

He turned around to look at Anne, nodded to her. She quickly sat up, her hand flying to her mouth, covering it in her disbelief over her own all-consuming happiness. She rushed across the room and threw her arms around her betrothed.

"It will be so wonderful, Jamie! You and me and our—" She buried her face in his shoulder. As he stood there unmoving, Hess urged him, "It's all right, my boy, you may kiss her. I know you want to. It's all right. Now," he checked his watch, "shall we go into dinner? And we'll plan the wedding. Shall we say next week? Since Anne is preg—"

Mrs. Hess, rising to lead the way into the dining room, coughed again.

"Under the circumstances," Karl Hess corrected himself, "we shouldn't delay too long. We'll have to check with Reverend Hubert about having the wedding at the church as soon as possible—"

Church wedding? No, it was impossible! Church ritual? No! A tide of nausea rose up within him. He had visions of religious processions, processions he had forgotten. Peasants walking through the streets, an air of unreality. There had been a kind of hysteria, always a hint of anti-Semitism suffusing the sweet spring day. And then there was "Green Thursday." How could any Jew who had witnessed a "Green Thursday" forget it? That day when a convert, that Jewish infidel, carried a statue of Jesus at the head of the procession. He would be getting married on a Sunday but for him it would be "Green Thursday" just the same.

But what of it? he demanded of himself. What did it matter to him anyway? He no longer was Yitzhak Markoff, son of David and Eve Markoff, a Jew . . .

As Karl Hess carved the leg of lamb, he told Jamie that he was presenting him with another five-percent interest in the junkyard.

"No, sir," Jamie protested. "I don't want it. I won't accept it, not for doing the only honorable thing." *A convert yes, a whore—no!*

As soon as the words were out of his mouth, that he was only acting out of honor, he realized that they were less than adequate words, and he tried again. "I can't accept a gift for doing what is not only correct, but my privilege, my pleasure." He didn't look at Anne as he spoke. He hadn't looked at her since she had rushed across the parlor to embrace him. Now, he forced himself to look at her and smile. He was going to have to get used to looking at her constantly, for the rest of his life. She was going to be the mother of his child, and a child—well, a child was a precious obligation.

"Very well put, Jamie my son. But I insist you have another five percent. After all, it's all in the family now, Jamie . . ." It was the first time Karl Hess had called him by his first name. It was the start of a new era.

Then the prospective father-in-law proposed a toast to the happy couple, to their future. The only thing to toast with was the milk, slightly off in flavor. Drinking it down, Jamie's stomach turned over. *To his future?* Maybe it was as sour as the milk.

Two weeks later, they were married in Galveston's Methodist Church, with a Champagne and wedding cake reception at the bride's home. The groom seemed somewhat preoccupied. The wedding guests laid that to a new husband's nervousness at what followed the ceremony—the honeymoon. Mr. Hess had, as a matter of fact, proposed to send the couple on a honeymoon to St. Louis, but the groom had declined. He had much too much to do. They were experiencing some engineering difficulties with the seawall. He couldn't, in all good conscience, leave at this time.

The truth was he couldn't contemplate spending that much time alone with his bride. So, instead of leaving on a honeymoon after the reception was over, Jamie transported his belongings from his boarding house to the Hess home. Karl—Jamie had been asked to call him that—insisted that, for the time being anyway, Jamie and Anne make their home with them. So it was in Anne's white bed in the blue and white room that Jamie spent his first night as a husband, dreaming not of his bride nor even of his unborn child, but of a procession, a parade and not with a convert holding a statue of Jesus marching in front, but two women, dressed as clowns, leading off the march. One was red haired, and one had black hair, black as the night.

Two months later. A Monday morning, ten past eleven. The phone jangled in the office of the junkyard. Before removing the receiver, Karl Hess glanced quickly over at his son-in-law who was concentrating on a ledger. After listening for a couple of minutes, Karl hung up and said, "We have to go home, my boy."

Jamie looked up surprised. Go home in the middle of the day? That had never happened before.

"It's bad news, I'm afraid. Anne . . . She's lost the baby."

They went upstairs to the girlish blue and white bedroom Jamie and Anne shared. Anna the maid followed them, agitated; she was like one of the family. Anne was lying in bed, propped up by a mound of white pillows. She was covered by a pretty quilt, white with small blue flowers sprinkled here and there. Her face was pale and she was sobbing—rhythmic, dry little sobs. To the left of the bed stood her mother, lips compressed, hands folded in front of her. Before Jamie could go to his wife to kiss her forehead, glistening with little beads of perspiration, murmur his few words of consolation and inquire how she felt, his father-in-law did these things then took up a position on the right side of the bed. He smiled at Jamie, a small, sad little smile of commiseration, as Anne lowered her eyes, stretching out a hand to him, almost beseechingly. Her arm was covered by the long sleeve of a white nightgown. Jamie's eyes moved to his mother-in-law. She wasn't smiling Karl's sad little smile but her eyes were intent on him all the same. Even as the little hairs on the back of his neck rose, Jamie spun around to see what Anna was doing. She was caught in the doorway, wringing her hands. A little chill coursed through him; he felt as if he were up on the stage of the Beach Pavilion, part of one of those tableaux they held there last summer before the Pavilion was washed away. He broke out in a sweat (summer had come early to Galveston that year); the room was very hot and quiet, silent except for Anne's dry little hard sobs. It came to him that a vital character of the tableau was missing.

309

"Where's the doctor?" he asked quietly. "Didn't you call him?"

Mrs. Hess looked at her husband. "Yes, of course. Dr. Hubbard, my doctor." She shrugged. "He could do nothing."

Jamie moved quickly now to the bed. Anne looked up at him with her habitual half smile, her soft, cowlike blue eyes. He pulled the quilt from her body, threw it on the floor. She lay there cowering in her high-necked nightgown, white and pristine, on the pure-white, pristine sheets. Jamie pulled up the long nightgown in one swift motion. Even Anne's body was white and pure, no bloodied rag between her thighs! Her thin high-pitched shriek rent the room.

"You forgot one thing," Jamie said. "You forgot that though I'm young and gullible, I *was* a country boy, a dealer in livestock, used to the ways of animals."

"What are you going to do?" Karl Hess asked him.

Jamie laughed bitterly. "What do you think I'm going to do?"

"You're not going to be so foolish as to walk out on ten percent of a business?" It was more statement than question.

"Aren't I? What the hell does your stinking ten percent mean to me, anyway? I have no say in the business. I don't get any money out of it except for the few stinking dollars you throw me by way of a salary. I live here in this stinking house where the windows are never open, where there isn't a fucking drop of anything to drink except for your stinking milk, where I can't even breathe. Not to mention that I have to fuck your stinking, lying bitch of a daughter whom I can't stand the sight of—"

When he saw Karl Hess wince, he decided to go on. He wanted to wound the son-of-a-bitch liar who had snared him for his daughter just as wild animals were snared—through trickery and deceit, duping him as if he were the world's biggest fool.

"No wonder you had to trick me into marrying her after you had thrown her at me for months. Nobody else wanted her because she's so repulsive and she had to get married quick before she was *really* too old to have babies."

"That's not so," Hess protested. "She's not old. She's not repulsive."

"It made me sick to fuck her—"

Karl Hess staggered, held up a hand as if to ward off Jamie's repugnant words.

"No wonder she attacked me every night. She was desperate to make love, desperate to get pregnant so that I wouldn't find out she was such a stinking liar, besides being old and ugly."

"I refuse to have you talking about Anne this way—"

"Who cares what you want, you stinking hypocrite? Anyhow, it's the truth. Don't you like the truth, you stinking, lying holier-than-thou hypocrite?" His mouth curled into a sneer and his eyes lit with malice. "I thought you Christians like the truth better than we Jews! How do you like that, Karl Hess? It was a Jew you were so hot to get for your daughter. It was a Jew whom you were pissing in your pants for. It was a Jew whom you wanted to fuck your daughter! That's right! You knew my name was von Marx before it was James Markson. What you didn't know was that it was *Markoff* before it was Wilhelm von Marx. I'm no German! I'm a Russian-born Jew!''

To Jamie's amazement, Karl Hess didn't blink an eye. In fact, he seemed to regain some of his composure, even his usual arrogance. ''But not much of a Jew, I'd say, Mr. James Markson. A *geshmott* Jew, a turncoat, is more like it, wouldn't you say?'' Now he laughed at the expression on Jamie's face. ''Did you really think I didn't know the difference between a German accent and a Yiddish one? I knew what you were immediately. I came from Germany when I was already twenty. Germany's full of Jews. All kinds. Orthodox ones, assimilated ones who consider themselves Jews culturally but are practically non-observants. And we also have the converts who embrace Our Lord, Jesus Christ. Like my mother.''

''Your mother?'' Jamie was incredulous. ''Then you're Jewish!''

''No, Mr. Markson, unlike you, I was never Jewish. My mother's conversion came before she married my father. I was a Christian from the day I was born.''

He said this so smugly, so arrogantly that Jamie wanted to hit him. He ached to hit him. Instead he said, ''We had a saying about converts in Slobodka. 'He who's a convert is neither a Jew nor a gentile.' But since you pretend to be such a good, American-German Christian, and you say you knew I was Jewish, what the hell did you want with me? Why did you want me so much you had to trap me? Was it that you loved the Jewish blood in your veins so much you wanted more of it for your grandchildren?''

Karl Hess felt strong again, no longer on the defensive. On the contrary, he felt now that he was going to win this battle. He raised an amused eyebrow. ''No, I neither love it or hate it, unlike some full-blooded Jews I could name. You had a saying in Slobodka; well, we had one in Germany. 'No one makes a better German than a Jew.' Maybe that's why a Jew is more accepted in Germany than anywhere else in the world. Accepted and respected for his special qualities, of which there are quite a few—love of education, love of family, and a special knack for business, an ability with money.''

''But why me? Why were you so obsessed with getting me that you had to lie and use trickery?''

''I'm a careful man, Mr. Markson, a thorough man. While you may scorn my daughter, don't you think for a second there weren't other men who would have been happy to have her and what goes with her. No, I *chose* you. You were the correct combination of those qualities I wanted to see reproduced in my grandchildren. Perhaps it was the German in me that wanted your physical perfection, your strength and your power, your beauty of face and physique. Strangely enough, you have the ideal Nordic looks we Germans admire. But I'm more American, I hope, than German. I've lived in this country for forty years. As an American, I wanted your courage and heroism, the fearlessness you displayed in the hurricane. And as a businessman with an eye for the future,

311

eager to establish a dynasty if you will, I saw something in you that you didn't even see in yourself. What kind of man, do you think, fights to save lives one day and goes about collecting the wreckage of the disaster that imperiled those lives the next day? I'd say a born business man with foresight, a man who sees a need and a source and strives to connect the two. To be part of the future a man needs a combination of common sense and imagination.

"As for you having been a Jew, that was all to the good. As a father, I thought of another saying we had in Germany— 'Jewish men make the best husbands.' They're industrious, good providers and faithful. And they love their children. No, there's nothing wrong with Jewish blood, if you don't go around proclaiming it. And you weren't proclaiming it, obviously. For your own reasons, which don't interest me. In the final analysis, I know that the best thing to be in the whole wide world is a rich, white Protestant American male, preferably of Anglo-Saxon heritage. And you can be that man. I think what you object to most strenuously in our whole sad affair is that you think you were made a fool of. Well, I say to you now: Don't be a fool! Don't walk away from what's within your grasp! James Markson, you can have it all! It's a new century in a still new country. And Texas is only in its infancy. We can still build together! Stay with Anne! Have children! What is only a salvage business today can be Hess and Markson Enterprises tomorrow. Stay, and the limits are only those you impose on yourself!''

Jamie was studying his father-in-law's face. *He thinks he has me!* He watched Hess pull his watch out from his fob pocket, a creature of habit, constantly caught up in the passage of time.

Yes, check your watch, you old bastard. Your time is running out.

"I'm going to give you another ten percent of the business."

"The hell you are. You're going to give me another forty percent."

"Then, you'll have fifty percent altogether."

"Obviously."

"You want too much."

"Under the circumstances, I don't think so."

"It's too much. You're being vengeful," Karl Hess accused.

Jamie laughed. "Of course I am. What did you expect? I'm also being greedy. But you can't complain. You were the one who laid down the rules."

"How can I trust you?"

"Trust me to do what? Or, not to do what? You can't really. We'll have a contract as we did last time but we'll still have to take each other on faith." He laughed again.

"I tell you what I'll do. I'll give you another fifteen percent so you'll have twenty-five altogether. And I'll give Anne the additional twenty-five percent."

"No."

"Why not? That's fair. She's my daughter. Why not?"

"You said it. It's because she's your daughter." He knew about daughters and fathers. In the end, the daughters always sided with their fathers. "But I do think you should give Anne something. What I have in mind is the Villa at 24th on Broadway.''

"You mean that Italian palace?'' He was outraged.

"It's just a villa. It only looks like a palace. It's for sale and I think Anne should have it.''

"It must cost a fortune!''

"So what? You have a fortune, I'm sure. Salted away that you'll never spend.''

"It's ostentatious and vulgar.''

"I like it and Anne will love it. I get the additional forty percent and Anne gets the villa.''

"Or—?''

"Or I disappear from sight. You'll never find me and Anne will have to wait years to get a divorce. By that time, nobody will want her. She'd certainly be too old to have children.''

They sat in silence until Jamie went up to his father-in-law and took his pocket watch from his vest pocket. Looking at it, he said, "You have five minutes to decide whether it's yes or no. In five minutes my share goes up to fifty-five percent.''

"You're a real bastard.''

"You chose me, remember? You have four-and-a-half minutes.''

"You win, Markson. Because I love my daughter. But I have to know that you'll be good to her.''

Jamie smiled again, savoring his advantage. "Some things you have to take on faith.''

"How do I know there'll be children?''

"Oh, there will be. I forgot to tell you another stipulation of our agreement. You're going to designate another twenty-five percent to Anne's and my firstborn child.''

"You're insane.''

Jamie said nothing, waited. Karl Hess was a man who understood about choices. Finally he said, "That will leave me with only twenty-five percent of my own business.''

Jamie saw no need to respond to that statement of fact. He and his father-in-law both knew how to add and subtract. "Are there any more stipulations I should know about?'' Hess asked. He seemed no longer angry but resigned.

"As a matter of fact, there is one more. I want a letter from you attesting to what you told me about your mother. That she was a convert from Judaism.''

"You are crazy! I absolutely refuse! Why would you want such a document?''

"I give you my word that I won't use it against you. I want it for—let's say, an emergency situation.''

"What kind of emergency? To hold over Anne's head?''

"No, not Anne's. Mrs. Hess's. She doesn't like me. Never has. Just in case you should die before my first child is born, she'd be holding fifty percent of the business and that could be a problem. She could even sell her share to a stranger. You can see how difficult it would be for me to have to operate with another partner, a stranger, who didn't value me the way my father-in-law would.'' Jamie smiled thinly. ''But, as I said, I won't use it against either you or her. It's just a safeguard. Don't look so worried. You'll have your fifty percent until that first child is born.''

Hess's mouth twisted in ironic reflection. ''And what about the second child? Don't you want me to give my remaining twenty-five percent to your second child?''

''Oh, I wouldn't want to take away your incentive for living. I'll take care of the second child myself, and the third. You can count on it.''

But of course only he knew there'd never be a second child or a third.

He told Selena Janus that he was through with the speech lessons.

''You don't speak as perfectly as you think you do. My ear still detects a flaw here and there.''

''Not everybody has your ear . . . And if I were too perfect, no one would quite believe me either. People don't trust perfection.''

''It's that you think you don't need me anymore.''

''You're right.''

''How am I right? That you think you don't need me or that you really don't need me?''

''Both.''

She gave him a sour smile. ''You used me . . .''

''Just as you used me. Everybody uses everybody else. That is something I just recently learned. Only I don't want to be used anymore. I don't intend to be, ever again.''

''So that's why you're leaving me? Because you don't want to be used?''

''Maybe. Does it matter? Maybe it's just that you don't have anything I want.''

''God, but you're a prick!''

He laughed. She had enunciated the word so exquisitely, she made it sound like a beautiful thing to be.

His laughter infuriated her, drove her to utter other words she didn't ordinarily employ. ''Bastard! Son-of-a-bitch!''

Now, he thought, she was both right and wrong. He had a very real, legitimate father, so she was wrong on that score. But she was right about his mother. Didn't a bitch love and nurture her whelp at first then cast it aside so that in a year's time, the bitch didn't even recognize her own offspring, didn't even know him from all the others?

Jamie and his father-in-law signed the papers in the offices of Hess and Markson Enterprises in the presence of two lawyers, one representing each partner. Karl Hess behaved in a proper, mannerly fashion—the result of many years of self-discipline and tight control. Jamie admired him for that, although he noticed that, for once, the black shoes were not quite as shiny as usual and the gold pocket watch and chain were missing. Was he beginning to unravel? Jamie wondered.

After they were through with the papers and the two lawyers had gone, Karl announced that he was joining a few friends for lunch at the Commerce Club and didn't know when he would be back. Since he now had a full and equal partner who was both young and energetic, he, Karl, could begin to enjoy a more leisurely pace.

Jamie smiled and nodded although he wasn't quite sure how to take his father-in-law's announcement. Then, just before he went through the door, almost as an afterthought, Karl pulled his gold watch and chain out of his coat pocket and deposited the watch on his son-in-law's mahogany desk, rattling the chain as he did so. "There you go, my son. Now you have everything! Now you're the keeper of the time."

Jamie was thoughtful after he left. He had vowed to himself that nothing was ever going to surprise him again, that he'd be prepared for anything, but now Karl Hess had just surprised him. He had never suspected that his father-in-law had a sense of humor.

PART FOUR

AVA

1902—1910

28.

As 1901 drew to a close and Jamie and Anne were about to move into their new home, the Italianate villa that was considered to be one of the most imposing houses in the entire City, Jamie couldn't help but be impressed by his own achievement. He added up his score. He had been in America three and a half years in which time he had been brewery worker, foreman on the railroad, and was now half owner of Hess and Markson Enterprises, no longer just a junkyard in the business of collecting and selling metal scrap, old glass and rags. Buying a block-square lot adjacent to the yard, they had opened up their own glass recycling plant; Jamie estimated that within two years, or possibly three, the revenues would double. At the same time, they had bought many properties for future development. At the top of the list for projected plans was their own smelting plant.

At first Karl Hess had objected to the expansion plans. Being of an essentially conservative nature, he had been appalled by the enormous debt the company would have to assume. He decried the dangers of too-rapid expansion. But Jamie quickly shot him down. Since he had met Karl Hess, the older man had been proclaiming Galveston's glittering future—how it would grow along with Texas even as Texas grew along with a burgeoning America, and how the astute business man would align himself with that golden future, more golden even than Houston's, Hess's *bête noire*. Jamie told him it was time to put his money where his mouth was.

Still, Jamie had anticipated more resistance than he actually received. He surmised that Hess wasn't the same man he'd been before they became equal partners, before Hess had compromised his integrity by foisting his daughter on him by trickery.

In addition to Jamie's success in business, there was also his standing in the community. With the completion of the seawall, he was hailed and applauded throughout the City as one of the prime moving forces in its execution. Already he was immersed in the development of the scenic boulevard that would run the length of the ten-mile wall. After that, there'd be the commercial development. Jamie had visions of shops and attractions that would be the wall's final adornment. Never for a moment did he doubt that the wall would do its duty as a protector of Galveston City, a strong and stalwart guard against the onslaughts of nature.

319

He tried not to think of all the things he didn't have. Or rather of those who were absent from his life, including a wife he could love—not even as his father had loved his mother, but one that he loved at all. Instead he tried to think of the child he would have, the child that wasn't even conceived as yet. His mother used to say that a child was the future and he still believed many of the things his mother had told him. In many ways, he was still his mother's son, a child himself. But he was still a few months away from being twenty-one and although in Slobodka he had been a man since the age of thirteen, in America, twenty-one was the age a boy became a man.

Jamie wanted the Villa completely decorated before they moved in; he wanted it to be perfect. He supervised everything himself, from the hanging of the draperies to the laying of the carpets; from the regilding of every cherub to the restoration of the gardens. Anne offered to help. Tearfully, she asked if she couldn't at least choose some of the furnishings, but he ignored her offers as he ignored all her conversation, all her attempts at apologies, explanations and reconciliations. Her "I only did it because I love you" fell on deaf ears. As for the decorating of his house, he didn't need her help. He had very definite ideas as to what he wanted and only scorn for her taste as he had only scorn for everything and everyone connected to her, except for her father's assets which were paying for the house as well as its appointments.

Love? He loved his business and he loved his house. He would love his child.

Of all the rooms in his house, Jamie particularly liked the great entrance hall with its *giallo antico* marble floor and four giant bronze chandeliers with opaline globes and hanging crystal pendants. On one wall a della Robbia plaque hung over a gold-encrusted coffer, and on another wall a marble fountain adorned with dolphins, spilling silvery water into a rippled shell, fit into a soffit. Overhead, there was a stained-glass skylight that cast a subdued yellow glow over everything below. It was from this hall that the soaring staircase of Caen stone, wrought-iron and burnished bronze swept upward to the second-floor bedrooms. It was up this staircase that Jamie carried Anne, now his bride of some months, on their first night in the villa, to a bedroom with carved and gilded boiserie and a satin-covered bed heavily draped and swathed in hangings to match.

Anne couldn't believe what was happening. Never, never in her sweetest dreams, before they were married and certainly not after, had she imagined that this night would come when Jamie would behave in this manner . . . like a man in love, like a man swept away by passion. She had been convinced that he would never love her, surely not as she loved him. She had been convinced that he would never forgive her her duplicity. And now this! This mad, impetuous, rapturous demonstration of a man desperately in love, carried away by the strength of his ardor.

Then unceremoniously he dumped her on the bed. She was bewildered, torn again by conflicting emotions. "What is it?" she cried out. "Are you going to make love to me?"

"Love? No. I'm going to do to you what you did to me. I'm going to fuck you!"

Her eyes grew big with fear, but in spite of herself she wanted him to do it—fuck her! He ripped her shirtwaist open from neck to waist, the little buttons flying. Then slowly and deliberately he removed the rest of her clothes, so deliberately she wasn't sure whether he was raping her or not, and she didn't care! She just wanted him!

She saw him ready to mount her and unconsciously she raised herself to meet him. "Don't move!" he warned her. "If you move, I'll strangle you!"

She believed him and she was both excited and terrified. "Why?" she gasped. "Why can't I move?"

"I told you why," he said, sitting astride her, pushing himself into her. She screamed from the force of his thrust. "Because you're not fucking me! I'm doing the fucking this time!"

She moaned, not sure herself what kind of a moan it was—one of passion, or one of anguish. He shoved and thrust and pounded, riding her as if she were a wild mare on the plains, not weak, timid, deceitful, plain Anne Hess. The blood roared in his ears, throbbed in his temples, and for a few seconds, in his fury and rage, he wasn't sure at all who it was lying under him, impaled, motionless, trying not to tremble, trying not to groan.

He didn't go near Anne for the next three or four weeks, taking a separate bedroom for himself. He waited to see if he had been successful in impregnating her, waiting to see if it would be necessary to fornicate with her again. It wasn't. Approximately nine months later, in the fall of 1902, his child was born.

The doctor, who had anticipated a long, difficult birth, was astonished when the period of labor lasted only four hours from start to finish. He flung open the door to shout his good news to the waiting family—Karl Hess, pacing to and fro in the upstairs hall; his wife, sitting stiffly in a high-backed chair outside the bedroom door; the new father, reading in his rose and cream drawing room. "It's all over! It's a girl!"

Jamie put down his book and made for the staircase, taking the steps two at a time. The Hesses had already gone into the bedroom and he was furious with himself for having allowed them to wait in his house for his baby to be born, to see it first.

The doctor was saying, "Under the circumstances, a first child, four hours . . . Remarkable! It was as if she had a rage to be born!"

A rage to be born? But of course! She's a Markoff! He threw back his head and laughed, but then he remembered he himself was no longer a Markoff and his laugh faded away.

He rushed past the doctor and brushed by the woman who had assisted him,

321

to get to the bed where Anne was holding his daughter in her arms, where the Hesses stood gaping in wonder. He looked at the baby and gasped! Anne's eyes darted from her child to her husband, sharing his astonishment. She herself couldn't believe that from her own undistinguished body she had managed to bring forth this girl-child of such exquisite beauty.

"Never saw anything like it!" the doctor's assistant marveled. "So much hair, and that color! Like the Texas sun setting over the Gulf! And those eyes! Who ever heard of a baby not having blue eyes at birth? Just look at them—green as emeralds!"

"And that skin! Most newborns are red and wrinkled but not this one! It's because she was born so quickly," the doctor exclaimed, wanting now to take some credit for this particular miracle of birth.

"And she's not even crying," Karl Hess said in awe. "I thought all babies cried. Anne did . . . for six months after she was born."

Mrs. Hess tore her eyes away from the child to say to its father, "I'm sure you're pleased to see that Anne is well too." These were more words than she had ever spoken to him at any one time, a reproof to remind him of Anne's existence as Jamie stood transfixed with eyes only for his daughter. *She was the image of his mother!* And beautiful without compare!

Anne herself was incapable of directing her gaze anywhere but toward her husband. She wanted to shout at him: *Aren't you satisfied? Aren't you pleased with me? Haven't I done well? In the name of God, look at me and tell me you're happy with me for growing this extraordinary child inside me for you, just for you! Love me! Kiss me!*

Jamie bent down and for a moment she thought he was going to do just that—kiss her, whisper that he loved her, if not for herself at least for this supremely lovely gift of life. But his only intention was to take this bundle of flesh and swaddling from her arms into his own.

Entranced, he carried the infant to the window the better to study her every feature, the tiny but perfect fingers, every wisp of the red-gold hair. A thrill coursed through him as the baby appeared to look directly into his eyes with her own green ones, clear as glass. The nurse rushed over, clucking, "The eyes are too delicate yet for this light. They don't see for weeks, you know."

Jamie ignored her; he knew better.

The doctor came over to stand by Jamie, looking over his shoulder at the baby. He shook his head. "That coloring sure beats me. With the two of you so blond and blue-eyed, I could have sworn that's what the baby would be. But you never know for sure. Most likely the hair will fall out before the real hair comes in and the eyes will change color. Wouldn't be a bit surprised if she ends up with big blue eyes and hair the color of corn."

But Jamie ignored the doctor's words as he had the nurse's. Again, he knew better.

An overwhelming surge of love poured through him for this—he searched for a word large enough to encompass his feelings—this treasure, this jewel, this gem among jewels. She was flawless. She was regal. She was a princess: And that's exactly how he would raise her, as an aristocratic American princess, even as if she were really of noble birth. As for the past it was done, gone. There was only his daughter and her royal future.

It was actually painful for him to relinquish the infant so that she could be put to her mother's breast. "The baby has to nurse so that the milk can start flowing," the nurse explained.

The Hesses went home but he himself was unable to leave the room. Rather, he sat and watched as the baby's rosebud of a mouth searched out her mother's nipple, and then fell asleep.

Twilight fell and the room darkened. The baby slept in her cradle now. Anne, watching him watching their daughter, thought that it was possible things might work out for the three of them, together. She saw so much love in Jamie's face as he gazed at the infant, surely some would spill over, even a few drops, just for her.

She asked softly, "What shall we name her?"

He almost said, "Eve," and was furious with himself. But it was hard to look at the baby and not think of *her,* even long for her at a time like this.

But she was behind him, she and what she represented. He had to try harder not to think of her, not to think of any of them. It was all a long time ago. Another world. Over and done with.

No, the baby couldn't be Eve. Even if the name didn't rake across his heart conjuring up all kinds of painful images, he couldn't possibly name the baby after his mother. Even though she might be dead to him, she was very much alive, and Jews didn't name their children after the living. He was still Jew enough to remember that.

Yet, even though his mother was gone from him she was still part of him just as his baby was part of him, just as they were all part of each other. His princess would be part of Eve. She would be Ava, a name that was close to the name Eve but yet not Eve. Certainly not Eve.

"Ava," he said.

"Ava." Anne rolled the name around on her tongue. "It's a pretty name," she said, wanting to please him. "A pretty name for a pretty little girl . . ."

Pretty? But he hadn't expected her to understand. She was incapable of understanding. She was just Anne. . . .

It never worked out the way Anne had hoped, the way she yearned for it to be—the three of them together, a family. From the very first, Ava was her daddy's girl, and it seemed as if there was no room for her, the mother. She never completely understood it. As for Jamie, she knew what she had done—tricking him into marrying her—was a terrible thing. There was no denying it. But why couldn't he, now that he had so much, forgive her? Why couldn't one tiny piece of his heart soften toward her and allow her into that special kingdom they, Jamie and his little princess, shared?

Sometimes Anne ached to shake him, shout: "If it weren't for me, you wouldn't have any of this—all these things you prize so highly—the business, the house, your place on the City Commission, your precious princess of a daughter!" But of course she didn't; she wouldn't dare.

She couldn't understand how, right from the beginning, how her very own baby, an infant, could be so much a stranger to her. Sometimes it seemed as if Ava wasn't really her child at all; as if, somehow, she, Anne, had only been a means, a vessel, chosen to deliver the child into the world, that Ava had really never been of her loins; wasn't part of her blood. . . .

Anne knew it was crazy to think like that, still, she couldn't help herself. The baby's coloring—where had it come from? She had asked her mother and father if anyone in their family whom they could remember had had red hair or green eyes, and they had told her no. Then she had asked Jamie the same question and he hadn't answered her at all, only shaken his head in what she assumed was some kind of a negative answer. It was a mystery . . .

Ava's personality was equally puzzling to her. As an infant she almost never cried, only looked straight into one's eyes as if she could see right through a person and disdained what she saw there. By the time she was two, she still didn't cry as children her age usually did, when they fell, or were tired, or even when they didn't feel well. The only time Ava cried was when she was frustrated in some matter, getting something she wanted, something she couldn't reach, another child's toy, or when she simply didn't want to obey some command. These were tantrums such as Anne had never seen, tantrums of a frightening fury, an incredible *rage*. Then Anne remembered what the doctor had said that day she had given birth . . . *It was as if she had a rage to be born.* Those were the doctor's very words.

She remembered the night Ava was conceived, conceived in Jamie's rage. Anne wondered if what she had once heard was really true—*a child conceived in rage shall never know peace* . . .

Painful as it was, Anne had to admit to herself that her daughter was as alien to her as was the daughter's father. Could it all have started when she didn't have the milk to suckle Ava and a wet nurse had to be hired? She wondered. She had been miserable about that, had felt so inadequate, a failure. Still, she wasn't the first woman unable to nurse a baby. Jamie himself had interviewed the wet nurses, had looked at her, Anne, not with contempt exactly, but as if she were a zero, a *nothing*.

Then, it seemed as if the child never turned to her for anything. She turned to the wet nurse, of course. And to the nannies Jamie hired, one after the other. Anne begged him not to; she told him that they had enough servants so that she herself was free to spend all her time with Ava—playing with her, feeding her, talking to her, reading to her. But Jamie wouldn't listen. He said he wanted Ava to have the benefit of women trained in these duties, women of many heritages, so Ava would learn many languages. Jamie was obsessed with languages. He hired first a German woman, then an English one, and then a French one.

Sometimes Anne wondered if he switched nannies so that Ava wouldn't get too attached to anybody except himself.

Jamie himself always found time to do some of the things he hired the nannies to do and the things they didn't—carry her around piggyback, or take her to the beach. He was always the one who tucked her in bed and told her a bedtime tale.

No, Ava never turned to Anne, or ran to her or kissed her. Maybe this was, in the final evaluation, that she who was so much her father's daughter, had sensed with her unchildlike perceptions what her Daddy felt, and emulated him, shut Anne out, finding her not beneath contempt, perhaps, but certainly not worthy of too much attention, of love.

29.

It was never his intention to be unkind to Anne. At the same time he didn't cry for her. If she was unhappy, it was her own doing. More hers than his, certainly. It was she who had to bear the responsibility for a marriage that provided her no pleasure. "Forgive me!" she cried, but it was no longer a matter of forgiveness to him. For all that was worth, he had forgiven her. But having done that, he couldn't make himself love her. And that was what she desperately wanted. She wanted . . .

"Unfair!" she cried. "Have mercy!" she cried. But Jamie had learned long before that there was room for neither fairness nor mercy in this world. His father himself had told him that even as he had strained to be both just and merciful himself. It was his father's very disbelief in man's potential to gain justice and mercy that had caused him to lose most of his faith both in the Almighty and in a better world to come. But Jamie didn't feel that his father had ever lost all faith; he believed that there was that part of his father that still clung to the hope that he would be proven wrong. Of course, at his father's side was his mother who, no matter what, both believed and hoped and kept urging him to do the same.

Jamie could only lament that neither one of them had been fair or merciful toward him; that, for whatever reason, the two of them had lost their faith in their son. Still he often had difficulty putting them out of his mind. He found it somewhat easier to resist the memory of Jennie. In the delirium of his happiness with his daughter he was able to rationalize that had there been a Jennie in his life, there wouldn't have been Ava.

From the second Ava was born, and with each succeeding day, week, month, he grew more enthralled, more beguiled, more bewitched. He was convinced she was a gift from heaven, if heaven did indeed exist. Even as Anne charged, he was putty in Ava's tiny hands. All she had to do was look at him and he turned to jelly. The mere sight of her running across the lawn, her red curls bobbing, filled his heart with joy and gave him reason to be alive. All she had to do was place her small hands on her little hips, green eyes glistening, and pout: "Daddy, please!" and he wanted to run and catch the world to lay at her precious feet.

But even as Jamie was so immersed in his daughter and his business, he couldn't manage to shut out completely the rest of the world. He read the newspapers and couldn't help but be aware of what was happening in the land of his birth. The Russo-Japanese War. The papers were full of it. Things were going badly for the Russians, and the worse the war went the more the momentum of revolution built. Then he couldn't not think of his mother and father, wondering what part they were playing in it all. He agonized about how much they were at risk. He knew they had to be involved. They had been working toward this end since he could remember. Why else had he himself become imbued with that spirit of rebellion? Why else had he killed the Governor-General on that fateful day that had changed the course of his life forever?

He followed the stories in the papers carefully. On a Sunday in January, 1905, thousands of working men and women led by a priest, carrying icons and singing religious songs marched to the Winter Palace to speak to their Little Father, the Tsar. Instead of Nikolai, they found bullets and death. The movement accelerated. There were strikes and student protests all across the nation, agrarian uprisings. They sprang up and multiplied.

Part of Jamie rejoiced. A part of him he had thought dead came alive again as his blood was stirred by passions he hadn't felt in years. At the same time he grew increasingly alarmed. Despite his attempts to suppress this anxiety he was besieged by it. He couldn't help feeling anxious about the family he told himself no longer existed for him, and he did what he had sworn he wouldn't do again—he wrote another letter to Slobodka. This time, he included a draft on his bank for approximately 1,000 rubles. He was careful to point out that this money could be used for whatever purpose they chose—to aid in the movement or for passage to America. He neither urged nor begged. He signed the letter Yitzhak, in care of J. Markson. He would worry about the problem of his identity when the time came, if it came. He was beyond caring about that—he only wanted them to be *safe*.

Each day he rushed home to check the mail. He pawed through it even before he went to Ava to toss her in the air and hear her delighted screams, "Daddy!" But no reply came and once again his heart hardened.

In October he read of the great general strike uniting Russia for the first time. Everyone went out the same day—railway workers, postal and telegraph employees, factories, businesses, even the smallest of schoolchildren. At first a thoroughly frightened Tsar granted some concessions to his people, but followed them up with punitive demonstrations, then with police-organized pogroms against the Jews, the better to channel the energy of the masses away from him and his.

The word "pogrom" struck terror into Jamie's heart. Seven years later and worlds apart, the word chilled his heart and set his blood to raging. Russia! Damn her vicious heart, her cruel soul! He yearned to tear the Tsar, his family and every member of their ruling class into a thousand pieces! He wanted to wing back to Russia on the back of some avenging angel and destroy every policeman, soldier, Cossack, every vicious son-of-a-bitch who tortured, killed, raped, burned and ravaged.

He looked at Ava and saw his mother—small but brave with the inner strength of hundreds! He thought of his father—big and strong and heroic but diminished by his tormentors, their cruelty and their weapons, their centuries of intimidating rule. And he cried.

He threw his pride to the wind and wrote letter after letter after letter. He sent enough money to bring them all to America—every last aunt and uncle, every last cousin, every baby with a drop of Markoff blood. But he never got an answer to any of the letters. He cried and was angry in turn. Some days he was tormented with guilt, blamed only himself for everything that had happened, believing that it was God's retribution for his having turned his back on his faith. Other days, he cursed them for having turned their backs on him. Sometimes he cursed only the Almighty for having turned His back on them all.

In the end the Revolution of 1905 was called the revolution that failed. Jamie wept some more and didn't know anymore for whom he wept—wretched Russia, his mother and father, or for himself.

He wiped away his tears and turned back to Ava. *Thank God for Ava!* She was the beautiful child of his loins. She was the wondrous child of his blood. More, she was the child of his soul. She was all that was left to him.

When Anne stopped going to church, no one asked her why. No one even wondered whether it was loss of faith, or just a general disinterest. Jamie didn't even take much notice. Her parents barely urged her to keep up her attendance. Even they decided it was unwise to badger her, or even question her too much. Anne was, more or less, withdrawn and that was the way it was. In the end, it was always better not to stir the pot too much.

Karl Hess offered to take little Ava to church with him and his wife on Sunday mornings. "Since you don't go yourself, James, being an agnostic . . ." There was a little smile on his lips, an ironic smile that he had developed of late after a lifetime of hardly smiling at all. "We'd be pleased to perform this little chore."

Little chore, indeed! Jamie thought. "I'm sure you would," he said curtly, refusing his father-in-law's offer. "But I don't think that will be necessary."

As far as he was concerned, it was enough, too much, that the Hesses were so frequently at his house during the week when he himself was at work, seeing more of Ava than he himself did. Karl Hess had just about stopped going to the office since Ava had been born, and he had transferred half of his remaining fifty-percent share to his granddaughter's name. "You don't need me there, Jamie. I know you'll take care of your own fifty percent, and I have no doubt you'll be watching over little Ava's twenty-five, so I'll just hope and trust that you'll take care of my twenty-five too," he had said at the time, with that little smile.

"She should be going to church, you know," he said now.

"She's only a baby . . ."

"She's three and she doesn't act like a baby. She never has. She's like a child of five, six. Never saw a child with a vocabulary like hers. Wouldn't be a bit surprised if she sat down and read a newspaper. She should be going to church," he said again.

Jamie looked at him coldly. "I don't think church attendance is mandatory, not now, anyway."

"But it's fitting, Jamie, fitting . . ." Hess urged in a soft tone, also something new to him. His voice had always been not loud but crisp, authoritative. "You want to raise her to take her rightful position in Society, to be a proper young lady, the most proper."

"Oh, she'll be a proper young lady. More, she'll be even regal. She'll be the most accomplished, the brightest and the best-educated. And she'll be wealthy and beautiful. I'd say that all those qualities will make her very proper. Even now no one can resist her."

Karl Hess shook his head. "It's not enough. Everyone will think it a bit peculiar if she doesn't attend church. Isn't confirmed. They'll speculate about it, whisper . . . You think about it, James. I think you'll come around to my point of view. You'll see what I say makes sense."

Ever since the day Jamie had agreed to stay with Anne for a price and Karl had told Jamie that the best thing to be in America was rich, white and Protestant, they had never discussed religion again. But now both Karl Hess's eyes and little smile were sending Jamie a message. *A reminder? That they shared a mutual secret? Jewish blood?*

Jamie didn't like Karl's smile, his reminder. "I don't see why you're so concerned about *my* daughter. I'd think you'd be more concerned about your own. About Anne's dereliction from *her* churchly devotions."

Karl raised his heavy blond-gray eyebrows. "Anne's not affected by what I say anymore. If anyone were to tell her what to do, it should certainly be you, not me. Anne? It really doesn't make that much difference what Anne chooses to do at this point, does it? Now, Ava . . . Ah, Ava. Ava is the future, isn't she, Jamie? In one way, she's all that's left for both of us. Isn't that so?"

Jamie didn't answer. While he had bested Karl Hess in most confrontations, he wasn't quite sure he had won the whole game. At best, it had been a narrow victory. He had never underestimated Karl Hess's shrewdness. He was an astute man, and what he said could never be completely discounted. He could see that his father-in-law was not far off the mark. A true American princess would have to have a church affiliation, regardless of how devout she might actually be. It was a necessary aspect of the image, a part of the whole.

He was not eager to attend services himself. He had been in church twice—the day he was married and the day Ava had been christened. She had worn a long, lace-trimmed christening dress, white batiste embroidered with white silk. He had been committed to that christening, but he hadn't enjoyed it any more than he had his wedding day.

But if anyone was to take Ava to church, it would be he himself and not his father-in-law.

They went almost every Sunday, beginning that spring. Little Ava always wore a white dress. She loved to wear white and she always insisted in her delightful determined little way on wearing what she herself picked out. She wore little white gloves and a white skimmer on her curls and white patent-leather slippers. As they walked down the center aisle to a front pew everyone looked at them with admiring smiles. What a delightful picture they made! The handsome young father, certainly one of Galveston's foremost leading lights, and that charmer of a daughter.

During the service they frequently played quiet little private games, inter-twining their fingers; swinging their legs in unison—his long leg, her little one; tapping each other in rhythm; exchanging private impish smiles.

Anne told him repeatedly that he was spoiling Ava but he shut his ears to her. He refused to listen to the ravings of a jealous woman. When she accused a child not yet four years old of guile, even cunning, he had to laugh. Either she was mad, or not only jealous of him but of her own child as well. Who could take her seriously? When Anne complained of tantrums that disrupted the whole household, he accused her of distorting the truth. He himself had never seen Ava throw a tantrum, nor even display an outburst of temper. What he saw was courage rare in such a young child, a pluckiness, a willingness to fight for what she wanted. Strong-willed, yes. It was the will of a person, however, with much self-esteem. Ava, he declared proudly, had a lust for life.

Even when Karl Hess, spurred on by rumors about Jamie and other women that he feared would besmirch his son-in-law's sterling reputation and ultimately reflect on his granddaughter, came running to warn him, to berate and beseech him, Jamie didn't have to laugh in his father-in-law's face, tell him to mind his own business, or deny the truth of the gossip; Anne herself refuted the accu-sations. Scathingly, furiously, even piteously, she cried: "Oh no, Jamie Markson has no women on the side! Jamie Markson has no time for other women, no room in his life for them, no place in his heart! He doesn't even have the passion to spare! There's only one woman in my husband's life—his daughter!"

Karl Hess was shocked by his daughter's words and he recoiled from the force of her emotion. He even grew frightened by the possibility of Anne's being "disturbed." He immediately dropped the issue of the gossip and cautioned Jamie, "You'll have to do something about Anne."

"What do you suggest?"

"Perhaps she needs a little rest, a vacation, some time by herself away from the responsibilities of this house, the care of little Ava."

Jamie nodded even though they both knew that Anne bore little responsibility for the running of the household, and none for the care of Ava. What Karl was saying and Jamie was agreeing to, was that maybe Anne needed some time away from her husband, her child.

"Baden-Baden? Her mother would go with her. There are fine hotels there and the baths, of course. Theater, concerts . . . They should have a fine time." Karl tried to sound enthusiastic.

"Why not?"

In less than a week, Anne and her mother left for the German resort. Between the ocean voyage and their stay at the fashionable spa, they'd be gone for two months.

Even with Anne gone, Jamie heeded his father-in-law's words of warning about women. Old Karl had an instinct for such things, and Jamie would be the first to admit that he was still young and inexperienced. The last thing he wanted was to bring discredit on himself, and through himself, on Ava. He owed it to his little princess to keep his own reputation spotless. Accordingly, he ended his affair with Catherine Dubloss, a fragile blonde from New Orleans whom he had hired to run Markson's, the shop he had opened when the Sea Wall Boulevard had been completed. Markson's specialized in French imports—gowns, accessories and perfumes—and catered to Galveston's more affluent ladies as well as to the summer people.

Ending this "affair of the heart," which had nothing at all to do with the heart, entailed no sacrifice on Jamie's part. While it was more serious than most of his dalliances, it caused him no undue pain to give Catherine up. Since he didn't wish to lose her expert services as manager of Markson's he decided to expand the shop, taking advantage of the availability of adjoining space. They would add a line of haberdashery for the discerning male, and Mlle. Dubloss would be manager over all.

When Anne returned from Baden-Baden there was an air about her—a most decided difference between the woman who had left and the one who returned. For one, she brought back several trunks full of all kinds of fancy feathers and boxes of stylish hats trimmed with great plumes. She was more expertly corseted too, with a squeezed-in waist that displayed her bosom to better advantage. She had, James had to admit, a much more seductive look about her, and he wondered. In the past, he had urged her to dress herself at Markson's but she had refused to avail herself of the French fashions their own shop boasted. She said, "We'll leave the peacock feathers to little Ava since I'm the plain Jane in the family." Instead, she'd clung to her "hair shirts"—modest, drab garments from which she must have derived some kind of perverse pleasure.

There was her flaxen hair, now elaborately coiffed in puffs, curls, ringlets and French knots where, before, she had worn only ordinary knots, plain buns, unflattering arrangements of braids. But more than fashionable clothes and fanciful coiffures, Anne's manner was different, especially towards him. She was coolly superior, even self-assured. Her old perpetual half smile had turned into a full-blown one—the smile of the cat that has swallowed the canary.

Jamie didn't have to speculate too long about what had wrought this spectacular change in his wife in so short a time. She couldn't wait to tell him that she had taken a lover in Baden-Baden. At first, he didn't believe her. There was no doubt in his mind that Anne had turned "peculiar." When he realized she was telling the truth, he was more surprised than displeased. Anne—a lover? Incredible!

"You're shocked, aren't you?" she asked, relishing his astonishment. "You can't believe that other men find me attractive. And what do you really know about it? You, with your floozies. You with your fancy-Dan clothes and your acquired Texas drawl. You're a joke. Do you know what you really are?"

For a moment, he expected *that* word, but she only laughed in her newly acquired artificial manner and said, "You're nothing but a callow, country bumpkin who doesn't have the wit or the worldliness to appreciate the attractions of a mature woman. European men are different. They're truly worldly, sophisticated, able to discern the difference between blatantly vulgar sluts and the subtle appeal of an older, cultured woman. Yes, they found me attractive! At the Lichtentaler Allee, there was titled aristocracy from all over Europe. They found me more than attractive, they found me *divine!* My lover, the Duc, said I was the most passion— Suffice it to say, *he* knew how properly to make love to a woman."

Jamie was only surprised that modest, repressed Anne had taken a lover, not that a man chose to be her lover. But he was kind and didn't point out that the so-called titled aristocrats of Europe, so famous for their adroit lovemaking, were also famous for being on the prowl for rich American women, and the older the better. The older they were, the more starved these women were for romance, avaricious for love.

He didn't even ask her how much money she had passed on to her Duc, especially since his father-in-law had insisted on underwriting all expenses for the rest cure. But one thing did pique his curiosity, and he asked Anne what his mother-in-law was doing while Anne's attractions were being so finely appreciated.

"She listened to the band concerts and she drank hot chocolate with mounds and mounds of whipped cream sprinkled with those shavings of delicious German chocolate, the dark kind."

Somehow, it was difficult for Jamie to picture sour, dour, unsmiling Mrs. Hess indulging in such a rich confection.

Anne went about town more than she had before, even learning to drive his new Benz roadster. Occasionally, she would take Ava along with her but not often. But then Ava had so many activities, so many for a little girl. She was already taking dancing lessons and elocution lessons, even French, and didn't have that much time free to go driving about with her mother.

Anne told her husband she'd be going to Europe every year, perhaps even twice a year. It was fortunate that Jamie's business ventures were doing so well that they could easily afford this.

As 1906 drew to a close and Ava was about to celebrate her fourth birthday, Anne was in the south of France enjoying the mild, sun-drenched days of the Mediterranean, and God knew what else. Jamie was glad that his wife was finding and taking pleasure in life, leaving him free to enjoy being Ava's father without her constant harping about how absurd it was for a child Ava's age to be studying dancing and French! What could she possibly know about the extraordinary talents one precious gifted being could possess? What did she know of nurturing?

For Ava's birthday, there was a party on the lawn with entertainment provided by circus performers Jamie had hired, and pony rides. If Ava demanded to be first to ride the pony, that was her right as the birthday girl. And if she demanded a ride for herself for each one her little guests took, that was her privilege too as reigning princess. For Christmas, he bought her a ranch on the outskirts of Houston so that he would have a place to take her riding. He wanted her to grow into the saddle, to know, as he had known in the old country, the pleasure of riding into the wind. Only here in Texas in cow country, there was sagebrush and no snow, more sagebrush than sunflowers.

30.

Certain dates, certain years, stand out in a man's life. For Jamie, 1898 certainly. That was the year he had left home to begin his new life in America. 1899, the year he had met Jennie. 1902 was the year Ava was born. 1905 was the year of the failed revolution in Russia and the year he made his last attempt to get in touch with his family in Slobodka. Milestones in a man's life . . .

1907 was the year Hess and Markson Enterprises became one of the biggest moneymaking companies in Texas, even among the many companies that were growing rich, ever richer, as the state itself expanded on its way to becoming one of the richest states in the nation. Jamie became not merely a wealthy man, but one of the "New Texas Rich," as they were referred to in the newspapers.

As the rest of Texas was only beginning to realize fully what oil, the black gold, would mean to the state's future and to the individual fortune, Jamie discovered "fat," the white gold.

It was early morning on a hot summer day and Jamie was on the way to his office down by the wharves when he rode past the meat-packing house. He had come this way for years without taking particular notice, but this morning the air was ripe with the high stench of the waste piled high and particularly aromatic in the already intense heat of the day as it waited to be hauled away. Looking at it with repugnance, he noticed that separated from the rest of the animal dross, there were barrelfuls of the huge slabs of white fat that had been slashed from the carcasses of the animals the plant processed.

Images filled his head. His mother and aunts rendering fat to cook with, to make soap . . . Old Mrs. Teretsky boiling the tallow to make the Sabbath candles that were her living . . . If anyone had a burn, or was stung by a bee, his mother running to get a dollop of fat to ease the pain, to help the afflicted flesh heal . . . He could even remember being in a peasant home when they used melted fat to rub their bodies for warmth. For the first time it struck him how many uses animal fat could be put to, from cooking to soap to fuel to lubricants. Salves and ointments; all kinds of medicines; glycerins and waxes . . .

He called out for his driver to stop and went in search of the packing-house manager. He discovered they were actually giving the fat away to the garbage collectors for nothing in exchange for its removal, and that they even had to separate the fat from the rest of their debris first. Without ever stopping to calculate his costs, Jamie made them an offer for the fat by the hundredweight and they grabbed at his offer. They thought he was crazy; no one had ever offered to buy the offal.

Before the day was out, Jamie had signed up every packing plant and slaughterhouse in Galveston. The next day he was in Houston and by the end of the following week he had traveled to every major city in Texas cornering the market in white gold.

It was a mystery to him why he hadn't thought of it sooner. After all, he had collected scrap metal only to resell it before he had opened his own smelting plant. And fat was as much salvage as scrap metal. If he could smelt metal, it would be that much easier to melt fat. Then he would sell that commodity to whatever industry needed it for its particular product, but the cooking fat end would be his. He had the land on which to build the processing plant; he had the metal to put the final end product into cans; he'd ship it all over Texas!

By 1908, the year he hired a tutor for Ava so that she could be schooled at home, he was shipping not only to points all over Texas, but to Arkansas, Louisiana and Oklahoma as well. When the causeway was finally completed and the railroad actually came to their doorstep, he would ship it all over the country, as far away as New York.

In 1909, he hired a governess for Ava instead of a nanny because she herself told him in no uncertain terms that she was too old for nannies. By this time Anne was spending more time away from home than ever. She had increased the duration of her vacations, or rest cures, from two months at a time to three months . . . four . . . .

In 1909 he added another department to Markson's on the seawall, a department featuring the finest in children's wear. Markson's was fast gaining a reputation not only for quality, but for the unusual. The store was drawing the discerning customer from an ever-widening area, and Jamie was beginning to think about further expansion. With the proliferation of the automobile and the causeway almost completed, Galveston was going to be more accessible to that many more customers and to more affluent customers as Texas itself grew and expanded. The dream of an extraordinary kind of department store that sold specialities from all corners of the world was fast losing its dreamlike quality and becoming very real.

Then it was 1910 and the causeway was finally completed. There was a great celebration in Galveston as the first train came chugging into town. Those on the committee for the festivities thought it only fitting to crack a bottle of the finest Champagne across the locomotive in the same manner ships were launched from the harbor. Since the City wished to honor James Markson for his part in bringing the causeway to fruition, the person chosen to christen the train was Jamie's Ava—Ava in a lovely white dress she had personally chosen from Markson's French imports. Jamie was only concerned that Ava's thin young arm wouldn't be equal to the chore since he'd been present when grown women had had difficulty breaking the Champagne bottle against the hull of an ocean-going steamer; little Ava wouldn't be eight years old until the end of the year.

But Jamie was wrong about the capabilities of his daughter; he hadn't reckoned with Ava's strength of will.

That same year, soon after the celebration for the completion of the causeway, Jamie received a letter, a letter that was to shock him to his very core. It was from his cousin Dorie, written in English and postmarked Palestine!

For a second his heart stopped. Then he picked up the letter, went into his study and locked the door. He sat down at the desk so that he could hold on to something as he read:

My dearest brother Yitzhak,

Do you mind that I address you as brother? We were raised as brother and sister, after all. Your mother and father are the only parents I have ever known. Oh, Yitzhak, it's been so long and I have so much to tell you, I don't even know where to begin. The world that we knew as children is gone, fallen apart. And oh, how we struggle to put it back together again even as we know it will never be the same for any of us again.

I suppose, dear Yitzhak, I should start with how I found you. But before I do, I must warn you. Brace yourself, for there will be things in this letter that will shock you, tear you apart. Please be forewarned.

As you can see from the address I have written out for you on a separate slip of paper, I live in Tel Aviv and I'm still a Markoff! Yes, I married Aunt Hannah's and Uncle Abraham's Joshua. Remember how you used to tease me about Joshua? I myself can remember as if it were only yesterday and not a lifetime ago. But I mustn't digress. It's only fair that I tell you the things that I must tell you as quickly as I can. I hope there will be other letters between us when we can write each other about things less urgent, less earthshaking. Maybe there will even be visits someday when we will take our leisure and talk only of pleasant things.

How it came to be that we're in Palestine, I'll get to soon. After I've explained how I found out where you are living and under what name, Mr. James Markson. How formal that sounds, dear Yitzhak! I hope you'll forgive me saying that I find the name strange on my tongue when I say it to myself. I'm afraid you'll always be Yitzhak Markoff to me, my beloved cousin, my brother.

But I must begin. About eight months ago, I met a woman, a very lovely woman near my own age. Her name was Markoff—Mrs. Jennie Markoff. Well, this is a strange land here and there are not so many Jews here yet that if you meet someone with the same family name, you don't get excited! And this Jennie Markoff talks so nicely. Naturally, the first thing I asked her was the name of her husband. When she said Yitzhak, you can imagine! I could have dropped dead right then and there! I was convinced already that it was you! And I couldn't believe that after losing track of you for all these years, you were in Palestine right under our nose! I begged her to take me to you that very minute so that what I knew in my heart would be confirmed—that her Yitzhak and our Yitzhak were one and the same!

But then she breaks into tears. She says she's a widow, then tries to convince me that, most likely, her late husband and my cousin are two entirely different Yitzhak Markoffs. But I'm crying myself. To find you one minute then lose you the next? I press her for details so that I can truly determine where the truth lies. I must find out if you are truly dead or if it was some other unfortunate Yitzhak Markoff. I ask her what her husband looked like, where he comes from, but she's evasive. She says this is too painful for her to discuss and before I know it, she's gone.

I was heartbroken. I didn't know what to think. I *wanted* to believe that it wasn't you who was her dead husband. I *wanted* to believe that you were still alive so that one day we'd find you.

But a week later, this Jennie searches me out. Here, you see, it's a small world. It's not difficult to find a person if you know whom you're looking for. The moment I open my door to her, I know she's come to tell me that my Yitzhak and hers are one and the same and I'm ready to pray for your soul . . . But no! She tells me first *yes*, that you both *are* the same person but I don't have to mourn just yet, that you are *not* dead. She tells me that she's not a widow at all, that the two of you never married.

Well, Yitzhak, as you well know yourself, it's quite a story she told me— answering some questions, but posing new ones. But before I go on, I have to tell you one thing. The reason this lovely Jennie was posing as your widow is because she's a mother! The mother of your daughter! She told me that you never knew about the child.

But don't doubt for a moment, Yitzhak, that this is your child. We've all seen her and once having seen her, no one could doubt. She's ten years old, with the blue eyes and the exact shade of yellow hair of the Markoffs. She has the Markoff nose, the Markoff chin with the cleft. And Sabra is her name. In case you don't know, Sabra is a cactus that grows in the desert, tough and prickly on the outside, soft within. It is a name that people like to give to a child who is born here, in the desert land of Israel, a true Israelite. And Yitzhak, you should only live and be well and see her! She'll gladden your heart forever. She's tall and straight as an arrow and dark from the sun. She is a beauty *and* a nice girl. The nicest. She's very mature, since living here does that to a child. It's serious business and Sabra's a serious girl. She's only ten and already dedicated to the future of this land. Of course she grew up on a kibbutz, since that's where Jennie went when she came here. Everyone has a job on a kibbutz and Jennie was a teacher. Life on these communes is especially hard and the smallest child is dedicated to turning the desert into a paradise. But that's another story.

Why was your Jennie posing as your widow? Not merely to hide her shame at being an unwed mother. It was for Sabra's sake. Here a bastard— forgive me for using that word—is supposedly estranged from the rest of the community. It's forbidden for a religious person ever to marry her. Sabra would have been an outcast, a pariah.

Before I go on with my story, I must tell you that having met your Jennie and your Sabra, all of us Markoffs here will never let them go. No matter what else happens, know that! We love them and they are ours, as much as if you yourself were here and with them! One more thing before I forget. Jennie's father passed on not long after Jennie arrived here. It's so sad to think that he came between you two and then, poof! He goes to his Maker and you and your daughter are across the world from each other and the child grows up without a father. To some things, there are no answers.

Well, after hearing Jennie's story, we were able to piece together the rest of it and were able to trace you. Jennie told us you were living as Wilhelm von Marx and working for the railroad in St. Paul, Minnesota. I wrote to the railroad and they informed me that you had left, leaving them a forwarding address of General Delivery, Galveston, Texas, in care of James Markson. Two and two make four—sometimes even five, if you get my meaning.

When we wrote to the Post Office in Galveston they were nice enough to inform us that no one in Galveston City didn't know who James Markson was and your address was certainly no secret.

So that's how you came to get this letter. And now I must tell you more—the most painful part of this long letter. From what Jennie told us we understood that once you had left Slobodka you had no more idea of what happened there than would a newborn babe. Jennie told us, you see, that you wrote your letter to both your mother *and* your father, so it's clear you had no idea what happened to father. The day after you left they executed him in the marketplace without even a trial! Not that a trial would have helped.

They were under the impression that it was he, father, who, wearing that Cossack uniform, killed the Governor-General. Everyone begged mother to say that it was *you*, since, of course, you were gone and they couldn't touch you. But mother was like a stone. She kept saying that it didn't matter *who* killed him. Someone had to pay. That if they didn't take someone, the whole town would burn—twenty, thirty Jews would die . . .

She never even told anyone it was you who had done the killing. No one ever knew it until Jennie said that you had told her about it, had told her yourself. Up until then, nobody knew except for mother herself and *me*.

That day, you see, mother had sent Asher and me to the schoolroom to go through all the books. I guess that she just wanted to get us out of the way, that she had a forewarning that morning of what kind of day it was going to be. It was a very hot day, if you can remember, and I was tired of going through those books. I told Asher that we should both leave and finish up the next day, but he wouldn't. So I left him there and went home. I guess I came back earlier than mother would have wanted me to. I saw them in the fields, just the two of them standing there with the sunflowers on all sides, all around them. But I thought they were fighting at first and so I hid. I saw

mother pounding him with her fist, heard her screaming, "No, David! No! I
can't let you! I won't let you! I won't! I won't! I can't! Oh, David, don't ask
this of me! I beg you! I can't let you go!"

She was hysterical and he kept trying to console her, to kiss her. He kept
saying, "But I must, Eve, and you must let me! Would you have me send
my son to his death? Would you really want me to let them kill twenty
innocent men? Oh, Eve, you always called me your hero, your man of
destiny. Would you deny me the right to be those things now?"

But mother kept crying. "I don't want you to be anything but alive! I
need you! I can't give you up . . . I want you to live!"

But he shook his head and said the most telling words I've ever heard. I
will never forget them, Yitzhak! He said to her that it was important how a
man lived, but sometimes it was even more important how he died.

Then I saw them go to the stable and a few minutes later I saw the three
of you come out and you got on your horse and rode away. The two of them
stood there, with their arms around each other, watching you disappear down
the road, and waving . . .

Still I hid. I knew they had to be alone. Together. After you were out of
sight they crossed the road, hand in hand, and they just walked through the
flowers together, stopping to embrace, to kiss, until *they* came and took him
away. I will never forget it. I wish I could. She clung to him and they tore
him away from her. She cried and he threw her a kiss. "Be brave!" he kept
saying over and over, and smiling at her. He kept smiling for her.

I never told anyone. I didn't think it was my right. I tell you now,
Yitzhak, because I think it's *your* right to know what kind of person your
father was. And your mother. Because she went to the execution the next
day. Everyone begged her not to, but she said she had to. She had to say
goodbye. The others, none of the family, could bear to go but I couldn't let
her go alone. So I went with her.

They wanted the execution to be a lesson to everyone, but there was only
a handful of people in the marketplace. Not even the peasants would come.
Even they couldn't bear to watch a good man die. They knew what David
and Eve Markoff had done for them through the years, and this was one day
at least when they were remembering it all.

Mother didn't cry. She kept smiling at him. He refused a blindfold and he
kept smiling at her. Until he fell. Then mother screamed just once and began
to chant, "*Loheyn baal horahamin . . .*" But she never finished the
mourner's prayer that day. She fell to the ground just as if they had shot her
through the heart too.

I've thought about that day for years now. I can't forget it. All these years
I keep seeing that picture in my mind. How neither one of them cried, how
they kept their eyes on each other and smiled! It was as if they were making
a vow to each other, more sacred even than their wedding vows. A silent vow

that there would come a time and a place when they would be together again, when they would love again.

Even now, years later, I cannot think about it, or write about it as I am doing this minute, without shedding my own tears.

Mother was in bed for two weeks without speaking or eating. When we were despairing that she would never recover, she got up one day and told us that we could stop worrying about her, that she was going on. She had no choice. She was going to have a baby! Oh, Yitzhak, the ironies of fate! For years, ever since you yourself were born, she'd been trying to have another child and now with father gone—a child!

To the rest of us it seemed like a *cruel* twist of fate, but mother didn't see it that way. She was convinced that the life inside her had been conceived out of her and father's great love but also out of some heavenly intervention. She felt that the Almighty, knowing beforehand that He had to take David from her, had sent this child in his place. She said that she *knew* it would be a boy and that his name would be David.

She was determined from the start that baby David would be born in America. She said that she planned on leaving as soon as she heard from you, so that she could go to you. She said that the three of you, baby David, herself and you, would be an American family and in that way father would live on—in America, as they had always dreamed.

She asked us all to go with her—all of us—the cousins, the uncles and the aunts. But Aunt Hannah cried and begged mother to understand that her own dream had never been to go to America but to Palestine. She said she had a burning to live among other Jews in a land of their own, and if it wasn't yet their own land, it was something to work toward. I think mother was heartbroken about this, but she told Aunt Hannah that of course she understood. Everyone had to follow his or her dream.

Once Aunt Hannah said that, Aunt Miriam said she would go wherever it was Aunt Hannah and Uncle Abraham went. That she was too old a dog to be separated from Aunt Hannah. Then all the cousins said that they wanted to go to Palestine too, even Aunt Miriam's daughters and their husbands. I was torn. Joshua, who had finally told me he loved me, had always been dedicated to the idea of Palestine. Would I go with him or would I go with the woman who had raised me and loved me as her own?

I told Joshua that I had loved him for years but I had no choice. I would never let my mother go to America alone. And who knew if they, all of them, would ever go to Palestine? Everybody had been talking about leaving Slobodka for years and nobody had done so except for my real father, Yacob, whom I had never heard from, whom I had never known, and you, of course. But I knew that this time mother was really going to America. She would not be deterred, and my duty was with her.

But who was I dealing with? Eve Markoff! She looked into my eyes and it was as if she was looking into my heart and she told me that my place was with the man I loved, whether it was in Slobodka or Palestine or wherever, and she would hear of nothing else.

So there we were, with mother planning on leaving as soon as she received your letter, and the rest of us *talking* about going to Palestine some time in the near future, when there was a proclamation from Moscow. One additional and final punitive action. The Jews had to get out of Slobodka! Every last one of us! Moscow said Slobodka was a hotbed of revolutionaries and we were given two weeks to leave! Two weeks, after a lifetime . . .

The first thing mother insisted on was that Joshua and I get married immediately. She said that one thing even the Tsar wasn't going to cheat her of was seeing her daughter stand under the *chupah*. This made us all laugh a little at a time when all our hearts were breaking. Of course mother cried at the wedding, insisting they were tears of joy. There were a lot of ghosts at that wedding. Aunt Hannah and Aunt Miriam cried too. I don't know if they cried for themselves or for our father David, or for my real mama lying there in the cold Russian earth. I myself cried but I knew why. It was hard to think of not seeing mother again for what was bound to be years.

It was on my wedding day that Uncle Hershel spoke up for the first time. None of us knew what he had been planning, going to America or coming with the rest of us to Palestine. Well, we soon found out. He planned on going to America, taking his son Asher with him. (Gershon would stay in Germany to finish his medical studies, and Daniel would remain in Moscow until he was through with his studying to be a lawyer.) But he planned on going to America as mother's husband!

He proposed right in front of us all as we held a little wedding celebration just among the family. Everyone was a little shocked at the proposal coming so soon after father's death, but those were extraordinary times after all. No one wanted to see mother going off alone. So everyone was kind of hoping she would say yes. At the same time, I doubted very much that she would. She didn't love him, not in that way, certainly not in the way she had loved our father. I didn't think then and I don't think now that she could ever love again in that special way. But Uncle Hershel was quite eloquent. He told mother that it was the duty of the deceased's brother to marry and take care of his widow and children. And it was her duty, therefore, to accept. He also said he loved her. That he had, ever since Aunt Ruth had died. He said his sons looked upon her as another mother and she had a responsibility to them because of that. Not to mention that David's unborn child needed a father.

Mother tried to be kind in turning him down. She told him that she couldn't think of remarrying. Not at that time, certainly. But no matter how nicely she tried to put it, Uncle Hershel was furious to have been refused. He said that if that was her last word on the subject, then he wasn't going to go to America at all! He'd go to Palestine, too. At least there, he'd be with his remaining brothers.

Then we had only one week left and still there was no letter from you.

Mother was distraught. She had already written to my father Yacob's brother-in-law, my mother Dora's brother—the one person you were supposed to have contacted on your arrival in New York, and he wrote us that he had never heard from you. She said she couldn't leave Russia without getting a letter from you. How could she leave without knowing where you were or where she could find you? She needed some more time to wait for your letter, which was bound to come soon. There was only one person she could turn to in her dilemma, Dr. Golov. (Her old friend, the Squire, was too sick to bother with her problems any longer.) As for Dr. Golov, that's another story. I myself was always convinced that he was in love with mother. I once said something like that to her and she laughed, said I was a foolish, romantic girl, like all young girls should be, just a little . . . But Dr. Golov came down from Vilno to take her back with him. He would take care of her and harbor her until your letter came. Since he was an influential man, he could arrange for the letter to be forwarded to Vilno once it arrived in Slobodka.

The day mother left with Dr. Golov was the day we all left Slobodka. The saddest day of my life. The saddest day, maybe, of all our lives, when we should all have been happy to leave that godforsaken place. We should have sung and we should have laughed. We should have danced in the streets. But we didn't. We were all leaving too much of us behind. Mother Eve was leaving her youth and her dreams and her great love. Me? My poor dead mother whom I had never known, the mother Mother Russia had taken from me. And Aunt Hannah and Uncle Abraham, how they cried for their Golda whom they were leaving behind in the ground. Even Uncle Hershel, as he kissed mother goodbye, unable to stay angry with her, wept. "Ruth in heaven will never forgive me for not going to America with you." But mother hugged him. She told him, "It doesn't matter *where* you go, Hershel. It only matters *who* you are when you get there. Ruth knew that."

The worst part for all of us, I think, was when mother rode off in Ivan Golov's carriage. Would we ever see her again? We assured ourselves that we would! It was the only thing that kept us from running after her, from snatching her from that carriage and keeping her with us by force. The truth was, of course, that while she was a Markoff woman, she wasn't related by blood to any one of us. Still, she was part of each of us in a way that no one else could ever be. She had been our mainstay and our strength. She had been the light of our life.

Finally, the carriage was out of sight and Aunt Hannah cried out, "God help me! I hope that I made the right choice. I've chosen the land of Israel over our little Evele . . ."

What happened there in Vilno is anybody's guess. I never asked mother and she never said. Some things you don't ask another, not even your mother. My guess is the good doctor asked her to marry him and, of course, she didn't. She had a mission and nothing could have deterred her. She was going to get David Markoff's baby born in America and since your letter didn't come in the next few weeks, she was determined to search for you. (Of course, now we know your letter couldn't have come since you still hadn't written it at the time.)

I don't have to tell *you* she never found you. How could she? We know now, from Jennie, that eventually you did write, but by then we were all long gone. And who knows what happened to your letter? Maybe even now it's lying under some snowbank in Siberia.

There's only one more thing you have to know. We haven't told your mother any of this. Under the circumstances, we didn't think it was our place. Only you can do this. Only you can decide. I will say only this—that, yes, it will probably break her heart to hear how you have been living. How, under the circumstances, could it not? On the other hand, I can't think of anyone with a more forgiving heart than our mother. And think what a joy it will be for her to discover her long-lost son *is* alive! That should make up for a lot.

So, I am enclosing her name and address. Her *married* name. Yes, she married again in America. And I *could* possibly tell you how and why, but I won't. You see, before she married Jacob Frank—perhaps you've heard of him since I understand that he's a very big and well-known financier and philanthropist in America—she wrote me a letter telling me all about it, how she felt about our father David, and how she felt about Jacob Frank. She said that as David Markoff's daughter, she wanted me to understand everything. But Yitzhak, that letter was from my mother to *me*. Straight from her heart to mine. A very private affair, so I can't share it with you. If you want to know the whys and the hows, you'll have to ask her yourself—if and when you choose to make yourself known to her.

I can tell you, of course, that she married him in 1902, that they met while she was working in the settlement houses of the Lower East Side in New York, which she still does. As a matter of fact, she is so dedicated to the plight of the American-Jewish immigrant, she's known as the Angel of the Ghetto. So you can see that no matter what her married name is, she's still the same Eva Markoff! Thank God! In a life where so much has changed, she, at least, has stayed constant.

One more thing. There's another child. Your half-brother, Elliot Frank! He was born in New York City in 1903 and he's named for mother's father, Elijah. At first she was going to call him Elijah but her husband talked her into Elliot. He said that an American boy should have an American name. Finally, she agreed. She was forty when she had little Elliot. She wrote me at the time that the Americans had an expression, "Life begins at forty." She changed that a little. She says life is *renewed* at forty.

I have also enclosed Jennie's address. I haven't told her either that we've located you. Whether you choose to get in touch with her and your daughter will have to be your decision.

I won't go into any news now about the rest of the family, about who is married to whom, and who has what children. I know your head is already spinning and your heart—your heart must be breaking a little bit. I'm sorry to write you of things that must hurt terribly, but I have also written you things that I hope gladden your heart.

No matter what you decide to do, Yitzhak, I love you, and I would love to hear from you. Please, please write!

For the most part, we are all well. True, life is hard here in Palestine. Very hard! But it is also good. We believe, as your very own Sabra does, in the dream of a state of Israel.

My love always,
Your sister Dorie

There were three separate slips of paper with addresses—Dorie's own, Jennie's, and Eve Markoff Frank's. He clutched them in his clenched fist, put his head down on the desk and wept. He didn't even know for whom. His dead hero of a father? His mother, who had lost a great man to the executioner's bullet? For Jennie, his lost love, who had borne his child alone and raised her alone? Or for his love child, Sabra, who had grown up strong and good without him? And then there was David, his brother who had been cheated of his birthright—his father . . .

Or was it only for himself that he cried? He who had given up his birthright and in doing so, had lost everyone and everything in the world that meant anything to him save for one lone soul—Ava.

31.

For days Jamie's mood alternated between elation and despair. Some days he felt completely alienated from the world around him. He was glad that Anne was away in Europe. While she wouldn't have questioned him, she would have looked at him with speculative eyes and that would have infuriated him. For a few days he didn't even talk to Ava. He was disoriented and stayed in bed without eating. He neglected his business. Sometimes he'd get up in the middle of the night and go into his library, unlock the desk drawer and take out Dorie's letter, and read it over again and again until every word was not only imprinted on his brain but etched into his heart.

Sometimes he'd feel rage against Dorie. How dare she call his mother her mother? How dare she call him brother? She was only a cousin—one of many. She wasn't even his mother's niece by blood. Then he'd be flooded with shame, thinking he wasn't even fit to wipe Dorie's shoes. She was the one who had remained true to everything they had learned in their parents' house; it was she who had remained the devoted loving child and he himself was the faithless one.

He dreamed and he had nightmares. In the good dream his mother cooled his fevered brow with sweet lips, murmured that she loved him, told him how brave and strong he was. In the nightmare he saw his father fall, felled from the executioner's bullet, saw his mother rushing to the bleeding, lifeless body, heard her shouting at him: "You Absalom, you've killed your father! You're unfit to live among decent, God-fearing Jews! I condemn you to be an outcast for the rest of your days on earth!"

The bad dreams outnumbered the good. His little brother, David, wearing his father's face, called him Cain. His half-brother Elliot, faceless, sucked at his mother's breast, lifting his head only to look at Jamie and cry out, "She's my mother, not yours! You don't deserve her!"

In a good dream, Sabra, tall and strong as Dorie described her, hugged him to her breast, calling him, "Father!" Then the good dream turned into a bad one and Jennie, as lovely and young as he had seen her last, dragged Sabra away from him, crying out: "He's not your father; he's a heretic!"

Some nights he sat in his leather chair hating his mother for marrying Jacob Frank, denouncing her in his tormented brain for having been so unfaithful to the memory of his dead father so quickly. Just as Dorie had suggested, he had heard of Mr. Jacob Frank. As a prominent business man himself, he could not

345

help being familiar with Frank's name. Frank was one of those bankers who had his fat fingers in every industry across the country, who financed railroads and oil exploration, who underwrote the largest companies, who lent money even to the treasuries of nations. In despair, Jamie wondered how his mother could have married such a man, one whose life could be measured in dollar bills instead of good deeds—she, who had been married to a man of ideals, a heroic figure who had dreamed of freeing other men from oppression. Then he was forced to remind himself of how that heroic figure had died and who had to bear the ultimate responsibility for that death, and then he cursed himself as he wept.

Some days he even dreamed with his eyes wide open. He pictured himself running up to his mother on Fifth Avenue in New York City where she lived. Screaming with joy, she dropped her purse and the packages she was carrying the better to hug him to her. Oh, she looked every bit as beautiful as the last time he had seen her. The twelve years that had elapsed since that time seemed as if they had never been. Not a word of recrimination passed her lips. There was only her delight in being reconciled with him. She took him home, introduced him to his two brothers. They were equally delighted to see him, looked up at him with admiring, loving eyes. Even Jacob Frank was pleased to meet him, to shake his hand, said, "I know your financial record, Jamie, my boy. You've done a splendid job, my son, in so short a time. Remarkable!"

Of course they talked, his mother and he. He explained *everything* to her— how and why his life had taken the direction it had. But she brushed everything away, his explanations, his apologies, his tears of self-recrimination. She said she understood everything perfectly. The only thing that mattered, she insisted, was that he was alive and well, had prospered in America, had learned to speak English so well, had educated himself.

In the daydream he told her about Ava and then she demanded to see her at once and he produced his beautiful daughter, so bright and so clever, the miniature of Eve herself. He explained to his mother that Ava's maternal grandfather was half-Jewish by blood, making Ava one-eighth Jewish on her mother's side, which made her more Jewish than not. His mother said, "It doesn't matter how much Jewish blood she has, Yitzhak! You should know that. It only matters what kind of a girl she is, what kind of heart she has." It was the kind of thing his mother always said. She hadn't changed at all. She wore satin and furs and beautiful jewels and lived in a fine house, finer even than his own, but she was still the woman she had always been. She was still Eva Markoff!

She talked to Ava and said, "Oh, Yitzhak, she's wonderful! She's lovely!" She said she was proud to have Ava as a granddaughter. "She makes everything you've done worthwhile!" Those were the words he had been waiting to hear and he wept again, this time with joy.

Then he explained to her about Anne, told her about Jennie and Sabra. Again his mother didn't blame him for anything. Rather, she raged against the intolerance of Jennie's religious fanatic of a father, denounced Karl Hess for his

346

deceitful trickery, placing his daughter's resulting unhappiness squarely on her father's shoulders, rather than on her husband's.

Then Eve thought about the situation for a while and came up with a plan (Eve could always come up with a plan of action) to reunite him with Jennie. To unite the four of them—Ava and him, Jennie and Sabra Eve even knew what to do about Anne. Eve was not only forgiving, she was also remarkably resourceful. She convinced Anne that she'd be happier herself if she divorced Jamie. She told Anne that a marriage conceived in a lie was doomed from the start, that a loveless marriage was a sin against God and that once freed from this marriage, Anne herself would find true love, true happiness. She told Anne that it wasn't too late for her to begin again. As long as there was life there was hope. His mother explained everything in a fair, just manner that was full of compassion and love. It was Eve's way.

But sometimes even the reverie turned into a nightmare. In the daydream-turned-nightmare, his mother said to him sadly, "Oh, Yitzhak, you've strayed *too* far. You've betrayed everything your father and I stood for . . ." Sadly but with conviction, leaving absolutely no room for doubt, she proclaimed, "Yitzhak, you're beyond redemption!"

In this same nightmare, his brother David cried out: "You've killed my father!" His brother Elliot pointed a finger, "You've broken my mother's heart!" His mother's husband intoned, "You're a disgrace to our people. Why couldn't you have been more like *me* so that your mother could have been proud of you? I've made millions but I've kept my faith! All New York, the whole country, Jew and gentile alike, look up to me, respect me. Your mother is known for her dedication to the poor and the sick, the underprivileged and the undereducated. And you! You're an embarrassment to us all!"

Then Sabra, proud and unsmiling, appeared, declaimed sternly, "You're no father to me! You turned your back on us. Now we must do the same to you." Jennie came to stand by Sabra's side, said wistfully, "If only you had been a righteous man, it would have all worked out . . ."

In a cold sweat he'd shake himself awake even though he hadn't been sleeping. Then he'd go find Ava, to hug and kiss her. He'd take her to the beach to run in the sand with her, away from everything. They'd run into the clear sea where everything washed by the waves eventually became clean and pure. They'd go to the ranch to ride under the big sky where everything was open, on the flat plains where nothing was hidden. They went for automobile rides across the causeway and down the scenic boulevard of the seawall so Ava could say proudly, "My daddy helped build this . . ."

Or he'd take Ava on an instructive tour of the junkyard, the glass plant, the smeltery, the fat-processing plant, the cannery, so that she could be proud of all his achievements, but she wrinkled up her little nose in all those places, complained that they didn't smell pretty. Usually, they'd end up in Markson's which *did* smell pretty, its air infused with French perfume, where Ava would

347

try on every bit of finery that caught her eye. She'd dress up like a princess for her father, or sometimes she'd put on something entirely incongruous to make him laugh. And he'd tell himself that his life was good, that Ava was worth everything, and at times he even believed it.

He had both good days and bad days, but more bad than good, until he faced that which he already knew, that there'd be no rest for him until he saw his mother. There was a burning in him that wouldn't be quenched until he saw her again.

He packed a suitcase, and ordered his Pullman car hooked up to the next train heading east. Briefly, he considered taking Ava with him, speculating that his mother would never be able to resist her. At the very least he'd be able to show his mother his one supreme accomplishment, but then dismissed the idea as premature. There'd be time enough for that later—if everything went well, and after his mother had recovered from the initial shock of seeing him . . . *after* she had heard him out and still accepted him as her son.

He also contemplated shucking the three-piece Western-style business suit he usually wore and putting aside his Stetson. He even thought of growing as much of a beard as he could in the time it would take to get to New York. But he abandoned that idea as well. If he did that, he'd only be compounding all the other lies of his life. Honesty demanded that he present himself to his mother as he was now. Then, in a burst of what he considered total honesty, he decided not only to wear the Western suit, a white one at that, but also his highest-crowned white Stetson and his most lavishly tooled cowboy boots, and even to shave off his blond mustache. It was almost as if he was out to test her power of forgiveness. Or was he only rubbing salt in his own wounds?

The days passed quickly, too quickly. Before he knew it he'd be in New York and facing her. As he stared out the train window at the country passing before him in panoramic splendor, he saw nothing. Rather he practiced and rehearsed over and over again in his mind what he'd say to her and imagined what she'd say to him. He was fairly certain how the first few minutes would go, before the questions commenced and the explanations followed. At first she'd scream with joy, cry and laugh and kiss him, again and again until finally, the truth was revealed. All of it.

He considered all the possibilities. He could reveal only that he was there, alive, but hide the rest—the name he lived under, the life he led, the church he attended every Sunday. He could reveal the whole truth to her at some later date or he could unravel it to her gradually, piece by piece. How would that go? he wondered.

He decided then that a gradual plan of revelation wouldn't work. The first question his mother and her husband would ask would be: *Where are you living?* And he'd have to say, Texas. His stepfather would then ask where in Texas; a natural enough question, and he'd have no choice but to answer: Galveston. Then his stepfather would have him checked out. No doubt about it. He was a big banker, one of the biggest. Bankers always checked people out. Then the cat would be out of the bag. The whole story would come out and he'd appear to be even more of a charlatan than he already was by the mere act of trying to hide what he was. A man, a real man, faced up to and admitted everything, once he *was* admitting.

Jamie drank bottle after bottle of bourbon, usually waving away the specially prepared meals the white-jacketed porter brought him. His thoughts whirled and he conjectured. Maybe Jacob Frank had already tried to track him down. It made sense. A very wealthy, powerful man meets a beautiful woman who's everything he ever dreamed of—beautiful, intelligent, very definitely the lady his position in life demands. He falls in love with her, wants to marry her, wants to make her happy. *How can he make her happy?* What can he offer her other than jewels and furs, trappings that have scant meaning for a woman of Eve's character? She is forlorn because she hasn't found her son who came to America before her. He decides the thing that he *can* do to make her happy, delirious with gratitude, is to locate her son . . .

But how far would he get? Dorie, who *had* found him, had had a place to start, but Jacob Frank had advantages Dorie didn't have—unlimited financial resources, influence. He could have hired some agency, Pinkerton's perhaps. They could have found out that he landed at Staten Island. Then stoking the right memories with bills of the right denomination, they might have learned that Yitzhak Markoff left Staten Island as Wilhelm von Marx, even if there weren't records to attest to this. But it wasn't likely they had traced him to Milwaukee, most unlikely. Anyhow, they hadn't found him in Galveston. Unless they *had* . . . and then Jacob Frank had decided *not* to tell his wife the truth since she was better off without her oldest son and he didn't want her heart broken by James Markson's defection. Then again, maybe Jacob Frank had never wanted him found in the first place because he was jealous of her prior life, her prior husband and child. As for little David, Frank was probably raising him as his own son, trying to cast him in his, Frank's, own mold . . .

By the time Jamie reached New York, he was torn apart by his conjectures, his own fabricated images. He couldn't even make up his mind which hotel he would stop at, the Plaza or the Waldorf-Astoria. Finally, he decided on the Waldorf. He pulled himself together; he would be decisive, and if necessary, hard. He would face the situation squarely. First, he'd see his mother and brothers, and then he'd be damned if he wouldn't go find Jennie and Sabra, too. He would—as they were fond of saying in Texas—tough it out.

When the cab pulled up in front of 661 Fifth Avenue, Jamie experienced a shock. He had, of course, presumed that the Jacob Franks lived well, but he had not expected that they lived *this* well. To begin with, the property was one block square, marked off by a high iron fence with a tiny but exquisite park encircled by a driveway which led to a magnificent porte cochere that fronted the main entrance to what could only be described as a palace.

It was difficult for him to think of the woman he remembered, Mrs. David

Markoff, living in this house as Mrs. Jacob Frank. Nearly impossible to believe she could be the same woman. Well, the answer to that had to be that she *wasn't* the same woman. In Galveston, the community of German-Jews disdained such opulence. They lived quietly and kept apart, unwilling to call attention to themselves. Obviously, the Franks didn't mind a public display of affluence. The reason for that had to be that they were pretty much assimilated. He had heard that about the rich German-Jews of New York, that they were Jews in name only. And that's what had happened to his mother—she had assimilated almost as completely as he himself! She had always dreamed of being a real American and now she was. An American and a Jew in name only.

For a moment, he felt reassured. Now, she wouldn't even be heartbroken to hear his story. She'd easily understand.

But then, another thought occurred to him. Was it possible that the people who lived in this house, Mr. and Mrs. Frank, didn't have to hide, not because they were well assimilated, but because they were honestly proud of their place in America and of who they were?

A sense of melancholy pervaded his being. However, how long could he stand here gaping through the fence? There was a bell. He must ring it. Then a servant would come and he'd have to announce himself. And what was he going to say? That he was Yitzhak Markoff who had come to see his mother? Or that he was James Markson of Galveston, Texas, and he demanded to speak with Mrs. Frank? It was a preposterous situation; he should have telephoned first. Now, he didn't know whom he was going to find—the woman he loved who had cared about everything and everyone, Eve Markoff, or an elegant, cool, even haughty Mrs. Frank? He was terrified of the confrontation. It was his mother who had said, "Always remember who you are and from whom you come." If Mrs. Frank wasn't Eve Markoff, who would she be?

He rang the bell and in a few moments a gatekeeper answered the summons, politely inquired what it was the gentleman wanted.

"Mrs. Frank."

"She's not in. May I take your card?"

"When will she be back?"

"Late this afternoon, sir. Your card?"

"I'll be back . . ."

He was relieved on one hand, and disappointed enough to almost cry on the other.

As he started to turn away he saw a young man emerge from the house followed by two boys, running and jostling one another playfully. The young man sought to restrain them. "Come on boys, we'll play some ball," he said, leading them to the garden area of the courtyard.

His brothers, David and Elliot! David, the older of the two and much taller, was impossible to mistake. The Markoff physique, the yellow hair underneath a small skullcap. *A skullcap!* The other boy, smaller, with dark curls, wore one too. Jamie wanted to scoop them both up in his arms and listen to them squeal as young boys did. He had an urge to yell to the gatekeeper, "Hey, let me in! They're my brothers!"

But the gatekeeper was already looking at him curiously, his hand reaching for another bell inside the gate. Obviously, he was getting ready to summon someone else. Calling for help?

Jamie laughed with a tinge of bitterness, walked away quickly. They weren't really his brothers, anyway. They were strangers. Two small strangers in yarmulkes . . . It seemed his mother had remembered from whom she came, after all.

He kept walking, not knowing even where he was headed. He had done everything badly. He should have told the gatekeeper who he was and asked to wait until Mrs. Frank came home. Had he done that, he would have seen her within a short time. Now more than ever, he had to see her. He had to know exactly who Eve Markoff Frank was.

Then, he had an idea. He knew how to find out who his mother was!

When he left the newspaper offices he was the possessor of an envelope brimming with clippings—a documented record of the activities of the prominent Jacob Franks. He headed back to the sanctuary of his hotel to pore over them.

He discarded those clippings dealing with his stepfather's financial affairs, or hyperbolic descriptions of social occasions—balls, dinners and teas; those had nothing to do with the *real* Eve Markoff. The clippings that remained confirmed her as he remembered her, as she was etched into his heart.

There was the Frank Education Center which was many things rolled into one—settlement house, library, night school, art school, gymnasium, community center, public forum. It was called the Frank Education Center but it was all Eve Markoff. There was the Eve Frank Yeshiva on Division Street. *Eve Frank? No, Eve Markoff!* There was a medical clinic, a nursing school, a milk program, an Eve Markoff Frank summer camp for the children of poor immigrant workers who only knew the tenement and the city streets. There was even an organization for the girls and women who worked in the sweatshops of the Lower East Side. It was called the Alliance of Women Workers, but it was Eve Markoff again, coercing and cajoling the working women into demanding better conditions for themselves, better pay. It was Eve Markoff up to her familiar old tricks. . . .

Yes, his mother had come to America but she had never forgotten who she was. Not for an instant. And he yearned for her as never before! But there was one more place he had to go before he went back to that house on Fifth Avenue.

He entered the great synagogue on Fifth Avenue—a stronghold of Reform Judaism that was dominated by the upper stratum of New York's German-Jewish community. Here, as Jamie saw it, was the final piece of the puzzle that was Eve Markoff Frank. His mother's sons wore skullcaps—they were bound to if they were enrolled at the yeshiva their own mother had founded—yet she attended *this* synagogue which was, possibly, as far away as one of the Jewish faith could get from Orthodox Judaism. He had researched the Temple with its Moorish facade before he came, had read that it endorsed "the Judaism of the heart, the

Judaism that proclaimed the spirit of religion as being of more importance than the letter.'' That sounded like his mother in one way, still, it was hard to picture her here within these walls, which more resembled a church with its pulpit and pews and handsome appointments than the synagogues of his youth.

But then he realized something else. Here, there were no partitioned-off sections for women. Here the women sat side-by-side with the men, and he knew why his mother Eve came to worship God here, where she didn't have to stand second in His eyes.

As Jamie was leaving, he saw an adjoining building with a connecting entrance to the synagogue. On the wall above the double doors leading to this building was the legend—*The David Markoff House of Study!*

Dazed, he entered. It was a research library of Judaic Studies. There were rooms and rooms filled with books and manuscripts. It was a place for men and women to read and study and contemplate the ancient lore. And David Markoff was remembered.

The tears pressing on Jamie's eyelids were hot and salty. Eve Markoff Frank had not only remembered *who* she was, but who David Markoff had been. And her husband, Jacob Frank, remembered David Markoff too; he had helped his wife dedicate this building of learning to him. His own younger brothers came to this Temple and saw that legend, and in that way they too remembered David Markoff. Only he, Jamie Markson, had forgotten the father who had died for him, had died in order that he would be free in America. Only he had denied David Markoff!

He went back inside the synagogue. There was no one else in the huge room, no worshiper, no cleric. He went up to the ark where the Torah was raised and enshrined. He closed his eyes, trying to remember the Hebrew words of the mourner's prayer so that he could pray for the father only he had forgotten.

But the words wouldn't come. They were gone from his memory. In English, he cried: ''Father, forgive me!'' Then he thought of his mother and his brothers, of Sabra and Jennie . . . He wasn't worthy of any of them. Then he thought of Ava. Was he worthy of her?

Twilight had already fallen when Jamie saw the gates of the Frank mansion close after the carriage. He raced across the street to stare through the posts of the wrought-iron fence at Eve Markoff Frank alighting into the porte cochere. He thought he wouldn't be able to restrain himself from crying out ''Mother!'' but he was strangely silent, strangely numb.

He saw his mother's sons, Elliot and David, dash out the front door to greet her. It was too dark for him to see her face clearly and he blinked his eyes to clear the mist away, but it didn't help. She was wearing a coat of dark green velvet with wide sleeves banded in dark fur and carried a little muff that matched. He wanted to see her hair. Was it still the color of a Russian summer sunset? But she wore a large-brimmed hat with a plume the shade of the raspberries he and Dorie had gathered in late spring, and he couldn't see her hair. With a pang of pain that slashed his heart he realized now that he'd never know.

He saw her laugh and bend down to kiss the boys and the ache spread all through him. He no longer was one of Eve's sons. Their paths had diverged too widely and he'd never know the touch of her lips again, the warmth of her sweet bosom.

It was all over. It wasn't that he didn't yearn for her, for he did. It wasn't that he didn't think she would forgive him, for he knew that she would. It was only that she could never be part of his life again or he of hers. They had walked down different paths; they had traveled too far from each other. And for him there was Ava! He had brought her up to assume the throne of the empire he had created for her—a genuine *American* princess. He had no right to tear her life apart with a grandmother and uncles from another world, another culture, an alien culture, different from anything she had ever known.

Just as his mother didn't really need him, neither did Jennie and Sabra. They had built a world for themselves in which he didn't belong just as they didn't belong in his and Ava's world. No, the best thing he could do was leave things as they were. . . .

They were going into the house now—Eve and her boys. For a second, she looked up expectantly as if sensing a presence and his heart turned over. But no, she hadn't seen him. He watched the three of them disappear into the house and a gasp issued unbidden from his throat, a silent cry.

The gatekeeper came over to make sure the gate was locked and saw him standing there. "You're the gentleman from this morning. If you wish to give me your card now, I'll tell Mrs. Frank you're here."

"No . . ." His eyes were on the closed door. "It was a mistake, all a mistake. An error of judgment . . ." He turned away and started down the Avenue, slowly at first and then at an increasing pace. He had to get home. He had already been away for too long. He had to get back as quickly as possible now. He had to get back to Ava.

Once the train heading west started moving, James Markson paced back and forth in his Pullman car, restless, unable to stop thinking, about everything, about the past. But he had to put it all to rest for good. It was the only way. Finally he sat down at the desk and took out an empty notebook, a pen, a bottle of black ink, thought for a moment and began to write:

I write down the following story not for others but for myself, not knowing at this time if anyone but myself will ever read it. At this turning point in my life I find myself impelled to do this so that in the future, even as recollections fade, as the faculties start to fail, I'll be able to recapture in memory, at least, all those fragments that make up a life. If it should ever be that, for any reason, anyone but myself shall find occasion to read these

353

words, I wish them to know that these words are truth as far as I can discern. I have lived a long time without truth and perhaps one loses the knack of it.

Of my personal experience I write explicitly. Of stories I heard as a youth, I repeat them in context much as I heard them. As for the rest, I have conjectured to the best of my abilities, trying to find the heart of the matter . . .

I do this because in spite of what I have done, of what my life has been, of whom I am now, I have a need not to forget who I am and from whom I come, for a man who doesn't know who he is, no matter how others know him, is no more than a speck of dirt and is lost forever.

I was born Yitzhak Markoff in the year 1881 in Slobodka, a small town in Lithuania, which had been under Russian rule for some one hundred years, and under Polish rule for four centuries before that. By the time I was considered a man, I was already tall and excessively burly. I was yellow-haired, yellow-bearded, snub-nosed and uncommonly strong as my father before me and his father before him, and had already acquired some fame in the countryside for my feat of lifting a horse from the ground and elevating the creature to well over my head.

My father was David Markoff, of the wild Markoffs, as they were known, all of an imposing height, of remarkable strength, livestock dealers who were men of neither refinement nor education but who were noted for their fearlessness. My mother was Eve Brodkin, who even in her youth was known for both her beauty and erudition. The truth of the matter was that in a time when, and a place where, no female was ever considered a person of consequence by a Jewish male, or a Jewess viewed as anything more than an object of contempt and derision by the gentile, either gentry or peasant, my mother was known as a great lady—a *somebody*. Even before I was born my mother Eve was already a legend in her own time in her small corner of the world.

Once he began to write he couldn't stop. He wrote into the early hours of the morning. Then, sleeping for only three or four hours, he arose and wrote again. He continued writing for all the days of his journey. Just hours before he arrived back in Galveston City, he finished. Then, even before he went in search of Ava to tell her that her daddy was home, he locked his journal away in the desk, along with the letter from his cousin Dorie. It was the past and he was finally ready to turn the key, locking it all away.

EPILOGUE

Having written it all down, the story of his life up until the time he was twenty-nine, he thought he was done with it. But then, from time to time, a compulsion came over him to add to the journal, to write in it again—notes of addendum.

November 12, 1912

Tonight was the dance recital. Ava was clearly a star. She radiated like a diamond in the sky. Dressed all in white, she was a fairy princess. She wore a tutu of white satin and net, silk stockings, little white satin toe shoes. On her head she wore a tiara of rhinestones. Her beautiful red hair hung well past her waist. She makes me so proud. There's nothing in which she doesn't excel.

March 9, 1913

They read Karl Hess's will today. It was something of a shock to us all. Karl left his personal fortune to his wife, but his remaining twenty-five-percent share of Hess and Markson Enterprises was left in trust for Ava. She's not yet eleven and she's now my equal partner. Anne has been totally ignored, left out of her father's will completely. I glanced at her as they read the will but could detect nothing in her face, no expression at all. But I felt sorry for her. It must be very hard for her to be rejected by a father after having been so special to him all those years. I glanced then at little Ava who smiled at me, her green eyes glistening. I had to smile back at her, amused by her childish delight over being an heiress.

July 16, 1913

They brought over the contents of Bertha Hess's safety deposit box today to turn over to Anne. I had been pleased for my wife that when her mother died, just three short months after Karl, she had left everything she owned to Anne. I wouldn't have wanted Anne passed over again, to suffer another rejection, even if it had been in favor of Ava. Thus, I was shocked by Anne's ugly display of temper over the ensuing incident.

She should have been more understanding of a young girl's natural interest in her grandmother's jewelry. All young girls are entranced by baubles and glitter and Anne could certainly have shown a little more tolerance, even humor, when Ava picked up Bertha Hess's diamond and emerald bracelet, tried it on and begged, "Oh, mother, can I have it for my very own? I love emeralds. They match my eyes . . ."

To take the entire contents of the jewelry box and hurl it at poor little Ava, shouting: "Here, take it all! You have everything else!" was not only unforgivable but incomprehensible. It took me hours to calm Ava down. Naturally, she was almost inconsolable over her own mother's behavior.

I'm at my wits' end with Anne. I've even suggested that on her next trip to Europe she consult this Dr. Sigmund Freud. I've heard of his work with women who suffer from chronic hysteria.

April 25, 1914

Today I sat at the breakfast table and when I picked up the morning newspaper I could not believe what I saw. It was a picture of my mother taken in Ludlow, Colorado, of all places. I excused myself from the table to go to the library to read the accompanying article away from inquisitive eyes. The photograph was taken at an encampment of striking workers of the Colorado Fuel and Iron Company. On the twentieth of the month, the workers' tents had been raked with the gunfire of two hundred company guards, and then soaked with kerosene and set ablaze. There were twenty-one dead and one hundred wounded. Mrs. Jacob Frank, the article stated, had come to Ludlow to offer whatever relief she could to the surviving workers. I studied the picture but it was blurred around the edges, even as my own memories were. I cut out the picture and put it into the drawer, along with my journal and my letter from my cousin Dorie.

When I returned to the table Anne said nothing as was her way. But Ava asked me if anything was wrong. I told her nothing was wrong in any world where *she* lived and she jumped up and came over to give me a big hug and a kiss.

September, 1914

There are mixed feelings here in Galveston about the war in Europe, with people choosing sides. There are many German-American families who are in sympathy with Austria and Germany, but at least half of our populace sides with the Allies. There are businessmen here making a great deal of money selling goods to the Allies and bankers who are even lending money to them. But since Russia is involved there's something in me that keeps me from being one of those businessmen. I refuse to take sides. How can I be on the side of Russia, the land that took my father? After all, America's not at war and I continue to export goods to European neutrals. Of course, it's a disappointment to us all that Anne will not be able to go to Europe this fall.

Ava was adorable and resourceful. She suggested that since her mother couldn't go to Baden-Baden, or the Riviera, she should go to Saratoga Springs in New York instead. Anne received the suggestion in stony silence but at the same time, she has decided to do exactly that.

September 20, 1915

Today, Anne's body was reclaimed from the water, the only victim of the great hurricane of 1915. The seawall has done its job. Anne, it seemed, had been beyond the protection of the wall, on the beach itself. I paced the rooms of my house. What had Anne been thinking of? Why hadn't she been safe at home once the winds started blowing in from the Gulf?

Of course, Ava is a consolation in my hour of grief and guilt. She put her hand in mine, smiled sweetly at me. "We still have each other, daddy."

Anne died intestate and rather than have the courts quibbling over what percentage of her estate should go to Anne's daughter and what to her husband, I requested that everything be put in Ava's name. What does it really matter? Everything I own will someday be Ava's, anyway. Everything has always been for Ava—everything.

November 7, 1916

We opened our Houston branch of Markson's today. Ava, who will be fourteen shortly, cut the white satin ribbon at the opening ceremonies. She looked very grown-up in her white pleated dress with the bright green sash. In fact, she wanted to put her hair up but I wouldn't allow it. I won't have her grow up on me that quickly.

Ava's thrilled about the new store in Houston even though we won't have the imports from France and England until the war's over. She'd been after me for some time now to expand into Houston. Of late, she's taken to calling Galveston "provincial." She's also started to deplore our involvement in what she calls our "repulsive" enterprises—junk and fat. She proposes that we sell off all our holdings and concentrate on department stores, putting a Markson's into every major city in Texas. While I have no intention of selling any part of Markson Enterprises, I'm charmed by Ava's intelligence and her interest in our business. I was entranced with the way those green eyes sparkled when she talked about opening "oodles" of Markson's stores.

Here I had intended to raise an American princess in the lap of luxury and she has her own aspirations—to be a merchant princess. I'm beginning to realize that my Ava wants many things out of life. At times I suspect that she wants everything!

March, 1917

It appears that we'll be in the war shortly. And there is revolution in Russia *again!* I had convinced myself that this was a world I had forgotten. I had almost, but not quite . . .

357

War! I am very busy at the junkyard and the refineries. Ava complains that I'm neglecting her. She also objects to attending Miss Adrian's School for Girls. She would much prefer the Duchess School in Houston, which is considered a more "elegant" school. But that's out of the question. I won't have her traveling back and forth every day and I certainly won't allow her to board. I've promised her that when the war's over, I'll take her on a tour around the world with a season in France and England.

"Do you promise?" she pouted prettily, and I solemnly promised.

Like most Americans, I pray for an end to the war. And like most Jews around the world must, I exult when I read about the Balfour Declaration—that the British government favors the establishment of a national home for the Jews in Palestine after the war. How can I not think of Sabra and Jennie, of Dorie and all the Markoffs in Palestine? Of what this will mean for them? They are a part of my life that is finished. Still, I have not quite managed to excise them from my heart.

Then, when I read that the Bolsheviks had taken over in Russia, I could almost hear the blood roar in my ears. The world of the Tsar and his nobility has finally fallen apart, and there is hope for a new and better Russia, land of my youth. How can I not think of Mother and how she must be rejoicing at the news that the people of Russia have been set free? How can I not think of my dead father, and of the day that I killed the Governor-General? How can I not think of my youth? Does one ever forget that world, that world when one is young and full of dreams and hope . . . even when that world is no more?

I realized at the Christmas Cotillion tonight that while Ava won't debut until this next year, she is all grown up. She wasn't able to wear white tonight (only the debutantes were permitted to wear that color), so Ava wore green satin instead, yards and yards of it, with little green bows sprinkled through her cascading hair. I wasn't the only one who thought she was the most spectacular sight ever seen in Galveston. She had more Texas boys mooning over her than any debutante there, even as I tried to discourage them by claiming at least one dance out of every three for myself.

For only a second, I suddenly thought of Sabra. I could not help it. I wondered how she looked now that she was all grown-up—older even than Ava.

Ava's commencement exercises are tomorrow. I had planned on her continuing her education but she is as willful as ever. She insists that she'd rather help run the stores. She has very gently reminded me that she is, after all, my partner. The fact is, she's richer than I since she also has her Grandfather Hess's personal fortune.

There has been talk of running me for Senator, a prospect that I have been dismissing. Being active in local politics is one thing—everyone knows me here, this is my hometown. But once I started campaigning for Senator there would be too many questions, questions I could not answer. If it were only myself that was at risk, I would chance it. But I cannot risk Ava's name and future.

Ava, of course, would love for us to go to Washington. She always says how dull it is for her in Galveston. Unfortunately, it is out of the question. That is one thing I cannot do for her.

August, 1920

I can see that Ava is restless although I allowed her to reorganize and revamp the Galveston store completely. I told her that after the branch in Dallas is completed in the fall, we can take off on the world tour I promised her. But she's informed me that she has other plans. She wants to go to Europe with a group of her friends, accompanied by a chaperone of course. The girls will have "a season" in Europe. She won't take no for an answer so I must let her go, but it's not without a sense of trepidation.

May 7, 1921

Today may well be one of the saddest days of my life. Today is Ava's wedding day. Today is the day my little princess becomes a real princess. Today is the day Ava, only eighteen, becomes the Princess De Lenko. She is marrying the Prince Alexei De Lenko, a White Russian exile from Red Russia. He is very handsome, tall, slim, dark-haired and dark-eyed, and wears a thin, black mustache. Ava, in her breathless, slightly Southern-accented voice, calls him divine, elegant. I call him a fortune hunter. I am a few months short of forty and I have the feeling that my life is over—the best part of it, at any rate.

Why did I ever let Ava go off to Europe without me, after chasing boys away from the house for years? It has been one of the worst mistakes I've ever made, and I've made many in my lifetime. I knew that it had become stylish for American heiresses to "do" Europe with the specific idea of bringing back a titled nobleman for a husband. Since they lacked for nothing, only a royal title would make them feel complete. But I never imagined my wise, practical Ava would be one of them. After all, she was already an American princess—what need did she have of a Russian title?

I should have realized that she was not only socially ambitious, but supremely competitive. If her friends were lassoing mere counts and dukes,

359

she would never be satisfied until she did them one better and snared a prince. But I think it's quite the opposite. I think it's he who has snared her.

And a *Russian* prince, of all things! What was I to say to her? That it was the Russian nobility who had made my ancestors' lives a living hell? That it was the soldiers of the Tsar, the soldiers of the Russian aristocracy, who shot my father down in a marketplace in a small town called Slobodka? How could I say to her that it had never been my dream for her to be a *Russian* princess?

No, I only told her what I thought of her prince with his elegant good looks, his debonair charm, his witty conversation. I told her that he was little more than a gigolo. I asked her if it was true that he didn't have a penny to his name. Instead of answering, she told me of the night she had met her sweet Alexei.

"Oh, daddy, it was so romantic. It was at the French embassy in London. The most wonderful ball you can imagine. The night just—radiated! Titled heads from all Europe were there—counts and dukes, barons and earls. And everyone wanted to dance with me! But daddy, no one could hold a candle to Alexei. I recognized at once that he was somebody special, *extraordinaire*. He literally swept me off my feet. He is the most superb dancer! And you must admit, he's very handsome . . ."

I admitted nothing. I only asked her what her prince did for a living. She said that she hadn't the slightest idea. It was clear that she didn't care. It was clear that she only cared about that title. Then I asked what he was prepared to do to earn a living.

Her eyes laughed at me. "Oh, work in the stores."

"As what? A floorwalker?"

"Oh, daddy!" she giggled. "You're so funny!"

"What will he do?" I persisted. There was nothing even slightly comical about this as far as I was concerned.

She stopped laughing. "I am an equal partner in the stores. I guess the owner of the Markson stores can always find a job in one of them for her prince of a husband."

May 8, 1921

She was the most beautiful thing I had ever seen. Her long red hair was done up in one great French knot, interwoven with ropes and ropes of seed pearls that matched the hundreds of seed pearls that decorated her wedding gown. The wedding veil was fastened to a diamond and emerald tiara that she had asked me for, accustomed as she was to asking me for anything she wanted. "Don't you think a princess should have a crown of diamonds and emeralds, daddy?"

The ceremony was Greek-Orthodox. What other kind of rites would suit a Russian prince? I fought desperately to hold back my tears as the bride walked down the aisle on my arm. She carried a white Bible and orange blossoms.

The reception was at our home. The house was filled with masses of white flowers—roses and lilies, gardenias and magnolias, camellias and oleanders. To me, it smelled like a funeral.

The wedding luncheon was served out on the lawns. Six hundred guests sat down to tables covered with white silk cloths, and protected from the bright Texas sun by white silk canopies supported by white columns. They sipped French Champagne and feasted on Russian caviar, poached oysters with truffles, giant Gulf prawns, *poulet farci parisienne*—an epicurean mix of Russia, Texas and France. My mother had always said that the Russian noblemen loved everything French. The wedding cake was tier upon tier, six feet high. There were two orchestras. The father of the bride danced with the bride only after the groom had danced with her first.

Since they had only recently left Europe, the couple honeymooned in New York, ostensibly to shop for imported antiques with which to furnish their new home, a French château of all things, to be built on *my* ranchland on the outskirts of Houston. Ava had requested the ranch as her wedding gift. She had always loved the ranch but, naturally, the old, small ranch house would never do for a royal couple.

May 9, 1921

I've hired an agency to trace down some facts about my new son-in-law. I've given the people there the only information I possess—his name and his title and the fact that Ava met him at the French embassy in London. The agency said they'd do their best, but that my expectations shouldn't be too high, that it's hard to get a fix on these exiles from Russia. There isn't a capital in all of Europe that isn't flooded with Russians who have supposedly fled the Reds, and each one with an alleged title, every one a supposed relative of the late Tsar. Half of them call themselves Romanov.

September 10, 1921

The happy couple have returned from New York. Ava is ecstatic. They had such a wonderful time! New York was an extraordinary place—so sophisticated, so alive, so much fun! All New York society feted them. Her friend from Galveston, Dolly Schopenhauer, introduced them to everyone who was worth knowing. And once they knew she was *that* Markson from Texas with a real prince for a husband, and so stunning to boot, they went mad over her! Dolly, she told me, had the most wonderful baronial mansion on Fifth Avenue since Dolly had married a baron from Germany. It seemed Dolly loved living on Fifth Avenue, much more so than she had loved living in Galveston. *Fifth Avenue!* It was indeed a small world.

Ava is full of stories—how they spent a week on Long Island at one of the Vanderbilts, with the Prince of Wales as a fellow houseguest. The Prince played polo and golf. "But he's nowhere near as handsome as Alexei," Ava gloated.

"Handsome is as handsome does, and I'd say the Prince of Wales has a much more handsome future, royally speaking," I responded, unable to resist the jibe. "Maybe you didn't play your cards correctly, Ava. Perhaps you should have waited for a prince who one day will be a king."

Ava had the last word, as usual. "I was thinking the same thing myself, daddy" she laughed throatily. "I had my eye on the ninny, and was thinking of trading in Alexei for Walesy but then I discovered I was pregnant. You're going to be a grandfather!"

I didn't know if the former part of her statement was true or not or if she was just teasing. But the latter part was definitely true. My daughter and her husband intend to spend all their time supervising the building of their Château De Lenko at the ranch. Ava wants it completed and furnished by the time her royal baby is born, and Ava always gets what she wants. That's how I brought her up.

April 1, 1922

The Prince Nicholas Alexander came into the world today. I asked my son-in-law for whom his son is named. "Why, for the Tsar, of course. May he rest in peace. He was my third cousin, once removed, you know . . ."

I must admit that it will be difficult for me to enjoy my new grandson. His name leaves a bitter taste upon my lips.

May 1, 1922

The investigative report on the Prince arrived in the day's mail. I had already been resigned to the possibility that under the circumstances of a Russia in turmoil, no information would be forthcoming, but here it was. After reading it, I almost wished that such had been the case.

. . .born Moishe Kaminsky! 1898. Parents, Rebecca and Abram Kaminsky, father, a tailor. Moishe disappeared from Odessa, fall of '17. Reappeared in Paris, spring of '18. Took up residence in London, '19. Launched into society under the sponsorship of one Lady Fullerton, a widow. Source of income at this time is unknown.

Strangely enough, I laughed, unable to stop. The Princess Ava De Lenko was really Mrs. Moishe Kaminsky, daughter-in-law of poor Russian Jews. I laughed, but I didn't know on whom the joke was—on me or on my daughter.

Perhaps if Nicholas Alexander, named for the late Tsar, and 13/16 Jewish according to my calculations which included Karl Hess's Jewish blood, hadn't been born, I would have rushed to the Château De Lenko to denounce my son-in-law to his proud wife, to point my own hypocritical finger in his handsome, lying face. As it is, the report has arrived about ten months too late. I will keep little Nicholas's secret as I have kept my own. I am almost forty-one and he is but an infant, and it is already too late for truth for both of us.

December, 1924

I've sold off the salvage business as well as the glass plant. I had been thinking of it for some time now, ever since Ava married the "Prince." The truth is, I've lost interest in all my businesses and Ava wants everything sold, except for the department stores. She says she wants to invest in other more dignified businesses, more suited to her title. Occasionally, I remind her that titles are not the fabric of America, but she ignores me.

In general I would say that Ava is more interested in her social position than in business. She and Alexei are constantly entertaining. The society columns are full of detailed descriptions of her parties at the château. Sometimes I'm invited, mostly I'm not. Ava says that's because I'm not always agreeable to be with. On my part, I'm not that interested in her guests. She often has very social friends from New York and Europe. The truth is, I think that we are drifting apart . . . I scarcely know her anymore.

June, 1925

My "fat" business that the Princess Ava found so disagreeable is gone. Now only the department stores are left and I try to bury myself in them. The truth is I am lonely, I am bereft. Ava has told me she's building a home in New York City and she's paying $1,000,000 for the land alone! She says the house will be necessary because she wants to open up a Markson's on Fifth Avenue, perhaps on 57th Street. She and Alexei and baby Nicholas will travel back and forth between Houston and New York. She doesn't even say that there will always be a place in her home for me.

July, 1925

Of late, I've been spending more time at home and less at my office since even my stores seem to have lost their luster for me. I've been doing lots of reading and studying. I've discovered that there's great solace in books. Peace, quiet, even security. You put a book down and when you come back to it, it's there waiting for you, unchanged.

August 15, 1925

There's a piece in this morning's society page describing a great weekend party at Le Château De Lenko. The guest list is long and illustrious—some of the country's most distinguished names in Society. One of the names stares out of the page—Mr. Henry Ford of Detroit!

363

At first I was only disturbed, but then I became angry! What was Ava doing with that scoundrel Ford? And it wasn't his cars that enraged me but his *Dearborn Independent* with its pages filled with despicable, bigoted venom. Henry Ford is a known anti-Semite and my daughter is hobnobbing with him at the ranch that was once mine!

I became so worked up, so outraged, that I called Ava at once. I demanded to know what she was doing with Ford.

"Doing with him, father? What do you think I'm doing with him? I'm not sleeping with him, if that's what you mean . . ."

If I had been talking to her face-to-face, I would have slapped her, something I had never thought of doing even once in her entire life.

"The man's a poisonous anti-Semite . . ."

"Of course he is. Anybody with any brains is. Mr. Ford is a patriot, a great industrialist. I'd say he's one of the country's foremost citizens. That's more than you can say for those filthy Jews. Everybody knows they're nothing but a bunch of Bolsheviks! If we're not careful, they're going to be the downfall of this country. Henry says that they're plotting to take over the whole world and that—"

I hung up on her. Oh my darling Ava! If anyone had ever told me I would want to slap her, that I would hang up on her, I would have said that person was crazy! I would have knocked him down. Now I only wanted to cry.

January 3, 1927

This morning, there's an article in the paper about a committee meeting held at Le Château De Lenko West. That's what Ava calls her home here in Texas now that there's a Le Château De Lenko East, ironically, only several blocks away from my mother's home on Fifth Avenue. The article lists the members of this committee, which includes some of the area's most public-spirited citizens. The committee has a high-sounding name: *Citizens for a Better America.* There's no one in Texas or Arkansas or Oklahoma or anywhere for that matter who doesn't know that the *Citizens for a Better America* is only a euphemism for one more chapter of the Ku Klux Klan, those defenders of the white against the black, the gentile against the Jew, the Protestant against the Catholic.

Since my son-in-law is not native-born and the Klan fulminates against foreigners, this means only one thing—Ava and Alexei are contributing large sums of money as well as the use of their home to make themselves more acceptable to these people who tar-and-feather, lynch, burn, murder and terrorize. My daughter! Eve Markoff's granddaughter! The champion of the Klan!

At first, I'm filled with rage which is swiftly followed by a sense of horror, then guilt, and then the greatest sorrow I have ever known—even

364

worse than when I first learned my father was dead and my mother was lost to me forever.

I try to think of what to do. Unmask my son-in-law to Ava as the Jew they both despise? Tell her that she herself is more Jewish than not? But what good would that do? It wouldn't change Ava where it counted the most—in her heart of hearts. It wouldn't change the fact that, somehow, I have created a monster.

I thought of going to her, of remonstrating with her, but I couldn't bear to hear the filth that I knew would spew from her lips—the jargon of the bigot and the demagogue. I am indeed lost. I have betrayed everything and everybody and now I am reaping my deserved harvest. I know that I can never face Ava again. I only regret that I cannot cut her off financially. I myself have arranged it that she's wealthier than I am but there is one thing I can do and I will do it as soon as I find the right person.

June, 1928

Today, I signed the papers in my lawyer's office. He will be the one to inform Ava that she has a new partner in the chain of Markson stores, one Hyman Goldberg, a recent immigrant who didn't like what was happening in Germany, was alarmed by the rising tide of anti-Semitism and elected to cast his future in America.

"I thought the best way to fix them," Hyman joked, "was to take my filthy Jewish money and get the hell out. That's what all the Jews there should do—stop supporting the economy of a country that has grown to hate them."

Unfortunately, all Jews are not as wise as Hyman Goldberg.

Much as the words hurt me, much as the words were like thrusts of a knife into my own heart, I had to warn Hyman about the kind of a person his prospective partner was.

"Oh, that's all right with me. I don't mind a good fight. We'll see who'll win out—" Hyman chuckled. Then, remembering that we were talking about my daughter, he put a hand on my shoulder. "I'm sorry, my friend . . ."

I wanted to cry. *My Ava!* "Not as sorry as I am . . ."

There is a remarkable irony in all this. Once I had kept silent and walked away from my precious mother in order to protect Ava. Now I will keep silent again, in order to protect my mother and her family from the embarrassment of the Princess De Lenko.

December, 1929

I have weathered the Crash. I can only hope that Ava has not, that she'll have difficulty in supporting her deplorable causes.

Although they are hardly adequate replacement for a daughter, I spend my days with books. I have again taken up the study of the Talmud and the

Torah, after having to relearn Hebrew once again. After all, it's been thirty years since I studied with Jennie. Ah, how much one forgets in thirty years! And how much one doesn't forget . . .

May, 1930

I am terribly concerned about what's happening in Germany. I keep reading about this "Handsome Adolf" Hitler who's growing ever more powerful, on the rise, riding on the coattails of a particularly virulent form of anti-Semitism. In Germany, the people are hungry and eager for scapegoats. Even here in America as the Depression deepens, it's easy for those eager for power to find an audience for the familiar old lies.

Every day I think more about Palestine, where a handful of idealists struggle to carve a land of milk and honey out of the desert. Every day I think about the daughter on whom I turned my back for the daughter for whom I gave up everything, even my last shreds of decency. But even as I think of Sabra, I can't stop thinking of Ava, although I am desperate to . . .

June 31, 1931

I have decided to invest my fortune in Palestine, in the future of the Jewish homeland in the land of Israel. I do this because it is the least I can do for my daughter for whom I have done nothing. Also, I do this in the spirit of the penitent. Not only the penitent father, but as a man in search of his salvation.

They need everything in Palestine—houses, agricultural equipment, sources of energy, hospitals, schools, even synagogues. But I know there's great need in my adopted country too. People are hungry here, too, in need. It is not America's fault that I have failed as a man. It is America that is responsible for my fortune. I have decided I will donate a dollar toward America's need for every dollar I invest in Palestine. It is too late to show my mother who I am, but perhaps it isn't too late yet to reserve a tiny place for myself in heaven.

June 17, 1937

Mostly, I have avoided reading newspapers and magazines. I scarcely turn on the radio. I have told myself that this is because, as a penitent, I must be removed from worldly things. But the truth is I avoid the news because even now I'm afraid to learn more of Ava's activities. In my heart I sit *shiva* for her every day of my life although officially the mourning period is supposed to be only eight days. Eight days after loving her so for every day of her life? It is not enough, it will never be enough . . .

I also cannot bear to read or hear what is happening in Hitler's Germany.

366

A thousand years of sitting *shiva* would not be enough to erase from memory the horrors of Nazi Germany.

But occasionally I weaken. Occasionally I can't resist opening ever so slightly the Pandora's box that is this world of the thirties . . .

Today, I see a picture in the paper of the Duke of Windsor, who is the former King of England and the former Prince of Wales, Ava's old friend. The picture shows the Duke alongside his wife, the Duchess, with their friend, Adolf Hitler. I read the accompanying article: it's the Windsors' honeymoon. Having visited Italy, where they were feted by Mussolini, they are now the houseguests of Adolf at his retreat in Berchtesgaden, accompanied by a retinue of friends. Among them is the American heiress, the Princess De Lenko!

What does a man do when his heart has stopped? He tries to take a deep breath and resume living. My mother once told me that to every man there comes a time when he must fight back. This time, Ava has gone too far! I must stop her! But how?

July, 1937

I have made arrangements with both lawyers and architects. The Markson Italianate villa on Broadway will become the David and Eva Markoff Institute for the Advancement of Judaic Studies. It will be one of the largest and best-endowed libraries in the Southwest. There'll be a simple bronze plaque on the door to attest that the building is dedicated and donated by the Markson Family.

Then I place in a box the following items: the letter I extorted from my late father-in-law, Ava's grandfather, Karl Hess, attesting to the fact that his mother was a Jew; the letter from my cousin Dorie; the picture of my mother Eve when she came to Ludlow, Colorado, to help the embattled strikers; the investigative report on the Prince Alexei De Lenko, ne Moishe Kaminsky. And then, as soon as I finish this last passage, this journal will be added to the rest.

I have two hopes—that it's not too late for me to make up with my daughter Sabra, and that it is not yet too late for young Nicholas Alexander, my grandson. He is still an innocent and maybe it is only the innocents who can save the world.

Those are my hopes, and along with the hopes there are always the regrets. Regrets? My life is full of regrets. But the most painful one of all is that I will never lay eyes on Eve Markoff Frank again! For no matter how much I repent, no matter how hard I try to make amends, it is impossible to turn back the clock. It is just too late for my mother and me. How could I possibly justify shattering the proud and peaceful existence that she, more than anyone else I will ever know, is entitled to in these autumn days of her life?

But I cannot resist. I take the newspaper picture of my mother out of the box just to take one more look—*Mama! Mama!*

I cry. My fingers even trace the outline of her face. But who can I rage against? This is my punishment—not ever seeing my mama again—but it is I myself who is handing down this judgment. It is a bitterly cruel punishment but it is just.

I put the clipping back into the box. One other regret is that I won't be able to look into the eyes of the Princess Ava when she receives this package, when she reads these words. Who knows what I would see there? Perhaps, God willing, sorrow, even regret. Perhaps then she will need her father even as I have so often needed mine, as I will always need my mother. But in that case, she will know where to find me for I am off to a land where I hope to be—at long last—a man. One who knows who he is and from whom he comes. And I don't go alone. There was a phrase in my cousin Dorie's letter about my mother—*she was part of each of us in a way that no one else could ever be* . . .The best part of Eve Markoff goes with me. . . .

Singer, June Flaum
   Markoff women